MONICA McCARTY

The Ghost

Pocket Books

New York   London   Toronto   Sydney   New Delhi

Pocket Books
An Imprint of Simon & Schuster, Inc.
1230 Avenue of the Americas
New York, NY 10020

This book is a work of fiction. Any references to historical events, real people, or real places are used fictitiously. Other names, characters, places, and events are products of the author's imagination, and any resemblance to actual events or places or persons, living or dead, is entirely coincidental.

First Pocket Books paperback edition June 2016

POCKET and colophon are registered trademarks of Simon & Schuster, Inc.

For information about special discounts for bulk purchases, please contact Simon & Schuster Special Sales at 1-866-506-1949 or business@simonandschuster.com.

The Simon & Schuster Speakers Bureau can bring authors to your live event. For more information or to book an event, contact the Simon & Schuster Speakers Bureau at 1-866-248-3049 or visit our website at www.simonspeakers.com.

Interior design by Leydiana Rodríguez

Manufactured in the United States of America

10   9   8   7   6   5   4   3   2   1

ISBN 978-1-5011-0881-5
ISBN 978-1-5011-0882-2 (ebook)

33614057584467

To all the readers who have been with me from
The Chief *to* The Ghost—*thank you!*

ACKNOWLEDGMENTS

WHEN I FIRST came up with the idea for "Special Ops in Kilts" (which is how I initially pitched the Highland Guard series), finishing twelve books seemed a long way away. Now, six years since the publication of *The Chief* in 2010, and I can't believe it's all over. Writing this series was pretty much a dream come true. I'll never forget sitting in Bella Andre's living room with Jami Alden (my critique partners) circa 2003, and telling them all about my "big" idea. It took me a while to feel confident enough to take on such a large project, but fifty single-spaced pages of an outline for all twelve books later, and I was ready. Getting it ready for you guys, however, took a lot of additional firepower.

Thanks, as always, to my fabulous agents, Annelise Robey and Andrea Cirillo at the Jane Rotrosen Agency, who believed in this project from the start. Thanks also to Kate Collins and the rest of the team at Random House for getting the series going, and to Lauren McKenna, Elana Cohen, Nancy Tonik, Faren Bachelis, and the rest of the editorial and production team at Simon & Schuster for finishing the series with such a fantastic bang. I feel extremely fortunate to have had such wonderful and talented people to work with over the years, and Lauren, I am really looking forward to what comes next.

I think I must hold the record for fabulous covers. All my covers have been fantastic, but a huge thanks to the art department at Simon & Schuster for putting a fresh twist on the last three, and for really capturing the tone and mood of the story—not to mention some rather exceptional, um, inspiration.

Finally, to the most important part of this endeavor, the readers who have made twelve books possible and enabled me to complete the series—thank you! Without your support, getting to *The Ghost* would not have been possible. If you have enjoyed reading these books half as much as I have enjoyed writing them, I'll consider it a great success.

The acknowledgments wouldn't be complete without a reference to my family. Dave, Reid, and Maxine, I could say something sappy, but you guys wouldn't believe me—which is why I love you.

The Highland Guard

Tor "Chief" MacLeod: Team Leader and Expert Swordsman

Erik "Hawk" MacSorley: Seafarer and Swimmer

Lachlan "Viper" MacRuairi: Stealth, Infiltration, and Extraction

Arthur "Ranger" Campbell: Scouting and Reconnaissance

Gregor "Arrow" MacGregor: Marksman and Archer

Magnus "Saint" MacKay: Survivalist and Weapon Forging

Kenneth "Ice" Sutherland: Explosives and Versatility

Eoin "Striker" MacLean: Strategist in "Pirate" Warfare

Ewen "Hunter" Lamont: Tracker and Hunter of Men

Robert "Raider" Boyd: Physical Strength and Hand-to-Hand Combat

Thom "Rock" MacGowan: Climber

ALSO:

Helen "Angel" Mackay (Née Sutherland): Healer

Joan "Ghost" Comyn: Spy

FOREWORD

*T*HE YEAR OF *our Lord thirteen hundred and fourteen . . .*
Robert the Bruce's war with England for the Scottish throne has reached a crucial juncture with nothing less than the freedom of a nation hanging in the balance.

For eight years, since the disastrous defeat at Methven that had him fleeing his kingdom as an outlaw, Bruce has avoided meeting the English in a pitched battle, army to army. Instead, he and the elite warriors of the Highland Guard have waged a "secret war," using pirate tactics of raids, ambuscade, and trickery to defeat his enemies—both English and Scot—and clear most of Scotland's important castles of their English garrisons.

But it isn't enough. Without a decisive victory in battle signaling God's judgment, Bruce's claim to the throne will not be recognized by England or the rest of Christendom. One day Bruce will have to take the field. But with the English army once again readying to march on Scotland, he must decide whether that day is now.

As the armies muster and prepare for what might be one of the greatest battles of all time, Bruce will once again rely on the secret warriors of his Highland Guard—both present and past.

PROLOGUE

Hagerstown Castle, Northumberland,
England, late September 1306

IT WAS A horrible, wicked lie! And had she not been eavesdropping on the two tiring women retained by her father to watch over her, Joan Comyn would have told them exactly that.

It couldn't be true. No knight could do that to a woman. Not even Edward of England, the self-proclaimed "Hammer of the Scots," could be so cruel and barbaric.

Could he?

A fresh stab of panic plunged through her chest. Though she never cried, her eyes prickled with tears as she slipped out of the alcove where she had been reading a book and trod soundlessly down the winding staircase of the castle that served as their temporary lodgings in the north of England. She wanted to put her hands over her ears to block out the offending words echoing in her head. Punish . . . traitor . . . *cage*.

No! Her heart raced and thudded wildly as she ran across the spacious Hall—ignoring all the curious faces that turned to stare at her—to her father's private solar. She pushed open the big oak door and burst into the room. "It can't be true!"

Her father's frown was dark and forbidding enough to make her start. She sobered, cursing herself for forgetting to knock. John Comyn, Earl of Buchan, hated to be disturbed, and though her father rarely turned his terrifying temper on her, the threat alone made her heart beat a little faster.

"You forget yourself, daughter. What is the meaning of this? As you can see"—he gestured to the half-dozen knights and barons seated around the table—"I am very busy."

She was instantly contrite. Clasping her hands before her, Joan bowed her head and did her best to look modest and respectful—the two qualities her father valued in women (and twelve-year-old girls who hadn't yet reached womanhood).

She lifted big eyes to his pleadingly. "Please, Father, I'm sorry to interrupt. But I heard something . . ." She lowered her voice, knowing well the risk in uttering the words. "About Mother."

She quickly looked down again, but not before seeing the bolt of rage strike her father's handsome features. In the best of moments, her father was irrational on the subject of his soon-to-be-set-aside wife, and in the worst he could become belligerent and unpredictable.

The room went deathly quiet. Tension and discomfort were thick in the air.

"Leave us," her father said sharply to his men.

They were only too eager to do his bidding, shuffling out quickly without looking at her. Not one of them would meet her eyes.

Her stomach dropped. Oh God, what if it *was* true?

Tears burning behind her eyes, she looked up at the man seated behind the large table. She would never have described him as warm and loving, but the cold, angry, bitter man he'd become over the past six months was nearly unrecognizable.

"If you speak of the treacherous bitch's punishment"—she flinched at the crude word no matter how many times he said it—"it is undoubtedly true."

Whatever blood Joan had left in her body drained to the floor. She swayed, lowering herself to the recently vacated bench opposite her father to prevent her legs from giving out. "But it can't be. I heard them say that she's been imprisoned in a cage high atop the ramparts at Berwick Castle . . . like an animal."

Her father's gaze hardened, his eyes two pinpricks of onyx with the unmistakable shiny gleam of malice. "It is true."

Horror made her forget herself. "But that is barbaric! Who could have thought of such a thing? You must do something to help her! The king will listen to you."

Even in England, the Scottish Earl of Buchan was not without considerable influence. Her mother, too, was important in her own right. Isabella MacDuff was the daughter of the previous Earl of Fife and the sister of the current earl—one of Scotland's most ancient and revered families. It was inconceivable that King Edward of England could punish any woman like this, but a lady—a countess—of her mother's position . . . surely her father would be able to put a stop to it?

His face turned florid and his eyes sparked with an unholy fervor.

Joan shrank back in the face of the temper she had unwittingly unleashed.

"I won't do a damned thing! The whore is getting no better than she deserves for what she's done."

Joan's throat choked with tears. *She's not a whore!* She wanted to scream in protest, but fear held her tongue.

Perhaps guessing her thoughts, he slammed his fist down on the table. The whole room seemed to shake—including her. "As if putting a crown upon the head of her lover wasn't enough, she is said to have taken the most notorious pirate in the Western Isles to her bed. Lachlan MacRuairi," he bit out disgustedly, spittle foaming in the corners of his mouth. "A bastard and a brigand. If she's being confined like an animal, it is because that is what the rutting bitch deserves."

Joan loved her mother more than anyone in the world. She refused to believe what they said about her. They were lies meant to discredit her and explain what people thought was unnatural bravery in a woman. They needed an explanation for how a woman would dare defy not only her husband, but the most powerful king in Christendom to crown a "rebel" king.

But Robert Bruce had been like a brother to her mother—not a lover. As for Lachlan MacRuairi . . . Joan remembered the scary warrior who had appeared in her chamber in the middle of the night not long after her mother had left Balvenie Castle for Scone to crown Bruce to explain why she'd been unable to take Joan with her as she'd wanted to. He had been in charge of the guardsmen sent for her mother's protection, that was all.

"She will freeze to death," Joan whispered weakly, probing for any ounce of mercy that might remain for the woman he'd been married to for thirteen years. The woman he'd loved so much he could barely let her out of his sight and always had her under guard to keep her safe.

At least that's what Joan had thought before. But maybe it was what her mother had wanted her to think. More and more, Joan was beginning to realize that something hadn't been right in her parents' marriage—that something wasn't right with her father—and her mother had tried to prevent her from seeing it. What Joan thought had been love didn't feel like love anymore. It felt like rabid possessiveness, control, and jealousy.

"Let her freeze," her father said. "If I had my way, I'd see her hanging from the gibbet. I told Edward as much, but the king is reluctant to execute a woman—even one who is deserving. Instead she will serve as a warning, a reminder to all who might think to support the usurping 'King Hood.'"

It was the name the English had given Robert the Bruce—the outlaw king. Nothing had been heard of Bruce and his followers in weeks. They were said to have fled to the Western Isles. They were hunted men. How long would it be before King Edward caught up with them?

Joan knew that help for her mother's predicament would not come from that direction. Robert Bruce and his men were too busy trying to save their own lives to rescue her mother.

Nay, it was up to her. If anyone could help her mother it was she. Her father cared for her, the "beautiful" girl who so resembled him. She had to get through to him, even if it made him angry.

Joan might be quiet and reserved, but she wasn't a coward. She had the blood of two of Scotland's most important earldoms running through her veins. Taking a deep breath, she tried to clear the tears from her throat and lifted her eyes to meet his. "I know you think she betrayed you, Father, but she was only doing what she thought was right."

"What was *right*?" her father exploded, jumping to his feet with enough force to cause the bench he'd been seated on to fall back with a resounding crash. Circling around the table, he grabbed her by the arm and hauled her to her feet. "How dare you try to defend her!"

Maybe she was a coward after all, because she was scared now. "I w-wasn't—"

But he was deaf to her pleas. "I will show you what is 'right' lest you be tempted to follow in your whore of a mother's treasonous footsteps. I wanted to spare you from this, but now I see that my coddling has only served to confuse you about where your loyalty lies. A daughter of Buchan—a Comyn—will never see anything *right* about a Bruce on a throne."

He dragged her across the Hall. One look at his face was enough to turn even the most curious of gazes in the other direction. She tried to calm him down, tried to apologize, but he was too angry to listen.

The cold blast of autumn air penetrated through the wool of her gown as he pushed open the door and pulled her down the stairs. He called for horses, which were quickly brought forward.

She realized what he meant to do. "No, Father, please. Don't take me there. I don't want to see—"

"Not another word," he bit out angrily. "You will do my bidding or I will see you punished with the lash. Would that I'd taken it to your mother and flogged the defiance out of her. We might have avoided this dishonor and blight upon our family."

Joan's eyes widened in disbelief. A lash? Her father had never raised a hand to her. But whatever regard he had for her had been forgotten by her defense of her mother. Not doubting that he meant what he said, she stopped protesting as he tossed her up onto a horse and they rode through the Northumbrian countryside the five miles to Berwick Castle.

By the time they passed through the gate, Joan had never been in such a state of misery in her life. She hadn't spoken a word since they left. Her father seemed a stranger— a dark, angry tyrant like the English king he defended.

It was dusk, and since she'd been forced from the manor house without a hooded cloak or gloves, her hands and ears were frozen.

What must it be like atop the tower in a cage?

She shivered or shuddered—maybe both.

Oh God, she couldn't do this! To see her mother suffering so horribly . . .

But any thought she had of pleading with him one more time fled as he plucked her off of her horse. Their eyes met, and she knew he was beyond reason.

She kept her head down as long as she could. But eventually, amid the crowd of gaping onlookers, her father ordered her to look.

She forgot her fear long enough to beg. "Please, Father, don't make me—"

"Look, God damn you!" He grabbed her chin and forced her gaze up to the ramparts. "See what happens to traitors and whores who betray their family to support false kings."

For a moment her mind refused to let her see the horror and barbarity of the sight before her. But the self-protective blindness could only last so long. Like the specters of a nightmare, the shapes began to materialize through the hazy mist of nightfall.

The wood latticed bars . . . the iron frame . . . the tiny square of a prison that was barely enough space to stand and open to the elements and the scorn of onlookers.

No! An involuntary cry escaped her lips as she saw a movement inside the cage. "Mother!" she sobbed, lunging toward the tower as if she would free her. Every instinct in her body screamed to go to her. To *do* something. To put an end to this travesty. How could they do this to anyone? How could her mother possibly survive? *Oh, Mother, I'm so sorry!*

But she'd barely taken a few steps before her father caught her and pulled her away. She started to scream and kick, but he quieted her with a warning. "You are only making it worse. Do you want her to hear you? Do you think she wants you to see her like this?"

She knew her father was only trying to prevent a scene—he didn't care about her mother's feelings—but it worked. Somehow she knew that it would kill her mother to know her daughter had been forced to stand witness to her suffering.

But she couldn't give up. She had to do something. Her mother needed her.

Past the point of caring about her father's anger, she tried again. "Please, Father, I'm begging you. Please do something to help her. You can't leave her like this."

But he could. And that's exactly what he did, dragging her sobbing and pleading from the castle.

Joan had never felt so helpless in her life. She'd failed. Her knees collapsed, and she would have slid to the ground had her father not been holding her up.

The pain and devastation on her face had finally penetrated the black haze of his anger.

Too late he seemed to realize that he might have gone too far. He held her up against him as if she were one of the pretty poppets he used to buy her as a child. "I'm sorry you had to see that, daughter. But it was for your own good."

She looked at him as if he were mad. How could that

possibly be for her own good? She would never forget it. Just as she would never forget his cruelty in bringing her here.

What he saw in her expression must have alarmed him. He looked truly uneasy as he wiped some of the hair back from her face. Feeling the chill on her skin, he jerked off his plaid to wrap around her. "Your mother is dead to us both. We will not speak of her again."

He was right in that. They didn't speak of her again. But it wasn't her mother who died, it was her father, who didn't rise from his bed after a fever struck him down two years later.

She didn't mourn him. He'd been dead to her since the day he'd taken her to see her mother hanging in a cage. Her father had taught her a lesson that day, although not the one he intended. The image of her mother treated so brutally and Joan's inability to do anything to stop it would stay with her forever, as would her hatred toward the king who'd put her there and the man who had refused to lift a finger to help her. She never saw her father in the same way again.

She would never see many things the same way again. No longer was she a spectator in the war between Scotland and England. From that day forward, seeing Edward of England defeated and Robert Bruce on the throne became all that mattered. She'd failed to free her mother from the cage, but she would do everything she could to ensure that her mother's suffering had not been in vain.

She should have taken the lashing. At least those scars might have had a chance to heal.

1

Carlisle Castle, Cumbria, England, April 16, 1314

"YOU ARE DRIVING me wild," the young knight said as he frantically pressed his hot mouth all over her neck. "God, you smell so good."

Joan wished she could say the same, but as Sir Richard Fitzgerald—the second-in-command of the Earl of Ulster's Irish naval forces—had cornered her after the midday meal, he smelled distinctly of smoked herring, which needless to say was not her favorite.

When he tried to press his mouth on hers again, not even the prospect of learning the movements of the entire English fleet could have stopped her from turning her head. "We can't," she said softly. The slight breathiness in her voice was not from passion, but from the effort of fending off a determined would-be lover tired of hearing no. "Someone might discover us."

Which was why she'd chosen this as a place to meet. It was private but not *too* private. She never left herself without a means of escape.

Deftly twisting out of his tentacle-like embrace with the ease of someone who'd had practice escaping men with hands like a hydra many times before, she looked around anxiously as if to prove her point.

They stood in a quiet section of the garden in the castle's outer ward, where she'd announced that she was going to take a stroll after the long meal. As she'd intended, Sir Richard had followed her there and had pulled her behind one of the rose trellises.

The young captain scowled, his face flushed with frustrated desire. With his light eyes, blondish-red hair, ruddy, wind-burned complexion, and sturdy build, he bore the marked stamp of his Irish forebears. He was not unattractive. Not that it mattered. She'd lost her weakness for handsome young knights a long time ago.

"No one would discover us if you would agree to come to my room. My squire can sleep in the barracks for the night."

"I couldn't," she said, as if the suggestion shocked her, though it was hardly the first time she'd heard it.

His smile might have been charming to someone with less experience in the ways of men. "Nothing untoward will happen," he assured her with a gentle brush of his finger on her cheek.

Right. Every time she heard false promises like that, it became more difficult to feign wide-eyed innocence. With some effort, she managed. "Are you sure?"

He nodded, his voice turning husky. "We can just spend a little time alone together. I thought you wanted that."

She gnawed anxiously on her bottom lip, as if contemplating the illicit offer. His gaze heated as he obviously contemplated equally illicit things about her mouth.

"Of course I do," she said. "But it's too risky, and there is plenty of time—"

"No there isn't," he snapped, losing patience with the two-week-long seduction that he no doubt thought would have progressed much further than a very few stolen kisses by now. She was supposed to be easy prey. "I received orders yesterday. I'm to leave in three days."

Finally, the information for which she'd been waiting! Joan had begun to despair of ever hearing anything of import from him. Young knights were usually so eager to boast and brag—which is why she targeted them (that and they weren't married)—but Sir Richard had been frustratingly closemouthed.

Until now.

She hid her excitement and relief behind a mask of concern. "Orders? You are leaving? But I thought you had until June to muster at Berwick."

"I'm not going to Berwick." He sounded distracted. His eyes had dropped to her chest again—a frequent occurrence. "God, you are so beautiful. There isn't another woman like you."

As he looked like he might try to kiss her again, she shuffled "nervously" and spoke quickly. "You're not? Has the war been called off, then?"

He glanced up from his lustful study of her breasts. She hoped he thought her as stupid as she sounded. If his amused but slightly patronizing smile was any indication, he did.

"No, the war hasn't been called off. But my duties are on the sea in advance of the army."

Which is why she was here with him. It was rumored that the Earl of Ulster—Sir Richard's commander who was currently in York meeting with King Edward—would be in charge of supplying the castles in advance of the English invasion. King Robert the Bruce would love to know of their plans. Though Ulster was Bruce's father-in-law, he was Edward of England's man.

She acted as if the news of his leaving was devastating.

"But where are you going? When will you be back? Will it be dangerous?"

Whether he would have answered her questions, she would not find out. The sound of approaching voices put a quick end to the conversation. Leaning over, he pressed a quick kiss on her lips that she could not avoid. *Herring.*

"Meet me later," he whispered before slipping away.

Not a chance in Satan's garden, she thought with a shudder. At least until she had a means of escape.

Cursing, knowing she might not have another opportunity like this again, she walked out from behind the trellis to greet the ill-timed interruption as the group of ladies came around the corner of a large hedge that surrounded some of the raised flower beds.

Joan had been so close. But her contingency plan had worked too well. She hadn't wanted to risk being alone with him too long. She didn't know how much longer she could keep putting him off. It was a dangerous game she played, and she knew only too well what a fine line she walked.

This was not the first time she'd encouraged a man to get information. She'd been spying for Robert the Bruce for almost six years now.

Shortly after her father's death, the Bishop of St. Andrews, William Lamberton, a loyal supporter of Bruce's who was being held in England at the time, had approached Joan to see if she would be willing to serve as an intermediary between Bruce and his imprisoned wife. Queen Elizabeth had been captured along with Joan's mother, but she'd been spared a cage for confinement under the supervision of Sir Hugh Despenser the elder—Joan's newly named guardian.

The bishop's offer was exactly the opportunity Joan had been waiting for to do *something*, and she'd agreed immediately. Although admittedly, at the time, she had no idea what she was getting into. Over the years her role had grown increasingly more important—and more dangerous—shifting from messenger to spy after she'd falsely been declared illegitimate, dispossessed of her inheritance, and sent to live with her cousin Alice Comyn, who had married Sir Henry de Beaumont, one of King Edward's most important barons in the north. Joan's position in de Beaumont's household had given her unexpected access to important information—and important men.

With her "tainted" blood, infamous mother, and no one to defend her, Joan had been easy prey. Men had targeted her for their unwelcome attention since she was fifteen. She'd been too young to protect herself then, but eventually, she'd turned it to her advantage.

Although some men—like Sir Richard—had a hard time hearing no, over the years she had learned to handle even the most determined of pursuers. Thanks in large part to the man who'd served as her personal sentinel since he'd first learned of her work for Bruce.

Lachlan MacRuairi, who'd freed and then later married her mother, had taught Joan how to move around without being seen, how to extract herself from unwanted situations, and, if necessary, how to defend herself. It was because of him that she'd been made a secret member of the elite Highland Guard, Bruce's highly skilled team of warriors who had been recruited for the most dangerous missions. Only Lachlan knew her identity; the other members of the Guard simply called her the Ghost.

The name fit, probably more than they realized. Most of the time she felt like a shadow. There, but not really there.

Seen, but unseen. Unable to touch or be touched, and incapable of feeling.

The ladies stopped to return her greeting but did not invite her to join them on their walk. As this was what Joan expected, she wasn't disappointed. It was a lesson she'd learned a long time ago. If you don't expect much of people, it won't hurt when they don't give it to you. Her father had been her first example, but many more had followed.

Realizing that it was getting late, and that her cousin would be looking for her soon to help her pick out what to wear for the evening meal (a process that seemed to take most of the afternoon), Joan started to make her way over the portcullis of the interior moat to the inner ward.

As the guardian of the castle for the king, de Beaumont had been given the largest suite of rooms on the top level of the new two-story tower that only had been completed a handful of years ago. As companion to her cousin, Joan had a small antechamber off the "lord's chamber." It wasn't large, but it had a window directly overlooking the countryside beyond the east wall, and most important . . . it was private. Unfortunately, her cousin intercepted her, and it was hours before Joan was able to seek the solitude of her chamber.

At first, she didn't notice anything amiss. She tossed the plaid she wore around her shoulders on the bed, kicked off her slippers, pulled the pins from her hair, and threw them on the small dressing table before moving to the window.

She froze. The tiny piece of silk thread that she'd tied to the latch on the shutter had been snapped.

Excitement burst through her. *Finally!* She had him. It was a game between her and Lachlan. Known for his ability to get in and out of anywhere without being seen, he'd been surprising her for years—and she'd been trying to catch him.

Trying. Unsuccessfully, at least, until now. A rare smile turned her mouth. The feeling that filled her chest was so foreign she almost didn't recognize it: happiness.

Moving swiftly to the ambry door, she pulled it open. "Hello, Father."

Calling him Father had started out as a jest to make him feel old—he'd just turned forty to her twenty—but she knew it wasn't just that anymore. The man her father had called a bastard, brigand, and pirate was much more of a parent to her than her own had ever been.

She heard a very un-fatherly curse before the big warrior materialized from behind her gowns. He scowled, although for a man with the war name of Viper there wasn't much behind it. "How did you know?"

She folded her arms across her chest and quirked a brow the way he did to her. "You don't expect me to tell you all my secrets, do you?"

Many people who knew him would be surprised to see how easily his mouth curved into a smile. The mean brigand with the black heart had changed, though he'd probably die before admitting it. He had a reputation to uphold after all.

"Not bad, little one. If all my men were so easily trained, my job would be a hell of a lot easier."

She grinned. Then realizing that she might actually be beaming, she sobered. "As much as I look forward to our little family reunions, I'm assuming for you to have risked climbing through that window your reason for being here is important."

He nodded and motioned for her to sit. She sat on the edge of the bed and he took a seat opposite her on the stone windowsill. He shot a meaningful glance to the door. She shook her head. "My cousin and Sir Henry are still in the Hall."

He nodded and continued. "Carrick plans to make an attempt on the castle tonight here along the east wall." He gave her a dry look. "I know it goes against your nature—God knows it's against your mother's—but try to stay out of danger and not go running toward it, will you?"

She laughed. "I'll do my best, and I appreciate the warning. But I hope the earl has a good plan. The English are tired of Bruce taking back all of his castles—they'll not give up one of their most important without a fight. I don't have to tell you how well defended it is."

"Nay, I had a devil of a time—" He stopped, his eyes narrowing. "If that's a trick to try to get me to tell you how I got in, it isn't going to work."

She blinked at him innocently, which he didn't believe for a minute.

"Christ, now I know where she got it from!"

Her brows drew together questioningly.

"Your sister. Christina gives me that look every time she's done something naughty—which seems to be a daily occurrence."

Joan couldn't prevent the tiny pinch in her chest. She'd never regretted the decision not to return to Scotland with her mother after Lachlan had rescued her—Joan had chosen her path and knew it was a solitary one—but she did regret not knowing her young half siblings. She had three now: Erik, who would be five in a few months; Christina, who was three and a half; and Robbie, who was almost eighteen months.

"You know what the Bible says: 'as ye sow, so shall ye reap.'"

Lachlan shook his head with a sigh. "That's what your mother says."

She smiled.

He told her what he knew of Edward Bruce's plan to take the castle, which in her opinion—and Lachlan's from the sound of it—seemed to be more a "why not take a shot as long as we are here" than a well-thought-through operation.

"So the bulk of the men will attack the main gate, while a small force in black cloaks to blend into the night will attempt to slip over the curtain wall behind the kitchens?" she summarized. "It seems like I've heard something like that before," she added dryly, referring to James Douglas's taking of Roxburgh Castle and Thomas Randolph's taking of Edinburgh Castle, which had used similar tactics.

Lachlan shook his head. "The king's brother will never be accused of inventiveness. But I think he is tired of hearing about Douglas and Randolph and wants to have his own 'miraculous feat of warfare.' Just see that you are nowhere near the kitchens after midnight."

"No late-night snacks for me, I swear it. Even if the cook makes apple tarts."

He shook his head and chuckled. "Now you sound like Erik. Don't turn your back on your sweets with that one around."

She smiled, but when their eyes met, she suspected he'd guessed what she was thinking—there was little chance she'd get that opportunity. At least not while the war was going on and while she remained undiscovered. She was too valuable here. If she were discovered . . . well, they both knew what would happen then.

"That reminds me. I have something for you," Lachlan added.

"A tart?" she jested, trying to cover the oddly emotional moment.

It didn't work. "Nay," he said seriously. "This. You are one of us now, and since a tattoo isn't appropriate, I thought this might suffice."

He handed her a gold bracelet. It was about two and a half inches wide and in the shape of a cuff. It opened with a hinge on one side and two tiny latches on the other. It was beautifully designed with a carved ornate pattern on the outside that reminded her of the old crosses in the church-yards back home in Buchan in the northeast of Scotland. But it's what she saw on the inside that made her gasp.

She looked up at her stepfather with her heart in her throat. The design lightly etched on the inside of the cuff was familiar to her, although she'd never seen it. The Lion Rampant and spiderweb was the mark tattooed on the arms of the members of the Highland Guard. Hers was personalized with something else that was important to her—two tiny roses. The pink rose had become a symbol among the people to protest her mother's cruel and bar-baric punishment.

She didn't know what to say. She feared if she said anything, he would know how much this meant to her, but hiding her emotions was part of the armor that enabled her to do her job. "It's beautiful. Thank you," she managed. "This means . . . a lot."

Maybe understanding more than she would have liked, he nodded. "Rock made it." Joan had heard of the newest member of the Highland Guard—and the feat he'd per-formed in climbing Castle Rock to help take Edinburgh Castle. "I don't need to tell you to be careful with it. Enough people know what that means."

She slipped it on. "I will."

"Leave it with the priest at St. Mary's if you ever need me." He looked at her for a few moments longer as if undecided about something. "I should probably go. The others are waiting for me."

She nodded. It was hard when he left. She always felt so . . . alone. Most of the time she liked it that way. But the short, infrequent meetings with Lachlan were the only time she could talk to someone without being on guard.

Lachlan pulled something out of his pocket and handed it to her. "I probably shouldn't be giving you this, but here is the powder you requested from Helen."

Helen MacKay—known as Angel—was the de facto physician of the Guard.

Joan tried not to wriggle under his intense scrutiny, but those eerie green eyes had a way of penetrating. "I've been having trouble sleeping," she explained.

She thought he might call her lie right there, but he refrained. "Helen told me to remind you not to mix it with spirits—the effects are intensified."

"I'll remember that," she said blankly.

He wasn't fooled. "You better be careful, Joan. If your mother finds out what you are doing . . ."

She lifted her chin. "I can take care of myself, Lachlan. I've been doing so for six years." Eight if she counted back to when her mother left.

"I don't ask you how you discover all this information—"

"Good," she said, cutting him off. "It's none of your concern."

He ignored her warning. "But I'm hearing rumors."

She stiffened and gave him a hard look. "You better than anyone know better than to listen to gossip."

The lies that were spread about him were far worse than anything they might say about her.

"Maybe so, but I also know there is usually a little bit of truth to them."

She pursed her mouth closed, signaling that she wasn't going to talk about it anymore.

He sighed. "You keep your thoughts hidden better than any warrior I know—your mother used to do the same thing—but don't think I haven't noticed how sad you seem lately. I can't remember the last time I saw you smile."

"I'm fine," she assured him. But seeing that she hadn't convinced him, she added, "I know you are worried, but you don't need to be. I know what I'm doing."

Whatever it takes so that no one else ever has to see her mother in a cage.

∞

The damned fools were going to get him killed.

Alex was riding at the head of the long train of English soldiers when they first caught sight of the smoke.

"Scot raiders," their scout confirmed shortly thereafter, having raced back with the news. "A few furlongs ahead."

Two years later and the word still made every muscle in his body tense with . . . frustration? Anger? A sense of futility?

Raider, the war name of his former partner in the Highland Guard, Robbie Boyd. The man who'd pushed Alex for seven years until he'd pushed him too far.

You raze me, I'll raze you more. The retaliatory raids that characterized the war in the Borders had driven Alex to London two years ago, yet here he was back in the north and the first thing that confronted him was fire—or the smoke from it.

"How many?" Pembroke asked. Aymer de Valence, the Earl of Pembroke, was the leader of the two hundred knights and men-at-arms who were making their way north to answer King Edward's call to muster.

Since he'd left Scotland and the Guard, Alex had been in the south of England able to avoid the fighting and the prospect of meeting his former compatriots across a battle-field. But no longer. King Edward had ordered him to march north with Pembroke ahead of the army to prepare for battle against Bruce. Like many of his Scot countrymen in Edward's allegiance, Alex served in an English earl's retinue.

"Not many, my lord," the scout answered. "Two score—perhaps less. The man leading them wore a surcoat of white with a red chevron."

Alex swore silently. That coat of arms was only too well known.

Pembroke could barely contain his glee. "By God, it's Carrick! We've a chance to take Bruce's only remaining brother. Ready your men," he ordered the knights around him, including Alex. "We'll circle around them from all sides. I don't want any chance of him escaping."

Despite the English being on the losing end of such confrontations most of the time over the last six years, it apparently never occurred to Pembroke that *they* might be the ones who would need to escape. English arrogance was one of Alex's many frustrations.

Though experience taught him that it would likely be futile, he tried to urge caution anyway. "Carrick wouldn't be raiding this far into England so close to Carlisle Castle with only forty men. Perhaps we should wait until the other scouts report back?"

Something about this didn't feel right, and Alex had learned a long time ago to trust his senses. He'd also learned that things like odds and superior numbers didn't matter to Bruce's warriors. And perhaps most important, he'd learned to never rush into battle without knowing exactly what you were up against.

They didn't even know the terrain they were working with—and it was getting dark.

Pembroke gave him a scathing glare. "And risk losing him?" His eyes narrowed. "You would think the brother of one of the most famed knights in Christendom would be eager to fight and prove himself. Perhaps you aren't eager to cross swords with your old compatriots?"

Alex ignored the insult and thinly veiled questioning of his loyalty—it had been his constant companion the past nine years no matter what side he was fighting on. Born in England and raised in Scotland, Alex was suspect to both. Sometimes he wondered if he would ever belong anywhere.

But it was much harder to ignore the reference to his brother. Sir Christopher Seton had indeed been one of the greatest knights in Christendom, Robert Bruce's closest friend and companion, and the person Alex most looked up to in the world. Chris had been executed along with Alex's other brother, John, eight years ago because of Pembroke's treachery. At the Battle of Methven, *Sir* Aymer had given his word as a knight that he wouldn't attack until the next morning, but he'd broken that word and sent his men into Bruce's camp in the middle of the night.

One of the reasons Alex felt he could no longer fight with the Highland Guard was that he was tired of furtive tactics and wanted to take the fight to the battlefield like a knight. Yet here he was taking orders from the man whose dishonorable treachery had cost him the lives of his brothers.

Irony was a capricious bitch.

It took everything Alex had not to respond and let the pompous bastard get away with the smug reference to his brother. But Pembroke was wrong if he thought Alex needed to prove anything. He might have at one time, but he'd proved himself many times over fighting alongside the best warriors in Christendom. The best of the best; that was why Bruce had chosen them. Each warrior of the Highland Guard had brought an important skill of warfare to the group. Except for Alex, that is. He was good with a dagger, but he'd been recruited because of his brother. Chris couldn't join—he was too well known—but he wanted his younger brother to be a part of it.

Alex had started out on unequal footing, and it had taken years for him to climb his way up from the bottom rung. But he'd done it. When he'd left, it hadn't been his warrior skills that were the problem. Hell, he'd even defeated Boyd, the strongest man in Scotland, in hand-to-hand combat, and no one had done that in years.

Though Alex would like nothing more than to prove himself to Pembroke—a fist through that smug smile would be a good start—he resisted the urge. Alex was here to help put an end to this, damn it. If it meant he had to work with arses like Pembroke to do so, he would. The people in the Borders—his people—had been bearing the brunt of this war for too damned long. *No more faces in the flames.* So he gritted his teeth and tried again. "I will be the first one to lift my sword if we determine Carrick is alone. Just give me a few minutes to find out."

"He could be gone in a few minutes," Sir Robert Felton, the captain of Pembroke's household knights (and even more of an arse than his lord), interjected. "It doesn't take long to steal a few dozen head of cattle." He gave Alex a hard look. "And I'll take the lead with Kingston, la Zouche, and Vescy. With your sword arm still weak, you won't be much use to us. You can stay in the back and protect the baggage cart with your men."

After a couple of weeks being around Felton, Alex had new respect for Kenneth Sutherland's ability to contain his well-known temper. Felton had been Sutherland's nemesis when he'd returned to the English fold as a spy a few years ago, and Alex didn't know how Sutherland hadn't ended up killing him. Alex would like nothing more than to do so right now. But then he would have to use his right hand. His arm was fine, but he wasn't ready to admit that yet.

This time not only were his teeth gritted, but his fists were clenched around his reins as well. "I take orders from the earl. I wasn't aware he'd put you in charge."

"He hasn't," Pembroke said with an admonishing glance at Felton. "I shall lead." In addition to Felton and the knights he'd mentioned, Pembroke added a few others, and then turned to Alex. "Felton was right. We need someone to protect the carts, and until your arm is strong enough you are the obvious choice. Stay here, and I'll send for you if you and your men are needed."

Had Felton not been the one to suggest it, Alex might have been glad not to have to face his former friends just yet. Hell, he was glad—Felton or not. He'd hoped to never be in this position.

A few moments later, the bulk of the army rode off, leaving Alex, the dozen men he'd brought with him from his estates in East Lothian, and the fifty or so servants and skilled laborers who accompanied the army, from the stable lads who tended the horses, to the smiths and their apprentices who repaired the armor and shoed the horses. The "small army" as it was called was a vital part of any conventional force, but it also complicated the process and prevented them from moving quickly. By contrast, the small strike forces that Bruce employed weren't hampered by all the added weight and logistics. That was part of what had made them so successful.

The first clash of battle sounded like a thunderclap; it filtered through the cold evening air as if it were a hundred feet away rather than a half-mile or so. The roar of the attack, the shouts of surprise, the clatter of steel . . . the cries of death. It was fast and furious. Or at least it should have been with nearly two hundred men to forty. But after about five minutes something changed. There was a shift in the sounds of the battle that told him something had happened. A short while later, he found out what.

One of Pembroke's men-at-arms came racing back. "Take what you can and make for the castle. The Scots are on their way."

Alex swore. "What happened?"

"Carrick's men weren't alone. The Earl of Moray and at least another fifty men were nearby and came as soon as they heard the attack. We were forced to retreat. Sir Aymer and the others are racing to the castle."

Being right didn't make Alex any less furious—or frustrated. Sometimes it seemed as if the wall he'd been banging his head against in Scotland had followed him to England. For two years, he'd been trying to get the English to stop underestimating their opponent so they would see a reason to negotiate and bring an end to this bloody war. But all that men like Pembroke seemed to see were their superior numbers, armor, and weaponry. Things that hadn't stopped Bruce's men for eight years. Pembroke might have double Carrick's men, but the arrival of the king's nephew would have changed the odds. Alex ought to know, as he'd been responsible for some of the Earl of Moray, Sir Thomas Randolph's, training himself.

Alex shouted orders for his men to take what they could

of the valuable plate and the silver Sir Aymer was bringing north to pay the garrison at Carlisle, rounded up the live-stock, and ordered the small army to follow the old Roman road to the castle, which should only be a few miles away. The small army wouldn't be hurt. No matter what horrible stories they told of the "barbarous Scots," Alex knew that Bruce had given orders only to kill those who fought against them. It was the cattle and coin to provision the army that he was after.

There was nothing barbarous about Bruce's men, but it wasn't until Alex had tried to cure the English of all their ignorant misconceptions and beliefs that he'd really understood it himself. The Scots might be terrifying and appear out of the darkness like brigands, but they weren't.

But unfortunately, unlike the small army, Alex and his men wouldn't escape death so easily if Bruce's men caught up with them.

Alex didn't delay, heading straight for Pembroke's cart to retrieve the silver.

He'd just shoveled the last of the fifty pounds' worth of coins from the wooden box into a linen sack to make it easier to fit in a saddlebag, when he heard the not-so-distant sound of approaching riders.

With a curse, he handed the bag to the last of his men and told him to go. They were leaving a lot of valuable goods behind, but there was no help for it.

Knowing Bruce's men would be on him at any moment, Alex mounted his horse and took one last look around. A movement out of the corner of his eye stopped him cold.

Bloody hell, where had she come from? A wee lass, not much older than five or six, had just emerged from the trees. Alex watched in disbelief as she started to cross the road that was directly in the path of the oncoming horsemen. He shouted a warning, but she didn't give any indication that she'd heard him. Couldn't she hear the horses?

She must have felt them. She stopped suddenly—right in the middle of the road—stared down at the ground, and froze. She had her back to him, but Alex didn't need to see her face to know that it was struck in terror.

Go, he told himself, looking in the direction of the road leading to the castle. *You can still escape. They'll see her in time.*

But it was almost dark, and she was wearing a black cloak . . .

She turned and saw him. Her eyes widened, and for one hideous moment, Alex's mind flashed back to another. He saw another little girl with wide eyes and full of terror staring at him, but this time from the open door of a loft in a barn with flames jumping all around her.

Flames that he had set.

Oh God, I have to reach her in time. Please let me reach her in time . . .

The memory cleared, but not the sense of urgency. He knew he couldn't take the chance that they wouldn't see her. He wouldn't see another innocent life put at risk—not when he could stop it.

He swore again and swung his horse toward the girl. He didn't have much time. The first rider had just appeared perhaps a hundred feet behind her. They weren't much farther away than Alex.

He sure as hell hoped his sword skills hadn't diminished as much as he feared in the past two years, because even if this worked, he was going to be fighting for his life in a few seconds.

With a snap of the reins and a click of his heels, his

stallion shot forward. Staying low over its neck, Alex held the reins in one hand and slowed just enough to lean over and wrap one arm around the girl's shoulders and drag her out of harm's way. Turning his horse in to the trees, he set her down. The pounding of horses stopped. Aware of the riders circling around him in the darkness, he told her to go.

Big, dark eyes in a tiny pale urchin's face stared at him mutely.

Nay, not mute, he realized, *deaf*. That's why she hadn't heard him or the horses. It was the feel of the ground shaking that had alerted her to danger.

"Go," he repeated again, pushing her in the direction of the trees. "You'll be safe."

She must have understood his meaning if not the words, because she gave him a frantic nod and scurried off into the trees.

Even before he looked up, Alex felt a chill of premonition as the men who'd surrounded him emerged from the darkness. The hand reaching over his back for his sword stilled.

Damn it, it couldn't be.

But it was.

The blood drained from his body in a violent rush. He muttered a harsh curse, recognizing the familiar blackened nasal helms, soot-stained faces, black leather studded *cotuns*, and dark plaids.

Hell, he wasn't ready for this. He wasn't sure he'd ever be ready.

His hand dropped to his side. After fighting alongside these men for seven years, he knew better. He was good, but single-handedly defeating nine warriors of the Highland Guard was beyond any one man's skills.

Alex had always known he might pay with his life one day for what he'd done, he just hadn't anticipated it being so soon.

A familiar voice broke through the silence. "I see you are still polishing that shiny armor of yours, *Sir* Alex."

2

ALEX BRACED HIMSELF for the condemnation and hatred, as he turned to face one of the most feared men in England, his former partner and hate-everything-English, Robbie Boyd.

But nothing could have prepared him for the stab of guilt that plunged through his gut when he saw the look of betrayal in the eyes of the man whose friendship and respect he'd struggled for so long to earn. At times Alex thought he had, and at others, it felt like all he was doing was banging his head against that wall.

You did what you had to do. He never trusted you anyway. You were never really a part of them. But the guilt coiling in his chest didn't seem to think that was enough.

"You didn't get enough of rescuing *fair* maids in Scotland, so you had to stab us in the back and go to England instead?" Boyd said.

Alex flinched. Though he'd anticipated the blow, it didn't make it any easier to withstand.

He didn't miss the emphasis—or the sarcasm. Boyd's wife was known as "The Fair Rosalin" after her illustrious ancestor "The Fair" Rosemund Clifford. When Alex had still been with the Guard, Rosalin had been taken hostage after a retaliatory raid in Norham to secure her brother's agreement to a truce. To say that Alex had clashed with Boyd over the taking of the hostages (Rosalin's nephew had been taken as well, although the boy had managed to escape) was putting it mildly.

Making war on women and youths was bad enough, but when Alex guessed that Boyd had taken Rosalin to his bed, the dishonor done to her while in their care had seemed the final blow.

Alex just couldn't do it anymore. He could no longer be party to such dishonorable acts done in the name of war.

Not just Boyd's, but his own as well.

Alex couldn't forget how close he'd come to doing something for which he could never forgive himself—that little girl's face in the flames was never too far from his mind. He'd reached her in time, thank God, and pulled her from the flames of the building to which he'd set fire in that same retaliatory raid in Norham. But that was the moment he knew something had to change. Holding the sobbing child in his arms whom he'd almost accidentally killed, something in him had snapped.

This wasn't right—no matter how just the ends—and he couldn't do it anymore.

He couldn't set fire to one more barn, see one more town razed, or one more innocent harmed. There had to be another way than the "eye for an eye," "you raze me, I'll raze you more" mentality that had defined the war in the Borders for so long on both sides.

In that child's tear-stained, smoke-blackened face, Alex

realized it was never going to end. Not like this. It had become a war of attrition that could and would go on for years, with Alex's people in the Borders—and little girls like this—the ones who suffered.

He knew he had to do something. Something drastic. Something that might make a difference. Something that actually had a chance of putting an end to the damned war.

It had become painfully clear that that something wasn't going to be fighting for Bruce with the Highland Guard. It wasn't that Alex had never fully embraced the pirate style of warfare, which went against everything he had been taught was honorable as a knight, but it wasn't getting them anywhere—not anymore. The skirmishes, ambushes, and raids that had given Bruce a foothold were never going to give him the definitive victory he needed to signal God's judgment in the righteousness of his cause and force the English to accept him as king. Only a pitched battle—army meeting army—would do that, but Bruce vehemently refused to do something so risky. Why should he, when he could go on as he was until the English gave up?

If Bruce wouldn't end the war with a battle—and God knows Alex had tried to persuade him—it would have to be done with a truce. And Bruce wasn't the one who needed to be convinced to parley. It was the English. The only thing Alex could do was to try to end the war from the other side, using reason, negotiation, compromise, and the influence he'd once had as a former English baron to help them see the value in peace and bring them to the bargaining table.

It would be a difficult task—hell, a Promethean one—but God knew, it would be better than raids, hostages, and burning barns with innocents.

When Rosalin decided she wanted to return to

England, Alex had "rescued" her—as Boyd had just accused him—by escorting her. Alex didn't know what Boyd had done to win her back, but it must have convinced her that he'd changed. For Rosalin's sake, Alex hoped so.

Unlike Rosalin, however, Alex hadn't gone back.

He told himself he was still fighting for Bruce's place on the throne, but he knew his former brethren wouldn't see it that way. To them he betrayed them—stabbed them in the back—and his reasons for switching sides wouldn't matter.

They wouldn't care that it was the hardest decision he'd ever had to make in his life. That he'd agonized over it for months. That leaving the Guard had been like cutting off his own arm—with the damage he'd done in removing his tattoo he practically had. That it had torn him apart for weeks . . . months . . . hell, it still tore him apart.

Now here he was facing not God's judgment in the righteousness of his cause, but his former brethren's.

He was a dead man.

Ignoring Boyd's jibe about the knife in the back, he said, "Aye, well, I didn't think you'd see her in time, and I doubt even someone who blackens their armor would let a little girl get run over if he could stop it."

He heard a sharp laugh from the man next to Boyd. "He has you there, Raider," MacSorley said.

But any thought that Alex might find sympathy from the always jesting and good-humored seafarer was lost when their eyes met. MacSorley's face was a mask of betrayal every bit as hard and impenetrable as Boyd's. They all were: MacLeod, MacSorley, Campbell, MacGregor, Boyd, Sutherland, MacKay, Lamont, MacLean, and one face he didn't recognize beneath the helm.

His replacement?

The sting was surprisingly sharp. Alex could never go

back. He'd known that, but seeing it staring at him in the face and condemning him was different. For seven years these men had been his brothers, and now they hated him.

It was hard to take—no matter how good his reasons for leaving.

MacSorley's sarcasm was just as heavy as Boyd's when he added, "Wearing a wyvern on a surcoat doesn't give someone a lock on chivalry and honor—even if Sir Alex seemed to think so."

Wyvern, not a dragon. That hurt. At one time Alex would have liked nothing more than to hear MacSorley refer to the emblem of his arms correctly. As a young knight the jest about the "dragon" on the Seton coat of arms had driven him crazy. But eventually, it had given him his secret war name among the Guard. By calling it a wyvern now, MacSorley couldn't have made it more clear that Dragon was no longer a part of them.

"I never thought that," Alex started to explain, and then stopped. He'd never been a part of them. That had always been part of the problem. Why would they understand him now when they never had before?

It was too late for explanations. They all knew that. He would not beg for understanding or forgiveness. He'd made his decision; he would have to live with it.

Or not live, as was the case.

Jaw locked, he turned to the chief of the Highland Guard, Tor MacLeod. "Do what you must."

MacLeod motioned to Boyd. Fitting, Alex supposed, that it would be his former partner to strike him down. They'd never seen eye to eye. About the war. About the way to fight it. About anything. But instead of pulling his sword from his scabbard, Boyd moved his horse a few feet forward and stopped.

"Was it worth it?" his former partner asked, his mouth a hard line of bitterness and anger.

The deceptively simple question took Alex aback. He'd never thought about it—perhaps because he didn't want to know the answer.

But he considered it now and answered truthfully. "I don't know yet." God willing, he could still do something to put an end to this. He'd made some inroads, but as today's precipitous attack by Pembroke on Carrick proved, he hadn't made enough. "But at the time I didn't feel as if I had any other choice."

He'd had to do *something*. He couldn't go on as he was, and trying to fight from the other side had seemed the best—the only—way of making a difference. If he never had to see another village razed, another family left to starve, another face in the flames, it would have all been worth it. No matter the personal cost.

Boyd's mouth clamped into an even harder line. "Because of Rosalin."

It wasn't a question, so Alex didn't attempt to answer. Rosalin might have been the final blow, but why he'd left was far more complicated than that.

Was it because his former partner had violated every code of honor and decency by seducing a woman in their care? Because Boyd had been ready to retaliate for a raid he thought was ordered by Rosalin's brother by burning down the castle she considered her home? Because Alex was tired of jumping out of trees and hiding in the dark, and wanted to fight knight to knight on a battlefield? Or because being a knight and living by certain codes actually meant something to him?

Was it because he couldn't stand the sight of one more injustice done in the name of war—by either side—that he was supposed to ignore as the ends justifying the means? Because he was tired of seeing the people in the Borders—his people—suffer for the misfortune of where they lived? Because he'd held a child he'd nearly killed in his arms and felt something inside him break? Because he knew Bruce would not risk the pitched battle that would bring an end to the war when he could wage a war of attrition and prolong that decision indefinitely? Because Alex thought he could do more to help end the war on the other side by trying to make the English see the value of the bargaining table?

Or maybe he just couldn't take it anymore—the war, the atrocities, the injustice, the constant disagreements with his partner, the feeling as if he was the lone voice of dissent.

Yes. That was the simple answer. It was all those things. But Boyd hadn't wanted to hear it when they were friends—or partners, at least—why would he want to hear it now when they were enemies?

They'd always had different lines in the sand. Boyd was willing to do whatever it took; Alex wasn't.

The two men faced off in the darkness, the tension palpable.

Why didn't he just get it over with? Was this part of their torture? Did they want him to beg? He wouldn't do it, damn it.

He couldn't have been more shocked when Boyd moved to the side to let him pass.

"You are letting me go?" Alex asked.

"This time," Boyd said. "Consider it repayment for what you did for my wife. You were right to defend her honor. I was wrong."

Alex had *thought* he couldn't be more shocked, but Boyd had just proved him wrong.

It sounded like an apology, and coming from Boyd, that would have been a first. But if Alex might have harbored an instant of wondering whether it might have been an opening, the door was quickly closed.

"But the next time we meet across the battlefield, *Sir* Alex, you will not be so lucky."

Boyd always did have a way of making his temper flare, and Alex couldn't resist responding, "Perhaps it is you who will not be so lucky, *Sir* Robert."

After all the shite Boyd had given him about being a knight, Alex still couldn't believe that his partner had been knighted. No doubt he'd done it to prove something to his wife. But as Alex had been reminded too many times in England, there was more to being a knight than wearing spurs and a surcoat.

Boyd hadn't missed the taunt. And the return flare of anger in Boyd's gaze told Alex that he had not forgotten who won the last time they crossed swords—or in that case, fists.

"I hope MacGregor can get someone to sell tickets," MacSorley quipped. "I can't believe I missed the strongest man in Scotland eating dirt."

Alex's gaze shot to Boyd's in surprise. He'd told them. Somehow knowing that he'd been hearing MacSorley's jabs for years felt like some form of recompense.

Without another word, Alex rode through the gap in the circle. He didn't look back. He *couldn't* look back. That was all too clear.

He'd thought the day he'd taken a knife to his arm and obliterated the tattoo that marked him as a Guardsman had been the most difficult. He was wrong. Coming face-to-face with his former friends, and seeing the way they looked at him . . . that had been far worse. They might not have killed him, but it felt as if eighteen knives had eviscerated him all the same. He knew how badly he'd betrayed them, but it wasn't until that moment that he'd really felt it.

He still couldn't believe they'd let him go. He'd half-expected MacRuairi to slip a dagger in his back as he rode by—

He stopped, all of a sudden realizing what he'd missed . . . and the significance: MacRuairi hadn't been there, and Alex knew all too well what that might mean.

Already riding hard for the castle, he quickened his pace.

The rest of the army was still straggling in as he came storming through the gate. After finding his men, he told them what he wanted them to do. He didn't identify MacRuairi by name, just that he thought one of Bruce's men might be in the castle. They were to tell him—and only him—if they saw anything suspicious, but not to approach. Fortunately, Alex was familiar with Carlisle—and MacRuairi's methods—and knew the likely places to look. But if the famed brigand had been here, he wasn't any longer.

Still, Alex knew MacRuairi's absence couldn't be a coincidence.

Maybe Pembroke had learned a little humility from his defeat earlier, because when Alex told him his concerns, he not only listened, he took them to the keeper of the castle, Sir Henry de Beaumont. Security was tightened, the guard was increased, and when the attack came later that night, they were ready.

∽

Edward Bruce's attempt to take the castle had failed. Though she'd been alerted to the attack by the noise with the rest of the castle, Joan had waited not so patiently all morning to hear the details. It wasn't until she was helping her cousin ready for the midday meal that Alice volunteered what she knew. By that point, Joan had been perilously close to breaking her rule not to ask her cousin direct questions. Though Alice was too spoiled and self-centered to focus her attention long enough on her "unfortunate" cousin to become suspicious, Joan didn't want to take chances.

"One of the Earl of Pembroke's men suspected what was happening with raiders in the area and foiled the rebel trickery when they attempted a diversion at the gate," Alice said proudly. "It was fortunate that the earl arrived when he did."

"Very fortunate," Joan agreed, hiding her anger behind a facade of polite interest. It wasn't just the missed opportunity to take the castle that infuriated her, it was also Pembroke's arrival. She should have known he was coming. How could she have not heard that one of Edward's most important commanders in the north, accompanied by at least two hundred men, was headed to Carlisle?

This was exactly the type of information Bruce was counting on her to uncover. That she hadn't—and Edward Bruce's men had been surprised—could well have been a disaster. Had Randolph not arrived when he did, the king's last remaining brother might have been taken or killed, and Joan would have considered herself responsible.

This was the first time she hadn't learned of something this important beforehand. Were the English keeping Pembroke's arrival a secret for a specific reason, or were they just being more careful with information?

Neither was a promising development.

Joan knew that the English were determined to uncover the well-placed spy who was feeding information to the Scots, but as women were beneath their scrutiny, she'd never felt the threat of suspicion—which didn't mean she wasn't careful. She always took care not to appear too interested in the war or politics, not to ask too many questions, and not to show any loyalty to the land of her birth. She tried to appear just as "English" as her cousin—although Alice's blood was every bit as Scottish as hers. You would never know it by looking at her or listening to her. Alice had fully embraced her adopted homeland and regarded Scotland as a rough "backward" place filled with "rebels" who must be conquered and civilized.

Alice shivered. "Can you imagine what might have happened if their plan had succeeded? We could be some barbarian's hostage right now." She gasped as if something had just occurred to her. "Do you think they would have ravished us?"

Good Lord, she sounded almost excited by the prospect. There was nothing romantic or exciting about having a man force you—nothing. But her beautiful cousin liked to be the object of male desire and thought their lust flattering. Joan knew differently.

Though a few years older than her twenty, Alice seemed far less mature. Joan had always been older than her years, and with everything that had happened since her mother was imprisoned, it sometimes felt as if she were Alice's mother rather than a young woman near her own age.

Though Joan wanted nothing more than to shake some sense into that silly head, she pretended to take the question seriously. "I suspect they might have. We are fortunate indeed that Sir Aymer's man figured out their plan. Who was he? Perhaps we should thank him for saving us."

Her tone must have been more curious than she intended. Her cousin's gaze seemed to narrow just a little. "I don't know. My husband didn't say. But I don't think that will be necessary. Besides, I doubt Sir Richard would like it.

He watches you like a hungry hawk." She frowned disapprovingly. "You need to be more circumspect, cousin. People are starting to talk, and it reflects poorly on Henry and me."

Joan tried not to choke on her tongue. Good Lord, that was the guilty cast as the accuser. Alice's rampant promiscuity was equaled only by her husband's, although Alice was fiercely jealous, whereas Sir Henry couldn't have cared less with whom his wife shared her bed—much to Alice's irritation. Her cousin seemed to equate jealousy and possessiveness with love. Joan had seen the fallacy of that with her parents.

Joan lowered her eyes as if embarrassed. "Sir Richard is leaving soon."

"Good," Alice said, standing from the chair she'd been seated at while Joan helped her with her jewelry. "I do not begrudge you your *flirtations*, cousin, but I do not like to hear you the subject of unflattering rumors."

In other words, she didn't like Joan being the focus of attention—even negative attention. That Joan had always been content to be in her cousin's shadow was the only reason Alice had taken her as a companion and tiring woman. Joan had never made herself a threat and needed to keep it that way. Fortunately, although Joan's looks appeared to resonate with the men, her cousin didn't view her as competition. With her dainty, well-curved figure, blond hair, blue eyes, and perfect doll-like features, Alice de Beaumont was a strikingly beautiful woman.

With a properly chastised nod that showed her gratitude for her cousin's benevolence, Joan followed her cousin to the Hall.

But the foiled attack, her ignorance of Pembroke's arrival, and Sir Richard's upcoming departure combined to make Joan realize that she was going to need to increase her efforts. She would not be caught in the dark again. If she was going to continue to be useful to Bruce, she had to take risks. Sir Richard had information, and she was going to get it. Even if she didn't like how she would have to do so.

3

J OAN COULD BARELY close the door behind her, her hands were shaking so badly. Actually, her entire body was shaking. Her skin was like ice. Fear and panic had invaded her body like a snowstorm in the dead of winter and wouldn't let go.

It's all right. You are safe. It's over. Nothing happened.

But it had been close. *Too close.*

She crept through the darkness of the corridor, winding her way down the stairs of the Captain's Tower from Sir Richard's third-floor chamber.

She felt clumsy . . . awkward . . . tentative. Her heart was still beating like a drum in her chest and ears. She couldn't shake the moment of terror. God, she could still feel his hands on her, pinning her down, not letting her move. The memories had come hard and fast and for one horrible moment she had been paralyzed with fear. It had been too similar. She'd thought he was going to . . .

But then her plan worked and the threat had collapsed in a drugged heap. The panic, however, remained.

Good gracious, she'd been so shaken she'd almost forgotten to search his room! A search that had resulted in a missive with his orders and details regarding the ports and shipping routes for getting the necessary supplies into Scotland for the war. An army of the size Edward was gathering would require far more than they could carry, even in an extensive baggage train. Now she knew how it would get there.

There were probably only a handful of people who knew the information she had discovered, and soon one of them would be Robert the Bruce. Thanks to her.

It had been worth it, she told herself. But her frazzled nerves didn't seem to realize that. The shadows seemed to jump out at her as she wound her way down the darkened corridors. At well past midnight, most of the lamps had already been extinguished for the night. She hurried down the stairs, going down faster than she should, trying to put as much distance between her and what had nearly happened back in that room, when her slippered foot landed awkwardly on one of the narrow stairs. The stairs were made of stone, and as they became worn with use, they could become slippery. She discovered this the painful way when her foot slid out from under her.

She tried to catch herself, and in doing so wrenched her ankle in the effort to find her footing. She tumbled down the last part of the spiral staircase, and likely would have landed in a painful heap at the base had someone not caught her.

"Christ! Are you all right?"

She was so startled to feel the man's hands on her, it took a moment for her to process his words . . . and his face.

But when she did . . .

God in heaven! A heart that she thought incapable of

catching did just that. If she still believed in handsome knights riding to the rescue, this man would have personified her fantasy. Dark golden-blond hair shimmered in the flickering light. Piercing blue eyes that were so crystal and clear they seemed to sparkle in the darkness. A finely featured face that might have been boyish were it not for the slightly skewed once-broken nose and the dark shadow of stubble shaped into a quarter-inch beard. Tall and broad shouldered, he had the lean solid build of a man who lifted a sword for a living. He'd caught her as if she weighed nothing, and the hands holding her were big and strong.

But even were he not wearing chain mail and surcoat, she would have known he was a knight. He looked like he should be riding on a white charger with his sword held high in the air ready to vanquish dragons and rescue fair maidens, which given their current position was appropriate.

Suddenly aware that he'd caught her in a way that might be construed as intimate—and the feel of her breasts crushed against the solid steel wall of his chest certainly felt that—she blushed (for real!) and tried to regain her composure as she pushed back to extract herself from his hold.

"I'm fine," she said unevenly, sounding more like a starry-eyed maid than she'd ever sounded in her life. "Thank you. I'm sorry to have troubled—"

She stopped suddenly, crying out in pain as she stepped back and put weight on her twisted ankle. She might have stumbled again had he not still been holding her arm.

"Careful," he said gently, steadying her on the stair above him. "You're hurt."

He had a very nice voice. Deep, soft, and soothing. There was something kind and almost gallant about it.

Good gracious, she really was getting carried away

with the knight fantasy, wasn't she? A long time ago she'd believed in the stories of handsome men in shining armor who not only espoused knightly ideals but also lived them. Now she knew differently; experience had cured her of *all* her illusions. Men like that only existed in faerie tales. With every lecherous look and dishonorable suggestion by the "knights" around her, they proved it to her. Honor, nobility, and respect didn't mean a thing when lust was involved. Men—even knights—only wanted one thing.

But this man wasn't looking at her like that at all.

Not knowing what to make of it, she frowned and told herself to give him time. He would probably try to turn his role of rescuer to his advantage soon. She could hear it in her head: *How can I thank you?* she would ask, and his response with a wicked smile, *I'm sure we can think of something*.

Aye, something that no doubt included mouths and tongues, and him trying to grope her chest.

Having successfully cleared the stars from her eyes, her voice (and heartbeat) returned to normal. "It's my ankle. I seem to have twisted it."

His expression shifted to one that seemed to be of genuine concern. "Are you sure it's not broken?"

She nodded. "It's a little tender, that's all. I will wrap it when I get back to my room, and I'm sure it will be fine."

She'd never noticed how tight and narrow the stairwell was—or maybe it was just because he was so big. His shoulders almost spanned the width. He seemed to have confiscated all the air. She was finding it difficult to breathe, and then when she did . . . her senses were filled with leather, wind, and the hint of something spicy . . . maybe cloves?

She was a tall woman at six inches over five feet, but even standing on the stair above him, the top of her head only came up to his chin. But their faces were close, and she was too aware of every inch between them—of which there were only a precious handful.

She studied his face again. He was even better looking than she'd realized initially. There was something vaguely familiar about him . . .

She gasped, shock making her forget herself for a moment. No wonder she thought he looked like a fantasy. He was a fantasy—*her* fantasy, as it turned out.

Joan had never forgotten the handsome young knight who'd caught her fourteen-year-old girlish imagination at the market in Roxburgh six years before. At the time, she hadn't realized he'd been with her mother. She simply thought him the most magnificent young knight she'd ever seen. Sir Alexander Seton. She'd learned his name in the intervening years, and his place in the Guard . . .

Suddenly, what else that meant struck her.

Her thoughts must have shown on her face.

"Is something wrong, my lady?" he asked.

Aye, something was wrong. Alex Seton wasn't a gallant knight by any cry of imagination—he was a traitor.

❧

Rescuing two young women in as many days was a bit excessive—even for him. MacSorley would have been making jokes at Alex's expense for weeks.

The fact that this was among his first thoughts after catching the woman falling down the stairs told him how much the confrontation with his former brethren still was weighing on him.

His other thoughts were equally troubling—especially

when he recognized the young woman in his arms. Having lustful thoughts about Bella MacDuff now MacRuairi's daughter shamed him. But Christ, the lass was even more stunning than he remembered (and old enough for him to notice, as opposed to the last time he'd seen her). With her dark-as-midnight long, wavy, and naughtily mussed hair, her wide, red mouth, snow-white skin, and take-me-to-the-bedchamber-and-ravish-me-senseless eyes, the lass was sin and sensual pleasure personified.

It didn't help that she looked like she'd just tumbled out of bed. She was wearing a dressing gown, for Christ's sake, and the soft, sensual, barely covered womanly curves had been crushed against his chest. He would have had to be a eunuch not to have been affected by such intimate and not-much-separating-them contact with a body divined for pleasure. Generous breasts, a dainty waist, slender hips, long legs perfect to wrap around . . .

He stopped. What the hell was wrong with him?

He knew exactly what was wrong with him, and it was bloody inconvenient to be reminded of it right now. Hell, he usually had better control. He *always* had better control.

But then again, he couldn't remember the last time he'd been alone in a dark stairwell with a beautiful, scantily clad woman in his arms in the middle of the night. Actually, as he realized that had never occurred before, he probably could be excused for the inappropriate direction of his thoughts and the swift reaction of his body.

Both of which vanished, however, when he realized she was hurt.

"My lady?" he asked when she didn't respond to his

question right away. She was looking at him so strangely. Almost as if she knew him. Had she noticed him all those years ago? He hoped not. God knows, any connection to the Guard could be disastrous for him. King Edward would be furious that he'd kept such information from him and would demand to know their secrets and their identities. Alex may have left the Guard, but that was a betrayal he could not stomach.

"Nay," she said hurriedly, lowering her gaze from his. "There is nothing wrong. I just realized I do not know who I should thank for saving me from a lot more than a twisted ankle."

"Alex Seton at your service, my lady," he said with a surprisingly lighthearted bow. He didn't usually go out of his way to charm young ladies—actually he usually avoided them—but he wanted to put her at ease.

Her mouth quirked, catching on to his game. "Lady Joan Comyn, Sir Alex. I would curtsey, but I'm afraid you might have to catch me again if I tried."

Just how much he wouldn't mind holding her again surprised him—as did the resulting wave of heat that coursed through his blood at the thought.

Remembering his role, however, he forced it aside. "Well, my lady, why don't I help you back to your room so you can tend to that ankle."

She looked alarmed. "I don't want to trouble you. I'm sure I can make it on my own."

"It's no trouble, and I insist. It isn't safe for you to be wandering the castle at night alone." Which begged the question . . . "What were you doing in here anyway? I thought the ladies were in the new tower?"

She blushed, lowering her gaze again. Her long, delicate lashes rested on her cheeks like wisps of a silken raven's wing. Christ, her skin was unreal. It was soft, powdery, and as flawless as freshly fallen snow.

"I don't remember, my lord."

He frowned. "You don't remember?"

She shook her head. "I sometimes walk in my sleep."

Alex nodded with understanding. "My brother used to do that when he was a child."

Her eyes widened; clearly she hadn't expected that. "He did?"

"Aye. It terrified my mother the first few times it happened—she thought he would fall down the stairs or walk into the sea beyond the gate and drown himself. But John only seemed interested in visiting the kitchens." He smiled at the memory. "He consumed an entire apple tart one night. I thought he was faking until I caught him myself." John's eyes had been open but eerily glazed over, and he'd acted as if Alex wasn't there. "She had special locks put on his windows and doors, but it seemed to resolve itself after a few years."

"He no longer does it?"

Alex shook his head; the wave of sadness that overtook him was not as sharp as it used to be, but it was still painful. "Both my brothers were executed eight years ago after the Battle of Methven. You have probably heard of Christopher."

Everyone had heard of Sir Christopher Seton. He wasn't surprised when she nodded.

But unlike everyone else, she did not go on about it or look at him with expectations that he could never hope to fulfill.

"I'm sorry," she added softly.

Alex acknowledged her sympathy with a nod, and then pushed the maudlin thoughts away with concern of his own. "Perhaps you should think about a lock on your door or having one of the servants sleep in front of it. Next time someone might not be there to catch you."

And Alex knew falling down stairwells wasn't the only danger in a castle like this—a castle populated largely by soldiers, some more rough than others. When he thought of how vulnerable she was in such a state . . .

Every muscle in his body hardened with rage that was both instinctive and, he recognized, disproportionate to the circumstances.

"You are right." As if sensing his anger, she put a hand on his arm. "I should have done so. It just hasn't happened in a while and caught me unaware."

Alex took one look at the very dainty, very soft and feminine hand resting on his arm and felt the strangest sensation. It was both instantly calming and instantly something else—something hot, jolting, and filled with awareness. He'd never felt anything like it, and the fierceness of the sensations took him aback.

Bella's daughter, he reminded himself. But that was too easy to forget when her very womanly body was only a few inches from his in a dark and suddenly excruciatingly small stairwell.

The lass was far too desirable for his peace of mind. He also felt a strange connection to her—as if he knew her. He didn't, but feeling as if he did was oddly disarming. *She* was disarming.

With effort, he forced his mind from bedchambers, thin chemises barely covered by velvet robes that did little to hide a body that he'd give his eyeteeth to see naked, silky, tousled hair that should be spread out on a pillow—or draped over his naked chest like a silken veil—and the faint scent of rose water.

"Come," he said, holding out his hand. "I will be forced to turn in my spurs if you do not let me help you back to your chamber."

She tilted her head, studying him with a slightly bemused expression on her face. "You take your knightly duties seriously, don't you?"

There was something dry in her voice that bordered almost on sarcasm. He frowned, stiffening. "I do."

She studied him a few moments longer before finally putting her hand in his. "Well," she conceded. "I wouldn't want to be responsible for interfering with a knight's duties."

The shock of contact was followed by a blast of warmth. Her fingers were so soft and small tucked inside his. He didn't want to let them go, but reluctantly he moved her hand to the curve of his elbow for support.

Alex liked that she was teasing him. He'd wager it was just as much a rarity for her as it was for him. "And I wouldn't be much of a knight if I let you think it was all duty."

Christ, was he actually flirting with her? He didn't flirt with anyone. He was too serious, too focused on the war, and had been since he wasn't much older than she. Women weren't to be trifled with, they were to be protected, admired, and treated with formality and respect.

Disarming.

He concentrated on helping her down the last few stairs, which wasn't easy, as she seemed reluctant to put too much weight on him or lean into him too closely.

Does she feel it, too?

He couldn't be sure—her thoughts were difficult to read. But the realization that he might not be alone in his attraction only made the situation more uncomfortable and fraught with tension. Every touch, every brush of their bodies made his body jump and his skin flush with heat.

When they finally reached the courtyard, he gave up. This was ridiculous, damn it. She was wincing every other step, and at this pace it would be dawn before they made it to the tower.

Taking matters into his own hands, he swept her off her feet and into his arms. Ignoring her gasp of shock at being carried like a bairn, he gritted his teeth and fixed his eyes straight ahead. He wouldn't think about how good she smelled, how soft the hair was that was brushing against his chin, or how her bottom bumped perilously close to the growing bulge in his braies with each step. A little lower . . .

"What are you doing?" she demanded, oblivious to his suffering.

He didn't need to glance down to see the eyes that were surely shooting daggers at him—he could hear her outrage in her voice.

"Carrying you," he said matter-of-factly.

"I can see that," she snapped back furiously. "But I did not give you permission—"

"You were in pain, and I knew you would object, so I decided to make it easy on you." He looked down at her with a smile. "You're welcome."

He could feel her eyes on him, studying his face as if looking for something. "Are you always so high-handed?"

"Only when I anticipate someone is going to be unreasonably stubborn." He laughed again at her expression. "Besides, I prefer to think of it as gallant."

"Is that so?" she drawled. "I guess that means I'm the helpless maiden in need of rescue to your Sir Galahad?"

Unknowingly, she'd hit a nerve. She wasn't the first person to call him that, though the other—MacRuairi—had done so with considerably more disparagement. Pushing aside the bad memory, he smiled. "Now you're getting the idea."

She shook her head as if he were an incorrigible bairn. "I hope you don't expect me to swoon."

She looked so adorably disgruntled he laughed again. "Nay, a simple thanks will suffice."

All too soon, they reached the door to her chamber. He set her down carefully—and maybe a little too reluctantly. "Now that wasn't so bad, was it?"

She looked like she wanted to argue, but her good nature won out. Her mouth twisted in a smile. "As it would be shrewish to argue when I have arrived so quickly and in such comfort, I think I'll swallow my pride and just say thank you."

He grinned. "Smart lass."

He was a moment away from dropping a kiss on her soft red mouth before he caught himself.

Christ, where had that come from? It was as if kissing her were the most natural thing in the world.

Perhaps guessing his thoughts, she sobered and took a cautious step back. "Thank you, Sir Alex," she said again before slipping into her chamber.

Alex stood staring at the closed door for a long moment before retracing his steps and returning to his own chamber. But the strange interlude with Joan Comyn stayed with him long into the night.

4

ALEX THOUGHT THE meeting would never end. De Beaumont—as keeper of the castle—and Pembroke—as an earl and the man of highest rank—had been measuring their cocks all morning, and frankly, neither had anything worth bragging about.

Two of King Edward's most important barons seemed more interested in the sound of their own voices than in planning this damned war. Posturing, positioning, vying for attention . . . that was all Edward's commanders seemed interested in, and Alex was bloody tired of it. At least when he was with the Highland Guard they'd always had a common purpose, even if they didn't always agree on how to get there. But these two were more worried about who would ride in what order and lead which part of the army than they were about tactics and strategy. After Alex's suggestion to request a parley with Bruce to see if they might come to terms before marching was swiftly (and decisively) dismissed, he had been only half-listening anyway.

Alex tried not to let the frustration get to him, but he was running out of time. The inroads he'd thought he'd made in London two years ago were harder to remember the farther they marched north. At first the king had seemed willing to listen to Alex's pleas for the people in the Borders and his warnings that Bruce was stronger than his numbers appeared. Edward had said he would consider Alex's suggestion of a parley.

He hadn't considered it for long. Thanks to the problems with his barons, Scotland had become Edward's rallying cry. His distraction. His way of proving to his people that he was his father's son, and a king they could believe in. Alex knew it was going to be next to impossible to dissuade Edward from his course. Which didn't mean Alex wouldn't try. But it was becoming increasingly clear that no one was willing to listen to reason—certainly not the cockmeasuring de Beaumont and Pembroke.

His thoughts turned to something far more pleasant. He wondered how Lady Joan's ankle was this morning. Perhaps he would seek her out after the meeting to check on her.

He found himself oddly curious about Bella's daughter. He knew that after she'd been falsely declared illegitimate, and her claim to the Buchan earldom given to her cousins, Lady Joan now served as a companion to one of those cousins—Alice—who was married to de Beaumont. He doubted anyone truly believed the lie that Joan was not Buchan's daughter (instead the product of an illicit affair between Bella and Bruce), but no one wanted to see the daughter of a notorious traitor rewarded with an earldom. He recalled some other contrivance about consanguinity—related godparents?—had been used as well.

They were a convenient pretense, that was all. Edward ensured the support of de Beaumont in his fight against the Scots—as de Beaumont would be fighting for his own lands—and no one cared about the daughter of a dead earl and a rebel "whore."

He wondered what Joan thought about it. Did she regret not returning to Scotland when she'd had the chance all those years ago? Ironically, Alex had been part of the team who had rescued MacRuairi and Bella from Berwick Castle when they'd been captured not long after Bella's return to Scotland. MacRuairi had given the then fourteen-year-old Joan an opportunity to go with them, but she'd declined, saying that her life was in England with her Comyn uncle and cousins. It had broken Bella's heart.

Given what had happened in the interim, Alex wondered whether she would make the same decision today. The lass had hardly been rewarded for her loyalty to the English cause.

It was close to the midday meal by the time the meeting finally broke up. Alex was going to go in search of her when he caught part of the conversation taking place in the group of young soldiers walking ahead of him.

"Long night, Fitzgerald? I thought you were going to fall asleep there for a while when de Beaumont was talking about whose men would sleep in the barracks at Wark and whose would have to set up tents outside the gates."

Alex had been about to doze off himself. He hadn't slept much last night. He'd been too busy thinking.

"I feel like I just swam from here to Ireland," another man answered. "I've never been so . . . *satisfied*."

From the way he said it—like a cat that had just lapped up a big bowl of cream—Alex understood what kind of satisfied he meant. Obviously the young redheaded knight had spent the night with a lass.

Alex recognized him now. He was one of Ulster's young sea captains. Sir Richard Fitzgerald was a promising young soldier from a powerful family and said to be one of the best seafarers in Ireland. Perhaps he'd give MacSorley a challenge one day.

Not that it would be any day soon. Alex knew there was

no one who could come close to the West Highland chieftain. Hawk—MacSorley—was the best seafarer not just in Scotland but likely in Christendom. He was also the best swimmer, as Alex could personally attest. Years ago during training, MacSorley had saved his life in the stormy seas near the Isle of Skye.

Why the hell was he thinking of that now?

"Ah, the lady finally succumbed, did she?" one of the men said. "And I use the term 'lady' very loosely. From what I hear the quiet, mysterious lady is a she-cat in bed. I wouldn't mind her sinking her claws into me. When you're done with her, of course," he said to Fitzgerald.

Alex stiffened at the crude talk. No man should talk about a woman that way—any woman—and it was worse, as these men were knights. They should know better, damn it.

Alex was about to remind them of that fact, when Fitzgerald spoke. "You should see her breasts," the young captain said with an exaggerated groan. "Hell, if she wasn't Buchan's bastard, I might be tempted to marry her just to bury my face in them every—"

He didn't get a chance to finish. Alex had him slammed up against the castle wall with his hand around his throat. The reaction was pure instinct, and if the black rage that was pounding in Alex's ears was any indication, the lad was lucky Alex hadn't killed him outright.

Fitzgerald's hands had gone directly to his neck and were trying to pull Alex's away from his throat, but the younger man might as well have been trying to pry steel. Alex's muscles were as rigid and fixed as an iron bar.

"I've heard enough of your vile lies," Alex said in a voice he didn't recognize. Hell, it had the low, deadly edge of MacRuairi's. "How dare you speak of a lady that way."

Fitzgerald's friends had finally recovered from their shock. "Let him go," one of them said, though he made no move to challenge Alex. "He can't breathe."

Realizing that Fitzgerald's eyes were bulging, Alex lightened his hold just enough to let the other man suck in a few gasps of air. Fitzgerald gaped at Alex like he was a madman—which wasn't that far off from how he felt.

"What . . . hell . . . Seton?" Fitzgerald said, pulling on Alex's hand some more to release him.

"What's going on here?" Alex recognized Pembroke's voice behind him. "Let him go, Seton."

Alex wasn't inclined to do as he asked.

"That's an order," Pembroke added angrily.

It took a few moments for Alex's head to clear enough to recognize the earl's authority. The king had put Alex under his command, damn it.

With a sound of disgust, Alex released his hold on Fitzgerald's neck with one more hard thrust against the wall. But the urge to kill still surged through his veins.

Seeing his expression, the young seafarer took a step back.

"What is wrong with you, Seton? I've never seen you like this."

That brought Alex up hard. Pembroke was right. For a moment Alex had forgotten himself. He'd been every inch the ruthless brigand he had been becoming in the Guard—not the chivalrous, conscientious knight the English knew him to be.

They'd never suspected his role in Bruce's army, and he wanted to keep it that way. But something told him he'd revealed too much.

Pembroke might be an arse, but he was a sharp one. "Your arm must be feeling better."

It wasn't a question.

Damn. Unthinkingly, he'd used his right arm to pin Fitzgerald.

Pembroke didn't wait for him to answer. "I'll expect you to start training with the rest of the men when we reach Berwick."

Alex nodded, cursing silently.

"Now explain to me what was happening here."

"I have no idea," Fitzgerald said first. "One minute I was talking with my friends and the next Seton was trying to kill me."

Alex stiffened. "I was defending a lady's honor from foul lies."

Pembroke frowned and looked at Fitzgerald. "I will not have ladies maligned—"

"It wasn't a lie," Fitzgerald said angrily. "I didn't realize Seton knew the lady." With his red hair and fair complexion, he couldn't hide the flush that came to his cheeks as he undoubtedly recalled his crude words. "I apologize for what he overheard, but it was the truth. I spent the night with Lady Joan."

Alex made a sound that was suspiciously like a growl, took a step toward him, and might have sunk one of the fists he had clenching at his side through Fitzgerald's teeth if Pembroke hadn't stopped him.

"Leave us," the earl said to Fitzgerald and his friends. "I will see to this."

With a few wary glances in Alex's direction, the young knights did as he asked.

"Your defense of the woman is admirable," Pembroke said to Alex, "but in this case unwarranted. The lady in question is gaining something of a reputation for enjoying the attentions of eager young knights. For all her quiet reserve, it seems the daughter is much more like the mother than she appears."

Alex didn't believe it. It didn't fit with the sweet, modest young lass whom he'd met last night. The English spoke lies about Bella, and now they must have spread to her daughter.

"I'd heard that she'd set her sights on Sir Richard," Pembroke said. "Did you not see them at the evening meal last night? Their heads were bent so close together I'm surprised either of them was able to eat."

Last night. Alex felt the blow like a hammer to the chest. Suddenly, it all slid into place.

"Nay," he said numbly. "I wasn't at the evening meal."

He'd been scouting most of the day and night chasing after any of Edward Bruce's remaining men. He hadn't returned until after midnight when he'd been climbing the Captain's Tower stairs and an angel had fallen from the heavens into his arms.

An angel coming from the very tower where Fitzgerald likely had a room who had claimed to be sleepwalking. Sleepwalking.

And he was fool enough to have believed her.

He felt like a damned idiot.

∞

He caught her before she entered the Hall for the midday meal. With surprising finesse for one so young, Sir Richard had Joan pulled into a storage room and pressed up against a wall with his mouth on her neck before she could react.

But she'd put an end to it—all of it—with ease. Sir Richard would not be propositioning her or demanding she come to his room again. Nay, Joan suspected he wouldn't come within a few hundred feet of her after this.

It had to be done. The trick with the sleeping powder wouldn't work twice. He already seemed confused about what had happened last night. She'd hoped he wouldn't remember anything, but perhaps she hadn't given him enough.

Tears poured down her cheeks. Crying was a skill that had been difficult to master but had proved useful more than once. She choked on a few more sobs and stared up at him incredulously. "What do you mean you won't marry me? After last night . . . you have to do right by me!"

The look of horror and fear on the young knight's face didn't dim any on the repeating. Her demand of marriage had cooled his lust as surely as a swift dunk in an icy loch.

"But I c-can't . . . surely you see . . . you're a bast—"

Fortunately for him, he didn't finish the word. She might have dragged this out a little longer just to see him suffer.

"But what of your honor?" she couldn't resist adding. "I thought . . ." She sobbed a little more for effect. "You are a *knight*."

As if that should explain it all. The fact that it *should* made it that much more ridiculous. Knightly code or not, a proud nobleman like Sir Richard wouldn't think of marrying a "bastard" with a less-than-maidenly reputation—even if he had actually seduced her.

What would she do if one of these "noble" men ever did the "honorable" thing? It would make her job a lot more difficult and it wouldn't be as easy to get rid of them, that was certain.

Joan had learned that the swiftest way to rid herself of a man she'd targeted who was growing impatient with "no," or might be beginning to suspect she wasn't the "easy" mark he'd been led to believe, was to mention one word: marriage. They scatted like frightened mice before a cat. It was shameful, really. But undeniably effective.

"I'm s-sorry," he stuttered, darting for the door as if the devil were nipping at his heels.

Without another word, he was gone, and that was that.

Joan sighed. It was hard not to be cynical when men never surprised her.

At least they didn't usually. But Sir Alex Seton—the man the Guard had called Dragon—had. She didn't know what she expected from the Guardsman who'd betrayed Bruce and his brethren (which now included her), but it wasn't the kindness, consideration, and yes, gallantry, that he'd shown her last night. For a few minutes she had almost been able to believe that she was as innocent and maidenly as he thought her.

Good gracious, when he'd lifted her in his arms to carry her up the tower . . . she could still feel the reverberation from the way her heart had slammed into her chest. She could also still feel the strength of the powerful arms wrapped around her, and the steely hardness of his shield-like chest.

She'd felt safe and secure, warm and protected. It would have been so easy to close her eyes, rest her cheek against his broad chest, and let herself forget—just for a moment. But she couldn't, of course. She wasn't a starry eyed, naive maid anymore, no matter how much he'd made her want to believe otherwise.

She should have been annoyed by his high-handedness, but the romance of the gesture had affected her more than she would have guessed. Perhaps her jaded heart wasn't completely hardened and impervious as she would like to think.

For more reasons than one, she would be wary. Alex Seton was dangerous. Dangerous not only for how he made her feel, but for what he knew. He might not know her identity, but he knew about the existence of a high-placed spy in the English camp. And although he might be a traitor, he was undoubtedly a highly skilled and savvy one. She would not underestimate him, or the threat he posed. She had to avoid him in the future at all costs.

He was a Scot fighting for the English—the worst kind of traitor in her regard.

But it wasn't fair. A traitor who'd betrayed his king and friends should have some kind of black mark across his face to warn her. He certainly shouldn't look as if he'd ridden straight out of Camelot.

She wondered if it was all for show. Was there perhaps one honorable knight left in England, after all?

Her mouth quirked with laughter at the silly thought. Alas, she would not be able to find out. Avoiding him was going to be her primary goal. She hoped he didn't make it difficult on her.

She need not have worried. As soon as she entered the Great Hall a few minutes later, she realized the gossip-mongers at the castle had taken care of Sir Alex for her.

One look at his face when he saw her was enough to tell her that he'd heard the rumors. The judgment in his hard, crystal-clear blue eyes, the disdain in the tilt of that sidelong glance, the mild distaste that turned his mouth as he took in her appearance—and the cut of her gown—shouldn't bother her.

Usually, she didn't mind that people thought her a "harlot" like her mother, because Joan had been "linked" to a number of men. Actually, as it helped her cause, she had never done anything to dispel the rumors. Her wanton reputation put her even more firmly beneath their regard and suspicion. In addition to making them underestimate her, it also gave her access to men she would not otherwise have had a cause to speak with privately.

But she couldn't ignore the blush that heated her cheeks

when Sir Alex's gaze dropped to the low-cut bodice of her gown or deny the pinch of disappointment—and maybe even hurt—in her chest when he turned sharply away.

So much for the fantasy of gallant knights. He couldn't have made his disregard or disapproval more clear.

Fine. She straightened her back and proudly thrust out the chest that seemed to cause so much attention. She had a job to do. And if men thinking her a wanton made that job easier, she would wear gowns that put the Whore of Babylon to shame. She didn't care what any of them thought. She knew the truth and that was all that mattered.

She was a ghost—they couldn't touch her, and she didn't feel anything.

When Sir Alex left Carlisle Castle not long after Sir Richard the following morning, Joan was glad. Two problems had been solved, leaving her able to concentrate on the only task that mattered: finding out whatever information she could for Bruce—and not getting caught doing it.

5

Berwick Castle, Berwick-upon-Tweed,
English Marches, May 16, 1314

JOAN FELT ALL eyes on her as she approached the dais. The gown she'd chosen for the midday meal was even more bold and daring than usual. Red had always been her favorite color, but she'd avoided it of late so as not to draw too much attention to herself.

But today she wanted attention, and the deep crimson velvet of the cotehardie seemed to be doing its job. Of course, it wasn't just the dramatic color. The gown was snug fitting in the arms and bodice and cut almost indecently low across the chest. If she could manage a deep breath—which she didn't think she could—she would be in danger of revealing the edge of her nipples.

The undergown was a rich contrast of gold damask, trimmed with fine beaded and embroidered ribbon. Her hair was loose and held back from her face by a simple gold circlet. The gossamer gold veil that covered the back of her head was so thin and transparent that she might as well have been bareheaded.

She only had a few pieces of jewelry remaining. Most of what her father had given her had been claimed by her cousins (mainly Alice) as part of their inheritance. The simple gold necklace, cameo, and small ruby earrings that Joan wore tonight had been beneath her cousins' regard. The bracelet that MacRuairi had given her was hidden, tucked under the sleeve of her gown. She didn't want Alice to see it and ask questions.

Joan had taken unusual care with her appearance, and if the level of appreciation in the male gazes staring at her was any indication, her efforts had been worth it. But there was only one gaze she sought. One gaze that she knew required boldness and flashiness to draw. Sir Hugh Despenser, King Edward's new favorite, only liked the best. Even as a young man, he had always surrounded himself with the finest, prettiest, and most rare.

Joan had known Sir Hugh for six years. His father—also

Sir Hugh—had been her first guardian after the death of her father. She'd liked the older knight, and although the younger Sir Hugh had been gone most of the time, he'd always treated her kindly.

As a girl, she'd been somewhat in awe of the brash young nobleman whose striking but refined dark-haired, dark-eyed handsomeness verged on prettiness. He dressed richly and colorfully in clothes fit for a king. Though arrogant, conceited, and with an undeniably high opinion of himself, his bold, boisterous charisma and unrepentant, lavish extravagance had always amused her. There was charm in someone who made no pretense about who he was and what he wanted.

He had an unexpectedly strong streak of honor in him though. As she'd grown into a young woman, she'd been aware that his gaze had lingered on her longer and with a different kind of interest. But he'd respected her position in his father's household and never attempted to cross that particular boundary—even when others had.

She hoped he would reconsider now when the boundaries no longer existed. She wanted to look in his direction to see whether his gaze was one that was turned toward her, but forced her eyes straight ahead instead. She didn't want her intentions to be too obvious or show too much interest in him—men liked to be the pursuers, not the pursued.

Joan knew she was taking a risk—a big risk—in setting her sights on Sir Hugh. He was both older and savvier than the young knights she usually targeted. But if the rumors that he held the king's confidence were true, it would be worth it.

King Edward had been mourning the death of his previous favorite, Piers Gaveston, Earl of Cornwall, for nearly a year. The reverberations from the execution of the much-hated Gaveston by some of Edward's barons were still rippling throughout the kingdom.

The exact nature of the king's relationship with Gaveston and others he picked out for his favor was speculated upon, but as the men were often married and involved with women—without the king's displeasure—Joan thought it likely something more than sexual in nature. The sodomy of which some accused him was almost too simple an explanation. What Edward felt for these men was beyond that—it was love, brotherhood, and friendship so deep and consuming that it bordered on obsession. It made him lose sight of everything else and not care that he was alienating his barons, his queen, and his kingdom with the largess he heaped upon his favorites.

The men already seated at the high table stood as she approached. De Beaumont held out his hand to help her take her seat beside Alice's younger sister, her cousin Margaret, who had arrived at Carlisle Castle just before they'd left for Berwick. When the royal party arrived, Joan would take her normal place on one of the lower tables, but with the few women at the castle at present, she was being honored with a seat on the dais.

"You look exceptionally beautiful today, cousin," Sir Henry said with a long look over her hand.

Joan didn't like the speculative glint in his eye—and apparently neither did his wife.

Alice's gaze narrowed. "That's a pretty dress, Joan. I don't recall seeing it before."

Joan swore silently. The last thing she needed was to have Sir Henry cast his lecherous gaze in her direction and draw her cousin's ire. At times, Alice's jealousy worked in Joan's favor. Indeed, they might not have left Carlisle Castle to travel with Sir Henry and his men to answer the king's muster at Berwick Castle were it not for her cousin wanting to keep a close eye on her husband. Alice suspected her husband had engaged in a liaison with one of Queen Isabella's ladies-in-waiting the last time he'd traveled to London (which he had), so when she heard the queen was marching north with the king, Alice had insisted they would go to Berwick as well.

Unlike the previous queen who had traveled with the first King Edward into battle all the way to Stirling Castle, Queen Isabella and the rest of the ladies would remain in relative safety at Berwick Castle when the king and his army marched on.

Despite the bad memories evoked by the castle that had been the place of her mother's imprisonment, Joan knew it was a great opportunity to be in the center of all the activity where she might discover information, and she'd been grateful for her cousin's possessiveness of her husband. But at other times—like now—it could be dashed inconvenient. The last thing Joan needed was to have a jealous Alice watching her.

"Thank you, cousin," Joan said, pretending obliviousness to Alice's concern. "Lady Isabella had it made for me before I left. It needed a few adjustments, but I was pleased that it still fit."

Her cousin's gaze dropped to the low cut of her bodice and her mouth pursed as if she might disagree about the fit.

But someone else spoke before she could. "I must thank my mother the next time I see her," a voice on the other side of Sir Henry said. Recognizing it, Joan felt a wave of satisfaction that only deepened when she turned and met Sir Hugh's appreciative gaze. "Her taste is as exquisite as the beauty of the woman wearing it."

Joan blushed prettily and gave him a nod to acknowledge

the compliment. She could still feel the heat of his eyes on her as she turned away and started a quiet conversation with Margaret—who was nothing like her sister—about their activities for tomorrow.

Joan didn't need to attract any more attention. The first spark had been lit. The question was whether it would catch fire.

∽

It was a conflagration.

Joan remembered Sir Hugh as bold, and he did not disappoint her. Barely had the first course been served when he made his way down the bench where she was seated and squeezed in between her and Margaret. For the rest of the meal, he entertained them with stories of some of the ridiculous things he'd witnessed at court. His witty observations had them both laughing until tears ran down their cheeks. She'd forgotten how amusing he could be, and for a while Joan could almost forget her purpose. But near the end of the meal, when Margaret was temporarily drawn into conversation with her sister, it was brought back to her in full force.

Sir Hugh inched closer on the bench, leaning his body toward hers until they were almost touching. "You have grown into quite a lovely young woman, Lady Joan. I must admit you surprised me."

"How is that, my lord?"

She could feel the heat of his gaze moving over the bare skin of her neck and chest. He made no attempt to hide his meaning—or his intentions. He wanted her, and he was letting her see that. She almost admired him for it. She preferred straightforward and matter-of-fact to lies and false promises.

"I didn't expect the quiet, reserved young girl who used to watch me when she thought I wasn't looking to become so bold and adventuresome." The hard muscle of his thigh pressed against hers. He was a big and powerfully built man, and it was not without effect. "You are adventuresome, aren't you, my lady?"

She did not mistake his meaning. "Under the right circumstances, my lord," she answered, and then added, "and with the right companion, of course."

The eyes that held hers were dark with understanding—and anticipation. Joan had to force herself not to shift and look away. Something about him made her uneasy. Sir Hugh Despenser was different from the other knights from whom she'd sought information. He was a man, for one. The others had been merely boys, and she was feeling the difference now. It was the difference between playing with a puppy and a wolf. She suspected that if Sir Hugh sank his teeth into her, he would not be easily shaken off.

"Of course." His hand moved a few inches closer, brushing her fingers with his own. "I hope we will have many adventures together while you are here." Not wanting to appear too eager, she didn't respond. After a moment he continued. "I don't like being indebted to de Beaumont, but in this case I think I must be."

"My lord?" She tilted her head in question.

"For bringing you here," he said with a smile. "I expected weeks of boredom and tedium in preparation for war, but now I am quite looking forward to my time at Berwick. I suspect it will prove extremely . . . entertaining."

Joan took advantage of the opening. "I'm sure there will be lots of entertainment when the king and queen arrive."

He seemed amused by her purposeful misunderstanding,

but indulged the shift of conversation. "Aye, I'm sure the queen and her ladies will not wish to be deprived," he answered. "Even in the midst of war. She loves games and tournaments almost as much as the king."

He really was quite handsome, she thought, if a bit too pretty for her taste. When an image of a dark golden-haired knight sprang to her mind, Joan pushed it away. Alex Seton might be her type of handsome, but the past month hadn't changed her mind about needing to avoid him. Knowing that she would see him here had been her one hesitation about coming to Berwick.

There was a lot about Alex Seton that made her hesitate. But she told herself there was no reason to overreact. He'd probably forgotten all about her, and it would be easy enough to avoid him. Most likely he would be at Wark Castle, where most of the army was mustering, and not at Berwick with Edward's commanders. The fifteen miles that separated the two castles would be a good buffer.

Joan turned her attention back to Sir Hugh—where it should not have left. "You sound as if you know the queen well, my lord."

His mouth quirked. "I am more friend to the king than the queen, but aye, I have spent much time in royal palaces the past year."

Joan acted suitably impressed. "You did not wish to travel with the royal party on the journey north?"

"'Travel' isn't what I'd call the plodding pace of the royal baggage train," he said with a laugh. "I journeyed with them as far as Newminster, and then was sent ahead with a message for Pembroke." His expression changed to dark and annoyed. "I was glad to leave. The squabbling between Hereford and Gloucester would drive a saint to perdition."

With that one offhand comment, Sir Hugh had already

proven himself useful. Bruce would be interested in knowing that not only were the two powerful earls answering the muster and bringing their impressive retinues to battle, but there was also discord in the ranks. But it was the content of the message that truly interested her.

"The message must have been important," she said, dying to ask more but knowing not to press.

Fortunately, she didn't need to. "It was." He seemed to be barely able to contain his glee. "It is no secret now. The siege at Stirling has lifted."

Her surprise wasn't feigned. "It has?"

He nodded. "Sir Phillip Moubray was granted safe passage and traveled to England himself to bring the king the news." Joan knew that Moubray was the former Scot patriot now holding the important Scottish stronghold for King Edward. "Moubray convinced Edward Bruce to agree to a truce. They agreed that if the English army doesn't relieve the garrison by midsummer, Moubray will surrender the castle to Bruce."

Joan's eyes widened.

Sir Hugh chuckled at her reaction. "Aye, it was a rash move on Edward Bruce's part, no doubt resulting from the boredom of laying siege rather than a tactical decision to benefit his brother's army. From what I hear, King Hood was furious."

Joan would imagine so. Laying down the gauntlet like that would force King Edward to respond by bringing troops into Scotland. Something to this point that King Robert had sought to avoid. The king must have also been furious that his brother had given up the chance to take one of Scotland's most important castles before the English came. With Bruce's recent success in taking back Scotland's castles from Edward's garrisons, it was a big prize to concede. It also gave the English a target and date.

She stopped. Was that the point? From what she knew of King Robert's only remaining brother, Edward was sometimes rash and overaggressive, but he wasn't a fool. Perhaps there was more than there seemed to this surrender. Could Bruce have wanted this? Had he done this so he would know when and where the English host would be headed when it marched into Scotland?

Joan feigned disappointment, trying to see what else Sir Hugh might volunteer. "By midsummer's day? But that means you will be leaving soon."

It would take time to march an army that far into Scotland to reach Stirling by the twenty-fourth of June. How much time, and what size the army, she hoped to discover.

He gave her a long, knowing look. "We still have a few weeks yet. It will take at least that long for the Welsh infantry to arrive."

She wrinkled her brow, hoping she appeared confused and not curious. "But the Welsh are already at Wark."

"The king sent out new calls to muster after Moubray arrived. This is going to be the biggest English host to march on Scotland since Falkirk sixteen years ago. King Hood will not escape this time."

"I imagine not, my lord. I've never seen so many knights and men-at-arms in my life here at Berwick."

"You should see Wark," Sir Hugh said. "There are thousands more there."

Joan leaned closer and gave him a look that was unmistakable in its invitation. "I should like that very much. Perhaps we might ride out together one day, and you can show me. It is so constricting at Berwick, don't you think?"

She knew the English commanders who had gathered

at Berwick so far: Pembroke, Lord Robert Clifford, and Lord Henry de Percy, as well as some of the Scots in Edward's allegiance—Robert de Umfraville, Earl of Angus, Ingrim de Umfraville, Alexander Abernathy, and Adam Gordon—but she wanted to see the others who had answered King Edward's call, as well as the numbers of men they had brought with them. A visit to the other camp would be perfect. Although she suspected Sir Hugh wasn't going to be as easy to put off as Sir Richard.

When his hand slid under the table to rest on her knee, she knew she was right. With a playful, chastising gaze she removed it.

Fortunately, Margaret asked him a question and gave Joan a moment to recover. She thought that it was Sir Hugh's touch that had made her skin prickle and the hair at the back of her neck stand up, but when she glanced to the back of the Hall she saw a group of men standing there, and one of them was staring at her with an intensity that seemed to burn right through her.

She sucked in her breath, startled by both the ferocity of the look and the connection. Alex Seton, it seemed, had not forgotten her.

❧

"Is something wrong, Seton?"

Alex drew his gaze from the dais to the distinguished knight at his side. Sir Adam Gordon had been a great Scot patriot in the early years of the war, but his fealty had always belonged to the deposed Scottish King John Balliol. Honor would not permit him to fight for Bruce, even though Alex suspected he hated having to ally with the English against his countrymen. With Balliol living in exile in France with little chance of ever regaining his throne—even as an English puppet—Alex wondered whether Sir Adam had been tempted to switch allegiance.

Alex admired Sir Adam greatly. The older knight was one of the bright spots since Alex had gone over to the English. Like Alex's lands, Sir Adam's holdings were in the lawless Borders where their people had taken the brunt of the war from both sides. Sir Adam, too, wanted to see the war and the suffering of their people ended.

Not only did they share the same goal, but Sir Adam was also the uncle of one of Alex's fallen comrades. William "Templar" Gordon had died over three years ago in an explosion while on a mission for the Highland Guard. Gordon was one of the best men Alex had ever known, and although Sir Adam could not know of the connection, Alex felt it.

He shook his head, ignoring the couple on the dais and forcing his body to relax—all his muscles were tight. "Nay, nothing is wrong."

Sir Adam looked at him with amusement. "So there is no reason why you are staring at Despenser like you want to sink a dagger between his pretty ribs?" His gaze slid to the woman beside King Edward's new favorite. "Who is the woman?"

Alex must have given away more than he realized. The lass must have gotten under his skin for him to betray his thoughts so easily. Why the hell should he care whom she bedded? "Joan Comyn."

Sir Adam's brow shot up. "Buchan's daughter?"

Alex nodded. "Aye, although some might argue that point."

The older knight's frown showed his distaste. "The way they have treated the lass is shameful. She has the stamp of Buchan all over her." His mouth quirked with a half-smile. "Although she is much more beautiful."

Alex didn't miss the question in the other man's gaze, but he didn't bite. "I think it has more to do with her mother than with her sire. That and giving de Beaumont a reason to fight in Scotland."

"Do you know the lass?"

"Nay." Alex paused. "I knew her mother."

And he knew how much Bella had loved her daughter. It would kill her to see what had become of her. From what he'd learned the past month, Sir Richard wasn't the first man Joan Comyn had been linked to, nor apparently—if the looks being exchanged between her and Despenser were any indication—would he be the last. The lass couldn't be making her interest more clear. And bloody hell, just look at that dress! It was a walking invitation, cut so low across the bodice that he was sure Despenser was holding his breath waiting for her to cough or sneeze. God knew, Alex did so every time she laughed or took a deep breath.

Sir Adam glanced around, although none of the other men who had come from Wark with them to report to Pembroke were listening. "Have care, lad. Your recent place in Bruce's army has made you suspect enough; a connection to one of Scotland's more notorious rebels isn't something I'd remind people of."

There was something about the warning that didn't sit right. Alex's brows drew together in a hard frown. "Am I being accused of something? I've given Edward no cause to doubt my loyalty."

"You are a Scot," the older man said. "That is reason enough for some."

Alex wished someone could have told that to Boyd. To his former partner, being born in England made him English—no matter that he'd lived in Scotland his whole life and considered himself a Scot.

Still Alex sensed there was something more Sir Adam was trying to tell him. "But . . . ?"

Sir Adam looked around again and lowered his voice. "Bruce is reported to have a high-placed spy in the English camp, and with the campaign ahead, the king has made it a priority to uncover him."

Alex was well acquainted with this spy. "The Ghost," as the spy was referred to in the Guard, had provided some key information to them in the last few years. But when he realized what the other man meant by it, he was incredulous. *Bloody hell.* "And they think it is me?"

Sir Adam shrugged. "Your name was mentioned as a possibility."

The ludicrousness and irony of the situation were not lost on him. Alex had made enemies of his friends and brethren to fight for the English, and the English thought he was still working with the men he'd betrayed. He drew himself up. "It isn't true. I despise subterfuge and deceit. Besides, how would I have been passing this information all the way from London?"

"I didn't say I believed them—or that it made sense. But your pleas for peace and urge for negotiation have not gone unnoticed."

"So because I am tired of seeing my people suffering and want an end to the war I am a spy?"

Alex knew Sir Adam understood—he was in the same position. As barons with lands in the Borders, they were caught in an impossible situation. Damned by the English if they supported Bruce and damned by Bruce if they didn't—with the brunt of the war being waged on their lands and their people being the ones suffering no matter which side they fought on.

"I feel the same as you, but they suspect anyone who is

not calling for Bruce's head. They don't want a peaceful solution. Edward will never recognize Bruce as king—he has that in common with his father, at least."

There was very little Edward II of England had in common with the powerful Edward I, the self-styled Hammer of the Scots, but Alex was beginning to think Sir Adam was right. Despite his efforts the past two years, Alex was no closer to persuading Edward to recognize Bruce's legitimacy to the throne—something that he knew Bruce would demand before a permanent truce could be reached. More and more, it seemed as if the only solution—the only way to end the war—was going to be on the battlefield by right of arms. The righteousness of the Scot cause would be determined by God. But if Bruce continued to refuse to take the field against Edward, what then?

This damned war could go on forever. And everything Alex had done would have been for nothing. Alex muttered a curse of frustration. He wasn't going to let that happen, damn it.

Seeming to understand the sentiment, Sir Adam put his hand on his back. "If it's any consolation, it isn't just you. They suspect most of us." Alex knew what he meant by "us": Scots in the English army. "Except maybe young Comyn," Sir Adam added wryly.

Aye, it would be a snowy day in hell before young John Comyn spied for the man who'd killed—many said murdered—his father before the altar at Greyfriars, the act that had launched Bruce's bid for the crown eight years earlier.

The English distrust of the Scots in their ranks wasn't new. The opinions and advice of the Scots were often given short shrift by their compatriots. It was one of the many—many—frustrations that Alex had had to deal with since joining the English.

But if the English thought he was the spy, they definitely weren't going to listen to anything he said.

All the sacrifices Alex had made to put himself in this position to try to end the war wouldn't mean a damned thing. He thought of the looks on his former brethren's faces the last time he'd seen them and knew what he had to do.

"I appreciate the warning," Alex told the other man. "But I intend to prove that it isn't me."

Sir Adam arched a brow. "And how do you plan to do that?"

It was simple. "I'll find the damned spy myself."

6

PEMBROKE WAS SURPRISED by Alex's offer but accepted it nonetheless. He had no reason not to. If Alex was successful, the English would have their spy, and if he was unsuccessful, they would be no worse off.

Pembroke undoubtedly thought that Alex would be in a better position to find a Scot spy being a Scot himself. Alex knew better than to think his offer would deflect suspicion from him, but as he had nothing to hide, he wasn't worried.

As he came out of the lord's solar where he'd met with

Pembroke, Alex glanced around the Hall, seeing only a handful of people still lingering over the meal—or more specifically, the wine. The dais and high table, however, were deserted. He was glad of it. What Joan Comyn did and whom she did it with were no business of his, but that didn't mean he wanted to watch it.

He spoke too soon. No sooner had he stepped out of the Hall into the corridor that led to the west postern than he heard a husky laugh that sent a bolt of lust straight to his bollocks. It shouldn't be familiar, and he had no reason to recognize it, but he did.

Instinctively, he stepped into the shadows. It wasn't necessary. It was clear the couple that had just slipped out of the alcove at the opposite end of the corridor hadn't noticed him. They were too busy doing God knows what, in the middle of the day, damn it, when anyone might happen upon them!

His teeth gritted. Was it his imagination or did that indecent gown look a bit rumpled? When she adjusted her bodice in apparent confirmation a moment later, his hands clenched into tight fists at his side.

That wasn't all that was tight. His entire body seemed to have gone as rigid as stone.

Alex didn't understand his reaction. The visceral, primitive response was utterly foreign to him. What was it about the lass that made him so . . . *angry*? Why should he care whose bed she slept in? It didn't concern him. He barely even knew her. She was nothing to him.

But her mother had been.

Maybe that was it. Maybe this irrational anger he felt at seeing Joan Comyn dishonor herself had to do with Bella. Bella was, or had been, his friend, and it was because of the Guard—well, MacRuairi, at least—that she had been forced to leave Joan behind in the first place. There might have been no choice, but that didn't make Alex feel any less responsible.

So when Joan left a moment later, Alex followed her. He was going to talk to her, that was all. It was his duty, he told himself. He owed it to her mother.

∽

Joan was already having second thoughts. She'd been right to be wary of Sir Hugh. He was nothing like the young pups she'd targeted before. Keeping him at arm's length was going to be a challenge.

Good gracious, he'd had her in that alcove before she'd even realized what was happening. Only the fact that she said her cousin was waiting for her had enabled her to leave with the "one kiss" he'd demanded as forfeit for letting her go.

Fortunately, he didn't taste like herring, but even the swift press of his mouth had alerted her to the danger. Sir Hugh Despenser knew what he was doing; he was obviously practiced at seduction. It was a good thing she was immune.

The "until tomorrow" that he'd whispered as she left had the distinct feel of a promise, and she was half-tempted to plead illness for their ride. But she couldn't waste the opportunity to gather information about the troops at Wark. It would be worth any difficulty, she told herself. Still, the cat was suddenly feeling very much like the mouse.

Instead of returning to the tower, she decided to take advantage of the lengthening day—it wouldn't be dark for at least a few more hours—to leave a message with her contact. Bruce would want to know about the additional

Welsh call to muster and the discord between the English leaders as soon as possible.

Fortunately, she'd brought a plain, dark hooded cloak for just this purpose. It covered the gown she wore underneath—which would hardly go unnoticed—and enabled her to blend in with the villagers going back and forth between the burgh and the castle.

Another benefit of her loss of status was the additional freedom of movement it afforded her. No one cared about the comings and goings of a bastard. She could largely move about as she liked without comment or notice, and unlike her cousins, she was not expected to take an escort or guard.

She was, however, careful and prudent about when she ventured into town by herself. Though she could defend herself if necessary, she didn't want to draw attention to herself by being forced to do so.

A quick trip into town in the late afternoon should be safe enough. The soldiers would be attending to their afternoon duties and the alehouses would not be crowded yet (in other words, she wouldn't need to dodge overamorous drunks).

Indeed, the high street was still bustling with merchants and shoppers as she made her way down the cobbled path to the mercery, where she would meet her contact for the first time. Though she knew Bruce and the bishop would have chosen the person with the utmost care, Joan admitted a bit of apprehension. The passing of information was when she felt her most vulnerable.

She missed her "Italian nun," but her former contact, Janet of Mar, had been forced to retire from Bruce's service a few years back when her identity had been uncovered. Since then Joan had had a series of contacts—mostly clergy—but this time it was the wife of the cloth merchant. Joan didn't know who she was or why she was trustworthy; all she'd been given was a name.

Joan was standing outside the shop, looking through the window to see if the woman was inside, when she caught the reflection of movement behind her that made her heart race.

It took a moment for her thoughts to catch up with her pulse. She couldn't believe it. The shock that someone was following her, and more significantly, that she hadn't noticed, quickly turned to anger. How could she have missed him? Perhaps it was her frazzled nerves after being cornered so easily by Despenser. That was the only explanation she could come up with for how easily he'd escaped her notice.

Sweet Jerusalem! She'd been seconds away from making contact and attempting to pass a message.

But who would be following her and why?

The answer came an instant later. Now that every one of her senses was flaring, it took everything she had not to tense as she felt the large presence move up behind her.

"Aren't you going in?"

The deep voice made her spine straighten and skin tighten. The reaction was anger and annoyance. She was sure of it. Mostly.

Very slowly, she turned to meet the penetrating gaze of Alex Seton.

If she needed proof of the danger and threat he posed, she had it. She'd been trained to evade, but he'd been trained to track—probably by the same person.

She *should* be thinking of how to rid herself of him as quickly and definitively as possible. Instead she was struck by the crystal-clear blue of his eyes—the color seemed almost unreal—and by the weariness of his expression.

He looked as if he'd barely slept in weeks. As if he had the weight of the world on his shoulders. He'd even missed a spot shaving this morning. The thin line along the left underside of his jaw seemed a testament to his exhaustion, and something about that made her chest clench. She felt the strangest urge to reach out and smooth a comforting hand over that stubbled jaw.

But why should she care if he was tired? Why should she want to comfort him? He'd followed her, she reminded herself. She couldn't allow that to happen.

She lifted her chin, eyeing him angrily. "Not that it is any business of yours, but not today."

"Perhaps you should reconsider," he said.

She frowned at his dark tone, at the same time noticing the tiny white lines around his hard-set mouth. He was acting angry, which didn't make sense. If anyone had a right to be angry it was she.

She crossed her arms. Putting a little more of a barricade between them seemed prudent; she sensed he very much wanted to put his hands on her. "Why would I wish to do that?"

"If that gown you are wearing is any indication, you need some new ones. Preferably with a bit more fabric."

She gasped—a few times—in both shock and outrage while staring at him incredulously. *Of all the . . .* "How dare you! What I wear is no business of yours. The last time I looked you are not my father or my husband. I have a guardian—I do not need another."

"You do if he lets you walk around in gowns like that." He paused, giving her a hard look. "Men might get the wrong impression."

She was holding on to her temper by the last wispy

threads, yet her voice was deceptively calm. "And what impression is that?"

If she expected him to back down, she was to be disappointed. Looking her square in the eye, he said baldly, "That you wish to bed them. Despenser clearly had that idea."

She might have admired his audacity if she wasn't practically sputtering with outrage. "And you can tell all this from a dress? What a unique talent you possess. What are my slippers telling you?" She gave him a sugary smile. "Let me give you a hint: it starts with go and ends with Hades."

He didn't seem to appreciate her sarcasm. "It isn't just the dress; your behavior has made you the subject of unpleasant rumors. How do you think it looks when you and Despenser come tumbling out of an alcove in the middle of the day?"

He'd seen her? Joan flushed, although she had no cause to, blast it! She hadn't done anything of which to be ashamed. She was using the tools she had in her power—turning what had once made her vulnerable into a strength—to find out important information that would help win this war. Her reputation was a small price to pay, but that didn't give him a right to judge her.

"I don't even want to think what your mother would say," he added.

She bristled. That there was more truth to his observation than she wanted to admit only made Joan more defensive.

But remembering her role, and her supposed alienation from her mother, she said, "My mother is a rebel and traitor to the king who left me when I was twelve. What she may or may not have to say is irrelevant." She gave him a hard stare. "You did not tell me you knew her—makes me wonder if there is a reason why. Perhaps you do not wish to remind people that not so long ago you fought for the enemy?"

The tinge of heat that flooded his face told her that her arrow had found its mark. He was a traitor—a man who had switched sides and betrayed his compatriots and king—and he thought to lecture her about appearances and behavior?

Was this judgmental, sanctimonious prig really the kind and gallant knight who'd carried her to her room last month? Perhaps she should thank him for curing her of all her illusions.

"This isn't about me," he said stiffly.

"How convenient," she replied dryly. "I don't recall making it about me either. Why should I not give my un-solicited opinion about your 'behavior'? I wonder what my mother would say about your switching sides. I think I'd rather be thought a harlot than a traitor."

The sudden darkness of his expression almost made her regret her words. The transformation was rather . . . *extreme*. She wouldn't have thought it possible for the golden knight to look so scary. It wasn't as difficult to imagine him as a nasal-helmed "Phantom" now.

Belatedly, she thought to take a step back, but his hand had whipped out to stop her. She'd never felt anything like it—or been so brutally aware of a man's touch. His grip was like iron, and she could feel the press of every finger like a vise wrapped around her skin.

Mother Mary, he was strong! And those hands . . .

She might have shuddered.

She'd almost forgotten that they were standing be-fore the mercery in the middle of the high street until he dragged her a few steps around the side of the building. He'd obviously realized that they'd been attracting attention.

"I am not a traitor," he said roughly. "I had my reasons."

She was sure he did—just as she had hers. Ignoring the fierce race of her heart, she lifted a challenging brow. "And I am not a harlot."

The words seemed to take him aback. He frowned. "I never said you were."

"Didn't you?" She reached up with the arm that wasn't clamped in his grip to pull aside her cloak. "But look at my gown."

He looked down, and just like that everything changed. The anger firing in the air between them turned to something else entirely. Something hot and charged and even more dangerous.

The weight of his gaze on her chest was as warm and heavy as the palm of a hand. Heat flooded her breasts with even more heaviness, and her nipples grew tight and hard under his steady perusal.

His jaw tightened.

Her belly clenched . . . low.

The tic below his jaw began to pulse and those tiny white lines reappeared around his mouth.

He wanted her, but he didn't look happy about it, and something about that stung. It stung quite a lot, and brought out a streak of heretofore unknown wickedness in her. Wickedness that made her want him to eat his words. Every last one of them.

If he thought her a whore, so be it. He was just like all the rest. *People always let you down.* Why would she have expected more?

She leaned into his hold, pressing her body against his. "And what of you, Sir Alex?" She blinked up at him coyly.

"Although I'm sure a chivalrous knight like yourself is too principled for tumbling out of alcoves."

Senses Alex didn't even know he had exploded at contact. It had been hard enough holding back his desire when those incredible breasts had been displayed only inches away for him to admire every mouthwatering ripe curve, every delectable point, and every tantalizingly deep crevice.

Christ, she was practically bursting out of the gown. The fabric seemed to stretch to the breaking point to contain all that straining flesh. All he had to do was reach down, slide his finger along the edge of her bodice, and he'd see the pink of her nipple. What shade would they be? A delicate light pink or succulent, berry red like her mouth?

Aye, looking was difficult, but having them crushed against his chest, that was torture unlike any he'd ever felt before. He ached to touch them, to feel the full weight in his hand, to rub his finger over the silky skin and pebbled tips, to squeeze and lift them to his mouth and tongue. Just thinking about it made him crazed with lust. His body was as hard as a damned spike.

Those siren eyes didn't help any. They dragged him in and made him think of pleasure. Of hot, twisted limbs in bedsheets, of sweaty, naked flesh, of sin and passion and lust.

She was temptation and base desire, and a damned fantasy come to life. It took everything he had not to pull her into his arms and cover that taunting, but achingly soft red mouth with his. He knew how good she would taste, how good she would smell. Like warm honey and flowers in the spring . . .

The fierce intensity of his reaction infuriated him. He knew what she was doing, damn it. She was only trying to provoke him. He should be repulsed by the obvious ploy.

But his body sure as hell didn't understand. It throbbed, ached, and tightened to the point of pain.

Ploy or not, he was good and provoked. He was going to take what she offered, damn it, and teach her a lesson about prodding hungry lions with a stick—or in this case, two very firm and barely covered breasts that he'd be picturing for too many nights to come.

He slid his arm around her waist to pull her even closer, groaning at how good she felt. She seemed to melt right into him. She gasped at the movement, and his mouth was about two seconds away from smothering the next one, when he suddenly swore and pulled back.

Christ, what the hell was wrong with him? He didn't teach women lessons like that. He sounded like a barbarian. Women were to protect, cherish, honor, and revere.

He released her so quickly she seemed to need to catch herself. But that didn't explain the slightly dazed look on her face. She blinked a few times, staring at him in confusion.

Clearly she'd expected him to kiss her, and just as clearly she'd been surprised when he hadn't.

But was there something else? Had she *wanted* him to kiss her? Had the ploy been less of a game than he thought?

He raked his hand back through his hair, and told himself not to think about that. The lass was confusing him enough. When he thought of how close he'd come to doing something dishonorable—maybe very dishonorable—it shamed him.

How the hell had this happened anyway? He'd only wanted to talk to her, but when she'd left the castle instead of returning to the tower he'd become curious about where she was going, and, admittedly, whom she might be going with.

He'd been angry—maybe more than angry—and so he'd acted like an arse.

He'd only wanted to protect her, damn it, but his well-intentioned warning had gone all wrong. Instead of the delicate diplomacy that the situation demanded, Alex had come storming in with the blunt force of a hammer. The only other person who could make him lose his temper like that had been Boyd.

He took a deep breath as if he could forcibly purge the torrent of emotions that still raged in his blood. "I didn't mean—" He stopped, and then started again. "I'm afraid I owe you an apology."

The wariness in the way she eyed him filled him with shame. This wasn't him, damn it. He didn't argue and lose his temper with young women—or threaten to ravish them against a wall.

Wariness, however, did not dull the blade of her tongue. "For what?" she asked. "For following me? For accosting me in the streets? For lecturing me about that which is none of your business? For being a sanctimonious, self-righteous prig? Or for nearly doing yourself that which you judge me for doing?"

His mouth hardened. She might be right, damn it, but he didn't appreciate the sarcasm. He was trying to apologize. "I was speaking out of concern—"

"I don't want, nor did I ask, for your concern."

He could feel the anger building again and tried to contain it, but his spine stiffened. "I don't think you realize the ramifications of what you're doing and the lasting harm it might do. I'm trying to protect you."

His words had no effect. She seemed to be struggling to contain her anger. "I don't need a knight in shining armor to rescue me from myself, Sir Alex. Despite your belief that I am not capable of thinking for myself, I know exactly what I'm doing and the *ramifications*."

"That isn't what I meant. I don't think you are incapable of thinking for yourself, damn it."

He couldn't recall ever forgetting himself and swearing in the company of a lass before. But she didn't appear to notice and acted as if he hadn't spoken. "You may have known my mother, but you are not responsible for me, nor does it give you a right to interfere, lecture me, or give me the wisdom of your opinion. All I want from you—the *only* thing I want—is that you leave me alone."

He suspected his eyes were every bit as flashing and sparking as hers when their gazes met. His jaw was locked; he didn't trust himself to speak.

What was it about this lass that made him so crazed? That made him act like an arse and feel like a barbarian? That made him tempted—even now when she was so obviously furious with him—to pull her into his arms and kiss her until she listened to him?

Bloody hell.

When she marched off, he didn't try to stop her. Leaving her alone was exactly what he should do.

7

IT RAINED THE next three days, delaying the ride with Sir Hugh, but Monday dawned bright and sunny— much to Joan's dismay.

She knew she should be anxious to go to Wark, but the brief respite had only increased her wariness where Sir Hugh was concerned. For three days he'd stalked her like a predator ready to pounce, and for three days she'd made sure she did not leave her chamber without the company of one of her cousins.

Proving his astuteness, Sir Hugh seemed suspicious when he commented about it at dinner one night. Whether he believed her explanation about her "duties," she didn't know. But his gaze definitely sharpened when he saw Margaret approaching the stables with her.

"Lady Margaret," he said. "What a delightful surprise."

Clearly it wasn't.

"I hope you don't mind my coming along," Margaret said with a bright, good-natured smile. "But after being cooped up in the castle for most of the week, I couldn't pass up the prospect of a ride."

Joan held her expression impassive as Sir Hugh's gaze flickered to hers before turning back to her cousin's. Margaret was more skillful with dishonesty than Joan realized. She'd asked her cousin to accompany them, claiming— honestly—that she wasn't sure she could trust Sir Hugh not to try something untoward.

"Of course not," he assured Margaret. "I am delighted to have the company of not one but two beautiful women."

Margaret blushed prettily and allowed him to help her on her horse.

When he turned to Joan next, she could see that he was unable to completely mask his annoyance. "I'm beginning to wonder if I misunderstood you, my lady," he said in a voice that only she could hear as he helped her up.

Joan feigned ignorance. "My lord?"

"Perhaps you are not as adventuresome as you claimed?"

She flushed, hoping he interpreted it as maidenly rather than as guiltily. "I'm sorry, my lord, this was . . . unavoidable. Margaret was so excited that I could not tell her no."

He held her gaze with an intensity that made her want to shiver. "Then you have not reconsidered?"

She shook her head.

"Good," he said, his dark eyes as hard as onyx. "I do not like feeling as if I am being led around by the bit like this horse."

She did not miss the warning in his tone. Sir Hugh was done with the chase. She wasn't going to be able to put him off with excuses much longer. But how much was she going to be willing to risk for information?

This was the first time she'd experienced difficulty with one of the men she'd targeted, and she wasn't sure how to handle it. Sir Hugh didn't respond the way the others had, and she feared she'd overestimated her experience in dealing with men. He was only the fourth man she'd attempted to get close to for information.

Targeting important young knights had seemed a natural extension of what she'd been doing before. She had a knack for being in the right place at the right time to hear information from her guardians, as well as listening while not appearing interested, shifting topics without notice, encouraging people to talk, knowing how to goad men into bragging with more information than they should, and "disappearing" into the background so people forgot she was there. Why shouldn't she be able to apply these skills to all the young men who pursued her? But the others had been, if not simple, then at least nothing she couldn't handle. She wasn't sure she could say the same about Sir Hugh—with or without sleeping powder!

He seemed to be waiting for acknowledgment from her.

Once she nodded, they were off. The guard that Sir Hugh had arranged to accompany them followed at a discreet distance, but close enough if any harm befell them.

Apparently satisfied by her assurances, Sir Hugh put aside his initial annoyance and proved himself again the charming host, regaling them with war stories and tales of his squirehood on the short journey along the Tweed.

She was enjoying herself so much that she was surprised when the castle came into view. Like Berwick Castle, Wark Castle was located on the important river that bisected a large part of the Borders—the Tweed ran nearly one hundred miles from the Lowther Hills just north of Moffat to the North Sea at Berwick. But that is where the similarities between the two castles ended. The single tower, simple gatehouse, and curtain wall of the motte-and-bailey-style Wark was nothing like the massive, multitowered, multidrawbridged royal administration center of Berwick.

Due to the limited grounds inside the wall, most of the soldiers at Wark were camped on the fields below the motte hill of the castle, and Joan could see the yellowed white of the tents peppered across the green grass of the countryside from quite a distance away.

She swallowed. There were so many of them. For the first time, she was confronted with the massive size of the army King Edward was gathering to march against her countrymen. At Berwick, where most of Edward's commanders had congregated, there were perhaps only a thousand men. Here at Wark there must be about ten times as many. And more would be coming in the next few weeks as the June tenth deadline to muster approached.

She looked in awe and horror at the tents that seemed to stretch on as far as the eye could see. Good gracious, would Bruce even be able to raise half this many men? A third as many?

The pit in her stomach seemed to grow a little heavier before she scolded herself for the worry that suddenly felt disloyal. Robert the Bruce had become known for his ability to defy the odds; he would do so again.

Her job was to provide information; the king would decide what to do with it.

But how many were there?

Joan could have kissed her cousin when she exclaimed, "My word, I've never seen so many tents! There are hundreds of them. Half the population of London must have answered the king's call!"

Sir Hugh smiled at the exaggeration. There were thought to be as many as eighty thousand people in London. "Not quite that many," he said with a wink and a smile. "Yet."

Joan hoped he was jesting. Forty thousand was impossible. Even the current king's father, the powerful Hammer of the Scots, Edward I, had only amassed an army of perhaps twenty-five thousand in his biggest campaign in Scotland sixteen years ago—when the English had decimated the Scots at Falkirk. The second Edward's popularity and power were nowhere near his father's. How many could he hope to raise? Ten thousand? By her estimation there must be nearly that many right now. She bit her lip. *Fifteen?*

Again she could thank her cousin for asking what she was thinking. "How many more men are coming?" Margaret asked. "And where does the king intend to put them?"

Joan laughed along with Sir Hugh, but waited anxiously for his answer.

"At least another few thousand when the Welsh arrive, and many more if the barons do their duty."

Joan weighed the risks and decided to ask, knowing another opening like this might not arise. "What of the other earls, my lord? Will more of them be arriving as well?"

Perhaps the biggest unknown—and what was causing the most whispers and speculation among the leadership (both Scot and English)—was whether the Earl of Lancaster, who held *five* carldoms and was the most powerful magnate in England, would set aside his differences with Edward to fight against the Scots. Similarly the status of the earls of Warwick, Lincoln, Arundel, and Warenne were also unknown. Given the number of men at these earls' command, if they decided to fight it could swell Edward's numbers considerably—especially in the numbers of deadly English cavalry—and be potentially disastrous for the Scots. Lancaster alone could command an additional five hundred horses. Roughly the same number as the entirety of the Scot cavalry.

Bruce thought they would find an excuse not to appear, but if she could get confirmation of that it would be a huge coup and a vital piece of information for him.

Sir Hugh didn't appear surprised or alerted by her question. It was undoubtedly on many people's minds. "The king is certain the earls will see the wisdom of doing their duty to their king."

"And if they do not?" Margaret asked.

He gave a shrug that harkened to his Gallic roots of generations earlier that said precisely nothing.

It wasn't long before they reached the castle, and Sir Hugh was giving them a tour of the grounds and practice yards where the ordinary foot soldiers, many of whom were farmers and yeomen inexperienced in warfare, were being put through extensive training by the battle-hard knights and men-at-arms who had been serving both Edwards in the Scottish wars for years.

Margaret was right. Joan had never seen so many men crowded into one area in her life. It was a little disconcerting. And with few women about they were attracting quite a lot of attention. She was glad for both her modest gown (the one she'd worn to the feast had done its job—maybe too well) and Sir Hugh's impressive escort.

Still, she and Margaret were subject to quite a few long, admiring stares. Not used to being the center of attention, Joan felt oddly conspicuous—like an exotic bird in a menagerie.

Her cousin must have been feeling the same. While they waited in the shade of a large tree—the day had grown uncommonly hot—for Sir Hugh to finish speaking with one of the captains, Margaret leaned over and whispered, "Why do I have the feeling some of these men haven't seen a lady in some time? If I ever need a boost to my vanity, I guess I know where to come." She gave a mischievous smile. "We probably shouldn't tell Alice about this. She'd be here every day. She likes nothing better than a boost to her vanity."

Joan gave a snort of laughter, which she discreetly muffled with her hand. Margaret had always had a sharp sense of humor that Joan had enjoyed. The two cousins had been extremely close as young girls, and if it wasn't for the war that had put them on opposite sides—though Margaret didn't know it—Joan suspected they would have remained that way.

She knew that Margaret attributed Joan's pulling away to the change in her status that had directly benefitted her cousins, but it wasn't that. Margaret hadn't made her a bastard and disinherited her; King Edward and de Beaumont had done that. Nay, she'd pulled away from Margaret because she was one of the few people in England whom she knew it would be painful to betray.

"Your sister is very beautiful," Joan said diplomatically, not wanting to appear disloyal.

"She is certainly that," Margaret agreed.

"You are as well," Joan pointed out. Margaret was lovely—perhaps not as perfectly beautiful as her sister, but few could be. Her hair was more brown than blond, and her eyes were green rather than blue, but her smile was full of good humor that her sister could never hope to emulate.

Margaret's mouth twitched. "You are kind to say so, cousin, but you don't need to worry about me. I know my strengths and weaknesses as well as I do my sister's, though I don't expect you to agree with me in your position." She meant as Alice's tiring woman. "Alice can be . . . difficult."

They both knew how much of an understatement that was. Joan gave her cousin a thoughtful glance. "How is it that you have not yet married, Margaret? I thought there was some talk a few years back."

A shadow crossed her cousin's pretty face, but it was quickly replaced by a smile and a shrug. "It fell apart when our families decided to fight for different kings."

Joan remembered now: Margaret had been promised to one of the Earl of Ross's younger sons. John, she thought.

"Is there no one who has caught your eye?"

Margaret gave her a sidelong look. "I suspect my brother by marriage has just as much interest in finding you a husband as he does me."

Joan suspected she was right. De Beaumont wouldn't want any husbands to interfere with his claims to Joan's inheritance—even from a sister.

"And what of you, Joan. Has no one caught your eye?" She gestured with her head to Despenser. "And don't say him. I don't think Sir Hugh interests you any more than he does me—although he is a charming rogue. Shameless and extravagant, but charming."

Joan hoped she hid her alarm. Margaret had always been perceptive—far more than Alice—but Joan didn't want her asking questions.

She was still trying to think of a way to respond when a loud roar rang out behind them from the group of men training nearby. Following the direction of the sound, she turned and something caught her gaze—or rather, *someone* caught her gaze.

She gasped, her body going utterly still. Her eyes were riveted. She couldn't have turned away if she wanted to. And really, if she were honest with herself, she didn't want to.

"What is it?" Margaret asked, but then following Joan's gaze her eyes widened. "Or maybe I should say *who* is it? My word, he's . . ."

She didn't finish. She didn't need to. What could she say that would suffice? He was magnificent? Incredible? Male perfection? Knee-weakening, belly tightening, and jaw-dropping? Aye, he was all those things and so much more. He drew the eye like a twinkling star, like gold shimmering in the sunlight, like the flame of a beacon in a moonless sky.

Joan found her voice, although it was lacking quite a bit of air. "Sir Alex Seton. He's part of Pembroke's retinue."

"Seton?" Her cousin frowned. "He's the Scot who switched sides a couple years ago, isn't he?" Joan nodded. "Interesting. Sir Robert certainly doesn't seem to like him much."

For the first time Joan's gaze turned to the other man whom she'd only been vaguely aware of. She recognized de Percy's champion Sir Robert Felton. The vaunted knight was also tall, well muscled, light haired, handsome, and bare to the waist, but for some reason she hadn't noticed him. Her focus had been entirely on the other knight.

Although admittedly, Alex Seton didn't look like much of a knight right now. She didn't realize he was so . . . overpowering. Good Lord! Stripped to all his primitive glory, he looked every inch the ruthless brigand. Her gaze absorbed every ripple, every rock-hard edge, every bulge and line of the powerful muscles on his chest and arms. She might have to rethink her golden knight fantasy. There was something to be said for brutal, fierce, and dangerous.

But he wasn't her fantasy, she reminded herself. He was a judgmental, self-righteous traitor who didn't know how to mind his own business. Lachlan used to refer to him as Sir Galahad—the idealized perfect knight who always spoke of doing what was right. Joan understood what he meant now. Obviously, Sir Alex had a moral compass that didn't flicker to gray.

She was still furious about the way he'd spoken to her, and everything about his attitude had rubbed her the wrong way. Which made her reaction that day all the more inexplicable. Could she really have wanted—even for a minute—for him to kiss her? She must have been out of her mind. She didn't feel desire for men. Not anymore. Not since she was fifteen.

She was glad he'd heeded her request to stay away from her. She hadn't thought about him more than one or twice in the four days since their confrontation on the street. Certainly not more than a handful of times. A dozen at most. Nor had she looked at the door every time a group of knights entered the Hall or held her breath every time she saw a golden-blond head across the crowd.

"Come," Margaret said, dragging her forward. "I can't see from back here."

For once no one seemed to be paying attention to them as the two women moved a short distance away from the tree, stepping carefully through the still muddy field to the circle of men on the makeshift practice yard. Everyone was captivated by the two men doing battle. The two cousins wedged their way between a couple of young soldiers to watch.

Margaret was right. The view was certainly much better up here. There were no heads or arms or shoulders to get in the way of the head, arms, and shoulders—not to mention the naked chest—that she shouldn't be so shamelessly ogling. Admiring. *Devouring*. But look at that stomach! She could count the bands, and his arms were much bigger than she realized, especially when they were flexed.

Alex turned slightly to deflect a blow and Joan gasped.

Margaret must have noticed the same thing. "Good gracious, I wonder what happened to his arm? It must have been a horrible injury."

Her cousin was right. The scar covered the entire upper portion of his right arm. It was a horrible, tangled briar patch of cuts and gashes that had healed some time ago, but still seemed to be troubling him. He was struggling against the other man, and the weakened arm seemed to be the cause.

Strange, it had seemed quite strong when he'd carried her—she hadn't sensed any pain or trouble then.

She wondered what could have caused such a horrible injury.

A sick feeling swam in her stomach as suspicion took

root. Of course . . . the tattoo. The scar covered the exact place where the mark of the Highland Guard would have been on his arm. The mark that was now obliterated.

But the scar was a badge of his guilt, and a reminder that she would not forget.

∞

Alex didn't notice the commotion right away. After being goaded into a contest with Felton that he regretted a moment after accepting (Sutherland truly did deserve some kind of award for not killing him), Alex was doing his best to not defend himself too ably, while at the same time to not get killed.

It wasn't easy. Felton was good—really good—and it was bloody difficult to fend off his blows and not give him the fight he so obviously needed. Alex was fairly certain he could have bested him two years ago, but he had barely picked up a sword since then, and even going full out, he wasn't sure he could do so now.

The realization infuriated him and made it even harder to take the trouncing Felton was giving him.

Like most Scots, Alex's pride had always been a weakness, and he felt it stirring now with a dangerous sting. But he knew he couldn't make his arm—the arm that he'd been claiming was too weak to use—appear fully healed. Pembroke was suspicious enough.

It was Alex's own fault. He should have known better than to let the deception continue. Subterfuge had never been in his nature.

Although the injury had been real enough when he'd first arrived in London. He'd done more harm than he intended while trying to remove the mark that would identify him as a member of the Highland Guard. Being attacked and thrown into the pit prison of Berwick Castle after he'd surrendered hadn't helped it any.

But even after the arm had healed, he'd continued the pretense. It provided him an excuse, a means of evading the truth that he didn't want to face: that by switching sides, he couldn't just wage his war in the corridors of some royal palace with words. There was every possibility—every likelihood with King Edward marching and his men mustering   that Alex was going to have to lift his sword against his former friends, brethren, and king. Men toward whom he inexplicably, even after all that had happened, still felt loyalty.

He couldn't avoid the truth and hide behind an old injury any longer. He'd given his loyalty to the English. If war came, he was going to have to fight—and not, unfortunately, against Felton.

God only knew how he would stomach it. But if it put an end to the war, stopped the atrocities and suffering, he would do it, damn it. Besides, what choice did he have? He'd made his bed.

A blow to his shoulder with the back of Felton's sword brought him harshly back to reality. The bastard was clearly enjoying himself and playing to the crowd, showing off his "superior" skill by toying with Alex. Felton knew full well that Alex's weak arm would hamper his ability to retaliate.

Felton swung his sword high, bringing it down full force on Alex's weak side. Alex blocked it, but Felton didn't let up, pressing down, lowering Alex inch by inch to the ground. He wanted to humiliate him.

The bastard was strong. Maybe not as strong as Boyd, but even if Alex wasn't feigning weakness, he may have had difficulty fending him off. As it was his arms were shaking from the effort to prevent the blade from descending onto his head or neck.

This was supposed to be practice, damn it. They weren't even wearing armor.

Yield. He should just yield. But even as sweat poured off his body and pain burned in every vein and muscle, he couldn't make himself say it. So he shook and burned, knowing that in a moment, when Felton succeeded in forcing him to the ground, he wouldn't have a damned choice.

Felton was smiling and preening as if he were on a tournament yard. His eyes kept flickering behind Alex. Soon he realized why.

"What say you, ladies?" Felton said. "Has he had enough?"

There were ladies in the crowd. Moreover, they were noteworthy enough for Felton to be showing off to. Alex wanted to turn around, but he dared not lose concentration even for an instant. Felton was close enough to taking off his head as it was. He was almost on his knees.

"It appears so, my lord," one of the women answered.

Alex didn't need to turn. He recognized that soft, husky voice easily enough, and the realization that the woman watching him suffer—watching him lose, damn it—was Joan Comyn reverberated through him like thunder and made his nerve endings flare as if he'd just been shot from head to toe with a bolt of lightning.

Her voice changed everything. His muscles no longer shook, they hardened with steel. He burned no longer with pain but with strength. It flowed through him—swelled through him—like a raging inferno.

He didn't stop to think. Instinct took over. Boyd had had him in this position too many times before—Alex knew what to do. Ignoring the blade pressing down inches from his head, he let his muscles go lax for a dangerous instant, using Felton's momentum—and the edge of Alex's blade—against him. The loss of resistance caused Felton to startle. When Alex angled his blade, Felton's skidded. The slipping of his sword was enough to enable Alex to twist away—with a hard jab of his elbow in Felton's ribs.

The other man let out a surprised "oof" and nearly fell to the ground himself.

It was a gutsy move that with any less precision could have resulted in a serious injury to Alex. Instead, he'd turned the tables, making Felton look like the fool.

And if the look on the other man's face was any indication, he intended to pay Alex back with death.

Practice, apparently, was over.

Let him come, damn it. Alex was done pretending.

Felton was already coming toward him with his sword raised when a small cloaked figure darted between them.

All that strength, all that steel, vanished in an instant as every drop of blood drained from Alex's body. For one horrible moment, he thought Felton wouldn't be able to stop the downward motion of his sword before he saw her.

Alex lunged forward, bloody well knowing it was useless. There was nothing he could do—no way to pull her to safety before . . .

Felton jerked to an abrupt stop, looking as pale as Alex probably did.

Apparently oblivious to the danger she'd narrowly avoided, Joan was clapping delightedly. She shot him a glance before turning her full attention on Felton.

Maybe not so oblivious, he realized. The look she'd given him had been filled with concern. She was worried about him; that was why she'd put herself at risk.

"Bravo, bravo! That was magnificent, Sir Robert." She

gave the other man a dazzling smile. "That was quite a show. My cousin told me that you were one of the best knights in Christendom, and now I see she did not exaggerate."

As Felton was momentarily confused, it took him a moment to respond. He puffed up like a rooster, obviously more than happy to go along with her pretense that he'd gotten the best of Alex.

Bloody hell, did she think him in need of rescue? And why did the very thought make his teeth grind together and Alex want to reach for his sword to prove her wrong?

Joan's cousin had come up behind her. "Oh yes, it was wonderful," Lady Margaret said. "But I hope we did not disturb your practice."

While Felton gallantly assured her that they had not, and the two women continued to fawn, Alex stewed.

What the hell were they doing here anyway?

He had his answer when the farcical party on the practice yard grew even larger with the arrival of Sir Hugh Despenser and his retinue.

"There you are," the young knight boomed, striding forward with all the pomp and circumstance of a royal prince. He even dressed like a prince in heavy velvets embroidered with gold, decorated with jewels, and (oblivious to the heat) lined with furs. Set around his mantle was a thick gold chain with a garishly large emerald pendant in the middle that Alex suspected had been a gift from the king. "I hope the ladies did not disrupt your training, Sir Robert," Despenser said to Felton.

Felton gave the other man a polite nod of greeting, but Alex suspected that Felton didn't like the arrogant young peacock any more than he himself did.

Despenser personified everything Alex despised about

the English: he was haughty, condescending, and solely concerned with his own advancement.

What the hell did she see in him?

Besides the obvious. As much as Alex disliked the other man, he couldn't deny that he was fair of face. If you liked men who were pretty as a lass.

"I was just assuring the ladies that we were done. Isn't that right, Seton?"

Felton's gaze was as hard as ice, almost daring Alex to disagree. Alex's jaw was locked so hard it was as if he had to pry the word out. "Aye."

For the first time, he felt Joan's eyes linger on him. They were fixed on the line of red dripping down his stomach from a cut he'd taken earlier in the fight, and despite his anger, despite the fact that she was with another man, the feel of her gaze on his naked body made him swell.

"You're hurt," she said accusingly, stepping toward him as if she might—Christ almighty!—put a hand on him. If she touched his stomach that close to something else, everyone here would know exactly what he was thinking.

He didn't know whether to be relieved or disappointed when Despenser stopped her. "It's just a scratch," the other man assured her.

Even though Alex had been about to say the same thing, he didn't like hearing it from Despenser. He liked the possessive way he tucked Joan into his body even less.

The hand gripping the hilt of his sword gripped a little harder. Gripped until his knuckles turned white.

Despenser hadn't missed the movement. His eyes narrowed with warning that might have been amusing in different circumstances. Despite the young knight's exalted new position as royal favorite, he was no match for Alex with a sword—"hurt" arm or not. If anyone should be worried, it was Despenser.

But proving his too-good opinion of himself, Despenser didn't recognize the danger. Instead, he seemed to be laying down a gauntlet, daring Alex to accept the challenge.

He wanted to. Damn how he wanted to. He didn't understand what it was about Joan Comyn that made him react with such intensity. Such possessiveness. Such anger.

She was undeniably beautiful in a sultry, wanton, "take me to the bedchamber" sort of fashion. But he'd known many beautiful women. Hell, the wives of his former brethren were undoubtedly some of the most beautiful in Scotland.

But he'd never been so attracted to someone before—even Rosalin—and to be attracted to the *wrong* someone was disconcerting. She was nothing like the sweet, innocent maid he'd pictured marrying after the war.

Rosalin Clifford now Boyd was just the sort of woman he'd imagined marrying one day. He might have contemplated making that day sooner, but it had been very clear she'd been in love with Boyd—whether he deserved her or not.

Marriage? Christ, why the hell was he thinking about that? He could never marry a woman who'd lain with another man—probably more than one—not when he'd held himself to a much higher standard.

Nay, it wasn't marriage he wanted from her, and as what he did want wasn't an option, he wasn't going to pick up Despenser's challenge—no matter how badly he wanted to.

"Aye, it's just a scratch, my lady, though I thank you for your concern."

Despenser's look of satisfaction—of thinking he'd made Alex back down—was almost too much to take.

As Alex's pride had withstood about as much thrashing as it could, he excused himself and moved away.

Joan Comyn wasn't for him, but leaving her to Despenser didn't sit well at all.

8

THE EXCHANGE BETWEEN Sir Hugh and Alex had not gone unnoticed by Joan. She understood that a challenge was being made, and that it had been rejected. Or rather, *she* had been rejected.

As she didn't want anything to do with Alex Seton, she didn't know why she felt a sharp pinch in her chest.

Maybe it was because she suspected his reasons. The always-do-what-is-right "Sir Galahad" as MacRuairi called him (it wasn't a compliment) wouldn't want a woman like her. Well, he might *want* her, but not in an honorable intentions kind of way—the only way she knew he would consider. To him, she was impure, unchaste, and thus, unworthy.

The fact that it was true made that pinch even sharper.

As little as she liked being a bone between two men, she liked Sir Hugh's possessiveness and his questioning of her "relationship" with Alex even less.

She masked her annoyance, however, and assured him—honestly—that she barely knew the man. He didn't seem convinced, and she was forced to explain that Alex's "protectiveness" stemmed from a previous family connection.

"Your father?" Sir Hugh asked.

She shook her head. Knowing it was dangerous but unavoidable, she admitted, "Nay, my mother."

She'd spent years distancing herself from the "rebel" Isabella MacDuff, severing any connection between them, and she hated reminding anyone of it.

His eyes sharpened with something that made her wariness seem warranted. "Seton knew your mother? How? When?"

"I don't know. You'll have to ask him."

He stroked his short, pointed beard thoughtfully. "I may just do that."

She didn't like the speculative edge to his voice and was glad when he let the subject drop. But she couldn't help but feel that she'd made a mistake. She didn't want Alex Seton's scrutiny, but she did not want to make trouble for him either.

And Sir Hugh Despenser was trouble. She had no doubt about that.

More trouble than he was worth.

Joan had escaped detection for so long because she knew when to back away, and every instinct was clamoring for her to do that now.

She always listened to her instincts.

But as she didn't look forward to telling Sir Hugh that she had indeed reconsidered, she was glad when they arrived back at Berwick to be told that her cousin "needed her immediately," and that she was to "find her the instant she arrived."

Thank goodness for her cousin's "emergencies." Joan wondered which hem had come undone or which stain "the stupid laundress" had not gotten out. For someone so concerned with her appearance, her cousin was not a neat eater or drinker. She had dribbles of wine and greasy fingermarks on her gowns after each meal. Stains that, of course, it was the laundry maid's responsibility to get out—not Alice's to keep clean.

But before Joan could answer her cousin's summons, Sir Hugh caught her by the wrist. She tried not to flinch. There was nothing offensive or repulsive about his touch, yet there was no denying that something about it felt that way.

"I will expect to see you tonight." His voice left no room for argument.

She pretended to misunderstand. "I will be at the evening meal if my cousin does not need me."

"See that she doesn't," he said, his gaze holding hers. "And I wasn't talking about the evening meal."

The surprise that widened her eyes did not need to be feigned. He certainly didn't waste any time.

She was tempted to tell him of her decision right then, but wanting at that moment only to get away, she merely nodded.

He released her, and she went to join Margaret, who had waited for her. "What was that about?"

Joan shook her head. "Nothing."

"It didn't look like nothing." Realizing Joan wasn't going to say anything, Margaret added, "Be careful with him, cousin. Sir Hugh is spoiled, and not used to being told no."

Once again realizing how astute—maybe *too* astute—her cousin was, Joan nodded.

A few minutes later they entered a maelstrom. Every item of clothing that her cousin possessed seemed to be strewn across all available surfaces of the bedchamber. A young maid—Bess—was standing before the fireplace twisting her hands and near tears. She'd never looked so relieved to see anyone.

Joan immediately took control. "What seems to be the problem?"

"Finally!" Alice said, turning from where she was buried under a stack of velvet, wool, and silk. "If I'd known you were going to be gone so long, I would never have agreed to let you go. I needed you."

Joan ignored the dramatics and didn't point out that she'd been gone only a half-day—less time than she'd told her.

Margaret rolled her eyes. Whereas Joan thought it easier to humor Alice, her sister did not. "Stop being so ridiculous, Alice. You knew exactly how long Joan would be gone. She is your companion, not your villein. She doesn't need your permission to enjoy a morning ride. Now, what dire emergency is it this time?"

Alice gave her sister a blistering glare, but did not argue with her. Though Alice was the elder by two years, sometimes it seemed the opposite.

"I can't find my new bracelet. One of the maids must have stolen it."

No wonder the girl looked close to crying. She probably thought she was about to be tossed into some prison cell or put in the stocks. Joan's mouth pursed in anger. Her cousin's dramatics were one thing, but her inclination to accuse the servants of everything was inexcusable and ugly. She hated when those in power took advantage of those who were not.

"I'm sure you just misplaced it," Margaret said. "Why don't you wear another one?"

"I can't wear another one! Henry gave me this one." She looked close to tears. "He loves when I wear his gifts."

Joan began to suspect that there was more than a bracelet at work here. "The gold and ruby bracelet?"

Alice nodded.

Margaret walked over to the maid and told her what she wanted her to do. Relief swept her face, and she nodded enthusiastically before rushing out the door.

"Wait! Where is she going?" Alice demanded.

"To fetch your bracelet," Joan said calmly. "The clasp came loose on our journey from Carlisle. You asked me to take it to the goldsmith as soon as we arrived. Bess has gone to fetch it."

"Oh," Alice said, oblivious to the terror she'd inflicted on the maid. "I must have forgotten."

Margaret gave her a look and shook her head. "I guess so. Much to poor Bess's misfortune. And look at this mess!"

Joan pushed a few gowns out of the way to clear some space and motioned for her cousin to sit. "Now," she said. "Why don't you tell me what this is really about."

To which Alice responded by bursting into tears—real ones, which was unusual for her cousin. Through the chokes and sobs Joan surmised that Alice suspected Sir Henry of having—or at least planning—another affair.

Alice's eyes hardened to a glittering and very icy blue. "He was talking with that shameless flirt Lady Eleanor. I know she's had her eye on him for some time." Joan very much doubted that. Lady Eleanor seemed to be fiercely in love with her dashing young husband, Lord Henry de Percy.

Joan had actually been surprised to see the Percys at Berwick. Having recently been freed from prison after his part in the execution of the king's favorite Galveston, de Percy did not seem likely to fight for the king who'd imprisoned him. He'd reportedly refused his summons. But he was close to Clifford, which she suspected explained his presence now.

Alice was still sobbing. "Now he claims that he has an important meeting tonight, which may go very late. He told me not to wait up for him."

Important meeting? *That* caught Joan's attention.

"What kind of important meeting?" Margaret asked.

Alice threw up her hands, exasperated by what she clearly thought an irrelevant and inconsequential question. "He said something with only the king's closest advisors. Pembroke, Clifford, Despenser, Henry, and maybe a few others, I don't know. But don't you see, it's probably an excuse."

"There *is* a war coming," Margaret said dryly.

Alice ignored her and wiped her tears, turning to Joan. "You'll help me, won't you?"

Suspecting what she was going to ask her to do, Joan smiled. "Of course."

∽

Alex stopped at the river before returning to the castle. Now instead of angry and slightly drunk, he was angry, mostly sober, and cold. Not a nice dulling, numb cold, mind you, but a shivering, freezing-to-the-bones cold.

The quick dunk in the water hadn't cleared his head or calmed any of the restless emotions teeming inside him. First he'd been called to Berwick for a meeting that he'd been excluded from at the last minute, and then he'd been forced to sit for two long hours while Despenser and Lady Joan made spectacles of themselves.

All right, maybe that wasn't fair. Maybe all they'd done

was share a trencher and smile and whisper a lot, but did they have to look so damned *intimate* doing so? Why not just shout out that they were sharing a bed?

Were they sharing a bed?

It wasn't any of his damned business, and he knew it. But that didn't mean he had to like it.

He didn't like it. He *really* didn't like it, but what the hell could he do about it?

Nothing

Which was precisely what he'd be doing to help end this war if he didn't find that damned spy. He'd joined the men after the meal tonight for the meeting to discuss some "new information," when Pembroke had stopped him and told him he wasn't needed.

Alex didn't need to ask why. Not long after he'd arrived, Pembroke had remarked upon his "miraculous" progress on the practice yard. Besting Felton required "great skill and strength."

Alex had cursed Felton for being Felton, Lady Joan for watching him, and himself for wanting to impress her. Thanks to his little slip today courtesy of his smarting pride, he'd given Pembroke more cause to question his dedication and loyalty. Despenser's questioning him with a smug smile about "his relationship" with Bella MacDuff hadn't helped either. He didn't have to guess where he'd learned that information.

So instead of participating in an important meeting where he might have been able to do some good—or at least impart some reason—he'd gone to the nearest ale-house and tried to cool his anger in more than one mug of ale.

He'd only been drunk a few times in his life (all before the age of twenty) and never intentionally.

But the drinking didn't work. If anything it only succeeded in making him angrier and edgier—which was the last thing he needed when he entered the Constable Tower and nearly ran right into Joan Comyn. He *would* have run into her, if she hadn't seen him first and let out a gasp that stopped him in his tracks.

Still, he instinctively reached out to grab her as if to steady her. Although maybe it was he who needed steadying. He felt the same way he felt every time he saw her—as if he'd slammed into a stone wall.

A stone wall that smelled like spring flowers and looked so lovely and desirable she made his heart stop.

Their eyes met and held in the flickering of the iron lamp that lit the tower entry. He didn't understand the connection between them, but neither could he deny it.

The snap and crack of the flame was the only sound until he broke the silence. "What are you doing here?" But even as the question left his mouth, knowledge pulsed through his already heated blood. His hands tightened on her arms for one moment before he let her go. "Sleepwalking again, my lady?" His eyes slid over the dark cloak that had parted enough for him to see the green velvet gown that she'd been wearing earlier. At least she was dressed this time. "Where is your night rail?"

Her eyes flared as an angry flush flew up her cheeks. "I'm on an errand for my cousin—not that it's any concern of yours."

"Is that what they call it now? An errand? Let me guess, your cousin had a message for Despenser? He has a room in this tower, does he not?"

He didn't need to wonder what she was thinking now. Her expression wasn't closed and mysterious, it was open and fierce. He liked getting to her. He hated when she closed up—it was like she wasn't even there. But she was all there right now. Her blue eyes were flashing dangerously, and that pretty red mouth was pursed into a thin line.

Christ, she was even more beautiful when she was angry. Seeing all that fire—all that passion—light her face was almost irresistible. Especially when that same fire and passion was racing through his own veins. Together they would be incredible. He knew it. Felt it. Wanted it. And it taunted him.

"As do most of the high-ranking lords and barons," she answered. "Including you, I might point out." Her mouth curved in a dangerous, catlike smile. "How do you know my errand did not involve you, my lord?"

She might as well have batted her eyes and sidled up to him; the sultry siren call was just the same. She was prodding him again, provoking him, but this time he was too wound up, too stripped to the ugly core from the drink, anger, and jealousy, to find the strength to resist.

Nor, if he were honest, did he want to.

The urge to take her in his arms and cover her mouth with his was both primal and undeniable. He didn't care that they were standing in an entryway, that anyone might come upon them, that she was the daughter of a friend, or that she might have just come from the chamber of another man. And he sure as hell wasn't thinking about the knightly code. All he could think about was that if he didn't put his mouth on hers—if he didn't finally taste her—he was going to lose his mind.

He wanted to stop the taunting, stop the torture, stop the crazed twisting of emotions wreaking havoc inside him. He wanted to feel her grow soft and weak with desire. He wanted her response. He wanted to know he wasn't alone in this madness.

He wanted it to stop.

Somehow through the haze he found control enough not to back her up against the wall and wrap her leg around his waist the way that he wanted. She might make him feel like a barbarian, but he wouldn't act like one. Instead, he slowly slid his hand around her waist and pulled her toward him, holding her gaze the entire time. The connection was like a powerful magnet drawing them together.

There was a poignant moment right before contact when anticipation made everything in his chest jump and his senses heighten. A pause where he wasn't sure it would happen but wanted it with every fiber of his being. He gave her about a second to pull away before his mouth found hers.

Finally. He groaned at the contact, and something slammed into his chest. It took him a moment to realize it was his heart, as he was too busy dealing with the explosion. Sutherland might have lit off one of his pouches of black powder right before his eyes, for that was the shattering effect that hit him when their lips touched for the first time.

He saw stars—literally. It felt as if a tight lid had been pulled off all the emotions, all the anger, and all the restraint that had been bottled inside him—releasing feelings he hadn't even known were there. He felt wild . . . unharnessed . . . unchained.

For the first time in his life, Alex wasn't holding anything back. Yet despite the almost frenzied urge to ravish—and the lust pulsing through every inch of his body (in some places more forcefully than others)—an overwhelming sense of peace settled over him. A sense of rightness. A sense of home. It was as if this was the exact place he was meant to be. That this was where he belonged. With her. Holding her in his arms. Kissing her. Cherishing her.

Aye, that was the feeling that surprised him the most. The intensity of emotion that swelled from somewhere deep inside him and made him tread gently where he would have raced wildly, and maybe a little roughly—hell, probably right up against the wall.

Instead he was filled with a surprising wave of tenderness. She loomed so large in his mind—and riled his temper so easily—it was easy to forget how young she was. She was so slight in his arms that he felt an overpowering desire to protect her and keep her safe.

He'd never felt anything like this before and he wanted her to know it. This was—*she* was—special.

He'd thought about kissing her from almost the first moment he'd seen her. But even in his darkest most erotic fantasies, Alex had never imagined how incredible it would feel. How her body would press against his in all the right places. How she seemed to melt right into him. How he would never want to let her go.

How good she would taste.

So good that he couldn't seem to get enough. He kissed her again and again, moving his mouth over hers in a gentle, tender wooing. He wanted to linger over every press, every sweep, every little taste.

But her lips were so soft and sweet that the gentle wooing soon gave way to something deeper and more insistent.

He slid his mouth over hers entreatingly, showing her what he wanted, urging her lips to part.

When they did, he growled, feeling a surge of masculine satisfaction that made him pull her a little closer as his tongue delved into her mouth.

Christ. Pleasure tugged low and hot, fierce in its

intensity. But it was nothing compared to the feeling of sheer happiness that zipped through him when he felt the tentative stroke of her tongue against his.

It made him dizzy.

He groaned again, sliding his hands through the warm silk of her hair to grip the back of her head to hold on to as he kissed her deeper and harder. As their tongues circled and pulled them closer and closer. As he started to spin into a whirlpool of pleasure so intense that he wasn't sure he'd be able to pull himself out.

Joan wanted to be angry. She wanted to push him away or bite down on the tongue that slid so deftly into her mouth. She wanted him to taste like herring.

She wanted to hate his kiss.

She wanted to hate him.

Alex Seton had done it again, jumping to conclusions about her presence in the tower—whether he may have had cause for those conclusions or not—and judged her guilty.

She was furious at herself for even trying to explain. She *had* been on an errand for her cousin, blast him.

It wasn't the first time she'd been sent to check on Sir Henry and make sure he was where he was supposed to be. He was, but the fool's errand—in this case a message for Sir Henry about a change in his wife's plans for the morrow—had enabled her to catch a glimpse of what appeared to be an important missive from the king. The wax Great Seal of the knight on horseback that dangled from the parchment from silk threads woven through slits in the parchment was easy to identify even from across the room.

The fact that the missive had been on the table before

Despenser hadn't escaped her notice either. It changed everything. That she might not be able to rid herself of Sir Hugh as quickly as she wanted to was weighing on her, which was probably why she hadn't noticed the man walking toward her until too late.

She wouldn't have ducked into the shadows, would she? She'd been doing nothing wrong; she had nothing to feel guilty about. No matter what he thought.

She'd been so furious—and yes, hurt—by Alex's accusations that she hadn't been able to resist taunting him. She might have even known what he would do. She might have even wanted it. If he'd ravished and devoured her with lust the way he was supposed to, she was certain she would have been able to push him away and revile him the way she should. He would be just like all the others.

But he wasn't like all the others. He was different. And his kiss was *very* different. It was gentle and tender— almost reverent.

She didn't understand it. How could he think her a wanton and kiss her like this? It was beautiful. Sweet. Shattering. With every smooth caress, with every gentle press, with every tender stroke, he ripped her defenses to shreds. He stripped her bare, revealing yearnings—desires—that belonged to another person. The person she'd been.

He kissed her like she meant something. Like she was special. He made her feel like a woman who was worthy of respect—not just a quick, lusty swive against the wall—and she hated it.

These feelings made her weak. *He* made her weak.

But she couldn't break away. It simply felt too good. That she felt anything at all was a surprise. She'd thought herself incapable after the horror of that day. But the numbness— the coldness—that she usually felt wasn't there.

She loved the solid hardness of his body against hers, which didn't make any sense. All that strength should be threatening. He could hold her down. Prevent her from moving. Instead it made her warm and melty. And maybe a little achy.

She couldn't help but remember how all those muscles had looked in the flesh. How they'd flexed and rippled as he moved.

She wanted to make them jump under her fingertips. She wanted to slide her hands up the hard ridges of his back and shoulders, over his bulging arms, and maybe even across the steely bands of his stomach.

She'd never felt desire so physically or viscerally—even that first time before everything had gone so terribly wrong—and the intensity of it took her by surprise.

Surely that was the explanation for the little gasps emitting from low in her throat. Gasps that seemed to be encouraging him to respond with a deep groan and a deeper swirl of his tongue.

His hands moved from cradling her head to down her spine and then to her waist and hips. He was folding her into him, bending her back, bringing her closer.

Confusing her.

All she could think about was the heat of his body, the dark, spicy taste of his mouth, and the sharp pull of sensation that drew her closer with every deft stroke of his tongue. He kissed wonderfully. With skill and purpose and something else . . . feeling? He didn't rush, smother, or slobber with eagerness. He was slow and calculated—as if all he cared about was making her feel good.

It was working.

His hand moved over her breast and she nearly jumped out of her skin. Heat gathered under his palm. Her nipple grew taut. He rubbed her, circling the pad of his thumb over the throbbing tip until she pressed against him. Arching into the firm cup of his hand.

He had great hands. They were so big and strong, but surprisingly gentle. He didn't grasp too tightly or squeeze too hard, or move too roughly.

At first. But then his control started to slip, and he moved a little quicker, a little harder, and maybe a little rougher. But she didn't mind. She liked it. She felt it in the increasing fierceness and intensity of his groans. The thick column of flesh wedged between her legs began to grind in slow, sensual circles reminiscent of . . .

That was when the memories returned. She jerked back suddenly. Harshly. Horror stripped the color from her face.

My God, she'd almost . . .

What was she doing? She couldn't do this. The fact that she'd wanted to—even for a moment—struck her cold. But the feelings had been so powerful, so overwhelming, so intense.

She knew better than to trust those feelings; she was more surprised that after all that had happened she still had them.

He seemed just as shocked as she about what had happened—and just as horrified. He recovered first. Somewhat.

"Shite." An instant later, he winced as if he couldn't believe he'd just said that. After raking his fingers through his hair, he stood a little straighter and tried again. "I must beg for your forgiveness. I hope you will accept my apology for the dishonor I have done you. I have no excuse. I do not know what came over me, but I assure you it will not happen again."

Joan couldn't believe it. The sharp sound of a laugh was

out before she could prevent it. Was he for real? There was something so charmingly old-fashioned and proper about him, she felt as if she'd slipped back in time into the pages of some faerie tale. Would he bend his knee and hand her his sword to do her will? Good gracious, she knew exactly what had come over him. Lust. Desire. Passion. It made people do things they never intended.

"You have much to learn about dishonor, Sir Alex. A kiss hardly qualifies."

She'd meant it more wryly than sarcastically, but she could tell by the way his jaw clenched and his eyes darkened that she'd offended him—unintentionally as it was. He gave her a hard look. "Maybe it is you who have much to learn about honorable men, my lady."

The reply took her aback. She stared at him. With a short bow of his head, he moved past her up the stairs, leaving her to ponder what he'd said.

9

"JOAN? I ASKED you a question."

Startled from her reverie, Joan turned to her cousin with a smile as they walked down the high street. It was Whit Monday, the day following Whitsun—or Pentecost—and one of the biggest celebration days of the year. Villeins would be free from service for the entire week and, as in most big towns, war or no war, Berwick was celebrating with a fair. The streets and markets were more crowded than she'd ever seen them. "I'm sorry, Alice, I was thinking. What is it that you asked?"

Alice's scowls tended toward petulance and this one was no different. "You've been distracted all week. Whatever is the matter with you? I'm getting tired of repeating myself."

As it was the truth, Joan could hardly argue.

Alice eyed her speculatively. "Perhaps Sir Hugh's leaving has upset you more than you let on? I doubt a week's absence will cause his eye to wander, although I suppose you are right to worry. He is a man."

Alice's experience with her husband's affairs had obviously colored her view of men in general. Not for the first time since that night in the tower Joan wondered the same about herself. "*Maybe it is you who have much to learn about honorable men.*" Was Alex right? Had her view of all men been colored by her experience with a few? She didn't want to think so. She'd met few honorable men and so many more who weren't. It was hard not to become cynical.

But she wasn't so cynical that she couldn't acknowledge that she might have misjudged Alex. Her first impressions may have been right. Despite his judgmental reaction to her "behavior," he seemed to truly believe some of the principles most men only parroted, such as honor, gallantry, and chivalry. Yet he'd turned his back on his friends and betrayed them.

She knew him well enough now to know that he must have had a reason—or thought he'd had a reason. Lachlan had been very closemouthed on the subject when he'd told her about it, except to say that "Sir Galahad" had never fit in, and he and Boyd had been a mismatch from the start. It just didn't make sense.

Nothing about him made sense, least of all her reaction to him. A week later and she was still confused by what had happened. She'd kissed him back, not because she had to but because she *wanted* to. She'd done what she thought impossible and welcomed a man's kiss.

More than welcomed, she thought with a grimace of shame. She'd kissed him openly and wantonly, no doubt only reinforcing his opinion of her. That was probably why he seemed to be making a concerted effort to avoid her all week. Though she had felt his eyes on her more than once. He must be wracked with shame for dishonoring himself by frolicking with a woman of her sort.

But she still didn't understand why he'd kissed her as if she weren't that sort of woman at all, but rather someone who was special.

Dear God in heaven, just listen to her! Could she really still be so naive as to ascribe sentiment to a kiss? The first man who didn't try to shove his tongue down her throat and she thought it meant something?

It was probably his seductive trick—making women think they were special.

But it hadn't felt like a trick.

She sighed, telling herself not to think about it. She had other things to worry about. Sir Hugh was due to return any day.

Undoubtedly the best thing to come out of that night was Sir Hugh being called away on a mission for the king. Although frustratingly, she'd been unable to find out anything about it. No one seemed to know the details, or if they did, they were being very secretive.

She would have to wait until he returned to see what she could find out. Instincts or not, it was clear she could no longer break things off with him—at least not right away. But at least his absence gave her a chance to breathe and figure out how she was going to handle him.

The sound of a stomp interrupted her musings.

"You are doing it again," Alice said, clearly annoyed.

"Leave her alone, Alice," Margaret said. "She does not need to confide all her secrets to you."

Alice gave her sister a skeptical frown. "What secrets could Joan have?"

You'd be surprised, Joan thought.

Margaret smiled at her as if she'd heard her. "We all have secrets," her cousin said softly.

Alice looked at her sister as if she knew what some of those secrets might be, and they upset her. She frowned and was about to say something when Margaret stopped her. "Isn't that the knight we saw practicing at Wark the other day? Alex Seton?"

Joan tried to feign disinterest as she turned in the direction of Margaret's gaze, but she suspected her sharp intake of breath had not gone unnoticed. Though she immediately averted her eyes lest their gazes meet, the quick glance through the crowd was enough to confirm his identity and bring a hot flush to her cheeks as memories hit with the subtlety of a sledgehammer. Her heart started to beat at an alarmingly accelerated rate.

It was nothing, she told herself. Just a kiss. She had no reason to be embarrassed or feel awkward. But there was no denying that she was both. The memory of that kiss—and how thoroughly she'd responded to it—was too fresh.

"Aye," she answered with as much nonchalance as she could manage. Then before he noticed them, or her cousin did something dreadful like call out a greeting, she took Margaret's arm to steer her away. "Come, I think I smell tarts."

There was no surer way to get them moving quickly—like her, both of her cousins loved tarts. It must be a family trait.

Unfortunately, they weren't quick enough. They'd only taken a few steps toward the stalls when someone—a big someone—blocked their path.

"Ladies."

The deep masculine voice sent shivers of awareness down Joan's spine that made her skin prickle and the tiny hairs on her neck stand on edge. Blast it, how did he do that? And did he have to smell so good? He was a man in full armor on a hot day. He should stink with sweat, not smell like he'd just stepped out of a steamy bath.

Her cheeks flushed hotter as that image came unwittingly to mind. His naked chest had been spectacular; she imagined the rest would be . . .

Nothing that she should be thinking about!

But if she were the type of woman to admire backsides—which she just might be—she would be in heaven. She couldn't help but notice the strong muscles of his flanks in the leather breeches when she'd been able to tear her eyes away from his bare chest the other day.

God in heaven, what was the matter with her?

Something about Alex made her feel like a lovesick maid again—before she'd had the stars wrenched from her eyes and her innocence stolen forever. Although she couldn't ever remember being so physically attracted to a man and filled with such decidedly *un*maidenly thoughts.

Annoyed by her silly reaction to him, she looked up with a purse to her mouth that faltered a bit when she found those spectacular crystal-clear blue eyes riveted on her. She feared she sucked in her breath again.

"My lord," she said with a curt bow of her head that was more to avoid that penetrating gaze than out of deference.

Had he noticed her flushed cheeks? She hoped he attributed them to the warm day. Her sixteen-year-old lass's reaction to him was bad enough without him being aware of it.

She wasn't to be so fortunate.

"Is something wrong, Joan?" Alice asked, waving her fan in her direction as if to cool her off. "Your face is as red as a beet."

And no doubt getting redder. Joan cursed her cousin and shook her head stiffly, not daring to look in Alex's direction. "It's a bit warm, that's all." With as much dignity as she could muster, she forced herself to meet Alex's gaze. "If you'll excuse us, my lord, my cousins and I were just about to get some refreshment."

She was being rude, and they both knew it. But all she wanted to do was get away. She sensed he felt the same—which didn't necessarily make her feel any better—but he looked behind them, frowning. "Where is your escort?"

Joan pointed to the young squire kicking the dirt with boredom a few feet behind Alice. "Right there."

"The lad?"

"My husband's squire," Alice interjected, looking back and forth between Alex and Joan with a slight furrow between her brows.

Joan nearly groaned. Wonderful. Was it so obvious that her oblivious cousin was noticing it? Whatever *it* was.

Alex turned to Alice and gave her a gallant bow. "Please, allow me to accompany you. The crowds can sometimes get unruly, and I cannot in good conscience let you go without proper escort."

"No." Joan's objection came immediately, which is

probably why he'd directed the request to her cousin in the first place. Aware of the three sets of eyes on her, she hastily explained, "I mean, thank you for your generous offer, but it isn't necessary. Charlie is quite capable of looking after us."

She looked in the squire's direction only to see that he wasn't paying attention to them at all. No longer bored, he was enthralled with a pair of young lasses who were standing a few feet away whispering and giggling behind their hands at the handsome young squire. Joan and her cousins could have had their purses cut—or throats for that matter—and he wouldn't have noticed. Both young girls were rather generously proportioned in the breast area.

"Aye, I can see that," Alex said dryly.

"We do not want to take you from your duties," Margaret said.

Joan could have hugged her.

But Alex didn't bite. His jaw was locked. She sensed a steely tenacity in him that would not be easily dissuaded. Which was exactly why she needed to avoid him.

"My duties can wait," Alex said.

Joan sensed he would rather they not, but apparently chivalry took precedence.

The matter apparently decided, Alex joined them as they strolled through the stalls of the market. She had to admit his presence was not without effect. People seemed to give them a wider berth with the imposing knight leading the way, and if any men in the crowd might have been inclined to look at and admire the three noblewomen, they quickly looked away. The women, however, weren't so shy. Joan noticed plenty of young—and not so young—women staring at the uncommonly handsome mail-clad knight. It irritated her for no reason—or at least not for one she wanted to admit.

Joan kept to the rear of the group and pretended not to listen to the conversations that sprang up between Alex and her cousins. But one struck her cold.

"Seton . . ." Alice said. "Ah, now I remember. My husband has spoken of you. I believe you are taking care of a little problem for him."

There was something about the way she said it that pricked Joan's curiosity.

Alex seemed inclined not to respond with more than a mumbled acknowledgment, but Margaret asked, "What kind of problem?"

"The problem of the traitor who has been feeding information to the rebels," Alice said angrily.

Joan was fortunate they'd stopped for a moment to take advantage of shade while they finished their refreshment or her step might have taken the same hitch as her heartbeat.

"Really?" Margaret asked, an odd note in her tone. "Who would do such a thing?"

"My husband has his suspicions, but that is what Sir Alex has agreed to find out."

Joan's stomach sank to her feet. Alex was searching for the spy? Good God, she was glad no one was looking at her because she feared that flush on her face had suddenly gone very pale.

"Have you any promising leads so far, my lord?" Margaret asked.

Alex appeared vaguely uncomfortable. "I've only just begun, my lady."

In other words, no. Joan let out the breath she didn't realize she'd been holding.

She felt his eyes on her and realized it might have sounded too much like a sigh of relief. Wanting to distract him, she said, "I'm surprised they chose a Scot for the job."

Then she added with what she hoped was the right amount of innocence, "Although maybe they think your recent experience in Bruce's army will be helpful?"

Apparently not innocent enough. His gaze hardened. "Aye, something like that, my lady."

Though she'd obviously made him angry, at least she'd succeeded in deflecting attention from herself.

For a moment at least.

"Joan," Margaret said. "Isn't this the shop you were talking about?"

To her horror, Joan looked over and realized they were standing beside the mercery. She'd mentioned it to her cousins, hoping to have the chance to make contact. But she hadn't anticipated having Alex Seton with her *again*.

"Aye," she said. "I noticed it on my last trip to town. They seem to have a large display of silks."

Alice perked up at the magic word. "We should go in."

Joan's smile betrayed none of her inward alarm. "It's getting late. We need to get back to the castle if you are to have time to dress for the midday meal. We can come back next week after the fair when the crowds are gone." She turned to Alex and finally she allowed their eyes to meet. If the shudder running through her was any indication, it had been a mistake. "I think we've taken enough of Sir Alex's time today."

❦

Alex knew she was anxious to get rid of him, and forgetting for a moment that he'd been just as anxious to avoid her, it grated.

He smiled, knowing how much he was about to annoy her. "I have all the time in the world, my lady. I am at your command."

Her mouth pressed in a tight line, and he had to force himself not to laugh even if what he'd said wasn't exactly true. He'd been pursuing a lead when he'd noticed the ladies—or rather one lady in particular—in the crowd. He might have let her go had he not noticed their lack of escort.

Letting her go is what he'd been trying to do for the past week. As he would be at Berwick for the foreseeable future—or at least until he uncovered the spy—he knew he wouldn't be able to completely avoid her, but he'd been doing his damnedest to try. Too often, however, he'd found his gaze straying in her direction.

He couldn't look at her without thinking about what he'd done, and that aroused very conflicting feelings in him. He was ashamed of his actions—he'd never treated a lady so dishonorably—but neither could he forget how incredible it had felt. Holding her . . . kissing her . . . it had felt so damned *right*. Which didn't make any sense as it was so wrong in every way.

Thus stymied, he'd focused his attention instead on identifying the spy, methodically going through what he knew about the information that had leaked and trying to match it with the most likely suspects. As much as he hated to admit it—and he *really* hated to admit it—Pembroke was probably right in that it was likely a Scot.

It made the most sense. The one English suspect, Ralph de Monthermer, Robert Bruce's former friend who most of the Guard assumed had been the source, had been away from England for much of the past few years patrolling the Irish Sea. Given the kind of information that had been passed, it was much more likely to have come from someone in the Borders.

Alex was actually certain of it. He had information no

one else in the English camp had. He knew the spy had been in the Roxburgh area a few years ago, as Lamont's wife, Janet—who'd been posing as a nun—had been the contact.

Unfortunately, narrowing it down to Roxburgh a few years ago didn't help much, as the Border stronghold had been second only to Berwick as a headquarters for the English army at the time of Edward II's first campaign. Most of Edward's commanders—men who would have been in position to hear important information—would have been through Roxburgh at that time, as would the Scot barons in the Borders. Men like Alexander Abernathy, the Umfravilles (both the Earl of Angus and Sir Ingrim), William de Soules, Sir David Brechin, and Sir Adam Gordon.

Gordon. There was another connection that Alex kept coming back to other than that Sir Adam's nephew had been a Guardsman. One he wished to hell he didn't know about. Janet's twin sister, Mary—Sutherland's wife—had been extremely close to Sir Adam. Alex also knew that Sir Adam secretly had passed on information about making black powder to Sutherland not long before Janet showed up in Roxburgh. Had that been all he'd passed on or was there more?

Alex didn't want to believe it was possible. Sir Adam was too honorable, too noble to be a spy. He was the last man Alex wanted to suspect.

But when he'd seen the older warrior leave the castle early this morning, Alex had followed him. Alex hadn't expected it to lead to anything, but Sir Adam had gone to the priory at Coldingham where Lamberton, the Bishop of St. Andrews and one of Bruce's most loyal compatriots, had been for years.

It could be a coincidence, and something told Alex it was, but he'd been on his way to confront Sir Adam when he'd noticed Joan and her cousins wandering the fair.

He'd been unable to resist. Just like he'd been unable to resist prodding her.

She was still glaring at him when her cousin responded to his offer to accompany them into the shop. It was the same mercery that Joan had been standing in front of before. The lass must like to shop through windows.

"You are very kind, Sir Alex," Lady Margaret said. "But I'm afraid my cousin is right. We had best get back to the castle."

"Then allow me to escort you," Alex said.

"That isn't—"

"I insist," Alex said, cutting off Joan with a devilish grin. What was it about the lass that provoked him to wickedness?

Suspecting he knew, he sobered. This attraction was damned inconvenient. Not to mention uncomfortable. All he had to do was stand next to her and his body responded. He knew he should stay away from her, but knowing was easier than doing.

He was glad when Margaret engaged her sister in conversation. Alice de Beaumont was undoubtedly a beauty, but she was also spoiled and vain. The kind of woman who expected to be fawned over and flirted with—neither of which he was going to do.

He and Joan walked in surprisingly companionable silence for a while. He had to reach out and steady her when someone in the crowd jostled her. The way she flinched from his touch stung. "Are you still angry with me? You have every right to be."

She gave him a sidelong glance that might have held a

hint of reproach for bringing up the subject that she was obviously trying to ignore. But that was like trying to ignore a purple horse.

"I am not angry with you. If I am mad at anyone, it is myself." She paused, shifting her gaze. "I shouldn't have provoked you."

She was blushing again, as she'd done earlier when her overzealous efforts to be rid of him had caught her cousin's attention. He had to disagree with Lady Alice, however. Joan's cheeks weren't the color of beets; they were a much prettier rosy shade of pink.

The girlish blush was adorable and so far from the seductive siren she was at other times, it was hard to jibe the two.

Actually they didn't jibe, and the incongruity intrigued him. *She* intrigued him. Was she the blushing, sweet young maid who'd charmed him the first time they'd met, or the practiced seductress linked to a number of men?

The more he watched her and the more time they spent together, the more something about the siren didn't feel right. But maybe that was just wishful thinking on his part? Maybe he wanted to believe that she might not be so wrong.

His mouth twisted in a wry smile. "Aye, well it wasn't without cause. I had no right to speak that way to you. My only excuse—and it's not a good one—is that I was not in the best frame of mind." He paused. "I know what you do is none of my business, but I just think someone should be looking out for you."

She lifted a brow. "Was that an apology?"

He grinned. "Aye, it was meant to be, although I guess it wasn't a very good one."

He was surprised and enormously pleased when she

grinned back at him. "Well, it is accepted. But you do not need to worry yourself on my account, Sir Alex. I do have someone watching out for me."

"Who?"

"The person in the best position to do so."

He understood the gentle reproach—even if he wasn't sure he agreed with her. "Yourself."

She nodded, pleased that he'd guessed.

They had just passed over the second wooden draw-bridge and through the final gate before entering the castle when he said, "You and I got off on a bad foot."

She looked up at him, and the feel of those velvety dark blue eyes on his gave him a little jolt. "Don't you mean bad ankle?"

He laughed. "Aye, well maybe you are right, but I should like to change it."

She peered up at him from under her lashes almost shyly. "I should like that, too."

"Good—"

The rest of what he'd been about to say was cut off by a man who'd emerged from a crowd in the yard.

"There you are," the man boomed, walking toward them.

Alex stiffened. Bloody hell, Despenser was back.

"I was about to come looking for you," he added. Despenser's eyes had been fixed on Joan, but now they slid to Lady Alice. "Your maid said you'd been gone some time."

"There was no cause for concern," Lady Margaret interjected, turning to Alex with an appreciative smile. "Sir Alex was generous enough to escort us."

"I can see that," Sir Hugh said through a very narrowed gaze directed at Alex.

His displeasure was obvious. Alex didn't give a shite, but Lady Joan hastened to explain. "The fair was more crowded than we expected. When we ran into Sir Alex he insisted on accompanying us."

Alex gritted his teeth. It was clear what she was trying to do. She didn't want there to be any misunderstandings about their relationship.

The explanation seemed to serve its intent in mollifying the young lord.

It didn't, however, have the same effect on Alex. He was getting that possessive, protective feeling again racing through his veins, and he knew he better remove himself before he did or said something to ruin the tentative truce he and Lady Joan had just forged. Like maybe smashing his fist through Despenser's pretty teeth.

With a short bow to the ladies, Alex excused himself and walked away. While he still could.

10

THIS WAS A mistake. Joan's instincts were screaming again, but she'd put Sir Hugh off for as long as she could.

It should be safe enough, she thought with an uneasy glance around as they entered the quiet stables. But the soldiers were still practicing in the yard nearby, and even if quiet now, the stables would not be for long.

Anticipating Sir Hugh's movements, she spun away

from him—and his embrace—as soon as they entered. "Now where is this great hero?" she asked playfully, hands on her hips. "You swore on your honor as a knight that the greatest hero in the castle slept in the barn. I hope it was not a trick."

Sir Hugh's smile held a hint of definite mischief. "You thought I would lie to get you alone? Well, I might, but in this case I did not. Come, see for yourself."

When he started to lead her toward one of the stalls in the back, she grew even more certain something was afoot. But she forced herself to keep walking. She could handle this. She could handle him. Something was going on with the English command, and she was determined to know what it was.

He stopped, leaning over the wooden gate to point at a small, furry black lump in the straw. "There he is."

Frowning, but undeniably curious, Joan leaned forward and identified the lump as a sleeping dog. A very small and ratty-looking sleeping dog. Suddenly the tiny creature looked up, leapt to its feet, and started barking crazily at her.

She winced at the sound, which was actually more of a high-pitched yap than a bark. But goodness, the little thing was so ugly it was cute.

Suddenly she understood Sir Hugh's riddle.

Even though this little beast had caused her Highland Guard brethren a lot of trouble, she couldn't help but smile.

Sir Hugh was clever, she would give him that. "This is the dog that alerted the guards and prevented the castle from being taken by the rebels two Decembers past."

Gregor "Arrow" MacGregor had had the dog in his sights, but he'd hesitated to shoot, and the dog's yapping had alerted the garrison to their presence, ruining their chance to take the important castle. According to Lachlan, that hesitation had made Gregor the butt of many jests in the Guard, but after seeing the dog, Joan understood. She wouldn't have been able to shoot either.

Sir Hugh looked mildly disappointed. "You weren't supposed to guess so easily."

"It was hard not to with that bark." She winced again as it continued. "This little guy is very well known throughout the Borders."

"So you agree, then? I will have my apology now. You maligned my honor by suggesting trickery," he said with mock gravity.

She laughed. "Very well, I apologize. You were right: the greatest hero at Berwick sleeps in the stables."

She bent over to quiet the dog and quickly realized her mistake when he came up behind her. "I think I'll require more of an apology than that."

His husky voice left no doubt of his meaning. She tamped down the alarm bells ringing in her head.

He put his hands on her hips, and knowing that she was seconds away from having her bottom pressed against a part of him she had no interest in feeling, she stood up quickly and tried to spin away. But this time he anticipated her movement, and instead he turned her into his embrace.

She gasped as her chest collided with his. "Now that's better," he said huskily, pushing her up against the wall of the stall. "God, you feel good."

Joan wished she could say the same. There was nothing objectively wrong with him. His breath didn't smell like herring, his lips weren't too puffy or his nose too long. His neatly trimmed beard wasn't peppered with crumbs from the midday meal. His body was hard and lean with enough well-sculpted muscle to make a woman's heart jump.

But hers was jumping for an entirely different reason.

She didn't understand this dread—this near panic. She'd been in this situation before and she'd never had such a problem detaching. But never before had it felt so *wrong*. Never before had she compared it to another. And never before had it made her feel as if she needed to dive into the loch.

Alex's kiss had stripped her of her armor of indifference.

One glance at Sir Hugh's face and she read his intent. Her pulse took another vicious jump. *He's going to kiss me . . .*

"You never told me about your journey," she blurted.

The slow descent of his mouth stopped. His eyes narrowed just enough for her to realize she had best be careful. Her vaunted subtlety in questioning had apparently deserted her.

"No, I didn't."

Her heart was hammering so loud she feared he could hear it in her voice. "It must have been important."

His expression didn't change. She felt a bit like a bug under a rock that had just been lifted. "It was."

"The king must value you greatly."

Misinterpreting her interest as she'd intended, he smiled. "He does."

He thought she liked his power and importance—she did, but not for the reasons he imagined. Unfortunately, it appeared Sir Hugh was not a boaster. She needed to find out about his mission.

He started to lower his mouth again, and she told herself she could do this—how bad could it be?—but at the last minute she turned her face so that his mouth landed on her cheek and jaw instead. He didn't seem to mind the detour, as his mouth descended to devour her throat and neck.

"I was bored all week," she blurted again, trying to think about anything other than what he was doing. But the feel of his mouth on her skin made it crawl as if a jar of spiders had just been poured on her. "There was so little to do. It stormed for a few days, and then everyone was getting ready for the fair . . ." She rambled on for a few more minutes, but nothing could distract her—or him.

His mouth left her throat to cover her mouth. It was that bad. Her body's rejection was instantaneous. She felt it in every fiber of her being. *No!* She wanted to scream. Her muscles tensed with the instinctive response to break free.

But she forced herself not to move. It was a job. It served a higher purpose. This wasn't her. She didn't feel anything. It was just a kiss.

But the cold detachment she'd always been able to muster wasn't there. She felt everything, and the sensation of his lips pressing intently—lustily—against hers . . .

Oh God, she couldn't do this.

She pushed away—or tried to push away—breaking the kiss if not his hold on her. "Wait!" she said in a gasp.

His arms tightened around her. She'd never been locked in irons, but she suspected the sensation was the same.

"Wait for what?" he said angrily.

"I . . . uh . . . anyone might discover us. Besides . . ." She smiled broadly and she hoped with considerably less trepidation than she was feeling. "We should get to know each other a little better first."

It was all she could think of to put him off. Goodness knew her trick with marriage wouldn't work with Sir Hugh—he would never believe she was foolish enough to consider marriage.

His dark eyes held a warning that he was not in the mood for delays or games. "I already know all I need to, and we know each other plenty well." He paused, eyeing her suspiciously. "Why are you suddenly playing the blushing maid? I thought you wanted this. Or maybe there's something else you want from me?" His eyes drew as sharp as daggers. "Did the queen put you up to this? Are you spying on me?"

"Of course not!" she exclaimed adamantly. But his accusation hit too close to the truth. She'd roused his suspicions, and knowing she had to put a stop to it, she didn't protest when his mouth covered hers again.

She tried—truly she did—for all of about three seconds. But when he attempted to push his tongue between her lips, the panic—the revulsion—was too overwhelming. She couldn't bear it. Not another moment.

She tried to push away a second time, but he wasn't having it. The arms that were wrapped around her were like chains of steel. He wasn't going to let her go.

She struggled, a moment of panic overtaking her as the memories came rushing back. But only for an instant. She would never let that feeling of helplessness take hold of her—she would never let a man hurt her like that again.

Her movements were smooth and quick, as if practiced a thousand times—which wasn't too far off. Lachlan was a difficult taskmaster and demanded perfection. She'd been glad of it now and had been more than once.

She moved her left hand to his right arm to grab the inside of his elbow and lifted her right to his left cheek. Neither movement was threatening, but when done together . . .

She pulled inwardly on his arm while the other hand pushed against his jaw to rotate his head. Using this simple yet elegant maneuver she was able to swing him around to change their positions, so it was he who was now pushed against the wall. His surprise enabled her to break free and step back.

It was done without a blow or strike. Her goal had been to gain her freedom, not hurt him, though she could have easily done so. And maybe even wanted to. But she didn't want to draw too much attention to her unusual skills.

In that she failed.

Alex slowly unfurled the hand that had been clenched around the hilt of his dagger. Despenser had been a few seconds away from having it buried deep at the base of his neck.

Alex wouldn't have missed. His skill with the blade was what had eventually earned him his place in the Highland Guard.

He couldn't ever recall feeling the urge to kill so powerfully. It had been bad enough when Despenser's mouth pressed against hers the first time. But when he'd kissed her again and Alex saw her struggling to break free, the urge had come over him in a red, primitive haze that even now still pounded through his blood.

Had she not extricated herself from his hold, Alex would have killed the king's new favorite. Happily. A man who would force himself on a woman deserved nothing less.

Perhaps in that Alex and his former partner were more alike than he realized. The vehemence of his reaction was unexpected. He'd never experienced the kind of hatred that Boyd had felt after his sister's rape—hatred that had fueled his vengeance against the English—but maybe he'd had a taste of it now.

Actually, he wasn't altogether sure his blade still wouldn't end up in the bastard's back—or gut, for that matter.

Despenser took a threatening step toward her. "What the hell? How did you—"

"Wait!" She darted away from Despenser. "I heard something."

Alex stilled. Had he made a noise?

"You heard nothing," the other man growled. "I paid the stable lads a shilling each to see that we were not disturbed for a while."

Alex had seen the two boys guarding the door not long after Despenser and Lady Joan had gone inside, which is why he'd slipped into the barn through the door on the opposite side used to bring the hay inside.

He couldn't believe it when he'd seen her go in the barn with him willingly. Didn't she realize what would happen?

His mouth fell in a hard line. Of course she did. And he was a bloody fool because he thought the kiss they'd shared might have meant something. It had to him. He hadn't realized how much until he'd seen her in another man's arms.

"So you *were* planning something," she said.

"Of course I was," Despenser replied angrily. "Any fool would have known what I planned. And whatever else you might be, Lady Joan, you are no fool. So either you are a tease or you had another purpose for leading me into believing you wanted to bed me." His eyes narrowed. "Which is it?"

Despenser had stopped advancing on her, and she stood to face him. Surprisingly, given the circumstances, she didn't look threatened or scared. Actually, she looked confident and strong.

Alex frowned.

"Neither," she said with a bold lift of her chin. "I just do not believe we will suit."

"*You* do not believe we will suit?" Despenser repeated incredulously. "Who the hell do you think you are? Since when does a bastard slut turn down one of the most important men in the realm?"

Alex's hand returned to his dagger.

He wasn't alone in his anger, although only a slight tinge of pink in Lady Joan's cheeks betrayed her fury as she responded to the taunt. "Since right now. I am sorry to have disappointed you, Sir Hugh, it was not my intention. But there is no reason to be cruel. We have been friends a long time."

The young knight's eyes blazed. Clearly, friendship was the last thing he was thinking about. Alex silently begged him to make a move. *Give me an excuse.* His hand was practically itching.

But she stopped him. "There's someone else," she blurted.

"Who?" The other knight demanded angrily, echoing Alex's thoughts.

She bit her lip, her hands twisting a little before her. "I'd rather not say."

Despenser eyed her with disgust. "You do not need to. I've seen the way you look at Seton. It's him, isn't it?" Alex froze. Was it true? He couldn't believe it when she nodded. Despenser cursed angrily. "You sure as hell don't waste any time, do you? Had your bed grown so cold in a week that you needed to fill it with the first man you could find? I'm just surprised that he took you up on your offer. Seton isn't known for dallying with whores."

That might have been the excuse Alex had been waiting

for, but Joan shifted just enough to block his direct line to Despenser.

"It's not like that," she said softly.

Sir Hugh must have seen something in her expression and gave a harsh laugh. "Unrequited lust, is that it? I'm not surprised. From what I know of Seton, he holds himself to rigidly high standards for a Scot. Still, he must have ice running through his cock to refuse a tasty piece like you in his bed."

Alex wasn't sure how much more of this he could take. Only knowing the embarrassment he would cause her prevented him from revealing himself right then and wiping the crude words from Despenser's mouth with his fists.

Joan stood in silence, but Alex sensed she was just as furious and anxious to defend herself. So why didn't she? Perhaps she just wanted it over? If that was the case, it worked.

Despenser closed the distance between them. She tensed at the same time as Alex, but there was no cause. The young knight walked right past her. "When you realize your mistake do not bother trying to correct it. It is too late."

"I am sorry."

"Save your apologies," he said. "I do not wish to hear them." He smiled coldly. "But I assure you, you will be *very* sorry."

The threat wasn't subtle, nor was it meant to be. In rejecting him, Joan Comyn had just made herself a dangerous enemy, and she appeared to know it as well.

She sank down on a bale of hay with a heavy sigh and a distinctly worried look on her face. Perhaps sensing her mood, the dog trotted out of the stall to collapse into a ball by her feet. For a creature that had caused so many problems for Alex's former brethren, it sure was a lazy little blighter. But Alex was almost jealous of it a moment later when Joan absently reached down to stroke it gently between the ears.

Alex should probably leave her alone. But it seemed he wasn't very good at doing what he should do when it came to Joan Comyn.

"Despenser will not forget the slight," he said, emerging from the shadows where he'd been watching.

She jumped to her feet. The dog that had roused a garrison barely lifted its head in Alex's direction—apparently its watch days were at an end. Joan recovered quickly and rounded on him. "I knew I heard something! You were spying on me!"

Alex didn't deny it. "It wasn't intentional. I was coming back from the river after practice when I saw you come in here with him *alone*. Damn it, Joan, what were you thinking? You had to know the danger and what could happen. He could have . . ."

The words were so repugnant he couldn't even get them out.

"Yes, I know ex—" She stopped. For a moment she looked haunted—devastated—but then the familiar defiance returned to her eyes. "I do not need you to protect me, Alex. I can take care of myself."

Ignoring for the moment that she'd used his given name—and how much he liked hearing her do so—he wanted to argue but realized he couldn't. She *had* extricated herself. Quite well actually. Her movements had been smooth and polished, as if it were something she'd done many times before. Perhaps she had. But something else about it niggled. Something familiar.

He frowned. "Where did you learn to do that?"

Joan knew that she'd made a mistake. Her third or fourth of the afternoon—so many she'd lost count. From thinking she could do what she had to do to avoid the confrontation like she'd just had with Sir Hugh, to nearly blurting out that she knew *exactly* what could happen, to reminding Alex of skills that she didn't want him curious about.

She could bite off her tongue. But she was more shaken by the episode with Sir Hugh than she wanted to admit. Alex was right: he would not forget the slight, and Joan knew she would have to be *very* careful around Sir Hugh for the remainder of their time at Berwick.

Just like she was supposed to be careful around Alex. Knowing that she would likely only arouse more curiosity if she pretended that she didn't know what he meant, she said, "My mother thought it was important that I learned how to defend myself."

The frown that gathered between his brows didn't release right away. He stared at her with an intensity that made her want to squirm, but she held her expression impassive. He must have trained with Lachlan many times; would he recognize something?

Finally, he relented with a nod. "That sounds like Bella. I'm surprised she did not have you practicing with swords."

"Swords were too heavy. But I do have this."

She pulled out her eating knife from the sheath on her girdle. The handle of horn was worn with use to fit perfectly in her hand. The four-inch steel blade had been honed to a razor's edge to slice easily through the toughest meat—or whatever else she might need to cut through.

Alex shook his head. "Why am I not surprised? You know how to use it?"

She nodded. Not as well as him, maybe—even Lachlan had conceded Sir Alex's superior skill with a dagger—but she could defend herself if need be.

He held her a little while longer with that too-penetrating stare that saw too much and made her want to shuffle her feet like a naughty child.

"Don't let it give you a false sense of confidence," he said. "A blade like that will do little against armor, and it can be defended against by someone with the right training." Like him, she supposed he meant. But she'd had training, too—not that she could tell him that. "You also have to be willing to use it."

She eyed him unflinchingly. "I am."

He didn't seem impressed by her confidence. If anything it appeared to anger him. His mouth tightened. "Keep meeting men in barns and I'm sure you'll have the opportunity to find out."

How dare he . . . ! The hot flush of anger flew onto her cheeks. She gripped the handle of the knife more purposefully, pointing it toward him in a manner that could only be construed as a challenge. "Does that include you, my lord?" she said with staccatoed sweetness.

He didn't move a muscle, which in no way lessened the threat. Instead it only made it more ominous. The air was thick with the coiled tension of a snake ready to strike. He wanted to knock the blade from her hand and prove the truth of his words so badly she could practically taste it. And she was ready for him to try.

Whether he would be able to, she didn't know, but she relished the challenge.

That was another mistake, which she realized when she

saw the flicker of surprise in his eyes. She'd given too much away. She'd reacted like a warrior, not a lady with some basic training. Bold and challenging were not the same as mysterious, quiet, and unassuming.

With an inward curse, she lowered the blade. Hoping to curtail any more curiosity on his part, she said, "I am sure your *advice* is well intentioned, but as I've said before, I can meet whomever I want in barns or anywhere else for that matter—it is no concern of yours."

The anger was back. His mouth hardened in a very formidable line, and the flare in his eyes . . . it burned with a strange light as he looked at her. "What if I wish to make it my concern?"

The declaration was so unexpected it took her a moment to realize that was what it was—and what he meant. And even then she didn't quite believe it until their eyes met. She drew in her breath, seeing the truth. He wanted her and not just in a dishonorable manner. He was offering her more. Maybe a lot more. Maybe everything.

The pang of longing in her chest was as unexpected as it was deep. It took her breath away, making her lungs burn.

It seemed inconceivable that any respectable man would want her under her present circumstances, let alone a paragon of righteousness and moral certainty like Sir Galahad. That he did moved her—and tempted her—far more than it should. For one illogical moment she let herself wonder if it were possible. If she could let herself be courted by this man who had already made her feel more than she thought capable—and more than she wanted. The man who'd filled her girlish dreams of handsome golden knights in shining armor since the first time she'd seen him all those years ago. Could she open her heart?

Try to have some semblance of a normal life that she'd thought impossible?

The longing was so strong that it took her a moment to come back to reality. But when she did it was with a hard thud. Good gracious, why was she even thinking about this? It *was* impossible. She'd made her choice years ago. There was no going back. Nor would she. What she was doing was too important. She was in a position—a unique position—to help the cause that she'd devoted her life to. Bruce needed her; there was no one else who could do what she did. And they were so close—closer than they'd ever been before. She couldn't do anything to risk that with a potentially war-ending battle approaching.

And Alex Seton was definitely a risk. She couldn't let herself forget who he was. He wasn't just any knight, he was a former member of the Highland Guard who was searching for the spy—her—in the English midst. If she allowed herself to get close to him, how long would it take him to discover her secret? What would he do if he learned she was a part of the very team he'd betrayed? She had no doubt that whatever he might feel for her now would change if he learned the truth. The always-do-what-is-right knight would probably feel honor-bound to turn her in.

She couldn't take that chance.

But it wasn't just that they were on opposite sides, even if he didn't know it. Joan also knew that she would never be able to live up to his standards. He lived in a world of gallant knights and chivalry, of innocent maidens who needed rescue, of right and wrong, and black and white. Joan's world was gray, where people did what they had to do. She wasn't innocent or maidenly. And one day, probably sooner rather than later, she would disappoint him.

Still, it was harder than it should be to get the words out. "Don't," she said softly, and then more firmly, "Don't make it your concern."

He gave no indication that her words had stung, but she sensed that they had. He drew himself up to loom over her in the shadowed light of the barn, seeming even taller than the few inches over six feet that she guessed him to be. She sensed that he wanted to touch her, but his arms were flexed rigidly at his sides. "Am I to be given an explanation? I heard what you said to Despenser. Was that just an excuse?"

She felt heat rising to her cheeks, embarrassed that he'd overheard that part of the conversation. Claiming there was someone else had been an excuse—a way to divert Sir Hugh—but it had also happened to be true. She did want Alex, and her feelings had made continuing the pretense with Sir Hugh impossible.

She would find another way to get the information she needed. But it would not be from him.

She did not need to feign discomfort. "I thought it would be easier if I gave him a reason."

Alex's eyes flared. He lost the rein on his control and reached out with one hand to take her by the arm. His fingers burned like a brand upon her skin. "Do you deny that there is something between us?"

"Nay." Hating what she was about to say, but knowing it must be said, she added, "But that is hardly unusual, and I find it never lasts long."

He flinched as if she'd struck him. The cold white lines etched around his mouth almost made her shiver. "I see."

Clearly, he did, and knowing what he must think of her made her ill. But it was better this way.

He let his hand drop with hard finality, relinquishing her arm and his hold on her.

She felt the loss like a knife in the chest. Feeling the urge to explain, she started, "It's just that . . ." What . . . what could she say? "I like my life, Sir Alex. I see no reason to change it."

It was true. Lachlan was wrong. She wasn't sad or lonely. She was alone by choice. Her work was what mattered—all that mattered—and whatever happiness she needed would come from that.

But which one of them was she trying to convince?

A gallant knight to the end, Alex gave her a short bow of his head before leaving her alone. Just as she'd wanted.

11

ALEX WAS ALREADY leading his horse out of the stable—trying not to think about what had happened there the day before—when Pembroke intercepted him. "You will not be riding out with us today. For the next few days I need you down by the river overseeing the loading of supplies onto the ships."

He had to be jesting. But it was clear he wasn't.

Alex gritted his teeth until his jaw hurt. After years of being a soldier, he knew how to follow orders, but that didn't mean he had to like them. Any more than he liked being rejected out of hand—with barely a pause of consideration, damn it—by the woman he shouldn't want but did.

So much for not thinking about her.

He'd been almost as surprised by his declaration as she'd been. But he'd known as soon as he said the words that he meant it. She might not be the woman he'd pictured, and God knows it was horrible timing with him riding off to war in a couple of weeks, but nothing had ever felt more right.

Except that she'd refused him. Which didn't make any sense. He knew she felt something for him, so why was she so determined to have nothing to do with him? He might have pressed her, but when she'd compared what was between them to her past experiences, he'd felt something hot, angry, and primitive burgeoning inside him. Knowing how close he was to acting like the barbarian she seemed to turn him into, he forced himself to walk away. The lass could strip away years of deeply engrained chivalry and honor with a few choice words. But if she thought this—whatever the hell *this* was—wasn't unusual and was anything like whatever fleeting fancies she'd had before, she was out of her damned mind. And he intended to prove it to her. If she thought he would give up, she was soon to be disappointed.

But maybe not as soon as he'd like with his shite job Pembroke was trying to foist off on him.

"Do you have a problem with that, Seton?" Pembroke asked.

Knowing how to follow orders also didn't mean Alex did so in silence. God knows he'd questioned half of Boyd's orders whenever his partner had been put in charge of a mission. But Alex wouldn't keep his mouth shut when he didn't agree with something. Pembroke, it seemed, didn't like it any better than Boyd had.

"Aye. The loading of the ships can be overseen by the captain and his men." Or any one of a dozen men of lesser rank in Pembroke's command. "I can serve you and the king better by accompanying you. I know the roads between here and Dunbar better than anyone."

If they were scouting for places the army could be attacked, there was no one who could help more than Alex. Pembroke knew that. They all knew that. Shouldn't they be trying to take advantage of his knowledge? Did they want to end the war or not?

Christ, what the hell was he doing here?

At times Alex wondered. The ineptitude was getting to him. Christendom might see the English as the "civilized" side, but clearly civilized didn't mean sensible or rational.

He was supposed to be doing some good, damn it. Somehow when he'd torn his guts out and betrayed his friends to try to put an end to this bloody war, he hadn't imagined himself overseeing the loading of the cargo. It was drudge work, plain and simple. It was like having one of your best leaders in charge of digging latrines—a waste. How was any of this going to prevent villages from burning and innocents from being caught in the flames?

"It was the king who suggested you for the job. Despenser said as much when he passed on the king's instructions."

Alex cursed angrily. He should have guessed. Lady Joan wasn't the only one who'd made an enemy of Despenser. Apparently Despenser was throwing some of the blame for his failed affair in Alex's direction. He'd wager the king hadn't said a word about who would oversee the loading of the cargo. But whatever Despenser had done last week, it obviously involved a meeting with the king.

"I'm surprised that the king thought it important enough to name someone for the task," Alex said, not hiding his skepticism.

Whatever else he might be, Pembroke wasn't a fool. He, too, probably questioned Despenser's message, but apparently had no intention of challenging the king's new favorite. "Aye, well, if I were you, I'd settle whatever score you have with Despenser, or I suspect you'll be attracting a lot of notice with the king."

Alex didn't know who angered him more: Despenser, for his underhanded attempt to settle personal grievances using his position with the king, or Pembroke, for going along with it even when it was clearly not the best thing to do to prepare for the battle, that if they were to relieve the garrison at Stirling Castle by midsummer's day, could only be weeks away.

Over the next few days Alex had a lot of time to think about it—and vent his frustration with the carrying of heavy crates and barrels. He had frustration aplenty. Not only toward the woman who practically ran the other direction when she saw him or Despenser for his juvenile vindictiveness and Pembroke for not taking advantage of his knowledge, but also for his continued exclusion from meetings of Edward's top commanders—meetings that he should be a part of, and had been a part of, until someone suggested he was the damned spy.

He was no closer to exonerating himself on that count either. He'd confronted Sir Adam about his suspicions yesterday, after the older knight returned from the scouting trip near Dunbar that Alex should have been on.

Sir Adam hadn't been surprised—or offended. "I would

have been suspicious of me as well," he said. "But I'm afraid you'll have to look elsewhere."

Not only did Sir Adam have an explanation for being in the priory—it was where his youngest son had been laid to rest when he'd died of a fever exactly a year before—he also provided Alex with information that made it extremely unlikely that he was the spy.

The night before Sir Adam had returned, a group of soldiers had stopped a monk after a night of revelry in town "to have some fun with him." Alex's mouth hardened. In other words, they were harassing him. "The monk seemed to be holding his pouch too tightly and grew agitated when they asked what he was hiding. It turns out he was carrying a missive with the approximate number of troops at both Wark and Berwick, including a breakdown of infantry and cavalry, as well as the names of all the barons who have arrived so far and the size of their retinues. My name was on it, as was yours." But unlike Alex, Sir Adam had not been to Wark, making it unlikely that he had passed on the information. Sir Adam paused significantly before continuing. "There was also a mention of who had not yet arrived."

Alex grimaced, knowing Sir Adam was referring to the earls who had not answered—and might not answer—Edward's call to muster.

"Aye," Sir Adam said, reading his expression. "I'm sure Bruce would like nothing more than to know that Lancaster and his fellow earls—and their cavalry—will not be joining the campaign. Although if it encourages King Hood to stay and fight and not scurry off into one of his fox holes, I almost hope they do not show."

Alex hadn't thought of that, but Sir Adam might be right. One of the reasons Alex had gone over to the English was because raids, skirmishes, and ambushes weren't getting them anywhere anymore. The pirate warfare, the so-called dirty war that Christendom accused Bruce of fighting, could only take them so far. The righteousness of Bruce's cause would only be proved one way: by fighting like a knight—in other words, by a pitched battle of army versus army. But that was something Bruce had adamantly refused to do to this point. Would the earls' absence change his mind? Could Bruce finally be brought from the trees and fox holes of ambuscade to the battlefield?

Alex didn't think so—Bruce had been adamant on this issue whenever Alex had brought it up—but he supposed if the odds were enough in his favor it was possible. But against such a powerful army, even without the earls, would Bruce ever think the odds in his favor?

"But this is interesting," Sir Adam added. "The note mentions Despenser's mission, but that is all. No details are given."

That was interesting. Whoever it was had probably not been at the meeting last week. That he hadn't probably only made them suspect him more.

"I assume the monk was questioned further," Alex said, referring to who might have given him the note.

Sir Adam nodded. "Fortunately, he did not require much encouragement."

Torture was not uncommon on either side, but Alex didn't like it. To him it was the very antithesis of chivalry and beneath the dignity and honor of a knight. Torturing a churchman—or woman for that matter—was even worse. The "do whatever it takes" and "ends justify the means" attitude wasn't reserved just for Scots. The English fought just as dirty, they just hid it beneath fine surcoats with colorful arms.

Right and wrong had always been so clear to him. Did

anyone actually believe the vows of knighthood and code of chivalry anymore? Sometimes he wondered whether he was the idealistic relic that Boyd had so often accused him of being. It was not a little disconcerting.

"*Un*fortunately," Sir Adam continued, "he was unable to provide much information. He claimed to be just a courier. Messages were left for him in the confessional and he picked them up and delivered them to another confessional in Melrose."

Alex nodded. It was consistent with the practice Bruce had employed a few years ago. The "couriers of the cloth," as Bruce called the monks and nuns who delivered messages and passed other important intelligence, were an important part of Bruce's intelligence network.

"So the monk never saw the person who left the message?"

"He claims not."

"I suppose that would be too much to ask."

Sir Adam smiled at the wry comment. "Whoever it is, they are careful. They've been doing this for a long time and aren't likely to make a mistake."

"People always make mistakes." Alex paused, an idea forming. "Although since we don't have much time we might have to encourage them into making one."

"How do you intend to do that?"

"I'm not sure yet. But I'd like to see the note. Who has it?"

"The soldiers brought it to Pembroke. I assume he still has it."

It didn't escape Alex's notice that Pembroke hadn't told him anything about it even though he was supposed to be searching for the spy.

When Alex confronted him about it later that day,

Pembroke wasn't surprised that Alex had learned about the captured communiqué and didn't object to Alex studying it. He handed him the folded piece of parchment with the broken wax seal. "It won't do you any good," he said. "There are no identifying marks. It's basically a list."

The English commander was right—there was nothing personal on the parchment, not even a greeting—but Alex took it anyway. Something bothered him about the handwriting, and he wanted to look at it a little longer.

By Friday, when he was done with his job to oversee the loading of the cargo, he was no closer to figuring out what was bothering him. About the note, that is.

He knew exactly what else was bothering him, and when he saw her walking back from the village—alone, damn it—he decided he'd waited long enough.

❧

Joan didn't delude herself that the dark, brooding stares she'd been the subject of for the past few days meant that Alex would heed her request. Or that she would be able to avoid him forever. She sensed he did not give up easily.

But he had given up before, hadn't he? On Bruce and on the Guard. Eventually he would give up on her; she only had to make him see that she didn't need a knight in shining armor to ride to her rescue.

For that was what this was about. She'd reached that conclusion over the past few largely sleepless nights trying to figure out what had motivated his declaration, and what he saw in her. As far as he knew, she was a dispossessed, illegitimate daughter of a rebel who'd shared the bed of more than a few men—hardly the type of woman a man would be anxious to have for a wife.

But Alex was a natural protector, and he obviously saw

her as in need of rescue. His honor wouldn't permit him to walk away, even if she clearly was not the sweet, innocent lass he surely had thought to find for himself. She suspected his friendship with her mother was also playing a part. Maybe he thought that by "saving" Joan, he was making reparations to her mother.

Whatever motivated him, it couldn't continue. Alex was interfering with her job. She hadn't identified a new target yet—she felt self-conscious every time she spoke with a man at a meal with the way she sensed Alex watching her—and it had taken her two days to pass the message to her contact at the mercery. He had her so jumpy she felt like she was being followed half the time.

But if she needed more reason, which she didn't, she had it folded up in the purse at her waist to be burned as soon as she returned to her chamber. When she'd returned to the mercery to pick up the silks for her cousin that had been the reason for the first visit, she'd been surprised to be handed a message. Knowing it must be important—Bruce rarely took the risk of contacting her—she'd taken a quick glance before sliding it into her purse. It had been easy to read, as there were only three words. But the meaning— and the warning—was clear: *Beware the Dragon.*

She'd always known Bruce had men watching her in case she was ever in trouble, but she hadn't realized just how closely they were doing so. But someone had obviously seen her with Alex and passed on the information. She winced, almost hearing Lachlan yelling at her for going anywhere near Alex.

Of the members of the Highland Guard, only Raider had been more betrayed by Alex's defection than her stepfather. The two men were opposite in every way. Lachlan had no rules, and Alex lived by them. From what she'd picked up over the years, it had taken Alex a long time to earn Lachlan's respect. And the fact that Alex had done so no doubt made Alex's leaving an added betrayal. Joan suspected that against Lachlan's inclination he'd come to like the young knight, making that betrayal personal.

Lachlan would be furious to hear that Joan was seen in Alex's company. If he ever found out Alex had kissed her, he would probably kill him. She paled a little, vowing never to let that happen.

She was nearly to the bridge when she felt the first prickle. Shifting the bundle of linen-wrapped fabric in her arms, she looked up to see him standing like a sentry with no intention of letting her pass.

A flicker of fear that he might be following her again dissipated on seeing his damp hair, and she realized that he'd just come from a wash in the river. He'd been working down there the past few days, and he must have finished for the day. She didn't know what he'd been doing and hadn't been inclined to ask, as she was just grateful for the time away from his too-penetrating stare.

Her heart jumped, of course, as it did every time their eyes met. She'd almost grown accustomed to it.

Almost.

But the warm prickle that spread over her skin and the feeling that every one of her senses had just come alive? She didn't think she would ever get used to that.

Nor would she get used to the golden-god-just-stepped-off-Mount-Olympus good looks and powerful, capable-of-vanquishing-dragons-with-his-bare-hands physique.

She'd never realized that she was so shallow, but it seemed she was susceptible to the superficial appeal of a handsome face and a few muscles. Her eyes scanned the broad shoulders, bulging arms, and rock-hard chest. All right, maybe quite a bit more than a few, but it was no excuse to be as weak-kneed and starry-eyed as a lovesick girl. She was a member of the elite Highland Guard, for goodness' sake. She might not wield a sword like her brethren, but her job was just as important—maybe even more so.

She had a task—a duty that she'd dedicated her life to and never strayed from since she'd seen her mother in that cage. It was disconcerting to realize how susceptible she was to feminine weakness from which she'd thought herself immune. By all rights, she should be.

Annoyed by her silly reaction to him, she gave him an acknowledging nod and tried to walk around him. No luck. He shifted to block her path, forcing her to reach out and steady herself against that chest she'd just been admiring or risk plowing right into him and probably ending up in a very undignified sprawl on her backside.

"Where's your escort?" he demanded angrily.

So much for niceties. She dropped her hand from his chest before she was tempted to do something like spread her palm over the steel-hard plane. Holding the package with both hands now, she took a step back to avoid the warm scent of soapy male—in this case myrtle—failing horribly.

"Why would I need an escort when I have you following me?"

"I wasn't following you."

She arched a brow.

"This time," he modified. "Although it appears maybe I should have. You shouldn't be walking around town alone."

She tried not to roll her eyes or let her temper spark. But clearly that protective streak of his made him deaf to her wishes. If he were her husband, he'd probably lock her in a tower somewhere. Though the thought was in jest, she couldn't help but think of her mother. But Alex wasn't anything like her father . . . was he? How well did she really know him? And how many times had she pointed out that it was none of his business?

"I thank you for your concern, my lord, but I have no need of an escort for a quick trip into town." She smiled. "Just as I have no need of unsolicited advice from overzealous knights in shining armor."

The only indication that he'd heard her was the slight quirk of his mouth. "What were you doing?"

She debated repeating that it was none of his business, but realizing that would only make him more curious and harder to shake, she said, "Running an errand for my cousin."

He eyed the package in her arms. "I presume that is the errand?"

She nodded.

He held out his hand. The standoff lasted about two seconds before Joan acceded to the inevitable and handed it over—but not without a scowl.

He grinned. But gracious in victory, he stepped aside, allowing her to pass. They walked in companionable silence through the gate. She liked him, she realized. Too much. As was becoming more and more evident. He was getting harder and harder to resist. She felt the noose of inevitability tightening around her neck, knowing that if she didn't do something soon it would be too late.

"From the weight of this bundle," he said, "I'm going to guess that you and your cousins finally made it *inside* the mercery?"

Normally the jest might have made her smile, but she

was feeling too much like a cornered hare. "Why are you doing this, Alex? I've told you how I feel."

The smile fell from his face, and his expression drew hard and impenetrable. "I don't think you have. I think you lied. What I want to know is why."

Heat flew to her cheeks. "Your arrogance is truly astounding. I'm sorry if I've hurt your pride, but I assure you it's the truth. We would not suit."

He grabbed her by the arm, and mindful of the people bustling around them, he pulled her around a building—the infirmary, maybe?—before hauling her up against him. "This has nothing to do with my pride, damn it. And we would suit perfectly. You know that as well as I do."

From the way their bodies practically locked together, she could hardly argue the point. God, he felt incredible. The warm solidness of his chest against her breasts, the strength of his arms wrapped around hers, the hard press of his manhood between her legs and against her stomach . . . everything fit perfectly.

Desire flooded her senses. Her mind was spinning in a thousand different directions. She had to stop it. "Is that what this is about?" She moved her hips against him in a way that could not be misinterpreted. She hadn't counted on having it affect her, however, and the shock of sensation nearly made her knees buckle. Somehow she managed to remember she was trying to get rid of him. "Haven't you heard? You do not need to court me to bed me. If that's what it will take to be rid of you, why don't we just get it over and be done with it? If your room is not convenient, I'm sure we can find an alcove somewhere."

The possessive flare of anger at the mention of the alcove he'd seen her slip out of with Despenser was so intense it took Alex a moment to realize that she was baiting him. It took an even longer moment for the haze of lust to clear. The feel of her hips circling against him set off dark, primitive instincts he didn't even know he possessed. He could imagine what it would be like to be inside her, and he wanted it so badly he thought he would go mad.

Why was she doing this, damn it? The reason flickered in her eyes. *She is scared*, he realized. Lashing out like a cornered animal. Trying to shock, anger, and disgust him into forgetting about her.

What she didn't understand was that it was already too late for that. He could no sooner forget about her than he could forget to breathe. She was his and had been since the moment he'd felt her lips under his. He hadn't realized how certain he was of that until this very moment, and nothing she could do or say would change it. But she was trying, that much was obvious. What he didn't know was why.

He shook her arm, forcing her gaze to his. "Why are you talking like this? This is not you."

The seductive mask slipped from her face, revealing just a hint of the torment underneath. She was so good at hiding her emotions that the fierceness of what he saw—if only for a moment—took him aback.

By the time she looked away, however, her voice was dull and devoid of feeling. "You don't know me, Alex. You don't know anything about me."

He tipped her chin, forcing her eyes to his. Wide set and seductively tilted, they were so blue he thought he might be content to drown in them forever. Christ, what was happening to him? This young girl had him utterly bewitched.

"But I think I do," he said, tilting her face to his. "Much more than you want me to."

Her mouth was too close, her lips too inviting, her eyes too full of longing. It was pure instinct to lower his mouth to hers and press her lips in a soft, tender kiss. The fact that it was the middle of the day, that anyone could walk by and see, that his honor had obviously gone to shite, didn't seem to matter. It was as natural as the sun rising in the morning and setting in the evening. As summer turning to fall and winter turning to spring. Nothing could hold it back—or turn it back.

Her lips were so impossibly soft and sweet he ached to taste her deeper. To slide his tongue into her mouth and possess her fully. To force her to acknowledge the force of the passion that burned between them.

But what was between them was more than passion—much more—and the tender, soft brush of his lips over hers, the gentle presses that lingered just long enough to elicit an ache in his chest and sharp yearning for more, proved it.

When she circled her hands around his neck and dissolved against him, surrendering with a sigh of contentment that seemed wrenched from the deepest part of her—the part that couldn't deny the bond between them any more than he could—Alex knew he'd won.

He lifted his head, keeping his fingers on her chin so she could not look away. "Tell me I'm wrong. Tell me that this doesn't mean something to you."

She tried to tear her gaze away, but he could see the sheen of tears dampening her lashes. "It doesn't."

"Liar," he replied angrily. "Why are you fighting this so hard? Why do you wish me to think the worst of you? Why are you pretending—?"

She wrenched away, pushing him back with a hard shove fortified by what he thought might be panic. "I'm pretending nothing. Dear God, what must I say to get through to you? Or do you always force yourself upon women who have made it clear that they are not willing?"

She might have slapped his face. The silence that echoed afterward was the same.

It was an unfair accusation to make. They both knew that. But it did not dull the impact or lessen the offense to his honor. He felt the blow to his chest like a swing from a war hammer. It left him cold and stunned, with a dull, hollow ache in his chest.

He had never forced her, and she had never been unwilling. But as he stood there, staring into her wild, tear-glistened eyes, he also knew there was some truth to her words. She might want him physically—and she might even feel something more—but she didn't want anything to do with him. Did it really matter what her reasons were? They were *her* reasons, and as a knight—as a man who tried to live with honor—shouldn't he show her the same and respect them?

Every instinct in his body clamored to say no. To pull her into his arms and kiss her until she surrendered to the maddening storm of emotion that had possessed him since the moment she'd fallen into his arms. He could make her his. He could make it so that she could never deny him. He didn't need experience to know that he could make her pant and beg and scream his name over and over in mindless orgasmic oblivion.

And just how badly he wanted to do that frightened him. He had seen men—brothers, friends—die on the battlefield, seen horrors that no human should be forced to witness, faced overwhelming odds and what should be certain death, faced ten of the best warriors in Christendom as a traitor, and never before had he felt fear like he did now. Because he knew just how close he was to losing himself— or the part of himself that he'd fought so hard to hold on to. The part of himself that had caused him to turn on his friends. The part that always just tried to do what was right.

He was becoming the very barbarian he'd feared.

Her face went white, as if she was shocked by what she said. "Alex, wait. I didn't mean—"

He didn't let her finish. "No, you are right. You have made your feelings quite clear. I will not seek to change your mind again. But if you change yours, you know where to find me—for a couple of weeks at least. After that . . ." He shrugged. It didn't really matter. Whether he came back from war or not, he knew she would not be waiting for him.

She looked stricken, as if the idea of him not returning had never occurred to her.

He didn't wait to hear her reply. With a short, stiff bow of his head, he handed her back her bundle and left.

12

*H*E WON'T DIE, Joan told herself. Alex Seton was one of the best warriors in Christendom, handpicked for Bruce's elite fighting force, even if he was now fighting for the enemy. It was inconceivable that he wouldn't survive the looming battle.

But deep inside she knew it was true: there were no guarantees in war. Even the best weren't invincible. Hadn't William "Templar" Gordon's death proved that? Joan hadn't known the young member of the Guard who'd died a few years ago, but she'd heard so much of him from Lachlan she felt as if she did.

Being the "best" also hadn't helped Alex's brother. Sir Christopher Seton was one of the greatest knights on either side of the border and reputed to be the third best in Christendom (behind his liege lord Robert Bruce, and Giles d'Argentan, the Frenchman who fought for the English). Yet Sir Christopher had been captured by his own countryman, the chief of the MacNabs, at Loch Doon Castle and executed at the start of the war.

The cold clamminess on her forehead spread over the rest of her skin in a sickly pale. She covered her stomach with her hands as if she could somehow steady the sway. Her entire body was in revolt—in panic—at the thought of never seeing him again. But what else could she do? What other choice did she have? She couldn't risk what she was doing, and any kind of relationship with Alex would surely do that. She'd finally done what she wanted and gotten rid of him.

Beware the Dragon. She hadn't forgotten the warning, but the thought of him not coming back, of him riding off into the mist to his death thinking the worst of her, had forced her to confront her feelings for him. She cared about him. Deeply. And it challenged her resolve like nothing before. For the first time, she could contemplate a future that did not involve being alone, and she was surprised how fiercely her foolish heart held on to the image.

Shouldn't she be beyond all this?

"Is something wrong, Joan?" her cousin Margaret asked when Joan waved away another tray of sweets—this one squares of apple tart. It was the late afternoon, and they'd gathered in Alice's sitting room to work on their needlework. "You don't look well."

Joan shook her head and tried to brighten but failed when her smile wobbled. "I didn't sleep well last night." That was the truth. "The men were up late."

"I heard them as well," Margaret said. "It must have been after midnight before they went to bed."

Alice looked back and forth between them, and then, clearly bursting to tell them something, leaned forward conspiratorially. "Henry told me not to say anything yet, so you must keep it to yourselves for now, but they have caught the rebel spy who has been feeding information to the usurper for years."

Joan hid her shock—barely—but the news caused Margaret to drop the cup of mulled wine she had been drinking. The fine pottery mug shattered on the hard wooden floor into dozens of pieces, spraying the pungent dark liquid all over their feet, although Margaret's hem took the brunt of it.

"Whatever is the matter with you, Margaret?" Alice said impatiently, as the maidservant hurried to clean up the mess. "You have been as jumpy as a hare of late. Henry said you almost fainted when he came up behind you in town the other day." Her small upturned nose wrinkled in a frown. "You never did say where you were going."

By now Margaret had collected herself, but her cheeks were still a warm pink. "He scared me," she protested. "And I am not jumpy, I am surprised. Why have we heard nothing of this? Who have they arrested?"

Margaret seemed almost as anxious to hear the details as Joan.

Alice savored her role as the keeper of the information and waited a few moments before responding. "They haven't arrested anyone yet. But they captured a monk who was carrying one of the spy's missives. It is only a matter of time before he is identified."

Joan's heart dropped. She tried to recall the exact wording of her latest message. Was there any way of identifying her? Would someone be able to trace it back to her? She was careful, but never before had one of her messages been intercepted.

Was that why she'd had this strange feeling of being watched of late? Did they suspect her? None of her fear and anxiousness showed as she tied a knot on the piece of thread she'd been working with before asking, "What did the missive say?"

Alice shrugged as if the details were unimportant. "I don't know. But there must be something incriminating, don't you think? Henry said your knight"—she waved her hand toward Joan—"insisted on taking it with him to examine."

Alex? Her heart dropped even lower. Good God, did he suspect something? Had he seen something in the note to identify its writer? Is that why he'd been so attentive of late? Was it all a ploy?

Nay, she refused to believe it. But the fact that he had the note did not sit well with her. Actually, nothing about this sat well with her.

And what of the monk? She assumed the mercer's wife had passed it on to him, but had he seen anything? She prayed the woman had been careful, and that the monk couldn't identify her. And what would the English do to him to find out?

Joan shuddered.

Margaret must have been having similar thoughts. "What has happened to the monk?" she asked with genuine concern.

Alice frowned. "He was questioned."

Joan winced inwardly. When her eyes caught Margaret's a few minutes later, she could see that her cousin realized what that meant as well.

"They did not hurt him?" Margaret said with more hope than belief.

"How would I know?" Alice said with obvious impatience. "But it is no more than he deserves for aiding the rebels. He cannot act like a traitor and then seek to avoid punishment by pointing to his holy robes."

Margaret looked as ill as Joan felt.

Although Joan and anyone else who dared to work for Bruce knew what they risked when they started, it was different somehow when confronted with reality. Her heart went out to the monk, and she prayed the English were not treating him harshly. But she hadn't been that naive since she'd seen her mother forced into a cage. There was nothing of which they weren't capable.

They let the conversation drop, but the quickening of her pulse and race of her heart stayed with her throughout the long afternoon. This was not good. Not good at all. She couldn't escape the feeling of doom hanging over her. But Joan would not overreact. No matter how desperate she was to learn what Alex knew, she wouldn't do anything rash. She'd survived this long by being cautious and patient. There was nothing on that parchment that could give her away. Even if every instinct clamored to try to fetch the missive back to make sure, she would wait for Alex to make the first move. If he had one.

But her cousin had other ideas.

As soon as Alice had left the room to rest before the evening meal, Margaret turned to her. She looked as if she was close to tears. "I need your help."

∽

It was late by the time Alex returned to the small chamber near Pembroke's that had been assigned to him while they were at Berwick. It wasn't much bigger than an ambry and didn't even have a small window to let in natural light, but what it lacked in size and amenities it made up for in privacy. He'd sent his squire to sleep in the barracks with the other lads, wanting—nay, needing—the solitude.

If he'd needed a reminder of why he was here, of all the horrors and injustices perpetuated in the name of war, of why he'd had to *do* something different, he had it.

After riding across the better part of the Lothian countryside with Pembroke since dawn, Alex felt all the bitterness, frustration, and anger that had driven him to try to find another way. Two years hadn't changed a thing— if anything it had only gotten worse. The devastation wrought along the Borders, on both sides, was horrible. It was as if miles of countryside had been swathed in black ash. Homes and crops burned or ravaged to feed the armies, livestock raided, the only signs of life the people starving and living in conditions that were almost unimaginable. Something needed to be done, damn it, and that was why he was here. It had to end. Even if he had to lift his sword again to do it.

But right now he didn't want to think about the looming battle; all he wanted to do was collapse on the narrow wooden bed and sleep. But after the hellish night before, he wasn't taking any chances.

When the serving girl set the jug of whisky on the bedside table, however, he felt a wave of self-disgust. The drink wasn't going to help. It wouldn't change anything. It wouldn't make him forget. He wasn't going to let her turn him into a drunk, damn it. Overindulgence of drink was for the weak.

Don't think about her. It's over.

As if it had ever begun.

He almost told the girl to take the jug away—that he'd changed his mind—but she was already halfway out of the room so he just let her go. His squire had helped him remove his mail before being dismissed, and Alex caught sight of it now, folded neatly on a bench along with his surcoat, gambeson, chausses, weapons, and sporran. He was about to pull off his shirt and toss it on the pile along with the rest, when the corner of a piece of parchment caught his eye.

He hadn't forgotten about the missive, but after the confrontation with Joan he'd had other things on his mind. Removing it from the leather purse, he read over it again, examining every line, every letter . . .

Letter. That's when it hit him. He knew what had been bothering him, but what he hadn't been able to put his finger on. The lettering was too pretty, too soft, too flourished. It didn't look as if it had been written with the quick, harsh, masculine lines of a soldier or knight—it looked distinctly feminine . . . as if it had been written by a lady.

A woman. Christ. Alex's mind reeled. He'd never considered that a woman might be the spy. None of them had. It wasn't just the danger involved, it was the quality of the information. Information that could have only come from someone high up in Edward's command—a man. At least that's what they'd all assumed, but Alex realized that it could also have come from a trusted wife, mistress, daughter, or servant of that man.

An educated servant like a lady's companion.

His bones turned to ice. There was no reason for his mind to go straight to Joan, but it did.

It could be anyone, he told himself. Hell, he wasn't even certain it was a woman, but now that the possibility had been broached, he could not dismiss it.

He tried to approach it analytically, going through all the ladies at court—both wives and mistresses—of which more than a handful were Scots.

But none of the other ladies were the daughter of Bella MacDuff, and that fact more than anything made him curse. He pulled on a pair of loose breeches, and not bothering with his surcoat, tossed a plaid around his shoulders before leaving his room.

Perhaps it was his disheveled, half-dressed, undoubtedly wild-looking state that prevented the guard on duty from questioning him overmuch. The tired young soldier made a brief protest that he could not permit Alex to see the prisoner without Pembroke's permission, but when Alex told him that he would be the one to wake the earl on a fool's errand—Alex was one of Pembroke's chief lieutenants and the man put in charge of finding the spy, after all—the guard quickly saw the wisdom of opening the door.

Ducking through the low stone doorway, Alex entered the small guardroom. The smell of piss and excrement—probably from the wooden bucket in the corner—struck him first. But he was relieved to see that although small, cold, and basic in the extreme, the temporary prison wasn't too bad. It was a hell of a lot better than the pit prison. Alex should know, he'd spent a few nights there when he'd left the Guard and escorted Rosalin Clifford back to her brother Robert, who was the Governor of Berwick at the time.

The noise of the door had caused the occupant to stir. The monk turned from his curled-up position on the plaid-covered pile of straw and glanced over in Alex's direction as he entered. Though the lamp Alex had placed on the single table in the room didn't offer much light, he was relieved to see that the monk didn't have a face full of bruises and a nose pointing in the wrong direction.

The thin churchman with tonsured head clutched the blanket around himself tighter and scooted back toward the wall. He was younger than Alex expected—probably no more than twenty—and had the kind of face that was neither plain nor attractive, but was unremarkable, which no doubt helped his role as a courier. He didn't stick out.

Realizing that he was frightening him, Alex schooled some of the fury from his face. Seeing a stool tucked under the table, he pulled it out and sat, hoping that by getting down lower it would make him seem less threatening.

It seemed to work, as the young monk's expression changed from frightened to wary. "What do you want? I've told them everything I know."

Alex didn't think he had, but he knew that confrontation and threats weren't the way to proceed. "I need your help."

The evenly voiced plea surprised the monk enough for him to sit up. Still, he eyed Alex as if he were a snake coiled and ready to strike. "What kind of help?"

"The woman you are trying to protect is in danger."

If he hadn't been looking for it, Alex might not have seen it. But there was a telltale flicker of shock in the monk's eye.

Christ, he'd been right. It was a woman. He cursed. The ramifications ran through his head and Alex had to fight to keep his emotions in check. *If she is bloody well involved in this, he was going to . . .*

"What woman?" the monk said an instant too late, and then added somewhat accusingly, "You are a Scot."

"Aye, with friends and family on both sides of the border, which is why I'm here. If I figured it out, how long do you think it will take the others to do the same? She is in danger, and I can help."

"I told them before, I don't know anything. I never met the person who left the note. I'm only a courier."

"Perhaps," Alex agreed. "But I think you know more than you are saying." He leaned forward, taking a stab in the dark. But he had always been good with a blade. "You saw her, didn't you?"

The monk wasn't old or experienced enough to have learned to control his expression, and Alex easily detected the flash of fear in his dark eyes. "No! I told you I never saw her!"

Her.

The lad quickly realized his mistake and, eyes wide, clamped his mouth shut as if it might make him mute. But it was too late.

Alex's face turned as hard as granite. "You did see her. Tell me what you know."

No wonder the English hadn't had to torture him; the lad fell apart at the first threat. Christ, what was Bruce thinking to rely on such innocents?

The monk started to babble and sob. "I didn't. I swear. I never saw her face."

He was too scared to be lying. "But you saw something," Alex said.

The lad wasn't a complete coward. He took a deep breath and tried to get himself under some semblance of control. "No," he lied.

Alex fought to control his impatience. He was tempted to drag the young churchman to his feet and give him a good shake. Instead, he clenched his fists at his sides. "I am trying to protect her, damn it."

"Why would you do that?"

"Because I have no wish to see a woman harmed, and if they find her, you can be assured she will be."

"But you are one of them."

He was. Though for some reason it made Alex grit his teeth. "Aye, but we are not all monsters." He paused, and then said intently, "Tell me."

"It's nothing."

Alex waited.

"She was wearing a dark cloak—the color of claret—trimmed with ermine, but I only saw her from the back. I arrived at the confessional a few minutes early by accident and saw her leaving."

Alex's heart was beating so fast he could barely get out the words. "Describe her."

"I didn't see her."

Alex's patience was set on a razor's edge. "Tall, short, thin, round?"

"Definitely not tall. She was short"—the monk stood and held up his hand to the middle of his chest—"about here. And definitely on the plump side."

Alex held his breath. His entire body seemed poised on the edge of a precipice. Joan was tall for a woman and slender. "Are you sure?"

"Aye." The monk seemed to sense the importance. "Do you know her?"

Alex shook his head and breathed a sigh of relief. "Nay. I don't know her."

And he'd never been so relieved about anything in his life.

This time when Alex returned to his room, he did collapse on the bed, and he didn't need the whisky to help him fall asleep.

∞

God, give her strength. She could do this.

Joan drew a deep breath as she stood outside the door. A few minutes, that was all. All she had to do was pretend for a few minutes. The powder would do its job, she would destroy the seal, and her cousin would be safe.

She still couldn't believe it. Not only had Margaret been sending information to Bruce, but she had also guessed Joan's secret. "You remember, cousin," she said. "I know you. I knew you as a girl, and I know you could not have changed that much. I know you were more interested in the war than you appeared, and I know you would not be with all those men without a reason. I also know how much you loved your mother."

Joan had been stunned silent.

Margaret, it seemed, hadn't accepted the broken engagement with the Earl of Ross's son. She and John were in love and hoped to marry once the war was over. So she passed information to the monk when she could to help the man she loved.

She'd only started recently. The idea had come to her when she thought Alice was getting suspicious of Joan. She thought two spies would confuse them, especially as she was at a separate castle at the time.

But her cousin had made a mistake. In a romantic

gesture, Margaret had used the imprint of a betrothal ring John had given her to seal the missive, and she feared that if Sir Henry saw it, he would recognize it. So Joan was here to destroy the evidence and prevent her cousin from being arrested as the spy.

Simple.

But it wasn't simple at all. It was Alex.

Without any more hesitation, Joan knocked, trying to ignore the way her hand shook.

She'd done this before; she could do it again.

But then the door opened and her stomach, heart, whatever else was in her chest, slammed to the floor. Dear God. She would have swallowed, but her mouth was too dry.

She'd never done *this* before. She'd never pretended to seduce a man—a half-naked man—who made her knees weak. Who made her wish that maybe it wasn't pretend.

He was gorgeously tousled; his blue eyes not their usual too sharp and penetrating, but soft and sleepy, and his dark golden-blond hair deliciously mussed, as if she'd just dragged him from bed—which undoubtedly she had.

But it was his state of clothing—or rather the lack thereof—that truly undid her. He wasn't wearing a shirt, and in the soft light of the single candle she'd brought with her, his chest glowed like a carved shield of bronze.

Good gracious, she'd thought he'd looked imposing on the practice yard, but it was an entirely different imposing when facing it in the middle of the night—alone—standing no more than a foot away, in a small, intimate, barely lit doorway where she could see up close just how broad his shoulders were, how big the muscles were on his arms, and how steely flat and hard was his stomach.

The breeches that looked to have been haphazardly

pulled on hung low on that hard stomach and narrow hips, revealing a thin trail of hair that she dared not follow, no matter how curious she was or how thick and long that column of flesh it led to appeared.

He slept naked, she realized. Which was something else she shouldn't think about, but her cheeks flushed hot and awareness flooded ever corner of her body as her gaze shot back to his.

She had to get the situation back under control—get *herself* back under control—but he looked warm and inviting, and entirely too attractive for her peace of mind.

Who was seducing whom?

He recovered before she did, which wasn't exactly a promising start. "What the hell?" He dragged his hand through his rumpled hair, which forced—for how could she not look?—her gaze back to his chest and the now flexed muscles in his arm. God in heaven! Something low and heavy did a little stutter step in her stomach. "What are you doing here?" he demanded.

Her mouth had gone dry again. With considerably more difficulty, she lifted her gaze back to his.

But dear Lord, a man shouldn't be so enticing!

That was her job.

Remembering what she needed to do, she straightened her spine and shook off the haze that had fogged her brain since he'd opened the door. Without waiting for an invitation—which she knew she would not be receiving—she pushed her way past him into the room, not giving him the opportunity to stop her. She ignored the smell of warm, spicy male as she stood there and tried to keep her knees from wobbling. "You said if I changed my mind, I knew where to find you. Well here I am," she said with a smile.

But he didn't look at all pleased to see her in his

chamber. His very *small* chamber. Despite her vow not to think about the intimacy of the situation—or any kind of intimacy, for that matter—a shudder of awareness ran through her.

Ignoring the forbidding frown being sent in her direction, she scanned the room. It didn't take long, as it was all of about ten feet by five feet. Other than the bed—which she wasn't going to look at until she had to—there was a small table, a chair, a trunk, and an iron brazier. She was relieved to see a jug on the table. It would have been awkward to send for something. The bag of powder suddenly felt very heavy in the hem of her cloak. She'd made a hole in the seam, which would enable her to remove it quickly and unseen.

This is wrong. You are playing with fire.

But what other choice did she have? How else could she get the missive away from him for long enough to make sure the seal would never be deciphered?

"You've changed your mind about letting me court you?" he asked suspiciously.

He was too smart. That was part of the problem. "Not exactly," she admitted. "But you were right."

Now he didn't just *sound* suspicious, he *looked* suspicious. "About what?"

Remembering her role, she attempted to appear cool and matter-of-fact, although her heart was beating like the wings of a not-very-brave sparrow as she nonchalantly walked over to the jug. Taking a deep breath, and making sure she positioned herself to block his view, she slid the powder from her sleeve and sprinkled a little in the cup before pouring a drink. She pretended to take a sip, before turning back to him with a face as if he'd tricked her. It was whisky, and not the wine she'd assumed.

"What we have is special," she said boldly—challengingly. "And I see no reason to waste it."

Courage . . .

Perhaps she should have drunk the vile brew after all. It was much harder than she thought it would be to push her cloak back from her shoulders and let it drop to the floor at her feet.

13

A LEX FROZE. EVERYTHING went still. Except for his heart. That was beating erratically and wildly.

This must be a dream. Please, let it be a dream.

For if it were a dream, he could reach out and touch her. If it were a dream, he could rip that diaphanous slip of fabric posing as a night rail off the body that he could see tantalizing hints of in the backlit candlelight, push her back on the bed, and give her exactly what she was asking for.

But it wasn't a dream, damn it. It was only too real.

Christ. A cold sweat ran over him. What the hell was he supposed to do? He couldn't think. His mind was too filled with illicit thoughts about what he *wanted* to do to the wicked enchantress who'd just invaded his chamber and offered him a bite of the apple. The most beautiful, succulent apple he'd ever beheld.

Eyes that heavily lashed and seductively tilted should be dark, but hers seemed impossibly blue as she stared up at him with her boldly carved features, snow-white skin, and wide crimson lips, offering to fulfill his deepest, basest desires.

He hadn't realized how many he had until that moment.

Quite a few of them would involve the high, generously rounded, and tautly tipped breasts, the generous size and exquisite shape of which he could easily make out under the thin swath of linen. He swore, his cock twitching hard as he made out the deep shade of pink of her nipples. He wanted to suck those little pearls of pink deep into his mouth and nibble them between his teeth until she arched and squirmed.

He forced his gaze away from her breasts. But the slide downward didn't help. The slim hips only made him think of holding on as he drove in hard and deep, and the long, slender legs were only too easy to imagine wrapped around his waist, squeezing him tighter . . .

He swore again and turned away, his body a rigid mass of throbbing steel. He was as hard as a rod and so primed for release he could come with one firm stroke.

She had no bloody idea how badly he wanted to take her up on her offer.

But he wasn't going to do this. No matter how much he wanted to—and every nerve ending in his body reverberated with wanting to.

It wasn't right. Not like this. The next time he made love to a woman she would be his wife. It wouldn't be one night of passion and lust without promises, it would be making love with vows and a future.

Still, it wasn't easy to get the words out. His mouth was pulled as tightly and angrily as the rest of him. "This isn't what I meant, and you know it. You need to leave, Joan. Now."

Those catlike blue eyes never flinched. She arched a very delicate, very dark brow in challenge. "Now who is pretending?" She walked toward him, holding the cup of whisky out to him. He waved it away. He didn't want a damned drink, he wanted her. "I know you want this. You need not fear your prefect Sir Galahad reputation will slip. I won't tell anyone."

He didn't like when she called him that—even in jest. It reminded him too much of MacRuairi, who *hadn't* said it in jest. Alex wasn't moralistic, damn it. Was it so wrong to have honor? To have codes and ideals? To try to do what was right? To want sharing such intimacies to mean something?

"You're wrong," he said intently. "I don't want this." He held the door open. "I want you to leave."

∞

Maybe if his mouth wasn't so white and his jaw so flexed Joan might have believed him. Clearly, he was furious at her for showing up in his room like this and wanted her to go. But just as clearly, he was fighting giving in with everything he had.

He just needed one more push.

She'd known it wouldn't be as simple as just showing up to his room. Known that Alex's honor would make things . . . *difficult*. She'd even realized what she might have to do. But she'd never been the seducer before, and the role didn't sit well with her.

Could she really . . . ?

She didn't finish the question. The answer was clear. Yes, she could. She would do whatever it took. Her cousin had been trying to help Bruce—help her—and she wouldn't let her come to harm.

She set the cup down on the table for a moment, to do what she had to do.

This isn't me, she told herself. *It's only a role. You are in control.*

But it felt very real as she leaned up against him and gave him that push, placing her hand on the part of him that could not lie. A part of him that from her experience thought very little about honor.

It was the first time she'd ever touched a man so boldly—so intimately—and the shock, the heat, the *size* of him would have made her yank her hand back if he hadn't made a deep sound low in his throat that was half tortured, half pleasure, and all desire.

It was working, and it gave her courage. "Liar," she murmured, the huskiness in her voice coming out all on its own.

He reached for her wrist to pull her hand away, but instinctively her fingers tightened around him. It was a good instinct. The hand that he'd wrapped around her wrist froze as he made another sound—this one deeper and more tortured than the last. For one long heartbeat he held her hand to him, maybe even pressing it a little harder against an almost imperceptible movement of his hips.

He liked it. Liked it a lot.

He was as hard as a column of marble. But instead of cold stone, he pulsed with heat. Heat that spread and enveloped her, as the realization of what she was doing and how much he liked it—how much *she* liked it—took hold. She wasn't scared, she wasn't nervous, she was undeniably, unexpectedly *aroused*. Very, very aroused. Her body felt as warm and melty as syrup.

This wasn't supposed to happen to her.

Their eyes met, and all thoughts of pretense and roles fled. What was between them was there in the open, raw, hot, and honest.

Maybe Alex wasn't the only one lying to himself. Maybe she wasn't here just for her cousin. Maybe the thought of him leaving and never coming back mattered more than she wanted it to. Maybe she wanted something to hold on to.

One kiss. Was that so much to ask? One kiss with nothing between them, and then she would have him drink the whisky.

"Joan . . ." His voice was a hoarse, strangled plea for her to put a stop to this.

But she wasn't going to do that. Not yet, at least. Leaning into him, she lifted her mouth to his. "Please, Alex, just kiss me."

∞

Every man had his breaking point, and Alex Seton had just found his. It had been hard enough to try to send her away when she appeared in his room like some erotic fantasy, standing one gentle push away from his bed in a chemise that revealed far more of her incredible body than it hid. But when she'd touched him, put her hand on his cock and squeezed, he lost whatever final vestiges of control he possessed.

It felt so good he didn't want her to stop—ever.

It shouldn't be that easy. He shouldn't be that weak. But there was no way in hell he had the strength to push her away again, especially with her soft plea echoing in his ears.

But he wasn't happy about it. She was manipulating him. He knew it, and she knew it. But it was working, damn it. He knew that if he sent her away, she wouldn't be coming back. And that he couldn't concede. He would hold on to her any way he could.

With a groan, he took what she offered and covered her sweet, red mouth in a hot, furious kiss. He'd never kissed her like this. He'd never kissed *anyone* like this. The bands of control, the chains of civility that had defined him had ripped free, revealing the fierce, primitive marauder underneath who wanted to plunder and conquer.

He took everything she offered and more, moving his mouth over hers in a wicked frenzy of lust and desire. He filled her mouth with his tongue, leaving no part of that sweet cavern unconquered and unplundered.

He kissed her until they both had lost their breath, until moans dissolved into pants that only increased the urgency. Until the fever that had taken hold of him inflamed them both. Everything seemed heightened—intensified. The smell of her hair was more floral, the honey taste of her mouth sweeter, the velvet of her skin softer. The passion between them hotter. The ache in his chest tighter.

This meant something. It had to mean something.

He was moving too fast, but he couldn't hold back. She wouldn't let him. She wrapped her hands around his neck, stretched against him, crushed her breasts to his chest, and returned the frenzied kiss with something akin to desperation.

He felt her urgency as powerfully as his. Her tongue circled and sparred, egging him on with every stroke. He couldn't get enough—couldn't go fast enough.

He touched her body as if it belonged to him. As if he had every right to cup her breast and run his thumb over the taut tip. As if his hands were meant to span the delicate circle of her waist. As if he'd held the taut curve of her bottom in his hand a thousand times to lift against him.

But pressing wasn't enough for either of them. He started to circle his hips in a slow, hard grind and his head nearly exploded behind his eyes. He could feel her heat through the thin layers of cloth, hear her moans of pleasure, feel her dissolving against him, and it drove him wild.

Heat and passion engulfed him, took over, and possessed him with a madness he'd never experienced before. He didn't recognize himself. The only thing that mattered, the only thing he could think about, was making her his.

He eased her back onto the bed and came down on top of her—or rather, half on top of her as his body stretched along the length of hers.

His mouth was on her lips, her throat, her breast. He didn't take time to open her chemise—he didn't have time—he just sucked and circled her nipple with his tongue through the fabric until he'd drawn her as tight as a bow. Until she was arching and straining and begging for his touch.

He gave it to her. Sliding his hand under the edge of her chemise, he found the soft place between her legs warm and slick with need.

The moan of pleasure she made when his finger slid inside her nearly undid him. He had to clench his teeth against the pressure pounding at the base of his spine. Pressure that had nowhere to go and wasn't going to be able to wait much longer.

But he would give her pleasure before he took his own release, damn it. God knew, he wasn't going to last long once he was inside her.

He stroked her. Soft and gently at first, and then with more urgency as her need intensified.

He stopped kissing her to watch as her lips parted with sharp, uneven little breaths, as color flooded her cheeks, as her back arched, and finally as her beautiful eyes fixed on his and widened with surprise right before she broke apart. *Surprise*, damn it. That had been new.

It was the most beautiful thing he'd ever seen, and the intensity of emotions swelling in his chest hurt.

But the cries of release were like a siren's call to his own need. Whether this was wrong or right no longer mattered. He couldn't have turned back if he wanted to—and he sure as hell didn't want to.

He didn't hesitate as he worked the ties of his braies.

⁐

The feel of him pushing between her legs brought Joan harshly back to reality. She jolted from the dreamlike haze with something akin to panic as Alex nudged the thick head of his manhood deeper and deeper inside her.

Wait! This isn't . . . I didn't mean . . .

It wasn't supposed to get this far. She was supposed to be in control. But then he'd started kissing her, and she'd completely forgotten about the powder and the missive she needed to find. After he'd touched her, she'd lost the power to think at all.

The feel of his thick, callused finger sweeping over her—touching her—so intimately had made every inch of her body come alive. She'd never felt anything like it. The need, the frenzy, building inside her had been indescribable. When the sensations reached the apex and seemed to break apart . . . she thought she'd died and gone to heaven. Literally. She swore her heart stopped beating.

It had been so wonderful, so beautiful, so perfect that

when she realized what was happening, guilt and shame made her panic.

She shouldn't have come here like this; it was wrong. What they had was special, and it felt as if she'd somehow tainted that by using it against him. He would hate her if he ever discovered the truth. She knew how much he hated deceit and subterfuge.

She made a sound of surprise when he closed the last few inches with a thrust. Surprise, not pain. At least not *that* kind of pain. He was a big man, and his size was making itself known with a certain amount of discomfort as her body struggled to accommodate him.

Their eyes met. She tried to pretend she did not see the flicker of disappointment in his gaze, but the knife of pain that twisted between her ribs proved otherwise.

She didn't know whether to laugh or cry. Had he thought it all a lie?

It wasn't. Not all of it, at least. And not the important part if that look in his eyes was any indication.

She was not a maid. She had lain with another man. But . . .

She wanted to tell him how different it was. How this was nothing like what had happened before. How what had been taken from her coldly and cruelly at the age of fifteen when a man she'd trusted—a man she thought she'd cared for—had held her down and forced himself between her legs, was nothing like what was happening between them now. How that man had taken something from her that day that she'd never thought to get back, but Alex had made her feel again.

But would it really matter?

He must have read some of the torment in her eyes. "Are you all right?"

She wanted to tell him everything, wanted to tell him of the man who'd forced her, wanted to confess her shame at her reason for being here, wanted to tell him that the feel of him inside her—of them joined together—made her feel alive.

Wanted to tell him that if things were different she could fall . . .

They aren't different, she reminded herself; she couldn't say any of those things. They would only make him ask questions that she could not answer. Questions that would be dangerous and could prevent her from doing her job.

So instead of telling him the whole truth, she told him only part of it. "I'm perfect." Their eyes met, and despite the intimacy—or maybe because of the intimacy—a blush stole up her cheeks. "You feel good."

It must have been the right thing to say, because he threw back his head and groaned. "So do you, sweetheart, so do you."

He started to move. Slowly at first, as if he could draw out every bit of sensation and every ounce of pleasure with one long stroke.

He felt so big and powerful inside her. Filling her. Possessing her. Loving her.

God, she was such a fool. But that was how it felt. Each tender stroke and circle of his hips seemed like a declaration. A silent vow. A promise. A claim to more of her heart.

Her body started to respond, her hips rising up to meet those incredible strokes with a message of its own. *Faster . . . harder . . . deeper. Give me everything.*

The sensations he'd stirred with his hand returned. Stronger this time, and even more intense because this time she wasn't alone. He was with her, and watching the pleasure building in his eyes and turning the shadowed lines of his handsome face taut with strain was something she would never forget. It transformed him; it made him hers.

The slow pace began to quicken, the tender strokes surging harder and deeper, claiming more and more of her. Her fingers dug into the solid muscles of his arms to hold herself steady against the shattering force of the powerful thrusts that tore her last defenses to shreds.

When she looked into his eyes there was no hiding the truth. A truth she thought she saw mirrored in his own.

"Oh God, sweetheart, I'm sorry . . . I can't . . . Too long. I'm going to . . ."

The words were lost in the cry of pleasure that tore from his soul. His entire body seemed to stiffen and then break apart. A warm rush shot between her legs and then spread through her as the wonder of the moment unfurled.

It was the most beautiful, romantic experience of her life.

And it was over far too soon.

No sooner had she felt the returning beat of his heart against her chest where he'd collapsed on top of her, than he stiffened again and swore. An instant later he rolled off her, and the connection that moments ago had seemed so strong and powerful snapped like a small twig.

∞

What the hell have I done? Alex stared at the ceiling in disbelief, not wanting to answer the question.

He knew exactly what he'd done. Quickly and rather furiously, which under the circumstances was probably to be expected.

Bloody hell.

Shame crawled over him, eating away at all the euphoria, all the joy, and all the tenderness, leaving only guilt and self-disgust.

He'd dishonored her and himself. Years of discipline, of waiting for the bonds of marriage, had been rendered meaningless. He'd done what he'd vowed he would never do again.

When Alex was nineteen, his brother had done him a "favor" and taken him to a whore to lose his virginity. Chris had had a woman in his bed since he was seventeen, and he didn't understand his younger brother's reluctance to accept one of the many propositions that had been thrown his way because of his "golden boy" good looks.

"If I had your face," Chris had said, "I'd never spend a night alone."

But the experience had been an unmitigated disaster. Alex's body had cooperated, but every minute of it had felt wrong, and when it was over, he hadn't felt like pounding his chest or boasting of his prowess and telling jests like the other lads did, he'd felt like retching.

Which is exactly what he'd done. Even after all these years, it was still humiliating to think about. He'd run out of there half-dressed and barely made it outside before losing the contents of his stomach in the innkeeper's flower box.

Chris had patted his back and cautioned him against drinking too much whisky, but Alex suspected that he'd guessed the truth. There had been no more "favors" or trips to the local inn.

Alex had vowed then and there that he would never dishonor another woman like that. He would never take someone to his bed for the simple reason of slaking his lust. Something so intimate had to mean something, and he vowed to give it the respect it deserved. He would not take another woman to bed who was not his wife.

He'd never told anyone of his vow. Most of his fellow

soldiers probably assumed he just kept such things private. Alex suspected that Raider and maybe a couple of the others had guessed—they'd spent too much time together to not notice him never taking a woman to his bed—but surprisingly no one had ever said anything.

Even when they could have. He cringed when he thought of all the self-righteous condemnation he'd heaped on Raider for taking Rosalin to his bed while she'd been their hostage. If Boyd had loved her, Alex had accused him, he should have proved it by marrying her, not seducing her.

Alex had thought himself above such base desires as lust and held himself to a higher standard. But look at him. He was every inch the unprincipled, uncivilized barbarian he'd accused his former partner of being.

He'd condemned his partner for the very thing he'd just done, and the irony was as bitter as it was unwelcome.

"Alex?"

He heard the question in her voice, and he wanted to say something to ease it, but he was too ashamed to even look at her. And maybe a little too angry as well. Not just for coming to his room as she had, but for not caring enough to realize this was special. For not realizing how much it meant. What had happened between them was incredible—special—how could she not see that?

When she leaned over and put her hand on his chest, he flinched as if burned and practically jumped off the bed.

The first thing he saw was the cup of whisky she'd set down on the table. It seemed he was weak after all.

He reached for the cup.

"Alex, no! Wait!"

She tried to grab his arm, but he ignored her and downed the cup in one long swallow. The trail of fire had barely reached his stomach before he reached for the jug to pour another.

Only after a third did he brace himself to turn to look at her.

She looked like a debauched angel. Her dark-as-night hair was gorgeously mussed with one long silken thread tangled in her lashes, her mouth was slightly swollen and as red as crushed strawberries, her delicate skin was pink from the scrape of his beard along her jaw and throat, and her chemise had come open and was slinking around her shoulders provocatively.

The visible proof of his dishonor should fill him with shame. Instead, his heart lurched when he realized she was close to tears. Christ, he was an arse. He was so wrapped up in his own head, he hadn't thought how she might be feeling.

"I'm sorry . . ." she said.

Why was she apologizing? It was his fault. He took a step toward the bed. "Nay, I'm . . ."

He stopped. What had he been about to say? He blinked a few times and then squinted through the haze that seemed to be fogging his vision. He reached out to grab the wooden post of the bed as the room started to tilt.

"What the hell?"

He was conscious of her taking his arm and easing him back down on the bed. "You're tired," she said in such a soft voice she might have been miles away. "Rest."

It was the last thing he remembered before waking with his head feeling as if it had been split apart by an axe.

He rolled the pillow over his head to block out the offending light. Thank God, he didn't have a bloody window. The sunshine would have been too much to bear.

Christ, how much had he drunk last night?

Last night. Suddenly it all came back to him, although with the grogginess it took him a few minutes to sort out the fantasies from the reality. He might have thought it all fantasy if his pillow didn't smell like flowers.

What had he expected? That she would still be here in the morning? Had she slipped out of the room in the middle of the night or waited until morning?

Both images filled him with distaste, and neither was going to happen again.

He knew exactly what he had to do. Joan might not like it, but it was too late for that.

With grim determination, Alex fought off the blistering headache and swirling stomach with a dunking of cold water from the pitcher, and began to don his armor. He was going into battle, and this was a war he wasn't going to lose.

14

J OAN LOOKED UP at the sound of the door, her pulse jumping like that of a startled hare. The needle she'd been about to push through the piece of linen stilled in her hand as she waited . . .

Bess. It was only the serving maid, bringing refreshment.

Her heart fell from her throat back into its normal position. Returning her gaze to her embroidery, she finished the stitch.

The deflating sigh that settled through her body was one of relief. It certainly wasn't disappointment. She was glad Alex hadn't come bursting through the door to her cousin's antechamber this morning after discovering her gone. Of course she was.

Her nervous edginess this morning—jumping at doors, startling at footsteps—was silly. He probably didn't remember anything. The drug had hit him so hard. In her nervousness she must have poured too much powder into the cup, and coupled with the amount of whisky he'd drunk, he probably remembered very little from last night. It must all seem a haze of confused dreams.

That explained why he hadn't come storming in here with his sword drawn demanding satisfaction—in this case, marriage. She knew him; his overabundance of honor would demand it.

She was relieved that he hadn't. Of course, she was. This way she didn't have to refuse him. She could pretend as if nothing had happened.

It was what she wanted, wasn't it?

The silly ache in her chest seemed to disagree. But what had she expected? Poetry and flowers? Platitudes and promises?

She was far too cynical for heartfelt declarations; she didn't need reassurance that she'd done everything all right. That she hadn't been the only one who thought what they shared was wonderful and amazing and special.

But she might not have objected to a few tender words afterward. And if she harbored a secret hope that he would remember something so important no matter what, she knew it wasn't fair.

As soon as Bess had set down the tray and left, Margaret turned to her. "Are you sure you are telling me everything?" She looked furtively at the closed door. "Nothing—"

"Nothing happened," Joan finished for her. "I told you it went exactly as I planned." Mostly. "As soon as the sleeping powder took effect, I searched his things and found the missive in his sporran." She neglected to mention that she was so upset she was halfway down the stairs before realizing she'd forgotten to destroy the seal and had to return to his room. "That's when I discovered that the seal had already broken off." Irony, that. Her deception—her seduction—had all been for nothing. "You have nothing to fear. Your secret is safe."

Margaret studied her face for a long moment, and apparently satisfied, she smiled and heaved a sigh of relief. "I can't tell you how happy I am to hear it. You've been watching the door so anxiously this morning I thought something had gone wrong."

Joan tried to return her smile and shook her head. "Nay, everything went perfectly."

"I'm so glad. I was so worried. I know you and Sir Alex . . ." Her cousin blushed awkwardly. "It couldn't have been easy for you. Is there any chance—?"

"No," Joan said, stopping her before she could finish. She couldn't let herself think like that. She needed to deal with reality.

Margaret held her gaze, perhaps guessing her thoughts. "I don't know how to thank you. If there is anything I can do?"

Joan shook her head, the gratitude making her uncomfortable. She just wanted to forget it had ever happened.

But how could she when it had been so perfect.

Right. Perfect until she'd drugged him—unintentionally doing exactly what she'd originally planned to do!

"Just promise me you'll be careful, Margaret. No more sealing missives with special rings."

Margaret gave a sharp laugh. "You have my word on that." After a moment, she frowned. "I suspect my days passing messages are at an end for a while anyway. Even before the monk's capture, I felt . . ." She shrugged. "I don't know, conspicuous maybe?"

Joan leaned forward. "Do you think someone was watching you?"

Margaret shook her head. "No, nothing like that. I suspect it's because there are so many people around."

Joan nodded. She'd felt the same. Since she'd arrived at Berwick Castle—which brought back so many bad memories anyway—doing her job had felt more dangerous. For good reason; it *was* more dangerous. As her cousin had said, there were many more people around. There was also Pembroke and Sir Henry increasing the efforts to find the spy.

And then of course there was Alex.

Joan startled as the door crashed open. Her foolish heart lurched, only to drop when Alice came bursting through in an excited flurry of pink satin.

Surprisingly, Sir Henry came following closely behind. Her cousin's husband rarely made an appearance in their donjon rooms during the day.

She was even more surprised to learn that *she* was the reason for that appearance.

"What do you know about Seton's sudden departure this morning?"

Joan couldn't have masked her shock if she wanted to. The color slid from her face. "He's gone?"

"Aye, he rode out of here this morning on some mission that no one seems to know anything about. He left a message for Pembroke that it was personal, but the earl is furious. He thinks he's turned traitor again."

Dear God, was it possible?

Despite a racing pulse, she managed to say evenly, "Has he given any indication that he might do such a thing?"

Sir Henry's eyes narrowed. "I was hoping you might answer that for me."

Joan was truly taken aback. "Me?"

"Alice says you've been spending time with him. That there is something between you."

Joan's gaze slid to her cousin's before turning back to Sir Henry. "Alice is mistaken, my lord. I have spoken with Sir Alex only a handful of times—and merely in passing. I know nothing of his intentions." It was painfully true. "Has he given any reason for you to suspect that he might turn traitor again?"

Could she dare hope?

Sir Henry waved the question off. "He's a Scot," he said as if that were all the explanation necessary, apparently forgetting that his wife, her sister, and her cousin were as well.

Joan returned her attention to the embroidery in her lap, picking it up once again before saying, "I wish I could be of more help, my lord, but I don't know anything about where Sir Alex might have gone."

She was aware of his gaze on her. When he was satisfied that she was not lying, Sir Henry said, "I am glad to hear it. I told Alice there could be nothing of significance between you." He looked with reproach at his wife. "As your guardian, I am responsible for your wardship and marriage, and Seton is not the right sort of man for you."

In other words, he wasn't the weak, ineffectual nobody who would never think to challenge her birthright.

She nodded, keeping her eyes on the piece of half-stitched

linen. It was to be a peacock, but all she could see was blue. "I understand, my lord. But marriage is the last thing on my mind."

It should be the truth.

∞

The next five days were some of the most miserable of Joan's recent memory. As if Alex's sudden abandonment wasn't enough, Alice was suffering from "head-splitting" headaches that were preventing her from sleeping, and she was taking her temper out on Joan, whom her cousin blamed for making her look "foolish" in front of her husband.

Apparently Alice failed to consider that it might be her own constant complaints and dramatic moans of pain that might be keeping her husband away from her bed at night, rather than anything Joan might have done.

In any event, last night had been the first full night of sleep Joan had managed in nearly a week—she refused to think of the first night when she'd gotten no sleep—as she'd finally become fed up with her cousin's whinging and distemper and given her what was left of the sleeping powder. It was welcome relief. She couldn't bear to look at the reminder of her perfidy and was glad to be rid of it.

On Friday morning, she woke for the first time to the feel of warmth on her skin and not a high-pitched screech in her ear. The novelty of feeling rested wore off soon, however, as the familiar questions began their daily—hourly—circling in her head.

Where had he gone? Why had he left? Did he intend to return? Did any of it have anything to do with her?

The one thing she knew was that he had not returned to the Bruce fold. She'd managed to get a message to her compatriots, and her answer had arrived yesterday. Seton was not in Scotland.

She hadn't really believed it possible, but the disappointment had been surprisingly acute.

So where was he? And why, even after nearly a week, did his leaving without saying a word still hurt so badly? He'd been so upset after. Did he despise her? Blame her? Or was he just avoiding her?

Joan didn't think so. Alex might have betrayed Bruce and the Guard—she knew him well enough to know that he must have had a reason—but he was not a coward.

With Alice still blissfully asleep, Joan crept out of her room and made her way to the Hall to break her fast. Margaret was already seated at one of the trestle tables, and Joan joined her. They spoke of nothing of import—and certainly nothing about their "treasonous" activities—but simply knowing that someone knew the truth was not only relaxing but oddly comforting. Joan wasn't alone, and for the first time, she realized how much she'd missed having a friend. A *real* friend—one whom she didn't need to deceive.

They were walking back to the tower to check on Alice ("Must we?" Margaret had groaned) when they heard the guards on the rampart call out excitedly that the king's banner had been sighted.

The two women shared a look of dread. They knew well what the king's arrival meant. The war that had largely taken a position in the back during the seven troubled years of Edward II's reign had finally moved to the forefront. The English king was determined to defeat Bruce, and the definitive battle that the Scots had sought to avoid for years was drawing closer.

Joan and Margaret, joined by what seemed to be most

of the castle occupants, raced up to the southern rampart (as the king was traveling from Newminster) to catch a glimpse of what was sure to be a magnificent procession.

They were not disappointed.

"Good God in heaven." Margaret had uttered the blasphemy under her breath. "Have you ever seen so many carts and banners? It must go on for miles."

It was not an exaggeration. The train of knights, men-at-arms, and their attendants, along with the carts of provisions, stretched like a long, colorful snake for as far as the eye could see.

"I'll give him credit," Joan said in a voice that only her cousin could hear. "Edward might not be half the commander that his father was, but he certainly knows how to look like a great general. Hail, Caesar!"

Margaret laughed. After a moment, her cousin added, "But it is something to see, is it not? All those banners flying in the wind, the colors of the surcoats as brilliant as jewels, and the silver of the mail shimmering in the sunlight . . . it's like a giant treasure chest."

It was true. The vast display of wealth, strength, and power was awe-inspiring.

It was also daunting as the realization of what they faced struck: the most powerful army in Christendom against a force of largely pikemen and foot soldiers.

Margaret must have come to the same realization, as she, too, fell silent.

Only when the procession of knights mounted on the fierce warhorses—clad in the same color and mail as their riders—drew close enough to make out the symbols of their arms did Margaret say, "Do you see them?"

Joan shook her head. She'd already been looking. She'd seen the squabbling earls of Gloucester and Hereford, but nowhere did she see the red and gold arms of Lancaster, or the arms for his fellow recalcitrant earls of Warwick, Lincoln, Arundel, and Warenne. "I don't think they are with him."

She heaved a huge sigh of relief. If England's mightiest earl and his cohorts did not answer Edward's call, Bruce would be facing considerably better odds—better as in horrible, not catastrophic.

"We'd best go down and take our positions," Margaret said. "I'm sure my sister is already wondering where we are."

Joan was sure she was right. She was also sure Alice would be furious that Joan wasn't there to help her pick out her gown this morning.

She was right about that as well. But fortunately, the first of the king's party rode through the gate, forestalling her scolding.

At times Joan almost envied her cousin. What must it be like to have your only thought be the color of your gown? To have your only worry be whether you looked your best? To have your own desires be all that mattered?

Vanity was simple and uncomplicated in a way that Joan could only imagine. Subterfuge and secrecy had played a part in her life for so long she'd forgotten what it felt like to not be on guard.

As the seemingly endless stream of knights rode through the gate, there were plenty that Joan recognized, including Edward's seneschal and captain of his household knights, Sir Edmund de Mauley, and one of the most famous knights in Christendom, the man reputed to be second only to Robert the Bruce, Giles d'Argentan. Riding not far behind him was the king himself in his red surcoat emblazoned with the three lions passant in gold.

Tall like his father and blessed with an unusually handsome face, King Edward II certainly looked the part of a king and great knight. But appearances in this case were deceiving. Though reputed to be an excellent sportsman and capable soldier, Edward had yet to live up to the expectation of his kingly robes. He was a weak monarch made weaker by the influence of his favorites.

She was so busy studying the king that she failed to notice the man who rode in behind him. Only the sudden ripple of whispers racing through the crowd and Margaret's elbow in her ribs alerted her to his presence.

At the sight of the yellow surcoat with the red wyvern, three crescents, and royal double tressure, her breath and heart caught somewhere in her throat.

"Seton is with the king?" she heard Sir Henry exclaim in outrage from a few feet away. "Why did I know nothing of this?"

Joan was curious as well, but the answer would have to wait.

Although perhaps not for long. Alex seemed to be scanning the crowd looking for someone. When his eyes locked on hers, she realized who it was.

The fierce intensity in the dark blue depths caught her in a hold from which she could not turn. Her skin prickled as every one of the tiny hairs on her arms seemed to stick up. Was it alarm, awareness, or a combination of both?

Something was happening . . .

After dismounting, Alex said a few words to the king and headed right for her. Her heart pounded hard in her chest, and she didn't take a breath for the entire time it took him to close the distance between them—even then it came out shallowly and unevenly.

He bowed formally before her. Aware of the eyes upon them, she executed a hasty and self-conscious curtsey.

"My lady, I would like to speak to you. In private, if you will."

Joan searched his face for an explanation but came up empty.

"What is the meaning of this, Seton?" Sir Henry interrupted angrily. "You most certainly will not."

Suddenly Joan realized the king himself had come to stand beside Alex. Edward had the oddest smile on his face as he addressed Sir Henry. "The lad will say his piece," the king said with a wink in her direction. Edward had always been kind to her the few times their paths had crossed in the past—guilt perhaps over what his father had done to her mother and what he'd done to her in declaring her illegitimate—but still the playfulness surprised her. "Come, Sir Henry," he said in a voice that brooked no argument. He was the king, after all, even if many in his realm wished otherwise. "I feel as if I've been riding across the deserts of Outremer and need some wine to quench my thirst. We shall talk."

Unable to object, Sir Henry followed the king, looking back occasionally at Alex and Joan.

But she wasn't paying attention to Sir Henry. All she could see was Alex. He was dusty and more tired than she'd ever seen him, yet there was a hard edge to his gaze that she'd never seen before. Steel, she realized. That was it. He had the look of determination in his eyes of a man who would not be gainsaid.

"What is this about, Alex?" But she feared she knew.

He didn't say anything but held out his hand.

She hesitated, feeling as if something momentous was about to occur. That if she put her hand in his, she wouldn't get it back.

Realizing she was being ridiculous, she slid her fingers into his. Maybe not so ridiculous, after all. Instantly she felt claimed—possessed—by the warmth of his big hand surrounding hers. It made her feel small and fragile and special in a way that she never had before.

She allowed him to lead her to the lord's private solar attached to the Great Hall. He motioned to the large cushioned chair—which she assumed was reserved for the king or his governor—for her to sit. He didn't seem inclined to do the same and paced (anxiously?) for a few moments before turning to face her. "I will not apologize for the dishonor I have done you, even though it is deserved. I think we both know it has gone beyond that. I would have spoken to you before I left, but under the circumstances, I thought it best not to give anyone, including your cousins and de Beaumont, any hint of my intentions."

The moment the king had winked at her, Joan had guessed (but didn't want to acknowledge even to herself) those intentions, and a strange mix of anticipation and dread had started to swirl in her stomach. By now it was a tempest. She looked down at her hands. "There is nothing you need say, my lord."

Reaching down, he took hold of her chin and forced her gaze to his. "How can you say that? What happened between us . . ."

His voice fell off, and his jaw hardened. But one look in his eyes, and any hope that he might not remember was put quickly to rest. He remembered *everything*, and she felt the heat rising to her cheeks as the memories hit her, too. Just being in the same room with him alone brought back the feelings of intimacy, the sensation of lying in his arms, the feel of his weight on top of her, the hardness of his powerful muscles against her, the fullness of him inside her . . .

She forced her thoughts away with a harsh twist of her head, freeing her chin from his hold and her gaze from the nearly irresistible pull. "What happened was regrettable, but it does not change anything." She stood, her voice shaking just a little as her fingers gripped the wool folds of her skirt. "Now if you will excuse—"

He stopped her before she could finish. "We aren't done here, and you won't leave until this matter is settled." Apparently she'd managed to rouse his temper, as his serious expression had definitely taken on an angry edge. "'Tis not the way I would have wished it—nor the proper order— but I owe you an offer of marriage, one I would have made had I not fallen into the sleep of the dead or had you been there when I woke up."

She ignored the none-too-subtle admonishment and turned away, unable to bear to look at him another second for fear that he would see her guilt and how much she wished it were otherwise. But they were at cross-purposes, and she did not delude herself as to how he would react if he knew the truth. Perhaps he would not clap her in irons, but he would despise her for deceiving him.

"You owe me nothing, Alex," she said quietly. "You better than anyone know that." She had not been a maid. She ventured a glance up at his face only to see his mouth turn white. Trying to douse the burning in her chest, she took a deep breath and added, "Besides, I came to you." *Under false pretenses*, she thought guiltily. "You need not fall on your sword to assuage your sense of honor. If there was any dishonor done that night it was mine."

She tried to move past him, but he took her by the arm. "This isn't about my honor, damn it. Don't you see? I *want* to marry you."

That effectively stole the argument from her mouth. She stared at him wordlessly.

Seeing her expression, he dragged his fingers back through his hair, loosening the imprint from the helm that he'd worn earlier. "Christ, I'm doing a piss-poor job of this. But I've never done this before."

He looked so boyishly discomfited. She smothered the impulse to comfort him with an equally awkward jest. "You do not propose to all the women you take to your bed?"

He gave her a strange look and frowned. "I do not take women to my bed."

At first she thought he was returning the jest, but when her smile went unreturned, it turned to incredulity. "You are serious?"

He didn't say anything, but it was clear he was.

"B-but surely that was not the first?" she sputtered. There'd been no indication . . . Her cheeks turned red at the memories. He seemed to know *exactly* what he'd been doing.

Perhaps guessing her thoughts, his gaze heated for a moment before he answered. "Nay, but the first since my brother took me to a bordel when I was a youth. It was not an experience I wanted to repeat, and I made a vow."

Joan didn't understand. "Like a Templar?"

His mouth quirked. "The Templars were disbanded a couple of years ago. Nay, nothing so formal—and I haven't been a monk. I just told myself that the next time I made love to a woman it would matter."

It took her a moment for the import of his words to hit. She stared at him in horror. Good God, what had she done? She'd wronged him even more than she'd realized. It seemed a man like him existed after all. And she'd made a mockery of what should be held dear. "I'm sorry, Alex."

He took her chin and lifted her gaze to his. "You misunderstand. I'm telling you this so that you understand the significance—so you see that it did matter. I want to marry you, and you would do me the greatest honor if you agree to be my wife."

Words she'd thought she'd never hear spoken by the only man in the world she'd ever wanted to say them. Though she knew what her answer must be, she let herself hold on to the moment for just a little bit, knowing it would have to last forever.

Muteness was not the response Alex had hoped for. But he could see the indecision—he hoped it was indecision—warring in her eyes and told himself to be patient.

It was not rewarded.

"I'm sorry, Alex, I can't."

She held his gaze, pleading for understanding. But he couldn't give it to her. He didn't understand at all. It was clear she wanted him, but something was holding her back.

"Why can't you?" An explanation occurred to him—one that made every muscle in his body flare. "Is there someone else?"

Her brow furrowed as if she were momentarily confused, but then a coy smile lifted one side of her mouth. "Isn't there always someone else?"

But there wasn't. He knew that, even if his jealousy had gotten the best of him for a minute. It was an act—he was certain of it—and he wasn't going to let her push him away with it anymore.

"Not anymore," he said flatly, his tone causing her to lift her gaze to his in surprise. "Whatever happened before today is in the past, and that is where it shall stay. It cannot be changed, but the future . . ." He let his voice drop off and gave her a knowing smile. "The future is a different matter, and I can assure you, my lady, I intend to keep you so well satisfied in my bed that you will never have want or reason to seek another."

She gasped in shock—and perhaps in something else as the sensual promise of his words penetrated.

They were standing so close he was tempted to prove it to her. But almost as if she guessed his intentions, she took a few steps back.

She shook her head. "I can't—it would never work. *We* would never work."

"I think we proved otherwise last Saturday. We work well together"—he gave her a heated look—"very well."

Her face turned so adorably red that he had to stop himself from laughing. She was the blushing maid again, and more and more he was certain *that* was not an act.

"You are trying to embarrass me," she chastised. "But that is not what I meant." She was twisting her hands anxiously in her skirts again. "I can hardly be the type of woman you were hoping to marry."

Perhaps she'd been right initially, but it wasn't true any longer. The idea of the sweet, innocent maid didn't hold the same appeal for him that it once had. Actually, he wasn't sure it had ever held appeal, it was just something he'd never thought about and just assumed. But now . . . a woman like that would be far too simple. He liked the edge that came from experience, and the challenge that came from wit and intelligence. He liked a little mystery and reserve. He wanted to be the one to learn her secrets and make her smile.

He also rather liked boldness in the bedchamber. He couldn't imagine a wide-eyed, blushing maid putting her hand on him. And Alex wanted Joan's hands on him—all over him. Aye, she could seduce him for a lifetime. "I wouldn't know," he said. "Until you there has been no woman I wished to marry."

She groaned as if he were torturing her. "God, why do you have to say things like that?"

He frowned. "Did I say something wrong?"

"Yes. No." She looked as exasperated as she sounded. "It's just sweet!"

His frown turned perplexed. "And that is bad?"

"It is when I must refuse you."

"Must?" It was a strange word to use.

Her flush deepened; she hurried to explain. "There are things you don't know. Things that might make a difference to you if you did." She hesitated as if searching for the right words.

But Alex, suspecting she was referring to other men, didn't want to hear any more. His expression drew hard and intractable. "I know everything I need to know. My mind will not be changed. Besides, it is too late for that anyway."

"What do you mean?"

"I mean the matter has already been decided. The king has given his permission, and unless you can think of a good reason why you cannot marry me—one that you wish to share with him—we will wed as soon as I return from Scotland. The first of the banns will be read on Sunday morning."

The flush drained from her face. She was pale as she stared at him with an expression that made him feel as if he'd just stabbed her in the back. "You have arranged this without my consent?"

Alex winced—a tad guiltily—at the betrayal in her voice. But it wasn't like that. "After what happened, I did not anticipate that I would be without it. I sought the king's permission because I thought I might need his help in convincing de Beaumont—not because I thought I might need it to convince my bride."

"Convince? You mean force!"

He tried to keep a rein on his temper at the scoff, but it wasn't easy. His jaw hardened. "Call it what you will, but the king is looking forward to it, and I do not intend to disappoint him."

"Sir Henry will be furious. What did you have to promise the king to get him to agree?" Her anger turned into a sneer. "Or perhaps you offered him something else? The king has an eye for handsome knights, does he not?"

Alex ignored the taunt—even if it was regrettably true. But he sure as hell hadn't pandered to the king's particular tastes. "Edward has a weakness for love-thwarted stories and enjoys being cast in the role of the facilitator."

"That is all?" she said disbelievingly. "He is willing to risk Sir Henry's anger to write a pretty tale?"

Alex shrugged, but not without a certain amount of discomfort. "I did agree not to pursue any claims on your inheritance until after the war."

The betrayal in her gaze cut him to the quick. "I see. How thoughtful of you to decide my future without consulting me."

He dragged his hand back through his hair. Bloody hell, it wasn't supposed to happen like this. He knew she might need some persuading, but he sure in the hell hadn't expected her to react like this. He wanted her to be happy, damn it. Like he was. Because despite everything that had happened, he was happy. "It wasn't like that. Besides, the war will be over soon anyway."

"You sound so certain, but for all you know, it could go on for years."

Not if he had anything to say about it. "It won't."

She stared at him, trying to find a crack where one didn't exist. "Don't do this, Alex. Please, I'm begging you to reconsider."

"Why are you fighting this so hard when I know it's what you want?"

"What *I* want?" she exploded angrily. "This has nothing to do with what I want. This is about *you*—about easing *your* conscience, assuaging *your* honor. I told you I *didn't* want this."

"Is that right? And when you came to my room, what did you think then, Joan? What did you *really* think would happen?"

She looked down, biting her bottom lip. "I didn't mean for it . . ." She shook her head. "I don't know."

She sounded so forlorn—almost lost—and it ate at him. He wasn't an ogre, damn it. Why was she trying to make him feel like one?

They'd gotten off track; he needed to get them back on. Gently, he took her in his arms. She did not resist, but the indifference was almost worse. His chest tightened as he tipped her face to his. "It was never my intention to make you unhappy. I was only trying to do what I thought was right. I thought after what happened that you would not be wholly averse to a match. I went to Edward because I knew Sir Henry would not support the match and would do everything to prevent it. The king may have granted permission, but I would very much like to hear you say yes." He took a deep breath. "Marry me, sweetheart. I swear to you I will do everything in my power to make sure you never regret it."

He quieted her objection—if she'd been about to make one—with a kiss. The moment their lips met, he felt something break apart inside him. All the worries, all the troubles, all the posturing and pleading he'd had to do with Edward were forgotten. It hadn't been six days since he'd kissed her last, but it felt like an eternity.

Christ, her lips were so soft and sweet. He wanted to devour them—devour her. But he forced himself to go slow. To ease her into the passion this time. To show her that it wouldn't always be fast and furious between them, that it could also be slow and tender but every bit as intense.

And hot. It was like a damned inferno. One touch of their lips and the air combusted between them, spreading heat in molten waves over them both. It threatened to pull him under, but he kept his mind focused on his task. This was a wooing, not another ravaging. He was going to make it impossible for her to refuse.

Where words hadn't worked, Alex used his mouth and tongue to persuade. He enticed. He entreated. He showed her with each sweep of his mouth over hers and each gentle caress of his lips why she should say yes. Why she *must* say yes. There was no other answer. What they had together was too powerful and right to deny.

He took his time savoring and drawing out every taste and sensation of her lips before finally giving her his tongue.

She moaned at the first stroke. And then he made her moan some more with each sweep, each circle, each long, slow pull. He made those pulls echo in her chest, until the yearning became palpable. Until it turned to moans of need.

They were the most beautiful sounds he'd ever heard, because he knew what they meant: surrender. She was surrendering to the passion, and he had no intention of letting her go.

He took her for a long, slow ride of touch and discovery. He tasted the soft, silky skin below her ear and kissed the long curve of her neck. He used the back of his finger to sweep the taut tip of her nipple and then to circle the heavy curve of her breast.

He tortured her with slow and gentle. He wanted her

to feel every touch and every stroke; he wanted to eke out every bit of sensation and every ounce of pleasure; he wanted to drive her mad with desire.

It was working. Her fingertips were digging into his shoulders. She was dissolving against him again, just the way he liked it, giving him free rein. Letting him lead and set the pace.

But those fingertips . . . they were driving him mad. He could feel her desire and it set off the sparks of his own. His mouth found her lips and covered them, as his hand found her breast and did the same.

It wasn't enough. He wanted her naked. He wanted her warm, velvety soft skin sliding against his. He wanted her hands all over his body. He wanted to be inside her. He wanted to feel all that dampness gripping him, all those tiny muscles spasming and contracting around him. He wanted to hear her scream his name as he made her shatter over and over.

She wanted it, too. Her breath was coming in low, soft pants, and she started to press against him, increasing the friction with increasingly insistent circles of her hips. It was so tempting to give her what she wanted—Christ, what they both wanted. He was so hard and throbbing he could explode with one touch. All he had to do was lean her back on the table, lift her skirts, and sink into her inch by silky hot inch.

But not yet, damn it. No matter how much his body was aching, the next time they made love, it would be with his ring on her finger.

Very slowly and very deliberately he pulled away. His heart was banging like a drum and his skin was hot and tight with passion and unspent lust. It would take a long time for his body to cool.

She mewled in frustration and tried to pull him back. He smiled and shook his head. "Not yet, sweetheart. Not until we are wed."

The frustration had not yet left her body, and her eyes fired a dark blue. "You are sure of yourself, aren't you? You think that one kiss will change my mind?"

"It isn't your mind I want to change."

He wanted her heart.

When she realized what he meant, the fight seemed to leave her. "Oh, Alex."

"Will you marry me?"

She nodded, it seemed helplessly. "Aye. I will marry you. Though God knows, we both might come to regret it."

He was too happy to heed the words of doom. But they would come to him later.

15

THE NEWS OF Alex's return and their engagement spread quickly, and the repercussions did not take long to be felt. Sir Henry was predictably furious, and Alice—although feeling vindicated—accused Joan of betrayal, treachery, and taking advantage of their "kindness and generosity" in taking her in. As it was true—albeit for different reasons—Joan's guilt gave her more patience with her cousin's dramatics than she might have had otherwise.

Alice was still harping the next morning as they readied to join the other women to go hawking—the queen had wasted no time in organizing the hunt to show off her prized falcon. The fact that this wasn't court and they were only weeks away from war didn't seem to bother her.

Joan put down the fur-lined plaid cloak she'd picked to go with her cousin's riding habit on the bed to protest yet again. "I had no idea what he intended, Alice, truly. Alex did not tell me where he was going. I was just as surprised as you to see him riding in with the king."

"You expect me to believe this?"

"It's the truth."

"Leave her alone, Alice," Margaret interjected. "You saw her face; you know Joan did not plan this. Besides, it is a good match. Surely you did not intend our cousin to remain unwed forever?"

They all knew that was exactly what she intended. But even Alice realized it would sound churlish and selfish to admit as much. "Of course not."

"Then what objections do you have?" Margaret asked. "Sir Alex is from an old and respected family, and is a baron of considerable lands on both sides of the border."

"He is a Scot," Alice said.

"So are we," Margaret reminded her.

"Exactly," Alice replied. She turned to Joan, adding with more astuteness than either Joan or Margaret gave her credit for, "It is your future I am concerned about. Your close connection to an infamous rebel makes your position here difficult enough, and now to marry a man who fought with the Scots two years ago and who is already under suspicion? Your loyalty will be in question even more."

"I have no connection to the woman who abandoned me," Joan said flatly. "Nor has my loyalty ever been in question." She tried not to sound as curious as she was. "And what do you mean by suspicion?"

"Didn't you know? Sir Alex offered to find the rebel in our midst to prove himself innocent."

It took her a moment to process what she meant, the idea was so ludicrous. "Alex a spy?" Joan was so surprised she laughed—and not just at the irony. "That is ridiculous. Anyone who has spent five minutes with him would know that is impossible. He hates subterfuge of any kind. He is straightforward and direct—deception is not his way."

It was hers. Though for the first time since she'd agreed to help Bruce, she wished it were otherwise. She hated lying to Alex; deceiving him felt wrong in a way that it never had before.

"For what it matters, I agree with you," Alice said. "He is the shiny knight type—the kind who actually thinks the code of chivalry is not just for children's tales." She laughed as if the idea were ludicrous. Joan shouldn't be surprised by Alice's insight into Alex's character; when it came to men, her cousin could be surprisingly clever. She, too, knew how to pick a target. "But I am merely passing on what was being said, and why you should be concerned." She paused. "Henry and Pembroke are determined to uncover this spy before they march to Stirling; I do not wish you to be caught up in their net."

It sounded almost like a warning, and for a moment Joan wondered if her cousin suspected something. But even if she did, what could Joan do? She'd tried to refuse Alex, but there was no excuse she could give him without rousing his suspicions. No matter how angry she was—and she was furious at the high-handedness in arranging the marriage without her consent that smacked too much of her father's controlling behavior and the kiss that had turned her mind to mush—she'd realized that it was best to go along with it. For now.

"I won't," she said with more assurance than she felt. "I thank you for your concern, cousin, but do not worry. The next few weeks . . ." Her voice dropped off. "Anything could happen."

Somehow she would find a way to break the betrothal—even if she feared that by then she might not want to.

Her fears were not unwarranted. No sooner had Joan and her cousins descended the stairs to join the other women in the courtyard than Alex appeared by her side.

"I've been conscripted as an escort," he said, by way of answer to her unspoken question.

Joan lifted a brow. "Why do I think you were not averse to the duty?"

"Aye, it's a nice break from the preparations of war."

"Is that all?"

"There might have been another reason or two."

She frowned. "Two?"

He quirked a decidedly devilish smile that made his already too-handsome face even more devastating and landed with a thump somewhere in the region above her ribs.

Dear God, would she ever grow used to how handsome he was?

He can be yours . . .

No, he can't. She had to force herself to quiet the voice of temptation. But every minute she spent with him, it grew louder.

He was everything she'd once imagined a knight could be: courteous, gallant, charming, and attentive. He made her laugh, made her feel like she was the most important person in the world, and seemed to anticipate her wishes even before she thought them. When one of the "ladies" in the queen's party tried to flirt with him—not seeming to care that Joan was right there—he gently but firmly cut her off. He only had eyes for one woman, and he made sure everyone knew it.

It was like a dream. She might as well have fallen back in time into the pages of her favorite stories: the fair maid being wooed by the gallant knight. He seemed to have forgotten her reputation, and she forgot the disappointment and cynicism that had helped construct it.

Maybe if she could have kept it at that it would have been easier to dismiss, but Alex was intent on drawing her in deeper and deeper with questions and conversations that made her realize he really wanted to know her. The *real* her. The person she hadn't been for a very long time.

The royal party had ridden for a few miles before stopping in a wide swath of moorland. As Joan had never had much interest in hawking—not only was it an extremely expensive sport, but frankly birds of prey terrified her—she had joined a few of the other ladies on an old stone wall to watch. After attending to his duties, Alex had ambled over to take a seat beside her. She didn't know whether to be annoyed or amused when the two ladies she'd been sitting with moved to give them some privacy.

It didn't take long for their light conversation to take a more serious turn. "I saw you once," Alex admitted. "A long time ago."

Joan was so shocked that he mentioned it that at first she didn't know what to say. She looked around to make sure no one was near and knew that she had to tread very carefully. "I thought I might have seen you once before as well."

He was clearly surprised. "You did?"

She nodded.

"At Roxburgh?" he asked.

She nodded again. "About the time of my cousin's wedding." She paused, debating how much more to say. "I believe you were with my mother."

He held her gaze with an intensity that made her want to turn away. Keeping her thoughts hidden from him was getting harder and harder.

"Aye, she was not very happy that I noticed you. You were far too young. Christ, you still are," he said half to himself.

"I haven't been young for a very long time. Having my mother imprisoned in a cage and knowing my father was one of the people responsible for her being put there, as well as being disinherited and branded a bastard, tends to make one grow up fast." Not to mention having her innocence taken from her by force at fifteen.

Though she'd said it lightly, maybe he heard more bitterness than she intended.

"Aye, I can see that," he said slowly. "Why did you stay? You might have returned to Scotland after your mother was released."

She shook her head firmly; this was very dangerous ground. "Why would I? My life has been in England for the past eight years. My family is here."

"Your Comyn family, perhaps, but what about your mother, brothers, and sister?"

The question pierced too deeply, touching on nerves that were more raw than she wanted them to be. She kept her voice as even and nonchalant as she could. "I barely remember my mother, and my brothers and sister I have never met."

"I have," he said. "Your sister resembles you."

"She does?" Lachlan had never said anything, probably guessing that the subject cut deeper than she wanted to admit. "People have always said I look like my father."

"You do, but there is more of your mother in you than I realized. Christina had just started to walk when I saw her last. She has blond hair like your mother, but there is something in the eyes, nose, and chin."

He studied her face until she grew self-conscious, but she couldn't stop herself from asking, "What about Erik?" Robbie had been born after Alex left.

"He has your color eyes and hair, but he looks just like his father."

There was an edge to his voice she couldn't ignore. "You don't like my mother's husband?" She proceeded slowly. "I suppose I shouldn't be surprised; Lachlan MacRuairi does not have the best reputation."

Alex gave a sharp laugh. "That is putting it rather mildly—and most of it is true. He's more brigand than knight, and as mean as a snake."

Viper. Lachlan's war name.

"And yet," Alex continued with a shrug. "Your mother saw something in him."

"And you did as well?"

He gave her another shrug. "Maybe at times. It was complicated."

Joan suspected that was the biggest understatement of the day. Not for the first time she wondered what had happened to make him leave.

They were quiet for a while, watching the hawks dive and soar, from their seat on the old wall. She might not like the birds up close, but they were absolutely beautiful to watch. "Why did you not say anything about seeing me at Roxburgh before?" Alex asked.

She could ask him the same. "I wasn't sure, and I didn't want to make things any more difficult for you."

He gave her a wry smile. "So I see you've heard that my loyalties are currently suspect?"

"My cousin mentioned something about your helping to uncover the spy to clear you from suspicion."

He shook his head, not without some disgust. "It's bloody ironic, isn't it? I turned traitor to one side only to be thought a traitor by the other. Everywhere I go, it's suspicion."

She'd never thought about it that way, but as a baron with lands on both sides of the border he didn't really have a side—he was caught in the middle. Was that it? She couldn't hold back the questions any longer, though part of her feared the answer. Alex's betrayal of Bruce and the Guard was the only thing keeping her heart at bay. It was easier not to know—it kept a wall between them. And yet she could no longer stop herself from asking, "Why did you do it, Alex? What made you decide to leave the Scots to fight for the English?"

There was an almost imperceptible stiffening of his shoulders. "There are many people who have changed allegiance throughout this war. It is hardly unusual."

He was avoiding the question. "But those men aren't you."

"What do you mean?"

"You live and breathe honor and integrity."

He smiled, his teeth a white flash against his already sun-darkened skin. "You make me sound like some kind of paragon, which I assure you I am not."

"Maybe so, but those things are important to you."

He gave her a wry smile. "And a man who betrays his compatriots cannot be honorable and have integrity, is that it?" She didn't say anything. "Yet that is why I left."

It was clear she didn't understand, and he seemed to be weighing whether to say more. Perhaps her patience and silence helped to convince him. "Do you know how to swim?"

The question caught her off guard. She blinked and nodded.

"I almost drowned once. I was swimming in the Western Isles during a bad storm. I remember struggling against the current and trying to fight my way out of it. But no matter what I did, no matter how hard I swam, I wasn't going anywhere. I couldn't feel anything anymore. I was so tired and cold, sapped of all my energy. The water was pulling me under, and I knew I was drowning."

She looked at him in horror.

"That's how I felt when I left," he said. "Like I was swimming against a current that was dragging me under, and I had to get out before I was pulled under."

From the tortured look on his face she knew there was more. "Why, Alex? Why did you feel like that? What happened?"

"There were things . . ." His voice trailed off. "Things done in the name of war that I did not agree with."

Joan could guess what he meant. She had to remind herself that no matter what she thought—or that it was necessary to have a chance against a much more powerful foe—the rest of Christendom saw Bruce as fighting an unchivalrous war. To a knight like Alex—a knight who obviously took the code of chivalry very seriously—the "pirate" warfare that Bruce had adopted would have seemed antithetical to everything he'd been taught to believe was "right" and "honorable." It wasn't nearly that black and white, of course, but Alex didn't exactly see a lot of gray, and the new style of warfare must have been hard to accept and a difficult adjustment for him. "You can't shoulder the conscience of everyone else, Alex, only yourself. Are the English so much better?"

Though she hadn't said it sarcastically, his mouth quirked as if she had. "Maybe not, but I wasn't shouldering other people's consciences, it was mine I was worried about. I came very close to doing something for which I would never have been able to forgive myself." She could hear the self-disgust and latent bitterness in his voice. "We were raiding Norham. I didn't want to be there. I was already fed up with all the back-and-forth raids that were destroying the Borders. But Clifford had raided our town so we had to raid his. I was in charge of removing the livestock from the barns and then setting fire to the buildings. It was maybe the second or third building that I'd set my torch to when I looked up at an open loft door and saw a face in the flames. It was a little girl—no more than six or seven."

Joan gasped in horror and instinctively put her hand on his arm.

He gave her a wry grimace. "The flames were licking at her skirts when I reached her. She was black with smoke and terrified, but otherwise unhurt." He gave a harsh laugh. "She'd been playing with a kitten in the loft where she wasn't supposed to be and thought the men were her father's. But that was when I knew I couldn't go on doing what I was doing. I had to do something different. Something that would put an end to the raiding, to the suffering, and to the pain experienced by the innocents who were bearing the brunt of the war."

Her hand squeezed. "Oh, Alex. I'm sorry. But why fight for the English? The same thing could have happened had you been with them. The Scots aren't the only ones who burn down barns."

"Aye," he admitted bitterly. "There is plenty of dishonor to go around. But I didn't see how I could put an end to all of it by doing what I was doing. Breaking my vow to Bruce and to the—" He stopped, but she knew what he'd been about to say. *To the Guard.* "To his men," he corrected, "was the hardest thing I've ever done, but I couldn't see any other way out." He gave a halfhearted shrug. "I'm sure some of them were glad to see me go. I never really fit in."

How could he say that? Did he not realize how much his leaving had devastated the others? But she wasn't supposed to know that. Instead she asked, "Why?"

He thought for a moment. "The men I was fighting with had a different line in the sand. They were willing to do whatever it took to win; I was not. I wanted to win, but not at the expense of being able to look myself in the mirror when it was all over. And secret warfare, lying in wait, hiding in fox holes, and subterfuge didn't feel much like winning to me. They may have given Bruce a foothold, but it became clear to me that pirate warfare wasn't going to win the war. The only way for Bruce to do that was to take the field. Which was something he refused to do. Why would he when he could go on forever as he was? Forever wasn't something I could accept. I couldn't watch my people suffer for it any longer." He shrugged again, almost as if he were embarrassed. "I saw two choices: I could stay fighting with Bruce doing the same thing for years and hope that there was a Borders left when it was finally all over, or I could go somewhere where I could actually *do* something that might end it. I thought that by coming here I could do some good." His mouth curved. "Apparently, I overestimated my powers of persuasion."

Joan was quiet for a moment, keenly aware of her own

"subterfuge" and role as a spy. "What did you hope to accomplish?"

"I thought I might be able to get Edward to see the value in negotiation—that much could be gained from recognizing Bruce as king. But I underestimated how much of his father he has in him," Alex admitted. "Perhaps it was naive to think one person could do anything."

Strangely, Joan understood. It fit with the old-time knight in shining armor. Alex expected the rest of the world to act and think like him. To be reasonable. To have the same honor and principles. But he was bound to be disappointed. Idealism had no place in war. "War isn't knights riding in tournaments, it's dirty and unpleasant. You have to fight with the weapons you have, even if it sometimes makes you uncomfortable." It sounded as if she was trying to defend her own actions. "And it isn't just the Scots who fight dirty," she pointed out. "The justice Edward dispensed to my mother was a far cry from honorable or chivalrous."

From the way his mouth set in a hard line, she could tell he didn't want to hear what she was saying. "I know that. Believe me, I heard as much from my old partner—over and over." He was referring to Boyd, and she could hear the deep-seated frustration and anger in his voice. "But there is no perfect answer. I had to do something—something that might have a chance of making a difference—and I did what I thought was right at the time."

At the time. Perhaps she was reading too much into the words—grasping at any thread to hold on to—but still it gave her hope where there had been none. "Do you ever regret it?"

He was so quiet at first she thought he hadn't heard her. But when he looked over at her, the bleakness in his eyes betrayed him. "It was the worst thing I've ever done. Breaking my vow to the king, who was like a brother to mine, betraying men whom I'd fought with like brothers for almost seven years—" He stopped. The rawness of his voice left her with no doubt that even now he felt the weight of that decision. "But at the time I made the only decision I could. God knows, I wasn't doing any good there; I thought I might be able to do more from the other side."

Beneath the emotion, she heard the frustration. "And have you?"

His smile was almost pained. "Like I said, I may have overestimated my ability to persuade and Edward's ability to listen to reason. But I haven't given up. Besides, regret would serve no purpose. I can never go back."

But what if he could? What if she could persuade him to turn once more? It could be an answer to her problems. But she did not delude herself: it wasn't going to be easy. She didn't just have to convince Alex, she also had to convince her brethren.

"You are certain of that?" Joan said.

"I am," Alex said. It was the one thing he was sure about.

Why was she asking him all these questions? Christ, this was the last thing Alex wanted to talk about. Not only did it border on treason, but what good would it do to tear himself up all over again? He'd known when he'd ridden away two years ago that there would be no going back— and seeing his former Highland Guard brethren again had solidified it. But he sounded defensive and knew it. How could he make her understand when he wasn't sure he understood himself anymore?

Her eyes were big, wide, and impossibly blue as she stared up at him. "And if the end of the war means Bruce's defeat? That doesn't matter to you? Did your differences with how the war was being fought make you lose your faith in Bruce as king?"

He eyed her sharply. It was a strange thing to ask coming from someone loyal to the English. And it was the one question he didn't want to—couldn't—answer. It did matter to him. More than he wanted to admit. He'd never stop believing in Bruce as a man or as king. But the cost had seemed too high. The way Bruce was fighting the war could go on forever—and that he couldn't accept.

"I lost faith that Bruce would ever take the field to lose or win, and the alternative was famine, burned-out villages, stolen cattle and grain, misery for the people who count on me to protect them, and little girls playing with kittens in a barn who get caught in the flames." He stood up and held out his hand. "We should go."

She looked over to where the queen and the rest of the entourage were readying to leave, as surprised as he that the hunt had finished already. "I'm sorry, I didn't mean—"

"We shouldn't be talking about this," he said, cutting her off. "It serves no purpose and could be misunderstood if overheard." He gave her a long look. "Why are you so interested? I thought you were content in England."

"I am," she said quickly. A light pink flush filled her cheeks. "I am curious, that's all. I want to know more about you. I didn't mean to upset you."

"I'm not upset." But he was—more than he wanted to admit. Her questions had struck old wounds that were more raw than he realized. He suspected they might never fully heal. "It's just . . ." How could he explain?

"Complicated?" she finished for him.

He smiled. "Aye, complicated."

They joined the others and the opportunity for more

private conversation was lost. He was surprised by how easy it was to talk to her—maybe too easy. The only time he'd talked about his reasons for leaving—very briefly— was with Rosalin as he escorted her back to her brother two years ago and submitted to the English. But still, something troubled him. He didn't know whether it was the subject of Joan's questions—rousing things he would rather not think about—or the fact that she was asking them.

After they enjoyed a light meal of wine, cheese, dried meats, and bread, the horses were readied for the ride back to the castle. The weather had cooled with the appearance of a few clouds, and the light breeze had turned sharper and more persistent. A few of the ladies donned heavier cloaks, including Joan and her cousins.

He hadn't realized how tall Joan was compared to her kinswomen. Both Alice and Margaret were probably not much above five feet, and Joan must be six inches taller— though they probably weighed the same. Joan was slender and her cousins were rounder—especially Margaret.

Short and round. Bloody hell. All of a sudden he noticed the color of Lady Margaret's cloak. It was a dark red, "the color of claret," trimmed with white—probably ermine— fur. The lady who'd left a missive for the monk had worn something similar.

It could be a coincidence. And he hoped to hell it was. But a claret cloak with very expensive ermine fur wasn't exactly common—and neither were ladies in a position to know key information. Margaret Comyn could well be the spy they sought.

He had no idea why she would agree to do something so risky for the man who'd killed her kinsman (Bruce's stabbing of John "The Red" Comyn before the altar at

Greyfriars had only made the blood feud between the families worse). But the far more pressing question was, what the hell was he going to do about it?

16

A LEX DIDN'T HAVE long to decide. Pembroke's new-est squire found him and gave him a message that the earl wanted to see him just as Alex was helping the ladies down from their horses.

"Is something wrong?" Joan asked, watching as the lad hurried away. "You seemed a bit subdued on the ride back."

He probably should be surprised how easily she already seemed to read his moods, but he wasn't. With at least part of the wall that she'd erected between them knocked down, their natural connection was being felt. "Perhaps a bit. There is a lot to be done in the next few weeks." He gave her a smile. "As much as I would like to focus on the betrothal, I'm afraid Edward and Pembroke will have different ideas."

She bit her lip in a way that could easily distract him, despite what he'd just said. "I hope it was nothing I said."

He shook his head. "It wasn't. But I'm afraid I will not be able to join you for the evening meal as I hoped. Pembroke has ordered me to attend him."

"Is there a problem?"

There wouldn't be if Alex didn't suspect her cousin was the spy.

He didn't want to lie to her so instead he just said, "I suspect he is wondering about my progress in uncovering the person who has been passing important information to Bruce."

"And are you any closer?"

The question was asked with polite interest—nothing more. But something about that bothered him. Perhaps it was the contrast with the impassioned discussion they'd had a short while ago. This almost sounded careful.

Did she suspect her cousin as well? Did she know something?

He hoped to hell not.

His gaze fixed on hers as if he could force her to reveal her thoughts. But she stared at him blankly, and he prayed, guilelessly.

"I'm not sure," he answered.

"That sounds promising."

Again, polite interest. *Careful* polite interest.

"Not as promising as I'd hoped," he said ambiguously if truthfully. He sure as hell had never expected a woman—let alone her cousin—to be involved in this when he'd offered his help to defray suspicion from himself.

It put him in an awkward position. As was made clear when he faced Pembroke a short while later in his private solar.

"You left on your 'errand' before you filled me in on the leads you were following," the vaunted English commander said, not hiding his continued annoyance at Alex's leaving the castle to find the king.

As Alex had already offered his apologies and explanation, he ignored the thinly veiled reprimand.

"What did you find out?" Pembroke finished.

Alex cursed. His duty was clear. He should tell Pembroke what he'd learned about the spy being a woman. But if he did that there was every chance the earl would suspect Joan—as Alex had. And he sure as hell wasn't going to tell him his suspicions that it was Margaret. As much as he despised subterfuge, even if Alex was certain it was her, he wouldn't condemn Joan's cousin to prison—or worse—especially when he wasn't sure of Joan's involvement.

Lies, subterfuge, treachery, and dishonor . . . these were exactly the things he'd sought to avoid, damn it. Yet here he was wallowing in them again.

Honor and loyalty demanded an answer Alex wasn't going to give. His line in the sand was moving. "Unfortunately, the leads I was following were less promising than I thought."

He could tell himself that it was not technically a lie, but no matter how carefully constructed the words he knew they were still calculated to deceive and wrong.

Pembroke frowned. "I was told you met with the monk very late the night before you left. Why? Did he tell you something?"

"I thought to catch him unaware in the hope that he might admit something useful. But after questioning him for a while, I am convinced that he never met the person who left the message. The young monk was indeed only a courier."

Another carefully constructed "truth." Alex hid his self-disgust beneath Pembroke's scrutiny. His commander gave him a hard look. "So you have learned nothing new?"

Alex shook his head. "Nothing helpful. I suspect the monk's capture has forced the spy to go underground for a while."

He hoped to hell *that* was the truth.

Pembroke considered him for a moment. "Perhaps you are right. But in any event, protective measures have been taken. The king is convinced that Bruce has somehow become privy to our shipping routes, as attacks have occurred with too much precision to be coincidence. He is furious and wants to ensure nothing else finds its way into enemy hands."

Alex knew the inability to get provisions to the English garrisons in Scotland for the large army that Edward intended to send north could be a severe blow, affecting their battle plan. They would be forced to take all the supplies with them, which would slow them down and make the large army even more unwieldy. How had Margaret managed to get that kind of information? Could de Beaumont have been that careless to share such detailed information?

But it was what else Pembroke had said that he was focused on. "What kind of protective measures?" Alex asked.

The other man waved him off. "It isn't your concern."

Alex held his temper—barely. "How can it not be when it is my job to uncover the spy?"

"A job that you have failed," Pembroke pointed out. "But you need not concern yourself with finding the spy any longer, I have another task for you."

Alex's teeth were grinding at the slight that was unfortunately warranted, but he managed to say, "My lord?"

"There is trouble brewing in East Lothian. The garrison commander at Hailes Castle is having some trouble with the local farmers, some of whom I believe are your tenants in Haddington."

Alex was immediately on alert. "What kind of trouble?"

"The captain believes they are conspiring with the enemy to provide them food and other necessities."

Alex bit back the curse that was about to follow, instead

saying, "That is ridiculous. Bruce's men raided that area not long ago in retribution for their supplying the garrison with grain. The same garrison that should have been protecting them," he added pointedly.

"I do not care about the details," Pembroke said. "I simply wish for you to do whatever is necessary to put the trouble to rest and bring any traitors to justice. I do not need to tell you how important the garrisons are as we make our way north."

Hailes was on the main road to Edinburgh.

"And if I find that it is the garrison commander that is the problem?" Alex asked.

"I am sure you will find a solution," Pembroke said.

In other words, justice didn't matter. The plight of the people in the Borders didn't matter. Just appease the damned captain.

By now Alex's teeth felt as if they'd been ground flat. He managed to nod, acknowledging the order.

"Good," Pembroke said. "You will leave at dawn. Take as many men as you need. I don't expect it should take you more than a few days."

Dismissed, Alex left the tower to find his men. He was so frustrated and seething with anger that he didn't look up until he heard a sharp gasp.

"Alex?" The soft, feminine voice was instantly familiar.

He didn't need to see the face hidden in the hood of the cloak to recognize the woman who came hurling into his arms a moment later.

Joan worried that she'd pushed Alex too hard and made him suspicious. But she'd been carried away by the prospect of a future beyond heartbreak, and the possibility that she could somehow convince him to return to his former compatriots.

He had clearly struggled with the decision to leave and didn't seem reconciled to it even now. *At the time* . . .

With what he'd said—and what she knew of him—she had a deeper understanding of what had motivated him to switch sides. It didn't seem as much of a betrayal now.

He'd been worn down, frustrated, and pushed to the breaking point by the brutality of war. Part Scot, part English, part knight, part brigand, Alex was torn between two worlds—two ideals—and unable to reconcile the fight for justice and chivalry. Eventually he'd snapped.

But whether it was the little girl, the trouble with Boyd, the style of warfare, his personal code, because he couldn't see an end, or a combination of all those things that caused him to leave, he'd done so with a noble purpose. He'd betrayed his friends and king because he thought he could do more good working for an end to the war from a different angle.

It was an admirable idea, but she guessed that it hadn't worked out the way he'd hoped. He'd counted on reasonable, honorable men like him—which were in short command. Moreover, the distrust and suspicion that Boyd had heaped on him for being "English" had followed him to England, where he was considered "Scottish."

She'd sensed Alex's frustration and had hoped to plant the idea to return. But she'd been a little heavy-handed with the seed, and now she feared she might have given herself away.

If he thought her sympathetic to Bruce, how long would it take him to connect her to the person feeding the "rebels" information? Perhaps he'd made the connection already. He'd been acting so strangely and purposefully evading her questions.

What a mess. The situation had become unbearable. She cared about him too much to continue to lie to him. But did she trust him with her life? Strangely, despite his betrayal of her brethren, she did. Unfortunately, there was more to it than trust. Telling him the truth would put him in a horrible position. He'd be forced to decide between her and his honor and duty. She didn't want to do that to him yet. Not until she was sure there was no other way.

But what did he know?

She'd followed him to Pembroke's solar to find out. As she could hardly listen at the door in the hallway, she gave proof to her spectral war name and passed through the wall like a ghost—or in this case, through the neighboring chamber with the unlocked door. She'd done this countless times before, but spying on Alex was different.

Though most of the castle was at the evening meal, just to be safe she hid behind the heavy tapestry that covered most of the wall. The partition was wood, but as it had been plastered, it muffled their voices enough to prevent her from hearing the entire conversation. But she heard enough to know that if Alex knew something, he had not passed it on to the earl. She also heard that he was being sent away, and that caused a surprisingly hard pang in her chest.

She was growing too attached. But how could she stop it?

She left the room not long after she heard him leave.

When she was sure there was no one coming, she made her way down the tower stairwell and out into the yard.

She glanced around, scanning the area, and her heart slammed into her chest. The air in her lungs turned so hot and acrid it hurt to breathe.

It hurt all over.

She hadn't waited long enough. Alex stood about fifty feet away near the entry to the chapel. She stepped behind the corner of the building, but she needn't have worried about him noticing her. He had his arms around a woman and was lifting her off her feet. When he started to spin her around and knocked off her hood, Joan could see that it wasn't just *a* woman, but one of the most beautiful women she'd ever seen in her life.

∞

Rosalin Clifford now Boyd was still laughing when Alex gave her one last squeeze and set her back down on her feet. He couldn't remember the last time he was so shocked to see someone. Shocked and very happy. She reminded him of . . .

He stopped the thought. His old life was over.

She reached up and put a hand on his cheek. "Oh, Alex, it's so good to see you. I've missed you."

He took her hand and brought it to his mouth. "And I've missed you, too, lass."

Suddenly, their location was brought back to him. They weren't in Scotland, they were in the middle of a castle full of English soldiers, and she was the wife of one of the most hated men in England.

Perhaps his darkening countenance reminded her as well, for she hastily adjusted her hood back over her head, hiding her remarkable features. Rosalin was one of the most beautiful women on either side of the border—a face like hers would not go unnoticed.

He cursed. She'd heard worse from him and didn't seem to pay it any mind. "God's wounds, Rosalin. What the hell are you doing here?"

She wrinkled her nose as if annoyed by the question and the tone in which it had been asked. "Lower your voice. We are drawing enough attention as it is."

He swore again and looked around. There were a handful of soldiers in the area, most of whom were looking at them curiously—and a few (who must have seen her face) enviously.

"Who is the woman?" Rosalin asked.

Alex frowned. "What woman?"

Rosalin looked around. "She was standing by the Constable Tower but she must have left. From the way she was looking at you, I assumed you knew her. Very pretty—sultry looking—dark haired." She frowned. "She looked familiar."

Alex swore again. Christ, Joan must have seen him. Sultry looking. He'd have to remember that—it fit.

"My betrothed," he said. He was going to have some explaining to do to Joan later. But first, he had to deal with the more pressing problem.

Taking advantage of Rosalin's shock at his announcement and noting the nearby chapel, he pulled her inside. Fortunately, it was empty.

"You are betrothed? Oh, Alex, I'm so happy for you. Do I know her? What is her name?"

"Later," Alex said. He folded his arms across his chest and gave her a look that warned her not to lie to him. "Does your husband know you are here?"

She bit her lip, having the good sense to look chagrined. "Not exactly."

Alex exploded, letting off a string of blasphemies and curse words that would have made MacRuairi proud. But his anger turned to something else entirely when she pulled back her hood again and unintentionally revealed something else—something he probably should have noticed when he was hugging her.

His face drained. "Good God, don't tell me you are with child?"

She made a face that involved a pursed mouth of distaste and a frown of displeasure. "Very well, I won't."

"Christ, you are!" he said incredulously. "Raider is going to kill—" He almost said "me," he was so damned used to being the source of blame, but he had nothing to do with this, which didn't explain how he somehow felt responsible. "You," he finished.

She didn't seem worried and shrugged. "I have every right to be here. Robbie and I have an agreement."

His eyes narrowed with suspicion. "What kind of agreement?"

"That I could come see my brother whenever I wished."

"I'm sure he didn't mean for you to come on your own with the entire English army camped nearby. Bloody hell, the king is here. There are soldiers everywhere."

The bite on her lip deepened. Funny, Joan did the same thing, but when Rosalin did it, he wasn't distracted at all.

"He is?" She may have winced with a little bit of shame. "I didn't realize, but it wouldn't have made a difference. I needed to see Cliff."

She was referring to her brother, Lord Robert Clifford, one of the highest ranking of Edward's barons and a longtime enemy of her husband's. Alex had no idea what she'd done to work out a truce between those two—hell, maybe he should have had her try to talk some sense into King Edward.

"And it couldn't wait?" he asked.

She shook her head, her expression suddenly despondent. "I had to see him before he left. I don't know how to explain it—it's just a feeling . . ."

Alex's mouth fell in a grim line. He didn't believe in premonitions, but he would not argue with one. "Have you seen him yet?"

She shook her head. "I was on my way to his rooms when I saw you. But I guess it was a good thing I did, as I suspect his rooms may have moved."

Alex nodded. "He's in the Captain's Lodgings. Pembroke has his old rooms in the Constable Tower."

"Indeed a very good thing, then. Sir Aymer would recognize me quite easily."

"I will take you to Clifford—and then I will take you back to wherever it is you came from."

"That isn't necessary—"

He held up his hand to stop her. "Don't bother arguing. Your husband already has a sword out there with my name on it, I will not give him another. And it would be deserved if I let you walk out of here alone. How the hell did you get in here anyway?"

From the way she blushed, he figured he wasn't going to like it.

He didn't. He exploded again. "You came in with some of the women from town? You mean some of the whores who make their rounds in the barracks?" He raked his fingers through his hair. This was just getting worse and worse. "And what if one of the men was 'interested'?"

"I just pretended to be with the women to get through the gate, and I have men waiting for me nearby."

Alex made a sound that was more of a snort. "As if they would have been any good to you in here."

"If you take me to them when I am done, they will see me safely back."

He started to ask back to where, but stopped himself. She must have understood why. When their eyes met, he could see the sadness in the realization that they were on opposite sides now.

He nodded. He would be able to return her to Boyd's men without too much of a detour from the route he would take with his men to Hailes.

"Now, tell me about this woman you are to marry. Do you love her?"

He winced, suspecting he was the one blushing now. "Christ, what a thing to ask, Rosalin."

"You do!" she exclaimed happily, throwing her arms around him again. "Oh, Alex, I'm so happy for you. Does she love you? Of course, she must. You are one of the most wonderful men I know. The quintessential perfect, handsome knight. Sir Galahad to the rescue," she said with a laugh.

Not her, too? Is that what everyone thought of him? Christ, how embarrassing. Not to mention untrue. It made him feel like some kind of fraud.

He extracted himself, uncomfortably going back to the question. Did he love her? He'd never put words on it, but aye, he did. And did she feel the same about him? He didn't know. She *liked* him, which was enough for now. "It wasn't like that."

"It was arranged by the families?"

"Not exactly." More like it was arranged by him and ordered by the king.

She stared at him for a long time. "No . . . you didn't?" She laughed, clapping her hands. "You did! I can't believe it. Maybe not Sir Galahad after all."

Now he was really uncomfortable. How the hell had she guessed? Did he have debaucher of innocents—he stopped, not letting himself think about *that*—branded on his forehead? "Let's just say I have a little more sympathy for your husband."

Though he said it lightly, the sentiments behind it were not. She knew the reasons for his leaving, including what he thought had been Boyd taking advantage of her when she was their hostage. Boyd had been wrong. But Alex had been wrong to think that forgetting his honor in the arms of a woman he loved was a sin that would never be laid at his feet. A sin that might be more complicated than it first appeared.

She put her hand on his arm. "I feel to blame for what happened. It wasn't his fault, Alex. I know you thought it was, but I wanted what happened as much as he did. I loved him to distraction. I still do. It was everything else I thought I couldn't live with."

Alex shook his head. "It wasn't you. As I told you then, it had been a long time in the working."

"But I know how hard it was for you. I was there—I saw what you were going through. I know Robbie is sorry for some of the things he did and wishes it could have been different."

"I very much doubt that," Alex said dryly.

"He does. You were like a brother to him, though he was too blinded by anger and vengeance to admit it. Maybe . . . do you ever think about going back?"

He wished he could say no. But he couldn't lie to himself. Every day he thought of what he'd given up. The challenges. The danger. The feeling as if he was part of something important. The camaraderie. Aye, most of all that. The Guardsmen had been the closest friends he'd ever had—even if it hadn't always felt like that. Walking away from them had been like walking away from part of himself. But he'd had to do it. He couldn't keep doing what he was doing. He just hoped to hell that in the end it would all be worth it.

"It hasn't been the same—Robbie hasn't been the same—since you left," she said, guessing his thoughts. "They need you, Alex."

Alex shook his head; she was wrong. "I saw them not long ago."

Her eyes widened in surprise. "When?"

He explained what had happened with the little girl and how he'd been surrounded. "They let me go, but your husband was very clear about what would happen the next time we met." He shook his head. "Nay, there is no going back."

"You are sure?"

He smiled; that was the second time he'd been asked that today. "I am."

"I suppose it would be difficult to explain to your new wife," Rosalin said with a smile that was just as sad as his. "She is probably from some illustrious English family."

Alex grimaced. He hadn't been holding back her name intentionally, but he hadn't volunteered it either. "Not exactly."

She lifted a brow. When he finally said her name, Rosalin gasped. Then she paled. "Bella's daughter? I knew she looked familiar. Good God, Alex, you can't marry her!

It isn't my husband's sword you will need to worry about, it's Lachlan's dagger. He'll kill you when he finds out."

It wasn't the first time the thought had occurred to him. "Why should MacRuairi care? He barely knows her."

An odd look crossed her face. "That won't matter. She's family, and he won't have her—" She stopped, embarrassed.

"Married to a traitor?" Alex said tightly.

Roslin nodded apologetically.

"Aye, well, we can't always pick our relatives. I'm sure Boyd has expressed similar opinions."

She laughed at that. "Maybe once or twice."

"Let's go find your brother. I wager he's going to have something to say about this as well."

Alex was right. Initially Clifford was just as happy to see her as Alex had been, but when he realized what she'd done, he'd been even more furious.

Alex left her with her brother with a promise to return in the morning and went in search of Joan.

But for the first time, he wasn't looking forward to it. He hoped Rosalin had been wrong that Joan had seen them. He didn't want to lie to her, but neither could he risk anyone knowing about Rosalin's presence in the castle.

After fleeing the courtyard, Joan had returned to her room and was helping Alice remove the pins from her hair when Bess arrived with the message that Alex was waiting downstairs and had requested to see her.

Alice waved Joan off. "Go, do not let your duties to me interfere. Besides, you have been as glum as a child staring in the window of a closed confectioner shop all evening. I hope it isn't a lovers' spat already?"

Actually, it sounded as if she hoped exactly the opposite.

"I'm tired," Joan said. "That is all. But I should see what he wants."

"Don't hurry back on my account," Alice said, sounding very sorry for herself. "One of us should have some fun tonight. Henry is in another one of his meetings."

That was the kind of information Joan should be focusing on—not why Alex had his arms around Robbie Boyd's wife.

But she couldn't get the image out of her mind. They'd looked so perfect together. The handsome, gallant knight and the beautiful "fair" maiden. With her blond hair, delicate complexion, and princess-perfect features, she looked to be in the first blush of womanhood and as innocent as an angel. It couldn't have been more brutally—or cruelly— brought home to Joan that *this* was the kind of woman Alex was meant to wed. The perfect English rose. The Fair Rosalin.

Once the initial stab of pain had relented, it hadn't taken Joan long to recognize the woman reputed to be one of the most beautiful in England. They had crossed paths from a distance a few times in the past at court in London when Joan had still been living with the Despensers. Joan had been as surprised as everyone else to hear that Rosalin Clifford had been taken hostage by one of the most notorious and hated Scotsmen in England, the Devil's Enforcer, Robbie Boyd. But unlike everyone else, Joan knew the truth that Rosalin hadn't been forced to wed Boyd, she'd wanted to.

So why was Rosalin here? And what, if anything, did it have to do with Alex?

Joan didn't need to be one of the best spies in England to know that Rosalin meant something to Alex—it had been as clear as day on his face.

What had surprised her was how much that meant to her. She'd been jealous and scared. Scared that she would lose him, scared that he would hold her up against this other woman and wonder what he'd been thinking, scared that she'd allowed herself to get too close, and most of all scared that it might be too late to do anything about it.

She had to try to pull away, while she still could. *Focus*.

He was waiting for her in the entry hall. The boyish smile that curved his lips when he turned and saw her cut like a knife through her heart. It seemed a taunt of everything she wanted that wasn't hers even if it seemed to be. It was all pretend. A glass house of illusions that could be shattered at any moment.

She forced herself not to show her hurt. To keep her expression cool and serene. "You wished to see me, my lord?"

He frowned a little at her polite tone. "Aye, I'm afraid I have something I must attend to at my lands in East Lothian. That is the reason Pembroke wished to see me. I should only be gone for a few days, but I must leave first thing tomorrow."

"I hope it is nothing too serious, my lord."

"As do I," he said, although he didn't sound convinced.

She could not hide all her emotions, it seemed, as her voice came out worried and entreating. "You will be careful?"

He smiled. "I will endeavor to return to you exactly as I have left you."

She returned his smile, appreciating the attempt at humor even if the idea of him being hurt made all those emotions she was trying to hide stir like a tempest. "Then I will wish you a safe journey, my lord, and see you upon your return."

She gave a short nod and would have turned away had

he not caught her. The feel of his hand on her arm made every nerve ending jump with awareness. She could feel his heat, smell the now-familiar scent of sandalwood soap, and the sensations raced through her blood in a hot rush, weakening her knees—and her resolve.

"I thought I saw you earlier," he said.

She gave no indication that the words had made her heart start to bang. "You did?"

"Aye, by the Constable Tower. Were you looking for me?"

"I may have been on my way to the chapel at the time."

He studied her face. Looking for some kind of sign of deception, perhaps? "I ran into an old friend."

"You did?"

Maybe she wasn't as good at hiding her feelings as she thought, because he nodded as if he knew she was lying and was trying to apologize. "A woman who is like a sister to me."

"You need not explain."

"I just didn't want there to be any misunderstanding."

"There isn't."

"It's just that it's . . . complicated."

He said it with a smile, but the easy humor of before seemed forced. Lies, deceptions, and half-truths had a way of doing that—she should know.

She could have let it go at that. But something provoked her to push—to test. Did he trust her enough to tell her the truth? "Who is she? Perhaps I will cross paths with her when you are gone."

Had she not been looking for the hesitation, she would have missed it. But if he considered telling her the truth, he decided against it. "No one you would know. But I'm afraid she was only here briefly and has already gone."

Joan looked him right in the eye and saw no signs of

deception. For someone who despised lying, he did it well. "How disappointing."

It was. Now she wasn't the only liar between them.

17

WITH ALEX GONE, Joan turned to her duties with renewed determination and focus. The date set by Edward Bruce and the commander at Stirling Castle for the English to relieve the garrison was less than two weeks away. King Edward would have to leave in the next week if he was going to make it in time. It would take at least a week of marching—maybe more—for the army to reach Stirling from Berwick.

So instead of wondering what Alex was doing, prevaricating over every word of their conversation, and thinking about what else he would do for Rosalin Boyd if he cared about her enough to lie for her, Joan concentrated on her cousin. Or more accurately, on her cousin and her husband. But Alice and Sir Henry proved surprisingly unhelpful and unusually closemouthed.

She didn't think they suspected anything, but she couldn't be sure. More likely it was merely a result of the increased effort by the king to find the spy and the tightening of information as the war drew near. But she couldn't shake the sense of disquiet.

Disquiet that only increased when she went to town to send a message to Lachlan that she needed to speak to him (not only to warn him about the betrothal but to start building the bridge that might allow Alex to return) and had the distinct feeling of someone following her. When she returned to the castle and saw a few of Despenser's men pass through the gate a short while after, she felt the first chill of fear.

She cursed herself again for the mistake she'd made with Sir Hugh. She never should have targeted him in the first place, but to make him feel a fool by appearing to discard him for Alex . . . that had not been smart.

He was a dangerous enemy out for blood, as she'd seen in his expression when he'd congratulated her on her engagement on the day of the hawking excursion. She'd dismissed the chill that had raced through her then, but now seeing his men . . . it didn't feel like a coincidence.

She knew she had to be careful—very careful.

There was one piece of good news. Upon returning to her chamber, Joan learned from Alice that Sir Hugh the elder had arrived with some additional men from Wales. Her former guardian had always been kind to her and had even tried to stand up for her with the king when Sir Henry first raised doubts as to her paternity. She would never forget the show of loyalty, and it was with true fondness that she returned his big hug at the midday meal under the watchful glare of his son beside him.

Before letting her go, the older man insisted that she come to his rooms later that evening (once he'd seen to his duties to the king) where she could tell him everything that she'd been doing since he'd seen her last, "including more about this knight who has won your hand."

She ignored the younger Sir Hugh's comment that from what he'd heard, she'd been "*doing* quite a lot," and promised the older knight to see him later.

With the queen's arrival, she and her bevy of ladies-in-waiting had taken over the higher tables, so Joan retreated to a trestle table farther away from the dais to join her cousin Margaret among some of Sir Henry's household knights.

She was only a few feet away when she stopped mid-step and gasped. The color leeched from her face as every ounce of blood in her body crashed to the floor. She had to grab hold of the edge of one of the tables to prevent her legs from collapsing.

Oh God, it couldn't be.

"Is something wrong, my lady? You look as if you've seen a ghost."

One of Sir Henry's men—Sir Bertram, she thought his name—must have seen her sway and had come to her rescue, offering her a steady arm to hold on to. She took it, not only for the solidity but also to block the person she'd seen from her view.

Only then did the shock dissipate enough for her to respond. Nay, not a ghost (irony, that), though she wished he were—there was no one in the world she would like to see dead more than him. "I felt a little light-headed for a moment," she said with a wobbly smile to the young knight. "But I'm fine now."

"Are you sure?" Sir Bertram asked with obvious concern. "You are shaking and your hand is as cold as ice."

Realizing that people were beginning to stare, she

forced a calm, serene mask to her face that she did not feel. "Perhaps a glass of wine would help."

Sir Bertram immediately jumped to do her bidding, leading her to the table and ordering one of the serving girls to bring the lady some wine.

Somehow Joan made it through the meal. She evaded her cousin's questioning glances and laughed and jested with the rest of the table as if nothing were amiss. But the cold sweat on her forehead and chill in her bones told differently. She was painfully aware of the powerful knight in Despenser arms seated not twenty feet away. *Let me go . . .* She could still feel his weight on her pinning her down as she struggled.

Though Sir Phillip Gifford had merely been a squire the last time she'd seen him, she would never forget the man who'd raped her.

When he'd been sent to Sir Hugh's lands in Wales four years ago, and she'd gone to live with Alice and Sir Henry, she'd thought to never see him again. But with the war and her being in such close proximity to the English leadership, she should have realized this could happen. She should have known. She should have been prepared.

But in truth, she feared nothing could have prepared her for seeing him again.

Alex. She felt his absence acutely. It wasn't that she needed his strength; it was as if his inherent goodness might somehow blot out the evil.

At the first opportunity, she excused herself to retire to her chamber where she could think and recover from the shock in private. Margaret offered to accompany her, but Joan declined—not ready to answer the inevitable questions.

She realized the hastiness of her decision a few

moments later when her path to the door was blocked by a big, mail-clad warrior in a white surcoat with the familiar black, yellow, and red arms.

Her heart pounded. She didn't need to look up to see the handsome features, golden-blond hair, and brilliant green eyes to recognize him. Recognition was visceral. She felt it in the disgust that crawled over her skin and the revulsion that slithered down her spine in a shiver. And if that weren't enough, the smell would do it. For months she hadn't been able to get his scent out of her nose or his taste out of her mouth. Brandy and licorice. Two things that she used to find pleasant, but after made her want to retch.

"Leaving without saying hello?" he said in that low, taunting voice that she'd once found so charming.

Now it made her stiffen. Every muscle in her body turned rigid and hard as steel.

She looked up, meeting the amused gaze of the man who at one time had seemed to be everything she'd ever dreamed of.

He was undoubtedly handsome, but now she realized he was just a pale imitation of the man she'd seen all those years ago and unconsciously tried to replicate: Alex. But compared to Alex, Phillip came up short in every respect. Most significantly in the color of his soul.

He wasn't as tall as she remembered, although he was considerably broader in the chest and shoulders. Most of it seemed to be muscle, but the belt around his surcoat cinched a gut that she suspected would tend toward portliness in a few years.

He still favored the short beard and longer hair that were popular among the nobility—although he wasn't. He was the son of a minor baron who with a lucky arrow had saved his lord from being attacked by a boar and earned his son a place in Sir Hugh's household. Joan's rank had been part of her appeal, and when it was gone, Phillip had lost use for her, but she'd been too much of a fool to see it until too late.

But she wasn't a fool now. She was no longer fifteen and trusting. She was no longer innocent and naive. He'd seen to that.

Her heart was now pounding in her ears and the shock that had weakened her limbs before was forgotten in the hot rush of anger and hatred that raced through her blood. Her instincts had changed, she realized. *She* had changed. She was no longer weak and helpless. She no longer cowered, rather she wanted to slip her blade from the scabbard at her waist and plunge it between his ribs.

Almost as if he knew what she was thinking, he took a small step back and frowned.

"Get out of my way," she said, clenching her fists into balls at her sides. "I have nothing to say to you."

He looked around as if concerned that someone might have heard. But they were well enough away from the tables—he'd seen to that—and the room was loud with its boisterous occupants.

"There is no cause to be impolite. We are old friends, are we not?"

The charming twinkle in his eyes and lazy grin that were probably fooling anyone watching them now seemed slimy to her. "We are not."

His gaze hardened almost imperceptibly. "From what I hear, you are quite friendly. So there is no use playing the frigid maid with me." He smiled again, with the glint of cruelty she would never forget. "Besides, I know differently." He gave her a long, slow look that made her skin crawl and leaned in to whisper. "Perhaps I should remind you later?"

He'd obviously heard of her reputation.

She held herself completely still. It took everything she had not to react, not to show him exactly how repugnant his "offer" was to her. Her body shook from the effort as she looked him in the eye and said very slowly, "I am no longer a helpless fifteen-year-old girl to be forced by a common brute." His gaze flared, she presumed at the word "common." "Unless you want everyone in this room to know exactly what you are, you will step aside and not come near me again."

His expression darkened. She'd angered him. Good. But he did not doubt her word. With a dramatic flourish, he bowed and stepped aside to let her pass. She held her back straight and strode calmly out of the Hall, not running until she reached the courtyard.

It was just after dark by the time Alex and his men rode across the wooden drawbridge. Fortunately, they'd made it just before the night bell and the porter locked the castle gates.

After dismounting, Alex pulled off his helm and gave it to his squire. He would have normally handed off his horse as well, but as the lad looked about ready to keel over with exhaustion, Alex led the palfrey to the stable himself.

He, too, was physically and mentally exhausted, as well as pushed to the breaking point by frustration and angry enough to kill someone—preferably the arse in charge at Hailes—but he'd driven his men hard to make it back tonight. He couldn't shake the feeling that something had been wrong with Joan, and with the shite heap of trouble that he'd just gone through in East Lothian, he needed to know that not all of his life had gone to hell.

He raked his fingers through his helm-plastered hair. *Christ, I need some sleep.* But it would have to wait. He needed to make his report to Pembroke. It was going to take everything he had not to let him see exactly what he thought of the English "lordship" in Scotland.

The garrison commander hadn't been so lucky. Sir Raoul had narrowly escaped with his life for what he'd done.

Damn it, this wasn't supposed to happen. He'd come over to the English to *prevent* things like this from happening. Alex's hand might not have been the one to light the fire, but innocent lives of people he was responsible for had been lost all the same.

The situation had been even worse than Alex anticipated. He should have known Pembroke's information would be skewed. He'd gotten the full story from his mother and Sir Alan Murray, a trusted captain of Alex's father who'd kept charge of their lands for as long as Alex could remember.

Alex's tenants had indeed supplied victuals to the castle soldiers, who'd in turn promised to protect them from Bruce's raiders. But they didn't. When Bruce's men had come, the bloody English cowards had refused to leave the protection of the castle walls to come to the farmers' aid. That hadn't stopped the castle soldiers from coming for more supplies later, however. When the farmers understandably refused—they had little left and even less inclination after being left in the lurch by English "lordship"—the English commander had raided their farms and villages, killing two men who'd been trying to free animals from a burning barn when it had collapsed on them.

Alex had left the English commander in no doubt of

what would happen if he ever did something like that again. He would also take the matter to the king, but he wasn't going to count on Edward to do what was right. Even if Alex could convince him of the unjustness of the situation—which was unlikely—he knew the king was too focused on the war to worry about a few farmers in Scotland, even if it was his duty as overlord and king. So Alex had been forced to take on the role of enforcer. It was ironic, given how much he'd hated it when his former partner, Boyd, had done the same.

Protecting the people in the Borders was what had driven Alex to the English, but he'd been unable to keep his own people safe from *English* raids. They were on the same side, damn it. Was this the kind of overlordship and protection King Edward intended for his Scottish subjects?

The last thing Alex needed on leaving the stables after seeing to his mount was to nearly run into Sir Hugh Despenser—a visibly sotted Sir Hugh Despenser—and a few of his toadies.

"Back already, Seton?" he said with a snide grin. "I see you learned from my mistake. But from what I saw earlier, I fear you may be too late. The lass works quickly, I'll give her that."

A few of the men with him chuckled. Alex stiffened, but in no other way reacted to the bastard's taunts. He didn't need to ask what Despenser meant; it was obvious he was trying to goad Alex into a fight by slighting Joan.

But Alex didn't for one minute put any store into what he'd alluded to. Joan cared for him. She'd accepted his proposal. Reluctantly maybe at first, but she'd come around. She wouldn't turn her sights on anyone else.

If thoughts of the past intruded for a moment, he pushed them away. He wasn't going to let Despenser get to him.

Ignoring the other men, Alex started to walk away. He

was headed toward Pembroke's rooms, but Despenser mistook his direction.

"You won't find her in de Beaumont's rooms," he taunted with a laugh. "The last time I saw her she was with my father. But I doubt she's there now. She's probably renewing old acquaintances with one of his men. They were supposed to be quite in love a few years back, as I recall. They made quite a scene cavorting at the midday meal today, didn't they, lads?"

The other men snickered and hooted like puppets on a string. Alex wanted nothing more than to put his fist through Despenser's malicious grin, but he wouldn't give the lies credence. He was sure there was an explanation.

But what the hell did he mean by "in love"?

Alex walked away; they didn't try to stop him again. Instead of heading to Pembroke's room as he should, he headed for Joan's. He knew he wouldn't be able to concentrate on a damned thing until he saw her. He was sure she would clear up whatever misapprehension Despenser was operating under in a few minutes.

But "in love"? Christ, the very idea made him twist with uncertainty and left his chest feeling as if it had been opened up and acid poured inside.

A few minutes later, he stood outside her cousin's door. *This is silly,* he told himself. Still, he knocked.

He heard voices inside and a moment later the door was cracked open a few inches by a young serving girl. "I'm sorry to disturb you so late," Alex said. "But there is something I must speak with Lady Joan about."

She looked worried. "She's not here, my lord."

"Who is it?" he heard Lady Alice demand from inside the room.

The girl looked to him.

"Sir Alexander Seton," he replied to the silent question.

The girl relayed his name to Alice, and then added, "He's looking for Lady Joan, my lady."

"Tell him she's not here. She's gone off somewhere again. She always disappears at the most inconvenient time."

The young serving girl's look of worry and anxiousness increased. "I'd best get back, my lord. I'm curling her hair with hot tongs, and I'm afraid I'm not nearly as good as Lady Joan."

Inconvenient indeed, Alex thought. He was glad Joan was nothing like her cousin, but he understood the barely opened door.

"I'm sorry to have disturbed you," he said again, and left.

He should have gone to Pembroke's at that point. But he didn't. He waited and waited at the bottom of the tower until the pitying looks from the guard on watch outside the door proved too much.

To hell with this. It had been a long time since he'd put his Highland Guard skills to use, but he still remembered what to do.

∞

Joan paused outside the door to Alice's chamber and turned to her cousin. "Thank you for insisting on accompanying me tonight."

Margaret grinned. "It was my pleasure. I'm not normally so pushy, but after what happened earlier, I did not want you to have to face that horrible man again—at least not alone. I'm just glad he was smart enough not to show his face; I don't think I would have been able to feign politeness."

Joan was glad Sir Phillip had stayed away as well. More than glad. Her cousin wouldn't have been the only one to find it difficult to feign politeness, and Joan didn't think her former guardian would have been as satisfied by the explanation as Margaret had been.

Joan had told her the truth—that she'd thought herself in love with him and he'd betrayed her—but omitted the specifics of that betrayal. Margaret had been content with the explanation that he'd lost interest when Joan had been disinherited.

"You, not pushy? Since when?" Joan laughed. "But seriously, I am thankful for the company. It was a delightful night."

"It was," Margaret agreed. "And fruitful."

They exchanged glances. Sir Hugh had been partaking freely of the brandy and had confirmed what they'd already guessed: the earls of Lancaster, Warwick, Lincoln, Arundel, and Warenne had refused to answer the king's call. Edward was understandably furious; Bruce on the other hand would be thrilled.

Joan met her cousin's gaze. "You are being careful, remember? I will take care of this."

Margaret nodded, but then looked at her worriedly. "You will be careful, too?"

"Always."

They bid each other good night, and Joan entered the darkened room without knocking. It was close to midnight, and Alice was likely sleeping. She didn't want to take the chance of waking her; her cousin was at her most unpleasant when roused from sleep (and that was saying something!).

A candle had been left burning, however, enabling her to immediately make out the empty bed. Sir Henry must have sent for his wife tonight. A fact that was confirmed a moment later when Bess lifted her sleepy head from the cushioned bench in the alcove near the window.

"I thought it best to wait for her," the girl said, explaining her presence in the room. "In case she returns."

"She won't be back until morning," Joan said. "But I can take care of her if she comes back earlier. You are safe to find your own bed in the garret."

Bess looked relieved. After the bracelet debacle, the girl was understandably terrified of upsetting Alice. "Thank you, my lady. But I will help you with your gown first."

She picked up the candle and they crossed the room to Joan's chamber. After opening the door, Bess set the candle on the small table by the bed and started to work the ties of Joan's gown.

"Oh, my lady, I forgot to mention. You had a visitor earlier," Bess said, pulling the tight sleeves of her gown down her arms.

"I did?"

"Aye." She helped her out of the overgown. The undergown came next. "Lady Alice said he was your betrothed."

She couldn't keep the excitement from her voice. "Alex is back?"

The girl nodded, handing her the velvet robe that she wore over her chemise at night. "He seemed anxious to see you."

Joan wrapped the robe around her and tied it at the waist, aware that she was smiling like a well-fed cat.

Good grief, just hearing that he was anxious to see her made her happy. But she was also relieved that he was back safely.

She was about to ask if he had said anything else, when she glanced over at the shutter and noticed that the wooden crossbar that secured it had not been pulled down all the way into the iron fittings.

Joan was in awe. How had he done it? This window was even less accessible than the one at Carlisle.

Another mistake? She couldn't believe that Lachlan would be so careless—and that she should be so lucky.

Her pulse quickened, eager to be rid of her company. "Thank you, Bess. I can finish the rest myself. You must be exhausted."

The girl gave her a quick bob. "Thank you, my lady. I will see you in the morning."

Joan's door closed, and a few moments later, the outer door closed as well. She turned to the ambry and pulled open the door. "That was fast, Fath—"

She stopped, shocked mute when Alex—not Lachlan—slipped out of the darkness. His expression was so dark it almost didn't look like him. When she managed to find her tongue, the word came out as a question. "Alex?"

"Expecting someone else?"

She hoped the room was too dark for him to see her face pale.

But the lapse was only momentary; she quickly got herself back under control and responded without hesitation. The ability to think of a lie quickly was one of the things that had made her so successful—although it wasn't anything to be proud about under the circumstances.

"Aye, I did," she said calmly. "I thought you were Fiona."

He looked at her quizzically.

"The girl that keeps the brazier lit for Alice at night," she explained. "It's a game we play. She likes to hide and try to scare me."

The lies that fell so easily from her tongue filled her with shame. God, she hated this. What once she'd not given much thought to now made her want to squirm.

Alex frowned. Not wanting to let him think too long—or ask any questions about a girl who didn't exist—she used another tactic: making him be the one to hold up the shield and not her.

"I think I'm the one who should be asking the

questions. What are you doing in my room, Alex? Spying on me while I undress?"

The tactic worked. Some of the darkness in his expression was replaced by sheepishness. From the way his gaze seemed to be avoiding anything below her neck, it was very clear that she was not the only one aware of her reduced state of clothing.

"I needed to see you. I've been waiting for hours. Christ, it must be midnight. Where the hell have you been?"

Joan's eyes widened at his tone and the blasphemy that seemed to surprise even him.

Good Lord, whatever was the matter with him?

Suddenly, she realized what was the matter. Realized what he thought. Realized what had caused him to lose his temper and blurt out the accusation. For that was exactly what it was. *He thinks I've been with another man.*

Given what he'd seen before, and what she'd let him think, maybe it was fair. Maybe it was reasonable under the circumstances.

But it still hurt. She'd thought—hoped—they were beyond that.

She arched a brow, giving no hint of the wound he'd just inflicted. "Where do you think I was?"

His mouth turned white around the edges and his face darkened. "Just answer the question, Joan."

She was tempted to tell him to go to Hades and let him think what he wanted. But she could see his torment and would not add to it just to salve her hurt.

"I was with my former guardian. Sir Hugh arrived at the castle earlier and invited me to his rooms so I could fill him in on what has happened since I've seen him last. We lost track of time. I didn't realize it was so late."

"And you were with him all this time?"

"I was," she answered. "You can ask my cousin if you don't believe me. Margaret was with us all evening." But she sensed something more behind the question. "What is this about, Alex? Why are you sneaking into my room in the middle of the night, hurling baseless accusations as if I've done something wrong?"

He raked his fingers through his hair in frustration, and for the first time she could see the lines of exhaustion on his face. From the dust and dirt on his surcoat and armor, she realized he'd probably come straight here after returning. Why such haste?

The question was answered a moment later.

"Because I rode back anxious to see my betrothed only to have the first thing I hear be that she was seen cavorting with another man."

She held his gaze. "And you believed this?" She took a step closer, smelling the leather and horse and the hint of sweat that was oddly intoxicating. "After what happened between us, do you really think I could share intimacies like that with someone else?"

He winced with shame. "No, yes, hell I didn't want to. But Despenser sounded pretty damned convincing. He said you knew this man."

"Sir Hugh?" she repeated incredulously. "Of course he has no reason to lie?"

He paused. "Despenser said you were once in love with this man. And then you were gone so late . . ."

Joan bristled. *Sir Phillip*. That was what this was about. Alex was jealous of the man who'd raped her. She would laugh if she didn't feel so much like crying.

God, if he only knew how wrong he was.

"Sir Hugh is feeding you lies, Alex. There is a knight who arrived with his father whom I knew as a girl, but I can assure you I want nothing to do with him. Which is exactly what I told him when he sought me out at the midday meal."

His eyes scanned her face, presumably for signs of untruth. "Then you did not love him?"

"I have only been in love with one man in my life, and I can assure you it is *not* Sir Phillip Gifford."

Her words didn't seem to mollify him; indeed they seemed to anger him. "Then who is it?"

She stared at him for a moment, shook her head, and laughed.

He scowled angrily. "I don't see anything amusing. I asked you a damned question."

Still laughing, she put her hand on his cheek soothingly. "*You*, Alex. I meant you."

18

ALEX STARED AT her dumbfounded. "You meant me?" She smiled so sweetly he thought his heart might break from overfilling. "Aye. Whatever else the future holds, you can trust that."

He was too stunned by her declaration to pay any mind to the odd warning of her words. She loved him?

God, he was an idiot. The luckiest damned idiot in the world. "I'm sorry. I've acted like a complete arse, haven't I?"

Her mouth twisted. "Maybe not *complete*. Although next time you climb a tower and crawl through a window, it might be easier to remove your mail first." She shook her head. "I should have liked to see you squeezing through that."

"It wasn't easy," he said wryly. He looked down into her beautiful upturned face and felt his heart swell all over again. "I've no excuse other than that I was out of my mind with jealousy at the thought that you might love someone else, when I am completely, thoroughly, and even more out of my mind in love with you."

She smiled back at him, eyes shining with happiness. "I'm glad to hear it."

He cocked a brow. "But not surprised?"

She gave him a distinctly female shrug. "I hoped that you might after what you confided in me. You've kept that vow an awful long time."

"Believe me, I know."

She laughed at his tone, but then sobered. "Still, I wasn't sure after . . ."

Her voice fell off, and he cursed inwardly, knowing what she'd been about to say. "She's an old friend, Joan. Nothing more."

"I know that's what you said."

"It's the truth." He thought for a moment and realized no harm could come from telling her now. "She's married to someone I once considered a close friend. She was here in secret visiting her brother, and I didn't want to say anything that might put her in jeopardy. You have probably heard her name mentioned before: it's Rosalin Boyd."

She didn't look surprised. Actually she looked *more* distressed. "You don't need to tell me this, Alex."

She tried to turn away, but he caught her chin and forced her gaze back to his. His finger swept the velvety curve of her cheek. "Yes, I do. I want there to be no secrets between us."

Now she looked pained.

"Did I say something wrong?" he asked.

She shook her head. "Nay, what you said is perfect. Too perfect."

He was having trouble following her logic. "Good. Then in case I wasn't clear, I love you, and only you."

Her eyes were luminous and shimmery—he hoped with emotion—as they looked into his. And her mouth . . . it was too damned inviting. Unable to help himself, he lowered his lips to hers and gave proof to his words with a slow, tender kiss.

God, her mouth was like honey. So soft and sweet and irresistible. He had to pull back before he sank in deeper.

But everything seemed to be conspiring against him. The bed that was right behind her was also too inviting—as was her very-easy-to-remove night robe. He tried to step back, but the room was too small, and it wasn't enough to break the invisible current pulling them together.

But he'd made a vow, damn it. Not until they were married. "I should go," he said firmly to remind himself.

He even managed a half-turn, before she caught his arm. "Nay, please. Won't you stay?"

As if it were the most natural thing in the world—which it was—she sidled up to him and curled against his chest as if she belonged there—which she did.

He would have had to be made of stone to resist the urge to put his arms around her. He wasn't—made of stone, that is, although part of him sure as hell felt that way.

He drew her closer, savoring the sensations as her body

melted into his. "You make it hard to do the right thing, sweetheart. I made a vow."

"And you can make another one," she said, moving her hands from his shoulders down his stomach to his belt. "Once I'm done with you."

"I should bathe—I've been riding all day."

She gave him a naughty smile. "Nice try, but you smell fine. And I suspect we'll both be a little sweaty soon."

Ah hell. Alex was done arguing. It was just making him hotter when she talked like that. He could feel the tug at his waist right before she succeeded in unbuckling his belt. He gave up the pretense of fighting it and tore off his surcoat. She was as efficient as any squire at helping him remove the heavy mail shirt and the padded linen aketon underneath. Only then did she hesitate—letting him see that she wasn't quite as confident as she appeared—but it wasn't for long. A moment later, his linen shirt was on the bed behind them and his chest was bare. She was quiet for a long time as she seemed to take in every inch of skin and muscle. Her gaze was soft with desire when her eyes finally met his. "I'm afraid I have to warn you that I might not be done with you for quite some time."

He swelled hot and hard at her words. God, he couldn't wait to be inside her. He reached down, unfastened the tie at her waist, and eased the velvet robe off her shoulders until it fell in a pool of crimson at her feet. "That's good to hear," he said. "But I think I'm giving up all vows but one when it comes to you."

She gave him a questioning look as her fingers trailed up and down the bands of his stomach. He had to grit his teeth against the urge to surge in her hand. But she appeared to have no idea of the torture she was exacting on him.

"And what vow is that?" she asked softly.

He swept her off her feet and carried her to the bed. "To love, honor, and cherish until death do us part."

∞

Marriage vows. He really was something out of an old tale. Joan knew she was a fool to let herself be this happy. That she was playing a game against time she could not win. That the love Alex felt for her might not survive the betrayal he was going to feel when he learned the truth. But she was going to live in this fool's paradise for as long as she could and hold on to every precious second.

The sense of borrowed time made her bold and forward. Although she'd been playing a wanton for so long, perhaps some of it had rubbed off, she thought with a smile. But they might not have another opportunity like this before he left, and she wasn't going to waste it. That he hadn't needed as much persuasion as she feared made her think that he might be feeling the same way.

No regrets. At least not about this. Others could not be avoided.

"I want there to be no secrets between us."

When he'd told her the truth about Rosalin, she'd been stabbed by such a deep knife of guilt she wanted to tell him the truth. If they were going to have a chance for a future, she knew she could not keep lying to him. As soon as she spoke to Lachlan, she would tell Alex the truth. Lachlan would undoubtedly argue (loudly) against it, but it was her decision.

And if she could convince Alex to turn . . .

God, maybe she was living in a fool's paradise.

All thoughts of the future, however, were lost when he gently laid her down on the bed and kissed her. Softly at first, and then as the passion ignited between them, harder and more insistently.

He was leaning over her, but not content with that, she pulled him down on top of her, wanting to feel his weight—and maybe something else. Even through his leather chausses she could feel the thick column of his manhood hard against her. Remembering how he'd feel inside her made her restless . . . anxious . . . impatient. It made her want to press herself against him and move.

She didn't realize she was already doing so until he pulled back and broke the kiss with a sharp, frustrated curse.

"What's wrong?" she asked in between gasps of air.

"Nothing, if you want this over in a few seconds. Otherwise, we're going to need to slow down." He gave her a wry smile. "You don't do much for increasing a man's stamina." His smile turned wicked. "I guess it's something we'll have to work on."

Joan wasn't completely sure she understood, but she had the gist. "I've never minded a little hard work."

He laughed. "Ah, love, you have no idea."

She looked down at the impressive bulge between them and said softly, "I think I do."

His eyes heated at the naughty innuendo. "Touch me again, sweetheart."

She did as he asked, reaching out to put her hand around the thick column straining against the leather.

His head fell back and his eyes closed with a groan at contact. But it wasn't enough for either of them. Their eyes met, and she knew what he wanted.

She started to work the straps of his chausses. He had

to help her remove them, but the linen braies underneath were much easier. Then there was nothing left between them.

God, he was . . . impressive. Thick and long, his manhood strained strong and hard against his stomach. It looked so red, though—and throbbing. "Does it hurt?" she asked, tentatively reaching out to trace her fingertip along the bulging vein that ran from root to tip.

He groaned again at her touch, seeming momentarily incapable of responding. His entire body seemed to be drawn up as tight as a bow. "Not in the way you think," he finally managed. "It's a good kind of hurt right now."

She nodded and then looked up at him. His eyes seemed to be burning with a low simmering heat. "Show me what to do," she said, her finger now circling the blunt tip of him. "I want to bring you pleasure."

"Everything you do brings me pleasure," he said in a— ironically—pained voice.

But he showed her. He took her hand and wrapped it around him, showing her how to stroke him.

She loved the feel of him. The thinnest, softest velvety skin over hot steel. But she loved even more what it did to him. The pleasure that overtook his face was something to behold. It made him look fierce and primitive and soft and gentle at the same time. She could feel the raw sensual energy reverberating in the air between them, and knowing that she was responsible, she was in control, was humbling.

She was just starting to get the hang of it when he stopped her. "No more," he said gruffly. "You are killing me."

"I take it that's a good thing?"

He gave her a decidedly wicked smile. "Why don't you tell me?"

He proceeded to show her exactly what he meant. Very methodically and very thoroughly. He exacted his sensual torture with his mouth, his tongue, and his hands, bringing her to the peak of pleasure before pulling away. Killing her. And it was definitely a good—a *wonderful*—thing.

First he tortured her breasts. He circled the taut tip through the linen with his fingertip and then with his tongue until she was straining against the fabric, until she barely noticed that he had rid her of the barrier and divested her of her gown. She was too hot and aching, too desperate to feel the warmth of his mouth on her skin to care that she was naked.

The warm suction of his mouth and the light nibble of his teeth set off sharp bolts of pleasure that shot to the very core of her. Which is exactly where he touched her next. She nearly shattered at the first sweep of his finger on her quivering flesh. Her hips rode against his hand. The pleasure he was exacting with his mouth on her breast collided with the hot ache between her legs. They were building, racing toward a cataclysmic finish, but he wouldn't let her go there—not yet.

Nay, he had other far more wicked plans in mind. At first, she had no idea what he intended. When his mouth suddenly released her breast, she wanted to cry out in frustration. But he hadn't removed his fingers—thank God—they were still stroking her to mindless oblivion. Which was her only explanation for how she didn't realize until too late that he'd slid down her body and that his mouth, instead of kissing her stomach, was now brushing the inner part of her thighs.

Shock broke through the pleasure. She tried to close her legs. "Alex!"

He paid her no mind, his big hands splaying her hips to slide around and cup her bottom.

"Trust me," he said, the warmth of his breath a teasing whisper. "You are going to like this."

She bucked her hips in protest. How could she like this when the intimacy of it mortified—

She cried out suddenly as his mouth brushed her right *there*. The feel of his lips and tongue . . . Oh God. He was right. It felt good. It felt *really, really* good. It felt so good that she forgot to be embarrassed. It felt so good that she thought she might never doubt him again.

She lost all sense of shame and gave herself over to the sensations. His mouth, his tongue, the scrape of his jaw, the very wickedness of what he was doing brought her to the very peak of pleasure. Her body tried to fight it, but he forced her over with the determined strokes of his tongue and the exquisite pressure of his mouth.

Sensation gripped her for one last paralyzing moment where it all came together in a powerful rush before shattering in sharp spasms.

∞

Alex couldn't wait another minute. Tasting her pleasure, feeling the force of her release against his mouth, was too much for him. Barely had the last spasm eased from her body when he lifted himself over her and started to push inside.

She was so wet, so warm, so ready for him, he had a hell of a time going slow. All he wanted to do was move his hips back and plunge in deep and hard. Sliding in inch by inch, as the tight glove of her body gripped him, was torture. Wonderful, agonizing, perfect torture, and he savored every minute of it.

Only when he'd gone about as far as he could go did he give that little nudge, that final thrust of possession that took him full hilt, eliciting a gasp of surprise that made him want to roar with primitive satisfaction.

He'd touched the deepest place of her and they were connected in a way that could not be undone. Their eyes met, and he knew she felt the significance, too.

Very slowly he started to move. Lifting his hips in rhythmic circles to slide back in and out in short, gentle strokes. But then the strokes got longer . . . and harder. His hips pumped and the erotic little gasps she was making every time their bodies slammed together grew louder and more insistent.

His jaw locked, his teeth gritted, and sweat gathered on his chest and face from the effort to concentrate, to stay in control, to not let passion overtake him again.

It was a battle he lost as soon as she started to lift her hips against his with increasingly frantic urgency. As soon as she started to grip him, clenching her body to hold on to him longer.

Her responsiveness undid him. She was so damned beautiful in her need he couldn't hold back another minute. She was going to come again, and this time, he was going to be with her.

He let himself go, releasing the clamp on the pressure at the base of his spine, and felt the shuddering waves overtake him as he thrust in deep, holding his body to hers and grinding against her until they cried out in unison.

It was intense. Cataclysmic. Out of control. He'd never lost himself so completely in anything. For the first time in his life he knew exactly where he belonged. With her. Forever.

When it was over, all he could do was collapse on top of her. Skin to skin, pounding heart to pounding heart, until fearing that he was crushing her, he found the strength to roll onto the bed beside her.

Not wanting to break the connection, he drew his arm around her and pulled her in snugly against the side of his body. One soft cheek and one small palm rested against his chest, and her knee was bent across his legs. It was a position that he suspected he was going to get used to very quickly. Absently, she traced the scar on his arm. It was strange that she'd never asked about it.

It was a while before she propped her chin on her hand to look up at him. For someone who had just been very thoroughly ravished, she looked impossibly innocent.

"What are you thinking?" she asked. "You are so quiet; I hope you are not feeling guilty again."

His mouth quirked to the side in a wry smile. "Not at all. I'm feeling an appalling *lack* of guilt, actually."

"Good," she said with something of a harrumph.

He smiled. "I was also thinking that I forgot to give you something. I brought it back with me from home." He laughed. "I think my mother feared I was never going to ask for it."

She was obviously perplexed. "For me?"

"Aye, for you," he said, pressing a kiss on her nose. He rolled over her and fished around on the ground beside the bed for his sporran. Digging inside with his fingers, he pulled out what he was looking for and got back into position with her nestled half on top of him before opening his palm.

She gasped, her eyes shooting to his in shock and accusation. "Alex!"

For a moment she just stared at the circle of gold and stone with the eyes of a starving child who had glimpsed a plate of sweets in a window. When she looked back at him her eyes were damp and shimmery. "It's beautiful." He could hear the emotion in her voice. "But I couldn't accept—"

"It's a *betrothal* ring," he said, cutting her off. "You have to accept it."

She looked like she wanted to refuse again, but eventually she nodded.

Taking her hand, Alex slid the ring onto her slender finger. It was a substantial piece of jewelry. The band was thick and engraved with an intricate design taken from the Seton arms, and a large sapphire—nearly a half-inch in diameter—was inset in the middle with another thick band of decorated gold around the edge.

It wasn't until he saw her holding it out to look at it on her hand that he wondered if she would like it. It had been in his family for so long he'd always assumed his bride would wear it. But perhaps she would like something more delicate and heavily jeweled.

"If you don't like it," he said, "I can have something made."

She snatched her hand back as if he were trying to take it from her. "I love it. It's the most beautiful ring I have ever seen. I would be honored to wear it for as long as you wish me to." It was a strange thing to say, and he might have followed up on it had she not asked him a question. "You said you got it from your mother. Was it hers?"

He nodded. "For a time. She gave it to my brother to

give to his wife, but when Chris died, Christina returned it to the family." Not only had his brother been one of Robert the Bruce's closest companions, he'd been married to his sister, Christina Bruce. "It's been in our family for generations, though." He smiled. "Family legend says that it was given to an illustrious ancestor by Charlemagne for deeds on the battlefield, but I think it more likely that it came from another ancestor, the Count of Boulogne—our arms came from him."

"The dragon?" she asked.

He tensed but could not completely stave off the pang that landed somewhere in his gut. "Wyvern," he corrected automatically.

"Of course," she said.

She'd turned her face from his, but he sensed something anxious—almost nervous—in her voice.

It was an odd mistake to make. Most women of her rank would have been raised to identify the symbols of arms easily and with the correct terminology. When Alex had been a member of the Highland Guard, Lachlan Mac-Ruairi had purposefully called it a dragon to annoy him. It had worked. It had also eventually led to his war name. Now it only brought back memories that he'd tried for two years to push aside.

Perhaps sensing his question, she explained hastily, "I saw the inscription on your sword."

Metuenda Corolla Draconis. Fear the Dragon Shield. Bruce had given him the sword some time ago, and he probably should have left it behind, but he'd been reluctant to get rid of it. But how had she seen . . .

"I noticed it when you were fighting with Sir Robert Felton."

She must have good eyesight. Accepting the explanation,

he held up her hand. "I'm glad you like the ring. It actually reminds me a little of your bracelet."

He thought she tensed a little as he brought her arm closer. "It's very fine work," he said, examining the intricate pattern of the cuff. "And an unusual style. Reminds me of some of the armbands the Romans were said to wear, but the design looks to be Norse. Where did you get it?"

He released her arm and she yanked it back.

She paused a shade too long before responding. "My father gave it to me."

She never spoke of her father, and he'd hesitated to ask her about him. John Comyn, Earl of Buchan, had been an abrasive, hard-arsed, ill-tempered bastard, and Alex had assumed they had not been close. But maybe he was wrong. "It must mean a lot to you," he said.

She shrugged evasively.

"I've never seen you without it," he added.

"But how . . . ?" She snapped her mouth shut.

He smiled. "I noticed it under the sleeve of your gown. I saw the imprint through the fabric."

She stilled again, but then looked up at him. "You are very observant, aren't you?"

He shrugged. "I learned from the best."

"Who?" she asked.

It was his turn to be evasive. "An old friend." Ewen "Hunter" Lamont, the best tracker in the Highlands. Returning to the bracelet, he asked, "Why were you hiding it?"

She propped her chin on his chest and said matter-of-factly, "I did not want Alice to see it."

It didn't take him long to realize why. When Joan had been declared a bastard and her inheritance taken from her, her cousins had been the ones to benefit. They were the heirs to Buchan and as a result would have been entitled to all his wealth, including jewelry.

He swore, his fingers sweeping a strand of hair from her lashes and lingering on the soft skin of her brow. "It's criminal what they've done to you. Anyone who knew your father can see the resemblance. I swear to you, when this damned war is over, I will do everything in my power to see it returned to you."

She put her hand flat on his chest as if to stop him. "Nay, Alex, I don't want you to do anything on my behalf. Truly, it means little to me."

He frowned. "How can you say that? Your father was one of the wealthiest men in Scotland."

Something dark and angry flashed across her features. But he wondered if he imagined it when she smiled, scooted up, and pressed her lips against his. "Do you really want to waste time right now talking about my father?"

The arm that was around her waist slid a little lower, enabling him to cup her bottom in his hand. Her very velvety and soft *naked* bottom. A fact that he was viscerally aware of as he instantly hardened.

"How's that stamina of yours now?" she asked playfully.

He groaned as her lips sent a trail of fire along his jaw and neck.

Before she realized what he intended, he flipped her on the bed and rolled on top of her. Those moves Raider had taught him had come in handy many times, but maybe never as handy as this.

It was funny, though. For a split second it almost seemed as if she *had* anticipated his movement. She tensed and started to move her leg as if to block him.

But there was certainly no resistance now. She practically melted under him. God, he liked her under him. On top of him. Whatever the hell position she wanted, as long as she was naked and he had full access to all that creamy, delectable skin.

Pinning her arms over her head, he started to kiss his way down her body. He couldn't wait to make her squirm and beg. "We have all night to find out."

Or so he thought, but somewhere after the third or fourth time of working on his stamina, Alex was roused from a deep—very deep—sleep by a sound.

Knowing Joan was just as exhausted as he, if not more so (he'd lost count after seven or eight of how many times he made her cry out), he was surprised when she immediately stirred as well. She was as alert as a warrior, he thought with amusement.

The sound of the outer door—for that's what he realized had woken him—was followed a moment later by the sound of a table or chair leg squeaking against the floor, and then someone crying out. "Ouch! Where's the blasted candle? Joan!"

Joan's gaze flew to his. "Hurry and hide," she whispered. "It's Alice. She must have seen the light."

They'd forgotten—or been too exhausted—to blow out the candle.

Hearing the unmistakable sounds of footsteps coming toward the room, Joan slid from bed, grabbed her robe, and threw it on as she raced for the door. Opening it, she slid outside, effectively blocking the entry and preventing her cousin from coming inside. By the closeness of Alice's voice, it was just in time.

"There you are," Alice said as if Joan had been hiding.

"Where else would I be?" Joan said with dry, exaggerated patience. "It's the middle of the night."

Alice didn't hear or didn't care about the subtle reprimand. "Henry can't sleep. He has a horrible headache. I told him about your magic powder, and he sent me to fetch some."

Magic powder for sleeping? Something about that struck him, although Alex couldn't put his finger on why.

He paused in his effort to put his clothes back on and get the bed linen back in some semblance of order.

There was a long pause before Joan responded. "I'm afraid it's all gone. You had the last of it."

"Can't you fetch some more?"

"Nay. I brought it with me from Carlisle."

"Well then, what am I supposed to do?"

Alex shook his head. Alice acted as if it were Joan's fault. He didn't know how Joan put up with it.

She wouldn't have to for much longer, he swore. He had even more cause to want to see this blasted war at an end.

"You could try a tincture of all-heal," Joan offered, referring to the herb commonly used to treat sleeplessness—valerian. It was used for many illnesses, including digestive complaints and nausea.

"He doesn't like that. He says it makes his stomach hurt."

It also sometimes had that effect.

"Perhaps just a posset of warm milk and ale, then?" Joan suggested patiently.

Alice made some exaggerated sound of exasperation. "Oh very well. But Henry won't be pleased. He was looking forward to your powder. I've never fallen asleep so quickly and slept so soundly."

Alice left soon afterward, and Alex reluctantly took his leave shortly thereafter. But something about that powder bothered him for the rest of the night.

19

JOAN FINISHED HER yawn with a deep sigh. She was exhausted, but happily so. She couldn't recall ever being this happy.

"There you go again," Margaret said. "You have that look of that big barn cat we used to have after he caught a mouse." She gave her a pointed look in the direction of Joan's hand. "Does it have something to do with that ring on your finger? I don't recall seeing it last night before you went to bed."

"Hmmm . . ." Joan murmured noncommittally. "Don't you?"

Margaret shook her head and laughed. "I won't ask, although I am interested in how he managed to get that to you before you left your room for morning prayers."

"It's a mystery indeed," Joan said with exaggerated piousness—which was fitting, as the two women were walking from the chapel to the Hall to break their fast.

Her cousin wasn't believing any of it and just laughed. But after a moment she sobered and said in a low voice,

"You will be careful, won't you, Joan? I don't want to see you get hurt, and Sir Alex isn't the kind of man not to take notice of things."

Joan wanted to dismiss her cousin's concerns, but she knew she could not. Margaret was right. Alex was far too observant—and smart for that matter. And although she would like to say she was being careful, their growing closeness was causing her to relax her guard and make mistakes. She couldn't believe she'd referred to the wyvern as a dragon. Good thing she remembered the sword inscription. And then there was his questioning about her bracelet, not to mention Alice's sudden appearance to demand her magic sleeping powder. Joan feared she'd lost every bit of blood in her face when her cousin mentioned it.

Joan didn't think he'd made the connection, but she never should have given Alice that powder. Of everything she'd done in the name of helping Bruce's cause, drugging Alex—accidentally or not—shamed her the most. She dreaded his ever finding out about it.

But to Margaret's point, she nodded. "I'll try."

"What are you going to do?"

"Tell him the truth."

Whatever it was her cousin thought she was going to say, it was not that. Margaret stopped just outside the entrance to the Hall and pulled her aside, away from the steady stream of mostly soldiers entering the Hall.

Margaret looked around to make sure no one could overhear and said in a low voice, "Are you sure that is wise? You are giving him a very big sword to hang over your head. Can you trust him?"

"With my life." She would need to.

"And what about what you are doing?" Margaret asked.

Joan knew to what she referred. "I will continue as long as I am needed, hopefully with help."

It took Margaret a moment to understand that she meant Alex turning back to Bruce. Her eyes grew as round as two large coins. "Do you think that is possible?"

Joan answered truthfully. "I don't know. But I hope so." Her future happiness depended on it.

"What are you two whispering about again?" Alice said, breaking away from a few of the ladies she was walking with to come up to them with a sharp stomp of impatience. "I swear, everyone is being so secretive lately, I shall be glad when this war is finally over."

On that they could agree, although Joan was dreading watching Alex ride away. What did they have, a few days? Four . . . five at the most? She felt a sharp pinch in her chest. Could she convince him by then or would she watch him leave, knowing that it was over?

She couldn't let that happen. Last night had been so perfect. Well, after the jealousy part, but perhaps that had been understandable. Sir Hugh was certainly trying to get his revenge. But she would not curse him for it, not when it had brought Alex to her room and led to a night she would remember for the rest of her life. She'd never felt warmth and closeness like that before. She'd never felt so relaxed and . . . happy. Without realizing it she looked down at the ring on her finger and smiled.

"What's that?" Alice said, reaching for her hand.

Joan resisted the urge to snatch it back. "I was just showing Margaret," Joan said. "Alex gave it to me. It's a betrothal ring."

Alice's mouth hardened. She dropped her hand. There was something on her face . . .

"It's very pretty," Alice said.

"I'm glad you approve, Lady Alice," a deep voice said with wry amusement. "I intend to see that Joan gets everything she deserves."

Joan turned, surprised to see that Alex had come up behind them. He was so blasted quiet! Maybe she should call *him* Ghost.

She gave him a sharp look—not for sneaking up on her, but for what he'd said to Alice. It could be an innocent comment, but despite her plea to him last night, Joan didn't think it was. She hoped Alice hadn't taken anything by it. Joan could not afford to have any kind of wedge between her and her cousin—not if she wanted to be kept within the circle of information. A circle that had definitely been tightening.

For once Joan couldn't tell her cousin's thoughts from her expression.

"What a pretty sentiment," Alice said. "My cousin is fortunate to have found you."

Ever the stalwart knight, Alex had come up by her side. He took her hand, put it in the crook of his arm, looked deep into her eyes, and said in a voice that no one could doubt, "Nay, it is I who am fortunate."

She felt her heart swell and her cheeks grow warm as she basked under the glow of his love for her.

The warmth and contentment lasted throughout the day, although unfortunately Alex was called away by Pembroke after breaking his fast, presumably to report on his journey to East Lothian.

He sent a message later that he had to ride out to Wark, and she was disappointed when he had yet to return by the evening meal.

Their handful of days had been whittled down by one. But what did she expect? There was a war coming.

To that end, she took the message about the earls' refusal to answer King Edward's call to her contact in the village under the pretense of purchasing some new fabric for a bridal gown. Avoiding blue—the traditional color of purity for a bride—she found a beautiful ivory brocade with an intricate scroll design in silk gold thread.

It was silly to buy it. It had cost a small fortune and a good portion of her meager savings. There was every chance she would never wear it. Still, she hadn't been able to resist. One of Margaret's attendants was a masterful seamstress, and Joan knew she could make her something beautiful at a fraction of the cost of a dressmaker in the village.

She'd stayed in the Hall to discuss it with her after the evening meal and had gotten so caught up in the excitement of all the details, hours had passed before she realized it was getting late.

No doubt Alice would be furious that she hadn't been there to help her ready for bed again—but Joan was too happy to care. Nay, not just happy, she was giddy.

Good Lord, she was acting like a besotted young bride-to-be with no other care than a wedding to plan, not a highly valued spy in the enemy camp with the biggest battle in Bruce's eight-year war just around the corner. But there was no reason she couldn't do her duty *and* carve out a few moments of happiness for herself—while she could. Even a wedding that could well be pretend was still fun to think about for a woman who'd never expected to have one at all.

She'd just entered the corridor when the bell rang for compline. She *had* lingered a long time. It must be half past nine or so. Outside the last vestiges of daylight were fading streaks of gray beneath the cloudy night sky, but inside where light had a hard time penetrating thick stone walls, it had been as dark as night for hours.

The bell from the chapel tower was still reverberating in her ear when she sensed a movement behind her and turned just as someone grabbed her.

"Hello, sweeting," he said, pulling her against him from behind and breathing down her neck. "I've been waiting for you."

Joan froze. *Licorice and brandy*. Even as her stomach rolled, the sound of Sir Phillip's voice conjured up the darkest memories of her worst nightmare—one that had been real—and filled her with an icy, mind-numbing terror.

Taking advantage of her shock, he pulled her into the storage room where he must have been waiting for her to pass by.

In one move, he closed the door, spun her around, and pinned her to it with his body.

"That's better," he said, wedging himself between her legs. "Feels like old times, doesn't it?"

The crude mockery in his drink-laden voice was enough to rouse her from her momentary terror-ridden trance. Fire replaced ice, and anger replaced fear. Instinct and training returned as well, causing her knee to lift forcefully against the offending bulge between his legs and come down just as forcefully on his instep.

He cursed in pain, bending over as if she'd folded him in two. "How does that feel, *Sir* Phillip? That is what *new* times feels like. I'm not a helpless young girl anymore who you can pin down and rape and who won't fight back. Touch me again, and I'll kill you."

She meant it, too. She was shaking with the force of her hatred. It would be so easy to slip her blade from its scabbard . . .

Too easy.

She had to go. She turned to open the door, and that's when Phillip made his move. "*Never turn your back . . . not even for a minute.*" Too late, Lachlan's warning came back to her.

"You fucking slut! You'll pay for this." He barreled his head into her like a charging bull, slamming her into the door. Her head took the brunt of it, snapping back with the force and filling with disorienting stars.

She'd been right to assume that Phillip wouldn't be able to recover enough to stand and stop her, but she'd underestimated his skill—or been overconfident in her own. She'd practiced many times, but this was the first time she'd ever had to fight back with force. It was different. Faster. Scarier. And Sir Phillip wasn't a young squire anymore, he was a full-fledged knight. A hardened warrior who'd trained for years, fought in countless battles, and knew how to fight dirty.

She wobbled, feeling for the door or wall to steady herself.

He took advantage of her dizziness with a sweep of his ankle behind her leg, causing her to fall back on the ground.

In her normal state she might have been able to roll away and fight back, but dazed and disorientated like this she was helpless.

Helpless. Oh God, no . . .

If she thought he'd been rough before, she was wrong. He backhanded her with a blow to the side of her face that made her cry out in fresh pain, kicked her in the ribs, and then knelt down on top of her to hold her in place. He was so heavy she couldn't breathe.

Writhing in pain from the blows, she was only half-conscious of his efforts to lift his long surcoat and untie the breeches he had on beneath.

"Maybe I'll make you suck it to make it feel better," he said, grabbing himself. "Would you like that, you fucking whore?" He reached down and squeezed her breast hard, pinching her nipple until she gave another cry of pain. He laughed. "Shall we see what my cock looks like with that pretty mouth wrapped around it?"

Revulsion surged up the back of her throat. She'd heard mention of such intimacies before, but it still shocked— and repulsed—her. *He* repulsed her. Her head throbbed with pain, but she managed, "You will sooner feel the bite of my teeth."

Her threat only amused him. "I see you have more spirit than you used to. I've always liked a lass with a little spirit, makes breaking them more exciting."

Joan's head felt like it was splitting apart. She could barely think beyond the pain, but she knew she had to do something. She shifted to try to roll him off her, but her movements were awkward and slow, and he had no problem stopping her.

She was rewarded for her efforts with another blow to the side of the head that made the lights start to flash again.

She tried to scream, but her crushed lungs couldn't find the air, and he only laughed at her efforts.

She could barely hear his taunts now; his voice sounded so far away with the ringing in her head. "I doubt you'd be much good with your mouth the way you are right now. Nay, this time, I'll have to settle for that tight glove between your legs." He laughed. "Although maybe it's not so tight anymore? Shame that I didn't get a chance to break you in a little more before I left."

Joan was going to be sick. *Do something*, a voice cried. But the voice was small and weak.

She felt air on her legs, and then a rough, callused hand tried to spread her legs.

"No!" she cried. A moment of clarity permeated the haze of confusion.

He was too occupied with trying to shove himself between her legs to hit her again.

Her head cleared a little more as the realization of what was happening caused her primitive instincts to flare.

Fight! You have to fight back. You have to try. Think . . .

But instinct was stronger than thought. He loosened his hold on her hands pinned above her head to try to fit himself between her legs, giving her an opening, and she reacted.

Her hand found the hilt of the eating knife at her side and a moment later the blade plunged up into the exposed skin of his groin. His eyes widened with shock. He said something, but the sounds in her head were blaring too loud to make it out.

It was as if time were passing at half-speed as her head fought to clear. He swayed for a long moment, and then toppled over.

She was sobbing as she struggled to get up, as near hysterical as she ever wanted to be. She looked at him, but the image was a jagged montage with the pieces scattered: pool of blood . . . his pants half-down . . . her knife lying next to him.

She'd killed him. Oh my God, she'd killed him.

What am I going to do? I have to get out of here.

She opened the door and ran to the only person she could think of who could help.

Alex had dismissed his squire after the lad had finished removing his weapons and armor. It had been another long and frustrating day. Pembroke and the king's reaction to the plight of Alex's tenants had been exactly as he'd feared—unsympathetic—and something was still troubling him from the night before. He'd taken the unusual step of ordering a hot bath to be brought up, rather than just relying on the river, in the hopes that it would help him sort his thoughts. He'd wanted to be alone so he would dry and dress himself as need be.

The lad didn't argue. Though after the ride to Wark and back, and the long day of ensuring that the soldiers were ready to march, the boy should be as exhausted as Alex; apparently some of the other squires were heading into the village to one of the alehouses, and he was going to join them.

Alex was just thirty, but there was nothing like a seventeen-year-old to make him feel very old and weary.

A few minutes after the lad left, Alex heard a knock on the door. Two men entered carrying the tub, and then for the next ten minutes or so they returned with buckets of hot water until it was full enough, and he sent them away.

He was just about to remove his shirt when he heard another knock. Assuming it was more water, he opened the door to repeat that he had enough, but the words died in his mouth.

"Joan?" He took one look at her and felt his insides twist in a coil of fear, horror, panic, and rage. The latter fueled by the nasty-looking bruise forming on the side of her pale, tear-stained cheek. Her face was bloodless, her hair half escaped from its pins, and her eyes glassy. He'd seen enough men in shock after a battle to recognize the signs.

When their eyes met, something inside her seemed to

break. She sobbed and collapsed against his chest in tears. He'd never seen her so vulnerable; it was so disorienting that he didn't know what to do. He caught her and held her tight, soothing her as best he could, but from what he didn't know.

Easing her into his room, he closed the door behind her, and then held her back to look at her again.

"God, what happened? Who did this to you, sweetheart?"

She mumbled something unintelligible between sobs. It was then that he looked down.

It was his turn to pale. It felt as if every drop of blood suddenly rushed out of his body. Her gown was covered in blood.

"My God, you're bleeding!"

He immediately reached for her, searching for signs of trauma, but she shook him off. "N-not mine."

He relaxed—infinitesimally. Leading her to the edge of his bed, he forced her to sit and went to the sideboard to pour her a drink of whisky to calm her. A memory jarred in his head, but he pushed it aside for later.

"Here," he said, holding the cup out to her.

She accepted it without argument and took a big gulp before putting it aside with the choking cough of someone not accustomed to the harsh drink.

The next few minutes while he waited patiently for her to tell him what had happened were some of the hardest of his life. And when the story did emerge, in choked sobs and heaving sighs, he felt a rage unlike anything he'd ever known take hold.

That bastard had tried to hurt her. If Phillip Gifford wasn't dead already, he was about to be.

"I didn't know what to do," she said finally.

"You did the right thing. I want you to stay here. I will take care of everything."

"But—"

He stopped her. "Let me handle this, Joan. I need to handle it."

"Please, Alex. No one can find out. I don't want anyone to know!"

He could see her rising panic and understood, but if that bastard was still alive, Alex was going to see him pay. "He needs to be punished, sweetheart," he said gently, trying to calm her down. "The king will have his ball—" He stopped. "The king will see justice served."

"Will he?" she demanded frantically. "Or will there just be more questions? Even if he is alive . . ." It was clear she didn't think that the case. She turned to him earnestly. "Please, Alex, I can't talk about it. Don't make me talk about it. I'm begging you."

Alex's mouth fell in a flat line. He couldn't deny her anything when she was like this, but he wasn't happy about it. He nodded. "I will do as you ask, but in return you are going to tell me everything that you just left out."

If possible, her face paled even more. Their eyes held. She didn't try to feign ignorance—they both knew she'd been holding something back in her retelling.

After a long pause, she nodded.

"I will be back as soon as I am able. Lock the door and wait for me here." He noticed her glance at the tub of water. "You can use it if you wish. You'll find soap and a drying cloth and whatever else you might need in the trunk."

She nodded, her lip trembling again. "You are being so sweet . . . thank you."

He shook his head, drew her into his arms, and dropped

a soft kiss on her mouth. "I love you, sweetheart. Never forget it."

She gave him the first smile—if a bit tremulous—since she'd entered the room. "I won't."

He left her—reluctantly—and paused to hear the door lock behind him before heading down the tower stairwell and out into the yard. He had just entered the corridor outside the Great Hall when he saw a door open and Sir Phillip Gifford straggling out, holding his hand over his hip.

Not dead, then.

At least not yet.

Rage unlike any Alex had ever experienced flashed through him like a lightning bolt. It didn't build or grow, it didn't give him time to think or rationalize, it was just there. Dominating. Permeating. Clouding his vision in a red haze.

Gifford barely made it out of the room before Alex's fist to his jaw sent him soaring back into it. Foolishly, he tried to get up. Alex hit him again. And again. Gifford tried to say something, but Alex wasn't hearing it. All he could see was the man who'd tried to rape the woman he loved.

He struck blow after blow, pummeling him to the ground until he didn't get up. And still it wasn't enough.

Alex drew out his dagger, lifted the "knight" up by his surcoat, and held the blade to his throat. For the first time in Alex's life he knew the kind of raw hatred and murderous rage that could make a man forget honor, chivalry, and whatever other tethers of humanity kept him fit for a society. *Brigand*. The old accusations he'd hurled at Boyd came back to him. Maybe he had more of it in him than he realized.

Gifford must have read the murder in his gaze through his swollen, half-lidded, and bloody gaze. "P-please . . ."

"Mercy?" Alex seethed. "Shall I give you as much mercy as you were going to show my betrothed? How does it feel, Gifford, to be at the mercy of someone stronger and more powerful than you?"

"I didn't do anyth—"

A fresh wave of rage surged through him. "Don't," Alex warned. "Deny it or say one word against her, and it will be the last lie you ever speak."

If Gifford's eyes could have widened, they would have. They flashed with fear. "S-sorr-ry."

Alex tossed him back with disgust. The man was nothing but a coward. He stood over him. "Give me one good reason I shouldn't kill you right now."

For once Gifford showed a spark of intelligence and didn't respond.

Alex looked down at him in disgust. He wasn't worth it.

Aside from the damage done by Alex's fists, he could see the stain of blood from where Joan's knife had penetrated near his hip. The same knife that was now at Gifford's waist. Reaching down, Alex pulled it from the belt and slid it in his.

"You will say nothing about what happened here to anyone. If someone asks, you were set upon by thieves on the way back to the castle from the village. Consider yourself fortunate that I do not take you to the king right now and have you thrown in the pit prison. But my betrothed wants to forget this ever happened, and I am very reluctantly honoring her wishes." Alex leaned down and lifted the other man up from his slump against the wall to meet his gaze. "If I hear you have even mentioned Lady Joan's name, I will kill you."

His tone left no doubt that he would like nothing more. Alex let him go and stood back up. He looked down at the beaten man like the excrement that he was. Gifford had started to recover and, realizing Alex wasn't going to kill him, his fear had been replaced by a look of burning hatred as he struggled to his feet. Some of his pride had returned as well. "You could try."

Alex just looked at him and smiled, knowing it wouldn't even be a contest. Gifford hadn't had half the training Alex had had—nor had he fought alongside the best warriors in Christendom for seven years.

Gifford seemed to read his thoughts—or the substance of them anyway—and his battered face flushed with anger.

But Alex had wasted enough time on him already. Joan needed him.

When he turned to leave, Sir Phillip Gifford made his last—fatal—mistake. He pulled a dagger from its sheath at his waist and was halfway to throwing it at Alex's back when Alex's blade struck him in the throat.

Alex was out of practice, but his aim was still true—and just as deadly. He was still the best

20

IT WAS A testament to her deep distress and shock that Joan didn't even hesitate to take Alex up on his offer to let her use his bath. She didn't care about the propriety of taking her clothes off in the room of a man who was not

yet her husband—or anything else for that matter. All she wanted to do was sink into that clean, warm water and wash the feel of Sir Phillip's touch off her skin and the blood from her hands.

She scrubbed and scrubbed until her skin was pink and not a trace of blood remained. If only the memories were so easily washed away.

She couldn't bear to put back on her ruined gown, so after drying herself with one of the linen cloths in Alex's trunk, she donned her chemise and borrowed a plaid she'd found in the same trunk to wrap around her shoulders. Then she sat and waited.

What was taking him so long? She grew increasingly worried as the minutes passed. What if Phillip wasn't dead? What if he and Alex had gotten into a fight and Alex had been hurt? Or what if Alex had been caught trying to clean up her mess, and someone thought it was he who had killed Phillip? She shouldn't have asked him to cover for her. She couldn't let him take the blame even if she had to tell everyone the truth.

The door opened, and she jumped from the seat she'd taken on the edge of the bed. One look at Alex's face was enough to ease her panic. He looked grim, but he wasn't hurt.

"What happened?" she asked.

"Your blade did not kill him." She didn't have time to figure out whether she was disappointed or not, before he added, "But mine did."

In short, concise, soldierly fashion, he explained how he'd found Phillip leaving the room—her blade had struck him in the hip, not the deadly groin area—and they'd fought. How Alex had beaten him to within an inch of his foul life, but had given him a chance to leave while still breathing. Phillip, however, hadn't taken the gift. He'd attempted to throw his dagger into Alex's back. He wasn't quick enough, however, and instead Alex's blade found him.

It was Phillip's misfortune that his cowardly act had come against the most skilled man with a dagger on either side of the border. Although Phillip wouldn't have known that—and she wasn't supposed to either, for that matter.

"I debated tossing him down the garderobe where he belongs," Alex finished. "But decided there would be fewer questions about his disappearance if I informed Pembroke, Sir Hugh, and King Edward of the truth." Anticipating her reaction, he said quickly, "Most of it anyway. I left out your part, telling them merely that Gifford and I had a disagreement, that it had led to a fight, and that he'd attempted to end it with a dagger in my back."

Joan would not falsely mourn the death of Phillip, and she was relieved that Alex had not killed him on her behalf, but she was horrified at the mess in which she'd embroiled him. It was a risk going to the king and Pembroke. It was Alex's word against a dead man's. That he'd taken the risk, however, didn't surprise her. Hiding, lies, and covering things up weren't his way. He would do the right thing no matter the personal risk or sacrifice.

She felt a flicker of disquiet that she forced away. He would never betray her—even in the name of "right."

"And they believed you?" she asked.

He gave her a wry smile, the first break in the grim exterior since he'd entered the room. "Aye. I suspect they knew our disagreement had something to do with you, but it seems my reputation comes in handy on occasion. They both knew I would not kill a man in cold blood—I imagine they would have been rather shocked to know how close I'd come to doing just that. But I did have some unexpected help from your former guardian."

"Sir Hugh?"

He nodded. "Apparently this isn't the first time Gifford has been accused of putting a knife in someone's back. He was seen fighting with a Welsh soldier, and when the man later showed up dead—with a knife wound to the back— Gifford was widely thought responsible but no one could prove it." He paused. "The Welshman reputedly had a very beautiful wife."

Joan's mouth pursed with disgust, although she was not surprised. She was glad, however, *very* glad that Alex was not in trouble because of her.

And Sir Phillip was out of her life forever. She would never again have to see the mocking eyes of the man who'd raped her. Was it so horrible to be relieved?

"Then it's over?" she asked, not daring to believe it.

He nodded and opened his arms. She rushed into them as she'd been wanting to do since he walked in the door. "Aye, my love, it's over."

She allowed herself to be swallowed in his embrace and take all the comfort he offered. His chest was a rock, his arms an anchor, and all that strength and solidity seemed to flow through her. She'd never had to or wanted to rely on anyone like this before, but it was . . . nice. She felt her pulse slow, felt the chill leave her bones, and felt her frayed nerves begin to unwind.

Taking a deep breath, she pulled away and took a step back. If he was holding her while she did this, she might cry. After all Alex had done for her, he deserved to know the truth about the man he'd killed.

Taking his lead from earlier, Joan spoke as matter-of-factly and dispassionately as she could about what had happened. But it wasn't easy; she'd never spoken of it before to anyone. It was her secret. Her shame. And she wanted to keep it that way. But Alex had a right to know.

"You were right. I was leaving something out. It happened a long time ago, and I've forgotten about it." She stopped. She would not lie to him. Not about this, at least. "Or perhaps it's more accurate to say that I've tried not to dwell on it. But there was more to my history with Phillip than I alluded to."

She dropped her gaze, but telling herself not to be embarrassed, she forced it to meet his again and drew a deep breath. "When I was fifteen, I fancied myself in love with him. I was young and naive and prone to daydreams of handsome golden-haired young knights." She paused to give him a wry look. "I'd seen one at Roxburgh not that long before who'd made quite an impression on me, and I convinced myself that Phillip—a new squire to my guardian—was the embodiment of every young girl's fantasy I'd ever had. He played the part well. He was charming, gallant, and doted on me as if I were a princess. I think he was genuinely wooing me for marriage." She shuddered at the idea. "For a time, that is."

She thought back to those seemingly happy days and frowned. "There were small signs he was not the man I thought." She recalled the time she'd walked in on him alone in the stables with a serving girl, whom he'd claimed to not know, and the time he'd come back from the village drunk with a mark on his neck that now she recognized as a love bite. "But I chose not to see them. Just as I chose not to see the subtle changes in his behavior toward me after I was declared a bastard and disinherited."

She could see the tension growing in Alex, and realized he'd probably guessed the direction this story was heading.

But he seemed determined to let her finish. It was one of the things she loved about him; he respected her not just with his words but with his actions. She hoped what she was about to tell him wouldn't change his opinion of her.

"Go on," he said encouragingly, but with a definite edge in his voice.

She drew a deep breath. This was the hard part. This was the part where her fantasy had been crushed, stomped on, and shattered—she'd thought forever. "We'd gone off a few times together before. Phillip had snuck a few chaste kisses, but never attempted anything more. He had always been so respectful, I never dreamed . . ." Knowing she was beginning to sound defensive, she stopped and tried again. "I *wanted* to spend time with him. Alone time. Perhaps it was wrong, but when he asked me to meet him for a private meal down by the loch, I agreed."

As the memories grew sharper, her pulse wanted to race, but she forced it to steady. "He was very sweet at first, and he seemed to have thought of everything. It was a feast—with my favorite sugared buns and tarts, and wernage. Aye, plenty of the sweetened wine. I must have been more nervous than I realized, because I drank more than I should have."

Alex broke his silence with a curse. "He wanted you to, damn it. That was no doubt part of the plan."

Joan smiled wryly. "I know that. But I should have—" She stopped. She couldn't go back and change anything—her actions or his—no matter how much she wanted. She just didn't want Alex to think badly of her—or think she was a complete fool. She should have pushed Phillip away the instant he started to kiss her. She wished she had. It wouldn't have changed what had happened, but it wouldn't have left her feeling so complicit.

"I welcomed his kiss at first. I didn't realize . . ." She forced herself to look Alex in the eye. "I didn't realize he wouldn't stop when I wanted him to. I told him to stop. I told him I didn't want this. I tried to fight back—I did!—but he was strong, and at the time, I had no idea how to defend myself. He pinned me down and forced himself between my legs." She took a deep breath to calm down before saying the words. "He raped me."

It was strange how such ugliness and so much pain could be boiled down into a couple of short sentences.

Alex hadn't moved, but she sensed the rage boiling inside him just under the surface, ready to explode.

"But you know the worst part?" she said. "When it was over, he acted like he'd done nothing wrong. Like I'd wanted it, and now I was just crying because I realized I'd given up for free what should have been bought with a wedding ring. For a while, he even made me question what had happened. But he raped me, Alex. I swear to you, I didn't want—"

Alex stopped her with a roar of fury. "Of course you didn't! God, do you actually think I would believe otherwise? For pity's sake, you could have been dancing around like Salome with her veils—or without her veils—and it wouldn't have mattered. You told him to stop. Whether you were drunk, let him kiss you, or anything else, the moment you wanted it to end it should have. That's what any man with honor or a damned conscience would do."

Joan was stunned. She knew that; she just hadn't known whether he would see it the same way. "I'm not making excuses for him."

"Good," he growled angrily. But she knew it wasn't at her but at the situation. Alex was a fixer. A rescuer by nature. It would be hard for him to hear this and know there was nothing he could do to change it or make it better. But he was making it better. Just by his reaction, he was making it better.

"I don't want to hide from my mistakes."

Alex's jaw tightened. "The way I see it, the only mistake you made was being fifteen. Hell, Joan, we all make mistakes when we are young. That doesn't mean we deserve to be punished for them with what that bastard did to you."

"Not everyone would agree with you. Some people would say I got exactly what I deserved for going off with him alone and allowing him to kiss me."

"Then some people are bloody idiots."

She smiled. She couldn't believe it. She'd told him what had happened, and she was actually *smiling*. She wouldn't have thought it possible.

He opened his arms. "Come here, sweetheart."

An instant later she was in his embrace again, and he was holding her. Comforting her. Hugging her. It was exactly what she needed. Not questions. Not judgment. Not an explosion of male anger. Just calm understanding and acceptance.

Well, maybe not complete calm—he was a man after all. A man who fought with his sword for a living. She knew that inwardly he was seething with rage.

Which is why his next words surprised her.

"I wish I hadn't killed him."

She drew back. "Why not?"

His expression turned so dark and menacing he almost reminded her of Lachlan.

"So that I could make him pay for what he did to you. Slowly and painfully."

He sounded like Lachlan, too. For all his noble knight persona, sometimes it wasn't hard to imagine Alex in a blackened nasal helm, black leather, and a dark plaid slipping in and out of the mist like a phantom with the rest of the Highland Guard.

She loved both sides of him. The fierce, deadly warrior and the noble knight. But it was his nobility that had renewed her faith in honorable men. His reaction to what had happened tonight only reinforced it.

Gazing up into his fierce, handsome face, she felt her insides squeeze. God, she couldn't let him go. She had to find a way to get through to him. But how?

∽

For Joan's sake, Alex was trying to keep a rein on his emotions, but it wasn't easy, damn it. He wanted to rage at the unfairness, lash out at the people who should have protected her, put his head in his hands and sob for the fifteen-year-old girl who'd been so horrifically betrayed, and kill the man who'd done it to her. As he'd already done that, perhaps he should say kill more painfully.

Had he really chastised Raider for his seemingly endless need for vengeance after the rape of his sister? Alex understood only too well the kind of pain and anger that could cause a man to lose sight of anything else. Every fiber of his being burned for vengeance right now.

Fifteen? Christ. How could anyone do that to a young girl? His heart broke for the loss of innocence. Not her virginity—he didn't give a shite about that—but at what must have been a cruel awakening to the ugly side of men. She'd already gone through so much in her life; the imprisonment of her mother, the loss of her father. To give her heart to a man, and then to have it so cruelly and brutally betrayed must have been a devastating blow.

He didn't know what he'd expected when she'd started

to talk, but it hadn't been this. Maybe he should have known. In many ways it explained a lot. Her initial reticence with him, her cynicism, her lack of trust, the seeming indifference to her reputation all made more sense now.

But he'd never felt so damned helpless.

He looked down into her eyes. "I'm so sorry, Joan. Christ, I wish there was more that I could say. I wish I could have been there for you." Had she gone through it alone? Though he suspected he knew the answer, he asked, "Did you ever tell anyone what happened?"

She shook her head. "At first I was too ashamed, and then later there didn't seem any purpose. Phillip had been sent away, and my wardship was given to Sir Henry not long after. In truth, I just wanted to forget it had ever happened." She laughed bitterly. "But it wasn't that easy. My situation didn't lend itself to meeting many honorable men."

Alex's jaw hardened with understanding. Men would have viewed her as ripe fruit from a low-hanging branch— easy pickings.

Bloody hell, where had Despenser and de Beaumont been? They were her guardians, they should have been protecting her.

"You changed that," she said. "You restored my faith in honorable men and gave me something I never thought to have: passion. After what Phillip did, I'd never thought I'd let another man touch me like that."

He was so busy fuming about her guardians' failure that it took him a moment to realize what she said.

"But you did."

She paused for a moment as if debating something, and then shook her head.

"But what about Despenser and Fitzgerald?"

She shook her head again. "No matter what it looked like—or what people say—you are the first man I have shared any kind of intimacies with since Phillip raped me."

Alex was stunned; he didn't know what to say. He was glad, of course. He'd never wanted to believe she was the wanton her reputation made her out to be. His instincts had been correct. She was more innocent maid than jaded seductress.

But how could Fitzgerald have gotten it so wrong? It wouldn't be the first time a young man had lied about being with a woman, but the young Irish sea captain hadn't sounded as if he was lying. How could anyone make that kind of mistake?

His gaze fell on the jug of whisky, and that niggle he'd noticed earlier got louder. A hell of a lot louder. Ever since her cousin had mentioned the "magic powder," something had bothered him. The night she'd come to his chamber, the first thing she'd done was offer him whisky. Whisky that she'd later tried to stop him from drinking. And after he'd done so, he'd fallen into the sleep of the dead. Nay. He didn't want to believe it. She wouldn't have drugged him.

But if she'd done the same to Fitzgerald, it sure as hell would explain his confusion.

He forced his mind from the whisky. "Why didn't you tell me? Why did you let me think you'd been with all those men?"

She dropped her gaze from his. "Because I would have had to explain about Phillip. And I suppose I wanted to see how much I mattered to you. I didn't think any man who believed what you did would make me an honorable offer, but you proved me wrong."

It was a good explanation, and he sensed it was the truth. But perhaps not all of it.

Was there another reason she might not want Alex to know the true nature of her relationship with these men? Could it be so that he wouldn't question what she was doing with them?

What she was doing with them.

He cursed silently. Fitzgerald was second-in-command of the Irish fleet for the Earl of Ulster. He would know the shipping plans. Just like the shipping plans that had made their way to Bruce. But Margaret was the spy . . . wasn't she? He'd wondered how she'd gotten that kind of information. What if she hadn't? What if she'd been helping someone else when she took that note to the monk?

"Alex, is something wrong?"

Her question shook him from his reverie. She looked so sweet and innocent, so heartbreakingly vulnerable, he told himself he had to be wrong. She couldn't have deceived him like that.

He took her in his arms again. "Aye. I want to make it better, but I don't know how."

She sighed against him, snuggling in closer. "Just hold me," she said.

He did as she asked—gladly. Wherever his thoughts led, whatever his suspicions, this was not the time. She needed him, and he would be here for her.

But things had begun to fall into place, and no matter how much he wanted to tell himself it wasn't true, he knew he had to find out for sure.

∞

Joan wanted nothing more than to stay with Alex all night, but she knew she had to return to her room before Alice sent someone out looking for her. Her cousin might suspect where she was, but Joan didn't want her to be worried.

Alice was self-centered and spoiled, but she wasn't without some cousinly concern.

Alex escorted her to the door of Alice's chamber, and asked her again if she was all right. "I'm fine," she assured him. "Although I'd be better if you decided to climb another tower tonight."

His mouth crooked in a half-grin and he shook his head. "I think my tower-climbing days are over—at least until you get a bigger window."

She laughed, and he bid her good night with a tender kiss that was over far too soon.

"Get some rest," he said, pulling away.

He turned to go, but she called him back. "Alex?"

He looked at her over his shoulder. For a moment, she thought she saw something pained in his gaze. "Aye?"

"Thank you."

He appeared perplexed. "For what?"

"For understanding. For believing me. For not questioning my version of events even with what you thought of my past. It . . ." She paused, emotion tightening her throat. "It means a lot to me."

"There is nothing you can't tell me, Joan—nothing. Do you understand? This only works if we tell each other the truth."

The odd intensity in his voice she attributed to the difficult events of the evening. But he was right. She had to tell him. Lachlan had better answer her missive soon. Maybe she should have sent the bracelet, but she hadn't wanted to alarm him. She didn't want to ask Alex to return to the Guard without first clearing the way with what was sure to be one of his biggest hurdles: her stepfather.

As Alex seemed to be waiting for her response, she nodded.

He waited for another moment, almost as if he hoped

she was going to say something more. She thought he looked disappointed when he turned to leave.

Frowning, Joan almost called him back. But it was late. Instead, she opened the door and slipped into the darkened room.

Almost immediately, her cousin lifted her head from the pillow sleepily. "You're back. Good. I feared I would have to send someone to make sure you hadn't fallen off the ramparts."

Cousinly concern apparently extinguished, Alice pulled the pillow over her head, rolled over, and went back to sleep.

Joan smiled and crossed the darkened room to her chamber. Someone had kept the small brazier going so she was able to light a candle. After making sure the window had not been disturbed, she started to remove what remained of the pins holding her veil in place. She never removed her bracelet—it was too risky—but she took off the small pearl earrings and matching necklace to put in the wooden box she used to store her jewelry that she kept in her trunk.

But after taking off the lid, she stilled. There, sitting in her jewelry box, tucked into the MacDuff broach given to her by her mother—a broach she never wore—was a piece of parchment. She looked around, half expecting Lachlan to materialize from some shadow. Had he put it there earlier? Had Margaret?

Carefully, she took it out to read. Her heart was pounding as she slowly unfolded it. The handwriting was not familiar, but the words turned her bones cold and sent chills racing through her blood.

You are in danger. They suspect the truth.

21

I**T HAD TAKEN** two nights, but Alex had his answer. Unfortunately, it wasn't the one he wanted.

As he approached the stones just after dusk for the second night to wait, he felt the sharp press of a knife against his back that confirmed his worst fear. There was only one man who could sneak up on him like that. He didn't need to turn around to know that the man behind him was Lachlan "Viper" MacRuairi.

Apparently Alex's leaving hadn't made the Guard change their method of contact in an emergency. An unusual oversight on their part, but one that had enabled him to summon his proof. He'd gone to the Standing Stones at Diddo a short distance from Berwick and placed three rocks in a pyramid at its base. The stones, circles, and cairns that littered the Scottish (and English) countryside were a favorite meeting place and place to leave messages of Bruce and the Guard—the three stones were the signal to come right away.

And who had answered the call but his betrothed's "father." That was whom Joan had been waiting for the night he surprised her in her room. That was what she'd started to say—*Father*, not Fiona. The maidservant had been a lie, as he'd discovered the morning after Gifford's death when he'd asked to see "Fiona." No one had heard of her.

Alex couldn't believe it. Joan was the spy; she was the

Ghost. She'd been deceiving him all along. The clues had been there, he'd just been too besotted to see them.

All the little oddities suddenly made sense. The deft move that had enabled her to escape Despenser in the barn and the instinct to block Alex's flipping her when they'd been in bed were because she'd been trained—no doubt by the very man holding the knife at his back right now.

Alex cursed. Of course, *the knife*! It had Norse carvings on the hilt just like the bracelet that she claimed to have received from her "father"—MacRuairi, not Buchan. How the hell had Alex not made the connection? MacRuairi carried an almost identical blade. And how could Alex not have realized her biggest mistake of all: dragon, not wyvern? She'd practically called him by his bloody war name. It hadn't been the sword; she'd known he'd been a member of the Highland Guard all along.

Suddenly the ramifications of that hit him with the force of a hammer in his gut. Had she been purposefully using him? Had she been spying on him? Had it all been a lie? The white-hot knife of betrayal sliced through his chest and burned with a new kind of pain. The pain of loving someone who'd been lying to him.

MacRuairi was the first to break the silence. "Give me one good reason why I shouldn't stick this knife in your back just like you did when you betrayed us."

MacRuairi's taunt might have had some effect if Alex weren't so furious. How could Joan have done this? How could *they* have let her do this? Heedless of the knife digging slowly deeper into his back, Alex snapped back, "I don't think Joan would like it too much if you killed the man she's going to marry in a few weeks." He paused and added sarcastically, "Shall I call you Father?"

MacRuairi cursed, and the press of the knife slackened

for one instant. Having anticipated it, Alex was able to use his former guardsman's moment of shock to twist away.

The two men faced off in the darkness, MacRuairi still wielding his blade and Alex retrieving his own.

"You hadn't heard about our impending nuptials?" Alex taunted. "You must be slipping, Viper."

"You are a liar as well as a traitor." MacRuairi's fingers tightened around the hilt of his blade as if he couldn't wait to attack. "Joan would never—"

He slammed his mouth closed and gave Alex a deadly glare that might have intimidated him once. It didn't any longer.

"What?" Alex seethed. "Marry me knowing what she knows about me? Is that what you were about to say? Don't stop now, there is no need for secrets between old *friends*," he said with the kind of biting sarcasm that could have come from the man opposite him. "I know everything." MacRuairi's weren't the only fingers tightening around his blade. Alex was practically shaking with the need to vent his anger on the man he held responsible. "I know Joan is the Ghost, damn it. I know you've been using her since she was barely more than a girl to spy on the English and send information back to Bruce. I knew you were a coldhearted bastard, Viper, but I never thought even you would let your wife's daughter play a whore for your own ends. Do you have any idea the kind of danger she's been in? Does Bella know what her daughter is doing?"

It could have been a trick of the moonlight, but he thought MacRuairi might have paled. "Leave my wife out of this. You don't know shite, you fucking English bastard. And we were never friends."

Alex's fingers were white, the intricate metalwork of the hilt biting into his skin. "Maybe you're right. But you know what? I don't care anymore. This isn't about me, it's about Joan. You can pretend ignorance, but you had to know what she was doing. Did you not question how she got close enough to Fitzgerald to get all those shipping routes?"

MacRuairi cursed again, but this time it didn't seem to be directed at Alex but at himself. His blade came down just a little. "You are wrong. I didn't know."

Alex took a step toward him. "But you suspected, didn't you? And turned a blind eye because it suited your needs."

"You don't know her at all if you think I had anything to do with it—Joan has her own mind."

He was undoubtedly right about that.

"But you helped her," Alex countered. "You taught her how to defend herself and wield that knife."

"Because I knew she would do it anyway, and I wanted her to be prepared. I was trying to protect her, damn it."

Alex didn't want to hear MacRuairi's bloody excuses. Alex looked at his former compatriot, at the man whose respect he'd fought so hard to earn. Though why the hell he'd wanted it so badly, he didn't know. MacRuairi was the antithesis of everything Alex believed in. But at times Alex had thought he'd seen more. He thought he'd glimpsed the man who a great hero like Bella MacDuff could see something in. "How could you, Viper? After what they did to Bella, how could you let Joan put herself in such danger? Do you want to see her in a cage, too?"

There was no mistaking the flinch this time—moonlight or not. MacRuairi lowered his blade completely, perhaps not even realizing it. "I told you I didn't have a choice. I've argued against it since I found out, but she and Bruce would not be gainsaid. But she's good—the best. Joan can take care of herself. She's escaped detection for a long time."

"Until now," Alex pointed out.

MacRuairi's eyes narrowed. "I warned her to stay away from you. I knew when you were spotted together in the village there would be trouble. What did you do? Trick her? Use your Sir Galahad routine to lure her in so you could betray her as well?" Another possibility appeared to occur to him and the knife lifted again. "If you touched her, I swear to God I'll kill you."

"It's a little late to play the concerned father, don't you think? And I have no intention of betraying her, I *love* her, you bloody arse, and she loves me."

Looking completely poleaxed by Alex's claim, Mac-Ruairi didn't say anything for a moment. But then his mouth turned in a slow sneer. "Are you so sure about that? Joan has been playacting a long time."

Alex wasn't sure about anything, but he wouldn't let the other man see it. "Do you think she would agree to marry me if she didn't?"

MacRuairi hesitated, contemplating the question. "She might if she didn't think she had any other choice. If you were threatening her with something. Is that it? Did you threaten to uncover her to force her to marry you?"

"Blackmail is more your method, Viper, not mine. And in case you missed it before, I said I love her. Do you honestly think I would betray her, knowing what they would do to her?"

"I think there is little you wouldn't do for the sake of your precious honor and knightly code."

Alex stiffened; MacRuairi always knew how to strike where it hurt. But the other man was right. Protecting her would not come without compromising Alex's honor and beliefs. He'd already lied for her, and he would have to do so again, forsaking his duty to Edward to ensure no one discovered what he had. He didn't like it, but he would do whatever he had to to keep her safe. "Her secret is safe. But it's over, Viper. Joan is done—the Ghost has provided her last intelligence. Find someone else to do your dirty work."

MacRuairi eyed him with something like amusement. "Fine by me if that's what Joan wants. I told you before, I was never a party to any of this. It was all her idea." He paused. "I assume you've explained this to her?"

The bastard knew very well that he hadn't. "She will agree. She will be my wife as soon as I return."

"Not if I have anything to say about it," MacRuairi said coldly. "But you have a lot to learn about wives if you think that will be enough. And don't you mean *if* you return?"

Alex didn't mistake the threat. "If you want to try to kill me you'll have your chance in a few days—assuming you take the field like a knight. But that isn't your way, is it? You've always been a pirate."

MacRuairi held his stare, and for one moment, Alex thought he saw something in his gaze. A flicker of emotion, of betrayal, and maybe of hurt. Right—as if an emotion like that were possible from Lachlan MacRuairi.

"You've always tried to make it so simple, Seton. But you never understood shite. Not everything is black and white. We all do what needs to be done when the time comes—even you. Like turning your back on people who trusted you." MacRuairi just stared at him, the accusation gleaming in his eyes. "How the fuck could you just leave like that? After everything we'd been through?"

Alex gritted his teeth, the words striking deeper and harder than he wanted. "Why the hell are you acting like you care? You made it clear from the beginning that I didn't belong."

"Aye, well I was wrong. You were one of us. You were the only one who never saw that."

Alex didn't know what to say. He felt as if he'd just had his legs cut out from under him. MacRuairi was the last person he ever expected to say something like that. Perhaps for the first time he understood the depth of his betrayal. He'd always told himself it had never really mattered to them—or some of them at least—but what if he had been wrong? That was something he didn't want to contemplate.

"I didn't think I had a choice." He hadn't seen any other way at the time. He'd just known he couldn't go on doing what he was doing.

"That's shite. You had a choice, you just chose wrong."

Even if he had, it didn't matter. It was too late. They both knew that.

Alex turned to go, but not without a warning. "Stay away from her, Viper. I will take care of her now."

MacRuairi shook his head. "Not until I hear it from Joan. Besides, we have protective measures in place in case something goes wrong."

"What kind of protective measures?"

The wily bastard just shrugged.

Suddenly Alex remembered a similar conversation he'd had with Pembroke and frowned. Pembroke had been talking about the spy, but at the time Alex hadn't realized it was Joan. Were they planning something?

Alex swore.

"What is it?" MacRuairi asked.

"Nothing, I hope. But I need to go find Joan."

"I'll come—"

"The hell you will, Viper. Your presence anywhere near here will only make it more dangerous for her. How long do you think it will take someone to make the connection if Lachlan MacRuairi is recognized? If there is a problem, I will take care of it."

MacRuairi looked as if he wanted to argue, but instead he forcibly clenched his jaw. "You better—or I'll be back. And next time you won't feel my blade."

Alex didn't need to guess what he meant. He wouldn't feel it because he would already be dead.

∞

Joan had been looking for an opportunity to talk to Alex in private since receiving the note, but with the men readying to march on Scotland any day, he'd been kept so busy with his duties that she'd hardly seen him. She told herself it had nothing to do with what she'd told him, but it was obvious that he was preoccupied with something.

She understood that only too well. Since receiving that note she'd been thinking of little else, not to mention jumping at her own shadow. Who had sent it? What did they know? Who else knew?

Margaret had been just as stunned as she—and just as worried. "You can't stay," her cousin had told her. "It's too risky now."

As much as Joan wanted to argue, she knew Margaret was right. Joan could not ignore the warning. Her time in England had just come to an abrupt end. For over six years, she'd done what she could for Bruce's cause; she had to hope it would be enough.

Her hand went to her wrist, unconsciously seeking the solid metal of the bracelet that was no longer there. She'd gone into the village earlier this afternoon and left it in the church as Lachlan had instructed when she'd moved to Berwick.

How long would it take Lachlan to come for her? A day? Two?

Should she just walk out of here and try to leave on her own? Though tempting, she wasn't going to overreact and do anything rash. How far would she get with no knowledge of the roads and little more than the clothes on her back in a countryside littered with soldiers? How long before they discovered she was gone and sent someone after her?

No, she had to be patient. Lachlan had promised to get her out when the time came. But if he didn't come by the time the army marched, she would try then. When it was safer. When there were fewer men who might come in search of her.

And after she spoke to Alex.

She couldn't leave without telling him the truth and trying to convince him to go with her. But he wasn't at the evening meal for the second night in a row. As they were leaving the Hall, she was about to ask Sir Aymer where she might be able to find him—or when he was expected to return—when a man came rushing up to the vaunted commander and handed him a message that the earl immediately took to the king.

"I wonder what that is about?" Margaret asked.

Joan did as well.

It didn't take her long to find out. With Sir Aymer unavailable, Joan had returned to her chamber, vowing to search Alex out later that night—in his room if she had to. She had finished lighting a few candles when Alice came in with Sir Henry. Immediately sensing the tension between the two, Joan bid a hasty good night and disappeared into her adjoining chamber.

Their voices, however, followed her.

"I am sorry our plans were interrupted," she heard Sir Henry say. "But this is important. The king has called an emergency war council, and I have to return to the Great Hall. This message could change everything. You want us to win this war, don't you?"

"Of course," Alice said weakly.

Joan was too caught up in the knowledge that something important—war changing—was happening to notice the oddity of that. Her cousin never spoke weakly.

"Then this is how it must be," Sir Henry said.

If Alice responded, it was too low for Joan to hear.

"Read it yourself," Sir Henry said.

Joan prayed for her cousin to say something about the contents, but all she heard was silence. She tried to peek between the slats of the door that separated them, but she was only able to make out shadows and movement. She would give her eyeteeth to know what was in that missive.

"When will you be back?" Alice said with apparent resolve.

"Late," Sir Henry said. Then as a concession, he added, "You can wait for me in my chamber if you like."

Alice must have nodded.

"Good girl," he said as if she were an obedient pup.

A few seconds later, Joan heard the sound of a door closing and Sir Henry's departure. Not long after that, it closed for a second time, signaling Alice's.

Joan debated all of a few moments, but she knew what she had to do.

"Change everything," Sir Henry had said. Had the earls decided to come after all? Had the English learned something key about Bruce's movements? She couldn't ignore

what she'd just heard. She had to take a chance and try to find out what important news the messenger had brought.

After donning a black cloak, she slipped out of her room through Alice's empty chamber and into the donjon stairwell. Exiting into the ward, she headed toward the Great Hall, which was situated in the south wall directly opposite. She didn't have a plan exactly, but she knew there was a narrow corridor between the Hall and Captain's Lodgings, and she hoped to be able to get into position to hear or see something. There were also a number of storage rooms in the vaults below that she could try. If anyone questioned her, she could claim to be hungry or to have lost something at the evening meal.

Though she was doing nothing wrong—yet—she was still undeniably nervous. Her usually light footsteps felt loud and ungainly, and despite the warm wool of her cloak, she was chilled to the bone.

It was that blasted note she'd received, playing on her normal composure.

Or was it?

Suddenly, she realized how quiet the yard was. There were very few people moving about, which was odd for this time of evening—the bell for compline had not yet rung.

The prickle of unease grew. Every hair at the back of her neck stood up. She told herself she was being ridiculous. Information like this didn't just fall into your lap . . .

She stopped suddenly. No, it didn't. *If it's too good to be true, it probably is.* Lachlan's warning came back to her just in time.

Joan knew better than to ignore what all her instincts were telling her. Something wasn't right.

Without another thought, Joan turned to the left and headed not for the Great Hall but for the chapel. If anyone was watching, they would see a woman going to pray—hardly unusual with the men about to march off to war.

The chapel was quiet and dark when she entered. There was a priest with his back toward her near the altar lighting a candle, but he appeared not to have taken notice of her arrival.

Stepping into one of the side chapels used for private prayer and confessions, she was about to kneel on the velvet-covered stool before the small altar when someone grabbed her from behind.

22

J OAN RECOGNIZED HIM right away. "Alex!" she exclaimed, twisting around to look up at him. "You scared me half to death." One glance at his face was enough to tell her something was wrong. "What is it? What's the matter?"

He didn't answer her right away. His expression seemed dark and forbidding in the flickering candlelight of the chapel. His entire body seemed to be radiating with dangerous emotions. His eyes burned with dark flames that she hoped were a trick of the candlelight. He didn't look like himself at all.

She could feel his fingers tightening almost imperatively on her arm. "Where are you going this late in the evening? And don't tell me it's to confess your sins—not that you don't have plenty of them, Joan." He leaned closer, saying with a low growl, "Or should I call you Ghost?"

No amount of training could have prevented the small gasp from escaping from between her lips or the draining of blood from every pore of her face. *He knows . . . Dear God, he knows.* And if the look of barely restrained fury burning in his eyes was any indication, he wasn't in any mood to listen to excuses or explanations, though she had to try.

"Alex, I know you are upset—and you have every right to be—but if you will just give me a chance to explain—"

"Upset?" He cut her off with a roar of outrage. The hand set like a brand around her arm gave her a hard shake and hauled her closer. "Now why would I be upset to discover that the woman who has agreed to be my wife and to whom I have given my heart has been deceiving me since the day we met? That she has *drugged* me"—Joan winced— "and spied on me? That she has acted the wanton to entice information from men? That she has put herself in unspeakable danger with no thought—" He stopped, apparently realizing that his voice had grown too loud, and took what she hoped was a calming breath. "When I saw you come out of the donjon and feared I wouldn't reach you in time . . . By God, you nearly walked right into their trap!"

It had been a trap. Hearing confirmation of what her instincts had told her should have filled her with relief, but instead her eyes narrowed. "I don't need you to rescue me, Alex. I figured it out myself."

"The hell you don't—"

"Is something wrong, my lady?"

Joan turned, realizing the priest she'd seen upon entering was standing a few feet away. He must have heard their voices. If he'd heard anything else, his expression gave no indication. He looked at her with concern and at Alex with suspicion.

Alex released her arm, his expression suddenly stony.

Joan forced a cheery smile on her face. "I'm sorry if our voices disturbed you, Father. My betrothed and I were having a small disagreement about the wedding feast—or rather about certain guests at the wedding feast. Perhaps you might settle it for us? Tell me, Father, do you think a man should be excluded from the list just for smiling at me?"

The priest seemed to understand the problem right away. Alex was being irrationally jealous—or at least that was what she wanted the priest to think.

The portly middle-aged clergyman smiled and said as gallantly as any knight, "Your beauty deserves smiles, my lady. I should think if that is a criterion for exclusion you would be left with a feast full of women."

Joan blushed prettily, as would be expected by the compliment, and Alex glowered, but the priest merely chuckled as he walked away.

"You lie convincingly, my lady," Alex said in her ear as he led her out of the side altar and into a small room nearby.

It wasn't a compliment.

Looking around, Joan realized they were in the sacristy. "Do you think we should be in here?" she asked as he closed the door.

Normally being in a small, mostly dark room with him would be making her senses jump with awareness, but now they were jumping with something more akin to trepidation. Good gracious, did he have to look so big and imposing? Where was her golden knight now?

"Don't worry, this won't take long," Alex said, adding to

the ominousness. "And this way we won't be interrupted again."

"How did you find out?" she asked, and then answered for herself. "It was the men, wasn't it?"

"You mean learning that you were not a wanton but only pretending to be one?" he said sarcastically. "Aye, among other things. But that doesn't matter. What matters is that I did, and if I can so can someone else. You may have avoided their trap tonight, but do not think that is the end. They are determined to find the person who has been feeding information to Bruce, and I sure as hell am not going to let that be you. It's over, Joan. As of right now, the Ghost is no more."

She bristled. It didn't matter that she'd come to the same conclusion herself, she didn't like being ordered and dictated to. It reminded her too much of her father. "That is for me to decide, Alex. Not you."

"You are dead wrong about that. If you think that I'll let this charade continue, that I will allow my wife to keep putting herself in danger, you are mad." *Allow?* "Do you even realize the horrible position you've put me in? I've had to lie for you, but I will not keep doing so." He paused, adding as if he knew her thinking, "And if you are thinking about running to your *father*, don't bother. I've already talked to him."

He'd seen Lachlan? If the *allow* comment wasn't enough to make her angry, that threw her over the edge. "By God, Alex, what were you thinking? Are you sure you are not the one who is mad? He could have killed you. God knows, he's been waiting for the chance."

"Aye, well he didn't. I pointed out that he might not want to stick a knife in the back of his future son-in-law."

Joan made a face. "I can only imagine his reaction to that."

Alex didn't say anything; he didn't need to. They both knew what Lachlan thought of him.

"I won't be ordered about, Alex. Not even by you. If you think marriage gives you that right, then you are mistaken. I have been doing this a long time; I am not a helpless maid in need of rescue. And if that is why you wish to marry me, you should reconsider. I know what I am doing, and I will continue to do whatever it takes to help our cause with or without your permission."

"*Your* cause," he corrected. "It isn't mine anymore. Whatever it takes? Christ, you sound just like Boyd. It doesn't matter who you hurt, who you lie to, and who you use as long as you win, is that it? God, I thought you loved me—or was that a lie, too?"

Guilt stabbed her. "Of course, I did—I do. I never wanted to lie to you, Alex. I hated every moment of it. There were so many times I wanted to tell you the truth, but I couldn't. You try to make it sound so simple, but it isn't. I did what I had to for the sake of the mission. Because I believe in what I'm doing. Because I believe in Bruce. Because I know the alternative and never wish to see anyone else's mother in a cage. So if it means I have to speak a few untruths, if it means I couldn't tell you what I was doing, if it means I have to pretend to be interested in a few men to get information, then I will do so. Gladly."

"Is that what you told yourself when you drugged me?"

She flushed with guilt. "That was an accident."

"So you didn't come to my room with the intention of knocking me out to search for the missive we retrieved from the monk?"

Her face heated some more. She shouldn't be surprised

that he'd figured it out. "Yes . . . no . . ." She gazed up at him helplessly. "I changed my mind."

"Before or after you planned to seduce me?"

"It wasn't like that, Alex. I never intended it to go that far. What happened between us was real. With what you learned about Phillip, you have to know that."

She'd won that point, at least. He didn't argue, but his mouth still flattened in a thin white line. "Justify it however you wish, but it was wrong, and it all comes to an end tonight. No more lying. No more spying. No more doing whatever it takes. I've been through this before; I won't do it again."

He sounded so final. So stubborn. So intractable. So confident in the righteousness of his view of things. "Or what, Alex? Will you do the same thing you did last time that someone didn't meet your stringent sense of right and wrong? Will you leave and turn your back on me just like you did your friends? Or maybe you will turn on me and betray me, too, for some idealized myth of chivalry that doesn't exist?"

Alex's ears were ringing and his head blared. His lungs felt as if he'd just swallowed a hot ball of fire. She'd learned more from Viper than how to use a knife and defend herself; she'd learned how to skewer and eviscerate with her tongue. She'd learned how to find a place of pain, poke it, and make it hurt some more.

Idealized myth? She'd reduced the hardest thing he'd ever done to a bard's tale. She made him sound rigid, idealistic, and uncompromising—as if he hadn't tried to think of another way.

But beyond the hurt, his body shook with rage and

indignation. How dare she accuse him of such after the hideous position she'd put him in. He had been tasked with *un*covering her, for Christ's sake!

"Betray you? To the contrary, I've *lied* to a man to whom I have a duty to protect you. It is not me who is the traitor here, Joan, but you. Turning you in is exactly what I should do, damn it." He let his voice drop off, his fists clenched. "But it was my misfortune to have fallen in love with a damned spy, who has now embroiled me in her treachery and made liars of us both."

She had the good grace to wince and looked up at him apologetically. How could she still look so damned sweet and tempting after what she'd done? How could he still want to drag her into his arms and kiss her when she'd deceived him so horribly?

"I'm sorry, Alex. I never meant for any of this to happen."

His jaw was like a block. "Aye, well it did. And lying and dishonesty might come easy to you, but they don't to me. All I've ever tried to do was what was right, but tell me how the hell it can be right to keep your secret while doing my duty as a knight to the king?"

"What if doing your duty to Edward is not right anymore?"

He stiffened.

She went on. "What if what is right is returning to Bruce and the Guard?" She paused and added gently, "I know you thought you were doing what you had to do when you left. You were worn down and disillusioned by what seemed an endless war that wasn't going anywhere and couldn't see another choice. But you have a choice now. You came here to help persuade the English to end the war by peaceable means. You gave it a valiant try, but it didn't work. The English are going to march on Scotland, and nothing you do will stop them. So now you need to decide whether you march with them or return to the place where you belong—where you can do some good. It's not too late, Alex. You gave up on them, but I don't think they ever gave up on you. They trusted you—even Raider, although maybe he didn't always show it."

He didn't say anything; his chest was burning too hot. Give up on them? He wanted to deny it, but after what MacRuairi said, he didn't know what the hell to think anymore.

"You were one of us."

Echoing his thought she added, "The fact that you are still standing here without any apparent dagger wounds after coming into contact with my stepfather should tell you something. It tells me something. He would never have let you go after what you told him if he didn't still trust you on some level."

Frankly, he was just as surprised as she was that Lachlan had let him go without a fight. Was she right?

"Come back, Alex. They need you. Bruce needs you. It's where you belong."

Her voice was like a siren's call, lulling him, beguiling him, fooling him. Making him think about things he didn't want to remember. "Nay," he said angrily. "I can never go back. I made my choice. What you want is impossible."

"Is it? Or is it your knightly pride speaking? Is it that you don't want to admit you might have been wrong? That war isn't black or white, it's gray—no matter what side you fight on?"

He hadn't been wrong, damn it. He'd done what he had to do to see this war end. To see the suffering of his people stop. To be able to keep looking at himself in the mirror.

He thought she'd understood that. But could someone like her ever understand? *Whatever it takes* . . . Christ, not again—*never* again. That was exactly the mind-set he'd wanted to avoid when he'd left, and he'd fallen in love with someone who was just as bad as Boyd. She wanted him to go back to that? To a war without limits?

His jaw clenched. "I don't want to talk about this, Joan. I've told you my decision. I'm not going to go back for you or anyone else. Do not think my feelings for you can bend me to your will."

She looked genuinely offended. "That is not what I'm trying to do. I'm trying to make you see that you can't straddle the fence anymore. You came here, I know with good intentions, but it didn't work. You tried to stop it, but war is coming anyway. Now you have to pick a side. You can't be both an English knight and a Scot patriot. You have to choose."

Perhaps unknowingly, she'd pricked old wounds. He'd heard the same damned refrain from Raider for seven bloody years. "I made my choice two years ago."

Her eyes met his with disbelief. "So you will fight against Bruce and your former brethren?"

He thought of that little girl, and the thousands of innocents like her who hadn't been so lucky. "If I have to, but you and I both know it won't come to that. Bruce won't take the field."

And the war would go on.

"And if he does and the English win? Would you see Scotland ruled by England with Edward as overlord? More English justice in the form of cages?"

"Edward isn't his father."

"No, he isn't," she conceded. "But neither is he Robert the Bruce."

She was too bloody right about that—much to Alex's frustration over the past two years. But until Bruce was willing to challenge Edward in open battle, he would never be recognized as king and the war would go on. If Alex thought Bruce could be persuaded . . .

Christ, listen to him! She had him so twisted around that he was letting himself consider what-ifs. But he wasn't going to let her force his hand. Even an English overlord was better than a war of attrition. "I'm sorry, Joan, but I won't do it. I won't turn traitor even for you."

It had nearly killed him the first time.

"You mean you won't turn traitor *again*. For don't delude yourself, Alex. No matter what you told yourself, no matter what justification and good intentions you might have had, the ugly truth is that you gave Bruce and the Guard your loyalty and broke it, and now when you have a chance to make it right, you are too stubborn and afraid to try."

Alex struggled to keep a rein on his temper, but it was whipping and snapping inside him like a sail unfurled in a maelstrom. "You seem to have such a firm grasp on the situation, Joan. So tell me, what is it exactly that you propose I do? Jump on my horse and ride into whatever forest or patch of heather Bruce and the Guard have made their headquarters? Boyd as much as promised that the next time he sees me, he will try to kill me. As you've pointed out, I betrayed them; they think I am a *traitor*. Somehow none of my former brethren strike me as the forgive-and-forget type. Do you have any reason to believe that they will welcome me back with open arms?"

She flushed.

"I didn't think so," Alex said.

"I didn't say it would be easy, but I can help."

"Now who is the one who is deluded?"

Her mouth pursed. "So what does that mean?"

"It means that when I leave for Wark tomorrow, it will be in the service of Edward of England, and when I return, you and I will do our best to forget any of this ever happened."

∞

Joan gasped. "Tomorrow?" She couldn't believe her ears. "You are leaving tomorrow?"

Alex's nod was grim.

"Why did you not tell me?"

"I only found out tonight when I returned—just in time—to discover that a trap had been laid to catch the spy. Pembroke has been ordered to ride ahead; the rest of the army will follow in a few days."

"I see," Joan said softly, feeling as if her heart were being torn in shreds. "That is it, then."

Alex tensed. "What do you mean, that is it?"

"We are on opposite sides. You can't really think I would marry someone who would fight against everything I believe in. Everything I have worked for since I saw my mother in a cage in this very castle."

Horror crossed his features. "Christ, you saw her?"

"My father thought I needed to be taught a lesson," she said bitterly. "It was not the one that he intended." She held his gaze. "I will not be told what to do, nor will I marry someone who would fight against my friends and brethren."

It took him a moment to realize what she meant. When he did, his face grew as dark as a thundercloud. "You are one of them. I should have guessed. Your skills at deception are unmatched." She flushed at the dig. "As is your obvious affinity for danger. Do you have any idea what the English would do to get ahold of one of Bruce's Phantoms?" He dragged his fingers through his hair and paced a few steps. "You will go to my mother in Winton tomorrow. I will talk to Edward and say it is an emergency. I can spare a few men to escort you."

"Alex, did you hear what I said? I can't—I won't—marry you."

His jaw clamped down with enough force to tell her that he was losing the battle on control. "You are angry right now—we are both angry. There is no need to make any rash decisions. Go to my castle at Winton, and when I return—"

"I'm not going to Winton, Alex."

"You can't stay here."

She didn't say anything, but he guessed her intent.

He grabbed hold of her and pulled her up against him. "I'm not going to just let you go."

Her eyes searched his face, memorizing every detail as if it might be the last. "Then come with me," she said softly.

He let her go and stepped back as if afraid to touch her. "I told you, no."

She sucked in a breath that felt like inhaling through shards of glass. "Then I'm afraid we are at an impasse."

Apparently, Alex wasn't much on impasses. He looked every inch the dangerous brigand when he leaned in threateningly. "I could force you to wait for me. Perhaps I should leave you tied up in my bed where you can't get into any trouble."

There was something in his voice that sent a shiver down her spine. She wasn't quite sure whether it was trepidation or something else. "That doesn't sound very honorable of you, *Sir* Alex."

He swore and took another step back, some of the fierceness leaving his expression.

"You could always turn me in," she offered. "That should salve your knightly code."

She'd pricked his temper again. "Don't bloody tempt me," he bit out angrily.

They stared at each other in the darkness for a few long heartbeats, the dark, dangerous emotions swirling around them both. But there was also longing and heartbreak, the understanding that the dream—the fantasy—was over.

"So that's it, then?" she asked, almost in disbelief.

Blue eyes bit into hers unrelentingly. "It is not me who wants this, it's you."

"It is the last thing I want, Alex. But what other choice is there? I cannot stay here and you will not come with me."

"As you said, an impasse."

He looked so remote. So angry. Her heart squeezed with such longing, it stole her breath. Why couldn't she have stayed as she was—a ghost, there but not there, unable to touch or be touched, incapable of feeling? Then maybe it wouldn't have to hurt so badly.

Slowly, she pulled his ring off her finger. Holding it out to him, she said, "This never belonged to me."

He flinched, looking at the gold band as if it was going to bite him. Finally, after a long, heart-wrenching pause, he took it.

She reached for him, letting herself touch him one more time. "I'm sorry, Alex. Truly. I never meant . . ."

He just stared at her accusingly, his eyes as hard and unyielding as sapphire, until she dropped her hand. Feeling as if each step she was taking was through a deep bog, she walked slowly back to her room.

He didn't try to stop her.

❈

Alex left at dawn. With tired, red-rimmed eyes, Joan watched from the tower window in Alice's chamber as he rode out the gate of Berwick Castle at the head of the Earl of Pembroke's two hundred knights and men-at-arms.

She waited anxiously for a sign. A look. A glance. Any slight turn of the head in her direction that would indicate a chip or crack—no matter how small—in his resolve.

Look up . . . please don't do this . . . please don't go.

But her silent pleas could not penetrate the stone walls of the castle or those that surrounded his heart.

His head remained fixed straight ahead. Not once did he look back.

Joan's heart felt as if it were being squeezed between a grinding stone, but there was still a part of her that refused to believe he would actually go through with it. He couldn't march on Scotland and fight against the men he'd once stood beside.

He can't just walk away from me.

It was wrong, and Alex would see that. She had faith in him. He was hurt and angry at her for her deception—as he had every right to be. He was thinking with his pride. But once he had a chance to calm down and think, he would do the right thing.

But he'd walked away on principle before. To him there was only right and wrong, and what she'd done was . . . *wrong*.

Oh God. Her heart sank. He had to forgive her. She

couldn't bear to consider the possibility that she might never see him again.

His friends needed him. *She* needed him. He was the only one who never saw it. Alex was their check, their conscience, their moral center. He reminded them of what was right and what was wrong, even when they didn't want to see it.

He'd reminded her.

She used to know what was right, but men like her father and Sir Phillip made her forget. Just because others were without honor it was no excuse to forget her own. If she hadn't gone too far already, that was the direction she was headed. But Alex had brought her back from a jaded abyss, restoring her faith in good, honorable men. A good, honorable man in war? Who didn't need that? She wished someone like Alex had been there to speak for her mother.

"What are you looking at?"

Joan turned in the direction of the door that she had not heard open. "Alice!" she said, surprised. "You are back early."

"You've been crying," her cousin said, walking toward her. "What is wrong?"

Joan might ask her the same thing. Alice looked as if she'd had as little sleep as Joan. There were dark circles under her eyes and her normally creamy complexion was pale and wan. Sir Henry must have gotten back late from his "meeting" to try to catch the spy.

Instinct had served Joan well last night, but she knew she could not wait for Lachlan any longer. She would leave tonight.

"Alex left this morning," Joan answered. "He rode out with Pembroke ahead of the army."

"And you are worried for him?"

Joan felt a hitch in her chest. "Aye."

Alice stared at her with unusual perceptiveness. "But that isn't all, is it?"

Joan shook her head, her eyes suddenly swelling with tears. She'd been fighting so hard to control her emotions, but sympathy from an unexpected source caused the dam to break. All the emotion and all the fear that she'd been holding back came rushing out. She crumpled into a ball of tears. "I-it's over," she choked. "I think it's over."

Alice came forward to stand next to her, and seemingly unsure what to do, put a tentative hand on her shoulder. "What do you mean it's over?"

Joan looked up at her, tears streaming down her cheeks. "I mean us—the betrothal."

Any chance she'd had at happiness. When that had become something she wanted she didn't know, but it had.

Alice looked shocked—but something else as well. Her paleness had turned ashen—almost as if she were ill. "It can't be over," she said. "Why? What happened?"

Joan didn't understand her cousin's earnestness but was too upset to think about it. "We had an argument."

"But that can't be the end. He was so fierce in his defense of you—he cares for you deeply."

"I betrayed him horribly."

Strangely, her cousin didn't seem curious about the nature of her betrayal. "Surely there is something you can do? You have to go."

"Go?"

"After him," Alice explained anxiously. She seemed so jittery, and her hands were flying all over the place. "Explain everything. I'm sure he'll forgive you. You should go as soon as possible—immediately."

Joan managed a tremulous smile, appreciating her cousin's

urgency on her behalf. "He's going to Wark, Alice, to march off to war. He's angry enough. He'd be furious if I showed up in camp."

"But don't you see? You have to go now. Otherwise it could be too late. What if . . ." She thought for a moment. "What if something happens to him? You can't let him march off to war with it like this between you. Do you want his last thoughts of you to be in anger or in love?"

Joan looked at her in horror and wrapped her arms around her stomach. "Oh God."

"I don't mean to cause you more distress, cousin, but you must think of all possibilities. I don't want you to regret not doing something. Go to him. Say whatever you need to convince him to take you back—to take you away from here. Just go now."

Alice had almost convinced her that it was worth the try. Joan loved him. Could she just let him go without a fight?

Since the day her father had dragged her to see her mother hanging in that hideous cage, Joan had dedicated her life to one thing: doing whatever it took to help Bruce's cause. Could she do anything less for her own?

She was going to fight for Alex. Even if she had to pound it into that thick male head of his, she wasn't going to give up. Alex belonged with Bruce—and with her.

"I will help you," Alice volunteered. She started toward Joan's chamber.

Joan startled from her thoughts. Alice, help me? Suddenly she was taking notice of her cousin's strange behavior. Why was Alice so anxious for her to leave? It was almost as if . . .

She knew something.

"Alice, what is going on? Why are you trying to help me win back Alex when I know you weren't happy about our marriage in the first place?"

"I made a mistake, Joan. I didn't realize. I thought . . ." She started to cry. "I'm sorry."

Her cousin's words didn't make any sense. Suddenly, the door opened. Sir Henry stood there, a handful of soldiers behind him. He looked with disgust at his wife, as if he knew what she'd been trying to do. Turning to Joan he smiled. "You weren't going somewhere, were you, cousin? You wouldn't want to forget this."

Joan masked the horror from her expression, but she could not prevent the dread that sent her heart crashing to the floor. In his hand he held a thick circle of gold that was painfully familiar to her.

Sir Henry had her bracelet.

23

BY THE TIME the army left Wark on Monday the seventeenth day of June and crossed the Tweed into Scotland, traveling the first fifteen miles to camp for the night in Earlston, most of Alex's anger toward Joan for deceiving him had faded. He hated that she was involved in any of this, but he understood why she thought she couldn't tell him the truth.

After another fifteen miles on Tuesday to Sutra in the heat and sun, while riding ahead of the enormous, excruciatingly slow, and drawn-out supply train to sweep the countryside for an enemy that did not appear to be waiting for them, he was regretting his harshly spoken words and replaying every facet of their conversation in his head. Over and over.

By Wednesday—and another fifteen miles to Edinburgh, where they were forced to wait two days for the infantry and supply train to catch up with them, necessitating a twenty-three-mile journey on Saturday all the way to Falkirk or risk not meeting the Monday deadline to come within three leagues of Stirling to relieve the castle by St. John's Day—he was wondering how the hell he was going to get her back. He might have to track her down, but he would find her, damn it. Somehow they would bridge the impasse.

After the last ten miles to Falkirk, his disgust and frustration at what had to be the worst-run military campaign in history—replete with not only an infantry at least a half-day's journey from the vanguard and squabbling commanders, but a king who refused to heed any caution or consider anything but utter victory over a clearly "inferior" foe—Alex wasn't just wondering how to get her back, he was also wondering, for God knows how many times, what the hell he was doing here.

But it wasn't until the evening of Sunday the twenty-third of June, after a disastrous first day of battle, when Alex stood in the crowded Royal Pavilion, which had hastily been set up in the middle of the boggy Carse of Balquhiderock just north of the Bannock Burn—within the required three leagues of Stirling—listening to the king and his commanders squabble, that Alex knew Joan had been right: he didn't belong here anymore—if he ever had.

Whether he'd thought he was doing the right thing two years ago no longer mattered. It had become painfully clear that it wasn't right any longer. Even before Joan's urging him to change sides, Alex had had second . . . third . . . God-knows-how-many thoughts. The early inroads he thought he'd been making with the English had been replaced by doubt and frustration. From the foolhardy attack on the Earl of Carrick, to them thinking he was the spy and shutting him out of meetings, to Despenser's petty machinations, to the English attack on his people near Hailes, the realization that his efforts were futile had been building for some time.

But he'd ignored all the gut twists and all the twinges. His rigidity and refusal to see anything other than black and white had prevented him from admitting that even if well intentioned, he might have made a mistake. As MacRuairi had accused him, Alex had tried to make it too simple. But since leaving the Guard, he'd changed. Age and experience had showed him that the world was more gray than he'd realized—especially in war. It wasn't always clear what was right and what was wrong. It wasn't always simple.

After what happened with Gifford—experiencing the kind of desire and hatred that might make a man forget his honor—Alex also had to acknowledge that his line in the sand might be more movable than he'd first thought. But he'd always had one—whether he wore shiny mail and a tabard or a blackened helm and a plaid.

Joan had accused him of giving up on his former brethren, and maybe he had. Maybe he should have stayed and fought harder. Maybe he should have banged his head until they listened to him.

But it was too late to go back and do it over. The question was what he was going to do about it now.

The events of the day had made it clear he had to do something.

Since leaving Falkirk that morning, Alex had been marching with the center or main body of the army, which was under the command of King Edward. But he'd ridden ahead to give information to the vanguard—under the disastrous joint command of the young Gilbert de Clare, Earl of Gloucester, the king's favored nephew, and Humphrey de Bohun, Earl of Hereford, the Constable of England and rightful commander—just in time to see one of the greatest (or most rash, depending on your perspective) displays of chivalric warfare by a king that he could ever recall.

Sir Henry de Bohun, the young nephew of Hereford, had caught sight of some of Bruce's men coming out of the New Park on the main road, where Bruce had positioned his men to block the English approach to Stirling. Realizing that one of the men was Bruce himself, de Bohun—no doubt thinking of the glory that would be his if he brought down the king in single combat—raced his destrier forward, lance in hand, intent on ending the war with one dramatic strike.

Rather than retreat into the forest of the New Park to avoid the charging knight, or leave his men to dispense with the attack as he should have, Bruce not only accepted the challenge, he skillfully maneuvered his palfrey at the last minute to avoid the lance, and then stood up in his stirrups to deliver a powerful blow with his axe into the helm of de Bohun that had not just cleaved through metal into the skull of the young knight, killing him, but had also broken the handle of the king's battle-axe.

This was a king to fight for. It was just the kind of extraordinary feat of warfare that had made Bruce an almost mythical figure to his men. The Bruce had more chivalry in his little finger than Edward would have in a lifetime. No doubt MacLeod and some of the other captains were reprimanding him for taking foolish, unnecessary risks—the entire Scottish cause might have died on the end of one lance wielded by a rash young knight—but the story would inevitably add to Bruce's popularity and his growing legend.

Some might also say that this one decisive single combat was a harbinger of things to come.

The spurious charge by de Bohun provoked an attack by the English cavalry on the Scot position before the New Park that was haphazard, ill-conceived, poorly executed, and ultimately repulsed by the Scot schiltron formations of pikemen. Alex had taken one look at his former compatriots across the battlefield and knew Joan and Boyd were right. There wasn't a middle ground. He had to choose, and he'd chosen the wrong side.

Hereford had tried to pull the men back into some semblance of order, but with no clear command it had been an exercise in futility. The English had been forced to retreat, giving Bruce if not his first victory, his first nondefeat of the battle.

The second had come slightly to the east of the New Park, where Clifford and de Beaumont, also in advance, had led a force of eight hundred cavalry on a quest to find an alternative route to Stirling through the boggy, inhospitable carse. They'd nearly surprised Thomas Randolph, the Earl of Moray, who with his men was positioned near St. Ninian's and was supposed to be guarding the flank for

Bruce. Moray recovered in time, and after a hard-fought battle, his schiltrons of infantrymen, too, forced the English into their second retreat of the day.

King Edward had arrived at the Bannock Burn to the shocking news that not only had the vanguard of vaunted English cavalry engaged the enemy twice—without his knowledge—but both times they'd been repulsed by Bruce's infantry pikemen. The flower of English chivalry defeated by farmers! It was inconceivable! Humiliating! At least it was to Edward. The armies weren't that unbalanced, of course—Bruce's men were skilled warriors—but to say that the mood among the English was disheartened was putting it mildly.

A situation that grew worse when the English were forced to set up camp for the night on the boggy, damp carse of mud, streams, and peaty "pols" of water, as the Scots called them. Most of the carts and infantry had to stay on the other side of the Bannock Burn, unable to cross, despite the doors and shutters that had been ripped down from houses to give them traction and make the ground more solid. There was plenty of water to water the horses, but moving them about in this type of terrain was slow and difficult.

It wasn't the retreats, low morale, or uncomfortable night that had convinced Alex what he had to do—no matter what the risk—it was the utter ineptitude of the English leadership. The army was unorganized and hampered by a ridiculously long train of supplies that stretched for twenty leagues—Despenser had even brought furniture, for Christ's sake, for the earldom of Moray that the king had promised him. Furthermore, King Edward had no real battle plan (arrogantly believing that Bruce would retreat or be no match for the "superior" English troops—despite recent proof to the contrary), and he'd not only failed to put an end to the squabbling among his commanders, he'd actually made it worse by fueling the bad blood between Gloucester and Hereford by appointing them joint commanders, leaving the important vanguard of the army without clear directive.

What chance did the English have to end this war when no one was in charge, the commanders were at each other's throats, and the king wouldn't listen to reason? And even if the English did manage to end it, could Alex count on Edward to protect the Scots in the Borders? Or would they just exchange one kind of suffering for another?

Alex listened in disbelief as Edward humiliated the very nephew he'd foolishly favored with co-command of the vanguard—young Gloucester—and ignored his sound advice.

"We have arrived in time to relieve the siege," Gloucester pointed out. "There is no need to force the Scots into a confrontation tomorrow. The men are tired after marching for a week. The carts and infantry are still straggling in. Let us rest a day, get the men organized, find better ground for our troops, and wait and see what Bruce will do."

"And give him a chance to slink back into his fox hole?" King Edward demanded furiously. "Are you a fool, nephew, or merely a coward?"

The word fell like the slap of a gauntlet. Gloucester's face turned nearly purple with anger.

Hereford, his enemy who'd been forced into joint leadership with Edward's favorite nephew, smirked.

And that is how it went in that crowded, hot, and pungent tent, teeming with angry and disheartened knights in battle-scuffed mail: fractious discord made wider by the king, and any effort to urge caution met with scorn and derision.

If Edward had troubled himself to walk around the camp through the boggy ground and look at the disarray and exhaustion of his army, he would have seen the truth. But like the unfortunate Sir Henry de Bohun, he was so caught up in the perceived glory of defeating Bruce and the Scots in a pitched battle that he would not heed caution. With nearly eighteen thousand men—three times as many as Bruce—Edward would not conceive of anything other than an English victory. *If* Bruce could be persuaded into taking the field, that is.

At least on that they agreed. Bruce needed to take the field. And if Alex wanted an end to this war—the right end—he knew what he had to do.

"It's not too late."

He sure as hell hoped she was right.

Despite it being close to midnight, the sky was not yet completely dark as Alex crept through the shadows, winding his way through the tents and fitfully sleeping soldiers. The English were on alert, half expecting a middle-of-the-night attack by Bruce. Still, Alex was stopped by sentries only once.

"I carry a message from the earl"—Pembroke, Alex meant—"to my men guarding the carts." The carts that were on the other side of the Bannock Burn.

They let him go.

It was partially true. When Alex arrived at the carts, he explained to his men what he planned to do and told them to be ready when the time came.

If the time came.

Though there were signs that Bruce might be considering doing what he'd avoided for eight years—meeting the English in pitched battle—Alex knew that prudence and caution would be urging the king to take the small victories he'd won today and slip back into the mist, leaving the fight for another day. Alex intended, however, to convince him to stay and fight.

So far Bruce had surprised him, and Alex wondered whether Bruce, too, *wanted* to fight. Was he looking for a definitive end to the war? Had he grown tired of the cat-and-mouse game they'd been playing?

The fact that Bruce had let the English army march unmolested this far—a complete change of tactics from the previous English invasion—and had stayed in the area to face them today, suggested that he might.

But Alex knew that if he did not act, there was every chance the Scots would leave the forest of the New Park by morning.

He couldn't let that happen. He knew with every fiber of his being that this was the chance Bruce had to defeat the English and end the war. So he swallowed his pride—knowing he would have to do so many times before the night was over—removed the surcoat that identified him as a knight, and told himself that even if he felt like a dog slinking back with its tail between its legs, he would do whatever it took. In this case, the ends definitely justified the means.

As he slipped through the English perimeter and headed toward the New Park, he entered the eerily quiet buffer of land between the two armies. After stumbling into a pit carefully hidden beneath leaves and branches and nearly becoming impaled on one of the wooden stakes at the bottom, he was more careful about where he stepped. But the honeycomb-like defensive pits dug by Bruce's men were one more indication that Bruce might want to fight.

Each step Alex took closer to the Scot camp he knew well could be his last. If one of their scouts didn't put an arrow through him first, he knew Boyd and MacRuairi would be fighting for the honor of doing so with a blade. But if he was going to die, damn it, it wasn't going to be fighting behind Edward Plantagenet's banner.

Joan was right; he had to take a chance.

He held his hands up in the universal signal of surrender as he approached, but that didn't stop the arrow that whizzed right by his ear—too perfectly directed to be a mistake.

Alex stopped and cursed. There was only one man skilled enough to make a shot like that. Of course Bruce had his best men on watch tonight; it was Alex's bad luck that he'd run into one he knew too well. "I'm here to see the king, MacGregor."

Two men stepped out from behind the trees. He didn't need to see their nasal helm–covered faces to recognize the shadows of Gregor "Arrow" MacGregor and Arthur "Ranger" Campbell.

Alex swore again. Christ, not one but *two* of his former brethren.

"I think your king is in that big fancy pavilion there on the other side of that burn," MacGregor quipped.

What had he expected, open arms? He'd known it would be like this. They wouldn't make this easy. No, they would make him pay for his betrayal—he knew that. And he would take it, damn it, until he convinced the king.

Alex gritted his teeth and said patiently, "I have important information that Bruce will want to hear."

"I'm sure you do," Campbell said. "And perhaps an assassin's dagger as well?"

Alex knew they had no cause to trust him—and every reason not to—but still, the accusation stung. Gritting his teeth some more, he removed his sword, dagger, and even his eating knife, and held them out. "Check me if you wish, but this is all of them."

Both men came forward. MacGregor took the weapons and Campbell, after a cursory search, stood back. "He's clean."

"This better be good, Seton," MacGregor said. "Make one false move and it won't just be my arrow that strikes you."

Alex understood. They would all be vying for that honor.

They took him to the king. Just outside the royal tent, which was about a third of the size of Edward's and not half as fine, Alex passed by a handful of tied up men whom he recognized; they were some of the more important English soldiers who'd been taken prisoner by Randolph today.

"Seton," Sir Thomas Gray said with obvious relief. "You're a sight for weary eyes. Did the king send you to negotiate our ransom already?"

Alex answered with a shake of his head. They would find out the truth soon enough.

After entering the tent—or rather being shoved through by MacGregor—a glance at the hardened visages surrounding him told Alex that he'd come at the right time. He'd interrupted the king's war council. For gathered around the king were his chief advisors: Douglas, Randolph, Neil Campbell (Arthur's elder brother and one of Bruce's most loyal and longtime companions), Edward Bruce, the Abbot of Inchaffray (who brought the relics of St. Columba), and every single member of the Highland Guard.

Perfect.

He ignored everyone but the king, who if his icy expression was an indication, was just as happy to see him as the rest.

"Sire," Alex said with a bow.

"You are either extremely brave or extremely foolish." Or maybe a little of both, Alex thought. "Say what it is you come to say, and then leave. As you can see, I'm busy."

Alex faced the man he'd always believed in—even when he'd turned his back on him. It was more difficult than he thought it would be. No matter what his reasons, he'd given Bruce his loyalty—his oath—and he'd broken it. Whether he had good intentions couldn't seem to stem all the shame.

Alex cleared his throat. "I made you a pledge nine years ago to help see you on the throne, and tonight I have come to fulfill that pledge."

"Is this the same pledge that you conveniently forgot about for two years?" The look the king gave him could have cut through stone. "I would never have believed that Chris's brother would have turned traitor."

Though the blow wasn't unexpected, it was powerful. It was also deserved. His brother had loved Robert Bruce like a brother; he would never have understood what Alex had done. But Alex did, and he realized that was enough.

He drew himself up, meeting the derision in the king's gaze directly. "Traitor for what I thought were good reasons," he said simply. "Which is the same reason I am here now. I bring you my sword and information." He didn't pause long enough to let the king comment. "The English army is disheartened, has lost faith, and is in disarray. Whatever authority Edward once had is gone. There is no one in charge, his leaders are too busy vying for position or squabbling. They do not expect you to really fight and have no battle plan if you do. You are not likely to get a better choice of terrain and know the benefits of the ground upon which they are camped."

He moved over to the crude map that was set out upon the table, not surprised when Boyd stepped in front of him. The two men eyed one another.

"Let him pass, Raider," the king said.

Boyd gave Alex a long, hard look meant to intimidate, which it might have years ago, and then reluctantly did as the king commanded.

Alex pointed to the spot between the Bannock Burn and the Pelstream Burn where the ground narrowed. "If you attack them with your schiltrons here in the morning, you will win." Schiltrons typically stayed fixed in one position, but what Alex was proposing was that they be dynamic—that they move—which he knew Bruce had trained them to do. "Most of the infantry are camped on the other side of the Bannock Burn. By engaging the first column of cavalry in this narrow area with your schiltrons, the second will be hemmed in by the burns and won't be able to reach them—you will take away their advantage of number. Nor will their archers be much help. In such close quarters, there will be too much risk of hitting their own men. The morale of the soldiers is so low they will scatter like frightened mice."

"And how do I know that you are telling me the truth?"

"I pledge my life on it, sire. Feed me to the wolves," he said, motioning to his former brethren, "if what I say is not the God's honest truth."

The king looked at MacLeod in silent question. The fierce Island chief and leader of the Highland Guard shrugged and looked to Boyd.

His former partner eyed him for a long moment. "He's too bloody noble to lie."

It wasn't a compliment—at least to Boyd—but it seemed to satisfy Bruce enough to let Alex continue.

"You have better leadership," Alex said. "Your men are better trained, and more important, they are fighting for something." He took a deep breath, knowing the king wasn't going to like what he had to say next. "I know you have had many reasons to avoid pitched battle to this point, but there are some who will never recognize you as king until you defeat the English army to army. This is the battle people want, my lord. Give it to them. You may never have a better chance."

The room was silent for a long moment.

It was Edward Bruce who was the first to speak. As Alex had never gotten along particularly well with the king's only remaining brother, he was surprised to hear his support.

"He is right, brother. We have them where we want them. And if it is half as bad in the English camp as Seton suggests, we can put an end to this. Victory will be seen as God's judgment and prove to everyone that you are the rightful king."

As Alex had been saying for years, a pitched battle was the only way of doing that. Bruce had to show he had a right to the throne, and in this case it had to be shown by right of battle.

One by one Bruce went around the room asking each man his opinion, and each—some with more reluctance than others—gave an affirming nod.

But the ultimate decision rested with Bruce. He didn't say anything right away, but stared at Alex until he felt like a bug under a rock.

"Well, Seton, you are either the messenger of destiny or the messenger of death. I guess we shall find out which."

Alex released the breath that he didn't even realize he'd been holding. He'd done it. He'd convinced the king, and in doing so, hopefully put an end to this war.

Dismissed, the men started to file out to find their pallets. But Alex did not think anyone would be sleeping much this night.

"What about him?" Boyd asked the king, indicating Alex. "Should I tie him up with the others?"

Bruce considered him for a moment, and then surprisingly one corner of his mouth lifted. "Give him back his weapons. Let him fight tomorrow. It's his life on the line."

They all knew there was far more than Alex's life on the line, but Alex had his second chance—from the king, at least—and he intended to do what he could to ensure Bruce did not regret it. Ever.

∾

The Nativity of St. John the Baptist,
Midsummer's Day, June 24, 1314

Midsummer's Day, which also happened to be St. John's Day, dawned sunny and hot. As the English woke from their uncomfortable and restless night, they stumbled out of tents to an inconceivable sight. The Scots were mustering for battle!

As Alex had foretold, the English were not prepared to face Bruce—and certainly not for a Scot offensive in broad daylight. The Earl of Gloucester was so hastily awakened he didn't even have time to don the surcoat that bore his arms. It would spell his doom, as when the Scot army of moving schiltrons attacked—led by Edward Bruce with Randolph and Douglas on either side—Gloucester, undoubtedly with the king's accusation of "coward" still ringing in his ears, mounted a quick charge against Edward Bruce and was cut down from his horse and killed rather than be held for ransom.

Alex watched it all unfold from his position fighting in the king's division, slightly behind Edward Bruce's. But to the English cavalry, which had little room to maneuver in the narrow ground between the two rivers, the Scot army must have seemed like one dense, moving wall of spears that they could not penetrate. The Scots kept pressing forward and the English kept falling beneath their pikes, men and beast skewered by the deadly points of steel.

It went on for hours, a fierce melee of pikes and horsemen. What was nearly the entire force of the Scot army was now pitted against the English front.

Only once did Alex come close to death. Ironically, it wasn't at the hands of the English, but at the hand of the man he'd hoped would one day be his father-in-law.

A small opening between the schiltrons had appeared, enabling a handful of English to penetrate. One of those men was Sir Edmund Mauley, King Edward's seneschal, who had lost his horse and was locked in a fierce battle with Boyd. Suddenly, another knight shot through the opening on a horse, intent on driving his lance into Boyd.

Alex shouted a warning. But Boyd didn't have a chance to react. Alex didn't think. He reached for his dagger and threw.

Out of the corner of his eye, Alex sensed the threat moving toward him even as he watched the horseman, now with a dagger in his neck, falter and drop his lance. Alex spun and lifted his sword, but only managed to block the blow from one of MacRuairi's swords. The other penetrated his mail and sank into his side—fortunately not in his gut where it had been aimed.

By this point, MacRuairi must have realized Alex hadn't meant to kill Boyd but to save him.

"Fuck, Seton. I didn't see . . . are you all right?"

Alex removed the hand that had gone instinctively to the hole in his side. Noticing only a small patch of blood, he nodded. "It's just a scratch."

MacRuairi didn't look like he believed him, but there wasn't time to say anything more. Another wave of men had appeared and they lifted their swords to fight them off.

The next time he looked over to Boyd, Sir Edmund was down. His former partner caught his eye and nodded in silent thanks. But Alex knew it didn't change anything.

The battle raged on, and Alex fought like a man possessed—or perhaps like a man with something to prove. Shoulder to shoulder with his former brethren they surged forward against the faltering English line.

He read the surprise, and then the hatred, on more than one face as his former English compatriots realized what he'd done. Despenser shouted something at him from across the battlefield—with an almost gleeful sneer—but his words were lost in the roar of the fighting. As Alex was only too anxious to meet him knight to knight, he was disappointed that was the last he saw of him.

It was mid-morning when Alex knew his faith would be rewarded. The fabled English archers, whose arrows might have penetrated the schiltrons of pikemen and made a difference in the battle, were deployed despite the close fighting and threat of hitting their own men. Bruce, however, was prepared. He ordered Robert Keith, the Marischal of Scotland, to attack with his cavalry that had been held in reserve for just this purpose.

The threat—and the only hope for an English victory—was eradicated.

The final blow came when Bruce brought forward his own archers, who sent a hail of arrows down on the rear of the enemy. The English resistance crumbled, and the army was in full retreat.

The melee became a bloodbath as the very ground that had constrained the English forces hampered their escape. The Bannock Burn, which stood in their way, became a giant burial pit as it filled to the top with bodies of men and horses. The Scots took to plunder—not only the bodies of the dead but the rich baggage train that Edward had laboriously brought with them.

And it seemed the biggest prize of all just might be

in Bruce's reach. Surprised by the aggressiveness of the Scot attack, and the inability of his cavalry to penetrate, King Edward had been caught unawares. Only thanks to the insistence of Pembroke and the famed Gascon knight Sir Giles d'Argentan was he forced from the battlefield, Despenser and de Beaumont fleeing alongside him.

Douglas was sent after them.

But with or without a royal hostage, Robert the Bruce had his great victory on the battlefield. The one that would finally ensure Scotland's independence and give God's validation to his claim to the throne.

Along the boggy carse of the battlefield, the grass and peaty pols now turned red with blood as the English fled and the Scots put down the last pockets of resistance, a great cheer went up. It was the cheer of a country that had fought for eighteen years for this moment—since Edward I of England had decimated Berwick in 1296, provoking the risings of William Wallace and Andrew Murray a year later. Scotland had its freedom.

Alex, who'd fought during the battle alongside his former compatriots but had hardly been welcomed, joined in, but perhaps without the enthusiasm of back slaps, happy embraces, and arm pumping.

He stood apart with his men who had joined Bruce at the start of the battle as he'd planned and started to take inventory of their injuries—his own would wait—when he sensed a familiar shadow move up behind him.

He stiffened—defensively—and turned.

"You saved my life," Boyd said, his expression stony. "I owe you my thanks."

Alex shook his head. "You don't owe me shite. Forget about it."

Boyd stood there staring at him, almost as if he knew

what Alex was thinking. He didn't want gratitude, but forgiveness was about the last thing he could ever expect from his former partner.

"What made you decide to come back? Not that it wasn't impeccably timed, riding into the rescue at the last minute. Bruce was ready to call for the retreat when you arrived with your information and persuaded him to fight."

"Does it really matter?"

Boyd held his stare and shrugged. "I guess not."

He started to walk away, and Alex felt the anger rise up inside him. "You were right, is that what you want to hear? I judged you for things that I shouldn't have. I tried to straddle both sides of the line, but just like you said, I had to choose. So I did. This is where I belong."

Boyd paused and looked at him as if he were an idiot. "It took you two years to figure that out?"

"Aye, well I was busy trying to do some good. And I guess you aren't the only one who is hardheaded and can hold a grudge."

Boyd's mouth might have actually quirked. "You always were too much of a damned idealist."

"Someone needed to be."

Alex said it mostly to himself, so he was surprised when Boyd responded.

"Aye, you're right." He looked like he was about to walk away again, but then he hesitated. "You weren't the only one who was wrong. I owe you an apology." Alex was stunned. Surely hell had frozen over? "I never gave you a fair chance—even after you deserved one. And you were right to do what you did for Rosalin. Defending her honor and trying to stop me from burning down her home." He made a pained face. "I was blinded by rage, and if you hadn't helped me see . . . she never would have forgiven me."

Alex felt his face heat. "Aye, well maybe not as right about defending her honor as I thought."

It took Boyd a minute to figure out what he meant, but he'd obviously been told of Alex's relationship with Joan—at least some of it. "Bloody hell." He shook his head. "I'd be tempted to gloat, but I almost feel sorry for you. You better hope MacRuairi never finds out."

Alex grimaced. "I intend to make it right as soon as possible." *If she'll have me back.* He looked around. "Where is MacRuairi?"

"He, MacSorley, Campbell, and MacGregor went with Douglas." He frowned. "Someone else was looking for him. Young Ross was around here a while ago with bad news—at least that's how he looked. I wonder what it was about?"

They found out soon enough. Bruce and his captains had returned to their camp in the New Park, and Alex, after seeing to his men and his wound—which was deeper than he thought—followed. Now that the war had been won, he was anxious to find Joan. Had she left Berwick? He hoped Bruce would know where she'd gone.

The moment he entered the tent he knew something was wrong. Bruce didn't look like a man who'd just achieved one of the greatest military victories in history. He looked upset and worried. Alex's instincts flared when he noticed the pitying looks being sent in his direction by Sutherland, MacKay, and even Boyd.

Joan.

He steeled himself. "What is it? What's happened?"

The room fell to a dead silence as if no one wanted to answer him. Finally, Bruce motioned to MacLeod. "Let him see it."

Alex read the short missive dated June 19 that had

finally found its way to John Ross, the Earl of Ross's youngest son. Each word felt like a sword in the gut.

Cousin imprisoned. I fear they mean to make her disappear. Send help. With all my love, Margaret.

Somehow Alex remained standing, but it felt as if every ounce of blood had been sucked from his body. His stomach lurched sideways and his head swam.

How could this have happened?

He turned on Bruce. "You were supposed to protect her! I thought you had men watching her."

"We did," the king said. "Something must have happened."

"Damned right something happened!" Alex said, furious. "You put her in danger and you screwed up."

"I'm sending a team to get her," Bruce said. "She'll be all right."

He didn't know who Bruce was trying to convince, Alex or himself.

Alex didn't need to ask what team he meant. He turned to MacLeod. "I'm going."

Chief's expression didn't flicker. "I'm not so sure that's a good idea."

Assuming it was because of his former place in the Guard, Alex clenched his jaw. "Do you need to see me crawl through the mud and beg your forgiveness? Because if that's what it takes, I'll do it—I'll do whatever it takes, damn it, but I'm going."

MacLeod's only reaction was a slight lifting of one brow. "I don't think that will be necessary."

"I wouldn't mind seeing it," Boyd quipped.

"Sod off, Raider," Alex shot back to him, not taking his eyes off MacLeod.

"Are you sure you can stay rational about this? I don't want any more rogue operators like MacRuairi when Bella was taken."

"I'm not like MacRuairi."

It turned out Alex was wrong about that, too.

24

AFTER ELEVEN DAYS in the hellish dark depths of Berwick's pit prison, Joan was beginning to lose hope.

They will come. Lachlan would search for her to the ends of the earth. But how long would it take for him to realize she'd been taken? And what if he *couldn't* come? What if he and the rest of the Highland Guard were fleeing for their lives right now?

Don't, she told herself. *Don't think like that. They will come.*

But what if it takes two years? God in heaven, how had her mother done it? Joan's appreciation for her mother's strength after what she'd endured at the hands of her English captors increased immeasurably. It also helped keep her from crawling into a ball of despair and giving up. Joan had the blood of one of Scotland's greatest heroes running through her veins; she would not let her down. She would not fall into a fit of despair and hopelessness. She would stay strong.

But it was hard.

Down here in the darkness and cold, with barely any

food and only the tantalizing trickle of water that seeped through the rock walls when it rained, she wasn't sure whether they meant to freeze or slowly starve her to death. Perhaps they meant to do both.

And then there were the rats. God, how she hated the rats. The vicious, sneaky, vile creatures that waited until she was at her weakest to sink their sharp teeth into her. She'd fashioned weapons out of old bones—she tried not to think too much about those—and gathered rocks to build a defensive wall around her when she slept. It didn't keep all of them back, but it slowed them down.

But even worse than the rats was not knowing what was going on outside of her prison. The only face she saw was that of the guard as he tossed down the occasional crust of dried bread or scrap of meat. But he didn't speak to her, and he certainly didn't tell her what they meant to do with her, or what news there was of the battle.

Had the English made it to Stirling in time to relieve the siege? Had Bruce waited for them? Were her friends alive? And most painfully of all, what had become of Alex? Had he ever looked back? Had he regretted the way they'd parted, as she did? Would he come looking for her or had he already put aside in his heart the woman who'd betrayed him?

For one horrible moment when they'd confronted her with her bracelet and accused her of being the spy, she actually thought Alex had done his duty and turned her in. Had he followed her and intercepted the bracelet before it reached Lachlan? Was that how he'd lured Lachlan into meeting him?

But Alice's tears and sobbing apologies had quickly pulled that knife from her heart. Alex hadn't betrayed her, Alice had. Her cousin had managed to convey that much before Joan had been taken away. Why she'd done it, Joan didn't know, but she'd obviously come to regret it. Unfortunately, not before the damage had been done.

Despenser had been only too pleased to follow up on Alice's suspicions. It was he who'd had Joan followed. It was he who'd had the church and every churchman inside thoroughly searched until they'd found the bracelet in the offertory.

They didn't know what it meant at first. But after the failed trap, Despenser had taken the bracelet out to show Sir Henry when Sir Adam Gordon happened to walk by. Without realizing the import, he'd caught sight of the lion emblem with the spiderweb and mentioned his nephew had one just like it on his arm, but without the roses.

Joan's fate had been sealed.

Despenser and Sir Henry accused her of being not only the spy, but one of Bruce's Phantoms, and had tried to beat the names of her fellow "traitors" out of her. Despenser had even threatened to have another cage built for her—just like her traitorous mother. She hadn't been able to completely hide her fear. But, fortunately, though her cuts and bruises had mostly healed—although her ribs still hurt—neither the promised torturer nor cage had appeared.

Indeed, since the second day—after which she assumed the army had left for Scotland—no one had appeared except for the solitary guard.

Did anyone else even know she was here? Would the men Lachlan had watching her realize something had happened?

The questions—and fears they produced—plagued her, even more so than the hunger. She wanted to get out. She wanted to find Alex and beg him to forgive her. She wanted to see her mother again, meet her siblings, and see the verdant hillsides and valleys of the land where she'd been born. She wanted to go home to Scotland.

She wanted a future.

Joan had always known what she risked, but it wasn't until she lay in that dark, wretched pit that she realized how much she didn't want to be a ghost. She wanted to live.

She had to do something. She had to think of a plan.

∞

When the trapdoor opened above her a few hours later, Joan was ready. Silently, she thanked Lachlan for giving her the idea.

She didn't wait for her eyes to adjust from the darkness; as soon as the head appeared above her, she threw the rock with everything she had. She'd always had a strong throwing arm, and her aim was true.

It was only when she heard the ding of metal and the deep Scottish voice say "ouch" that she stopped and focused.

Gradually the nasal helm came into view. The feeling of relief that crashed over her was indescribable. They'd come for her. They'd found her.

Though she'd seen the face beneath the helm only a few times, she recognized the fierce warrior well enough. "I'm sorry about that, Chief."

"I suppose she got that from you," he said to someone next to him. "Bloody hell, no wonder you let me go first." She heard another voice, but he told him to shut up and wait. He looked back down at her. "Are you all right, lass?"

"I am now. Or will be in a few minutes."

"Where is she, damn it?"

Joan gasped, recognizing the voice. A moment later a second face appeared beside MacLeod's. Alex? But how?

My God.

"I thought I told you to wait outside with the others until I brought her up," MacLeod said angrily.

Alex let out a string of curse words that would have done a pirate proud, and in no uncertain terms told Mac-Leod exactly what he thought about that. If Joan wasn't already in deep shock, she would have been—she'd never heard Alex speak like that to anyone, let alone the fierce chief of the Highland Guard.

"God, you even sound like him," MacLeod said. "I knew you weren't going to be reasonable."

Apparently Alex was done with talking. A rope was thrown down, and in what seemed like a heartbeat he was pulling her into his arms with a groan of relief. "God, I was so scared. I thought I'd lost you."

Still half in disbelief that he was really there—with her brethren, no less—she collapsed in his arms. Her strength had given out.

"God, sweetheart, forgive me. Please, forgive me. God, what did they do to you? You are so thin."

She looked up in the semidarkness at the handsome face that had always seemed like a beacon in the night. "You're here. It's really you. But I don't understand."

He smiled. "Aye, it's really me. I'll explain everything once we get you away from here."

He swung her up in his arms like a bairn and carried her to the rope. He made a loop for her to sit in. Doing her best not to wince against the pain in her ribs, she held on tightly as MacLeod and Lachlan—she could make out her stepfather now—pulled her up.

Both men took one look at her and swore.

She touched her face self-consciously. Apparently her cuts and bruises weren't as healed as she thought. "Is it that bad?"

"Who beat you?" Lachlan demanded.

From the shivery tone of his voice she could guess why he was asking.

Alex had come up behind her. His expression darkened to something decidedly terrifying when he took in her appearance. "He's mine, MacRuairi. I'm going to tear the bastard to pieces."

MacLeod swore again. "Neither of you are going to do anything right now. We have to get out of here. They aren't far behind us."

Joan didn't know who "they" were, but there was not time for questions as she was led out of the guardroom— past the dead guard—and into the courtyard where the rest of the Guard were waiting for them. No one said anything as they slid through the moonlight to the rear postern. She was surprised to see so few people around—the castle seemed almost deserted. Where were all the guards?

Suddenly a hooded figure appeared by the door. Joan recognized her instantly. "Margaret!"

She rushed toward her and the two cousins embraced.

"I don't understand," Joan said. "How did you—"

"Alex will explain everything," her cousin said. "But you have to hurry. The guards will be back soon."

She held a big iron key ring (how had she gotten that?) and carefully unlocked the iron yett. Knowing her cousin was somehow responsible for all of this, she gave her another hug. "Thank you," she said.

Margaret nodded, tears in her eyes. "I hope we will meet again . . . soon."

Joan knew she was thinking also of John Ross. If there was any justice in this world, Margaret would find her happiness. "As do I."

An eventless few minutes later, Joan was lifted up onto

a horse, sharing the saddle with Alex, and they rode away from the giant shadow of the formidable castle.

After eight years, Joan was finally going home.

∞

Most of Joan's questions would have to wait, but what Alex had managed to convey while they rode away was enough to keep her mind reeling.

She couldn't believe it. Not only had Bruce won his great battlefield victory, but Alex had been a part of it. He'd gone back. Her faith in him had been rewarded, after all.

But apparently, despite his timely changing of sides, not all was well between Alex and his former brethren, as she discovered when they stopped not long after leaving the lights of the burgh behind them.

First it was an argument between Alex and Tor MacLeod, upon which she'd been called to intercede, when Alex—after learning that it was Despenser's man who'd beaten her—announced that he intended to stay and wait for him while the others took Joan to safety. In this case, he had the support of her stepfather, who said he would join him.

When Tor objected to their plan, Alex told him in stinging and not very pleasant terms that he no longer answered to him, and that he—Tor—could take his opinion and do something with it that was physically impossible.

Only Robbie Boyd's intervention with Tor, and Joan's plea with Alex that she needed him with her, prevented a physical confrontation between the two men.

When Alex stormed away with her stepfather, she turned to Robbie. "What is the matter with him? I've never seen him like this." Alex wasn't foolhardy, but taking on the greatest swordsman in Christendom certainly qualified.

Robbie just shook his head. "He's lost his bloody mind.

He's been out of control like this since he found out you were taken. Never thought I'd see the day."

From the way he smiled, he actually seemed *pleased* by the whole thing.

It was from Robbie that she learned some of the details that Alex had left out, most important how his turning had come at a key moment in the battle when the king had been about to retreat. It was Alex's timely intelligence and persuasiveness that had convinced Bruce to stay and fight.

She would have told Alex how proud she was of him, but he was locked in another confrontation. This time with her stepfather.

Good gracious, that didn't take long! Alex and Lachlan's temporary alliance hadn't lasted all of about five minutes. She had just sat down to eat some of the beef and cheese that Alex had left her, when she noticed the two men arguing.

From the way they occasionally glanced in her direction, she didn't need to guess what they were arguing about. She could tell from Lachlan's expression that he was making threats, but Alex seemed completely unmoved. He waited until Lachlan was done, and then said something while pointing to his side. It was chillingly effective. Lachlan's face went white with anger—and maybe worry?—and a few minutes later he stormed off.

She stood as Alex approached. "What was that about?" she asked.

She wasn't sure he was going to answer her. He put his hands on her waist to lift her back up onto the horse. After making sure she was comfortable, he said, "Your stepfather didn't approve of my change of plans."

She turned around to look at him as he settled in behind her. The warmth and strength of his body felt so good she almost forgot what she'd been about to ask. "And what change of plans is that?"

"To stop at my castle in Winton on the way to Edinburgh."

She frowned. Winton was on the old North road that ran mostly parallel to the coast. It was the road the first Edward had taken into Scotland, but not the road taken by Edward II nine days ago. "Does he not think the road is safe?"

"That isn't the reason for his objection." He distracted her by putting his hand on her face with such tenderness it made her heart catch. "I'm going to kill the man who did this to you, but first I will see you cared for."

"I'm fine, Alex, truly. Especially now." She didn't want him going anywhere—and certainly not to take on Sir Hugh Despenser and whatever remained of King Edward's army. From what she'd been able to gather, Lachlan and a few other Guardsmen had caught up with Alex after failing to track down King Edward before he'd reached the safety of Dunbar Castle, where he'd found temporary refuge with one of the few remaining loyal Scotsmen, Patrick, Earl of Dunbar. King Edward and the men who'd seen him to safety—including Despenser and the Earl of Pembroke—had reportedly left Dunbar for Berwick by sea and were probably not far behind them. None of which would explain why Lachlan was so angry. "What objection does he have, then?"

With a snap of the reins, the palfrey moved forward. "To the wedding."

Joan froze, but her heart was beating fast. *Very* fast. "What wedding?"

"Ours."

That fast heartbeat went still. "And when is this wedding to take place?"

"Before the sun sets on another day, because the next time I go to bed you will be beside me."

In case she hadn't gotten his meaning—which she had—the arm wrapped around her waist just under her breasts pulled her in a little tighter, and he slid her bottom back in the saddle. Aye, there was no mistaking that meaning—she could feel every inch of his meaning riding hard and solid against her.

Good God, could he . . . like this?

She wasn't frozen anymore. Her skin was suddenly warm. But she forced all the shivering and quivering aside and straightened her back to give him a sidelong reproachful frown. "Haven't you forgotten something?"

"We don't need to say the banns. I secured a dispensation from the Abbot of Inchaffray before I left Stirling."

She lifted a brow. He was quite certain of himself, wasn't he? "How thoughtful of you, but I was referring to me. Do I not have a say in all of this?"

"No."

"Alex!" she exclaimed, turning fully around this time.

He shrugged. "It's your fault. You wanted a brigand, now you have to deal with it."

His smile took away most of her outrage. Most. She gave him a long look. "I think I like you better with the shiny mail."

He laughed and pressed a kiss on the top of her head. "No more bossing around after this, I promise. I'm done switching sides. I'm right where I belong."

Her heart squeezed, hearing the bigger promise. He was hers forever. "I'm glad to hear it," she said softly.

He leaned down and whispered in her ear. "You were right."

She shuddered. And not just from the warmth of his

breath against her skin. The hand tucked under her breast had taken the opportunity to roam under her cloak, and his fingers were caressing little circles in sensitive places. *Very* sensitive places.

"I was?" It wasn't the jarring of the galloping horse or the wind that made her voice so breathless.

"Aye. I was so convinced that what I was doing was right, my pride wouldn't let me see when it wasn't anymore. You can say I told you so all you want—*after* the wedding."

She laughed, shooing his hand away before she started moaning. "How many times?"

"As many as you want. Although I may need a few minutes' rest between."

She had the feeling they weren't talking about "I told you so's" anymore. "A few minutes?"

"Give or take. I'm still working on my stamina." She laughed, and he pulled her in tight again. "I'm not letting you go again, sweetheart. I love you."

"If that is a proposal, I accept." She turned, meeting his gaze in the moonlight. "And I love you, too."

He grinned, and she thought he looked more like himself, until he caught Lachlan's gaze. The look he shot back at him was every bit as venomous as her stepfather's.

Clearly, it was going to take more than a wedding to make it right between them. But she was determined that one day it would be. Alex didn't just belong with her and Bruce—he belonged with the Highland Guard.

"What did you say to him to convince him?" she asked.

Alex took a few moments too long to respond. "I told him we would have another celebration with your mother and siblings when you had had a chance to recover. He saw the wisdom of not having Bella see you like this."

Joan didn't blame him. Joan could imagine her mother's

reaction to her injuries—and what she would have to say to Bruce, Lachlan, and Alex about them. But she knew that wasn't all. "Why did you point to your side?"

Alex's face might have been in the shadows, but she would swear something resembling shame crossed his features. "I might have threatened him with something."

"What?"

"I can't tell you."

"Alex . . ."

"I made a vow."

She knew it wasn't an accident when he flicked the reins and kicked his heels to urge the horse to a gallop, and the opportunity for conversation was lost.

But she wasn't worried. She would get the truth out of him tonight. She would have to remind him about his vow to give up vows when it came to her.

25

THEY ARRIVED AT the castle shortly before dawn. Alex's mother had taken one look at the half-starved, beaten young woman in his arms—Joan had been asleep and he refused to set her down after she'd woken—and immediately whisked her away. After losing a husband and two sons to the war—her sons in horrific executions—Lady Agnes Seton had endured more than her share of tragedy, but had done it all with a strength that had never faltered.

Alex knew there was no one who could care for Joan more capably than his mother—except maybe her own—but it was still hard to let her go.

As he stood in the Hall and watched the two women disappear into the donjon stairwell, he felt a fist tighten around his chest. The rage that he'd experienced on first seeing Joan emerge from that pit—beaten, starved, and barely resembling the strong, passionate woman he'd left eleven days before—had turned inward. This was his fault. He'd done this to her.

He hadn't realized his former partner had come up beside him. "Get your sword."

"Why?"

Boyd didn't answer.

Despite being exhausted—God knew the last time that he'd had more than a couple of hours of sleep—Alex followed him out to the practice yard.

It didn't take him long to figure out the answer to his own question. Alex needed to vent his anger, and there was no place better to do it than battling his former partner.

It took only a few minutes for the light sparring to turn to no-holds-barred combat. That's how it had always been between them. They never gave half-measure. The two men exchanged blow after blow, until Alex felt as if his arms were going to fall off. Until he could barely find the strength to lift his sword or block the powerful blows.

Christ, the bastard had only gotten stronger in the past two years—which was saying something for the strongest man in Scotland. The fact that Alex was out of practice only made it worse. But he didn't give up. Finally, Boyd took mercy on him and put down his sword.

Dirty, thick with sweat, and exhausted, both men sat—collapsed—on the stacks of hay that the men used as benches.

After they'd caught their breath, Alex said, "Thanks."

"My pleasure. If you want to beat yourself up, I'm always happy to help." Before Alex could tell him to go to hell, Boyd turned serious. "There was nothing you could have done."

The fact that Boyd knew he blamed himself made it worse. Alex was almost too tired to argue—almost. "You're wrong. If I hadn't been so stubborn, if I'd admitted that I made a mistake and swallowed my damned pride a little earlier, this wouldn't have happened."

"That's shite. The only thing that would have changed was that we would not have won the war. If you'd come back any earlier, you wouldn't have had the intelligence that you did to convince Bruce to fight. Joan still would have been arrested."

Alex didn't want to hear Boyd's blasted reason right now. "I could have protected her."

Boyd—the arse—laughed. "How? Did you intend to take on the entire English army yourself? They were coming for her whether you were there or not. All you would have done is get yourself killed or tossed down there with her."

"I should have sent her here to my mother or at least made sure she got away safely."

"It was too late for that. Margaret told you she was being watched even before you left. There wasn't time to get her away."

Alex shot him a look of fury. "You have all the bloody answers, don't you?"

"Took you long enough to see the light."

Alex told him to bugger off, but Boyd just laughed. "If you are done with the self-flagellation, you might want to work on the foul temper before the wedding or the lass might reconsider."

Christ, Alex thought, dragging his fingers through his hair. The bastard was probably right. "I've been a little out of sorts."

Boyd laughed again. "That's an understatement. You've made Viper seem pleasant the past two days, not to mention challenging Chief like that. What the hell were you thinking?"

Alex winced. "I wasn't. I should probably apologize."

"Aye, but if I were you I'd wait until after the wedding when the drink has been flowing for a while."

Alex quirked a brow, surprised. "You are all staying? I assumed Bruce would be anxious for you to get back."

Boyd shook his head, looking at him as if he were an idiot again. "He is, but he'll understand. You think we'd miss this?"

Of course, how could Alex have forgotten. Joan was one of them. He shook his head. "I guess not."

Boyd frowned, suddenly solemn. "Besides, I won't be going back right away. I have to see Rosalin and tell her in person."

Alex nodded in understanding, not envying Boyd's task. It turned out that Rosalin's urgency to visit her brother had been prescient. Lord Robert Clifford, Boyd's former enemy turned brother-in-law, had fallen along with Sir Giles d'Argentan in a noble, but ultimately failed, attempt to rally the troops after seeing the king safely away.

"She will be devastated."

Boyd nodded. "Tom"—Boyd and Rosalin's firstborn son who would be two in November—"and the new babe when it comes will help. But you know how close she and Clifford were. I'm just glad she had a chance to say goodbye."

Alex's brows shot up. "I thought you'd be furious when you heard."

Boyd gave him a sidelong look. "I was. At first."

Alex looked at him questioningly.

Boyd shrugged. "She told me you were there. Between you and Clifford I figured she was as safe as she could have been."

The show of faith took Alex aback. "I appreciate the confidence, but I'm not sure it is deserved after what happened to Joan. God knows, I never would have been able to save her without you and the others. I know you didn't do it for me, but I still feel I owe you a debt I can never repay."

"You're wrong on both counts, Dragon."

At first Alex assumed the use of his war name was a slip of the tongue, but when he realized that it wasn't—and what Boyd meant—he was both shocked and humbled. They'd done it for him as well. He might not have been completely forgiven—and they sure as hell wouldn't be throwing him any welcome-back feasts—but the door had opened, and the long process of reconciliation had begun.

Alex hadn't been the only one who'd made a mistake, and he knew this was Boyd's way of acknowledging it and making his own amends.

"We might have won the war," Boyd said. "But Edward has suffered a severe blow and a humiliation that he will not soon forget. There is still much work to be done."

"I'll do whatever it takes."

Boyd arched a brow at that.

"Within reason," Alex qualified.

Boyd laughed. "You had me worried there for a minute. Where the hell would we be without Sir Galahad to remind us of right and wrong and point out that line in the sand?"

Alex shook his head. "Go to hell, Raider."

He didn't add that his line in the sand wasn't as rigid as it used to be. He'd learned that when Joan was taken. There was nothing he wouldn't have done to get her back safely. Nothing. He was a man, not an ideal.

Alex had been looking for honor and nobility in the wrong place. It wasn't in codes or rules of chivalry—those were ideals that didn't exist—it had been right before him all the time. These men—and women, he added, thinking of Joan, Bella, Helen MacKay, and Janet Lamont, who'd all done more than their part for Bruce—were the most honorable he knew. They might push that line every now and then, but it was always there.

"Come on," Boyd said, standing. Alex was pleased to see that his legs wobbled a little, too. Maybe he wasn't as out of shape as he thought. "You have a wedding to get ready for, and that river out there is calling your name. I know you've already anticipated the wedding night, but if you have any questions—"

"Sod off, Raider."

Boyd laughed and slapped him on the back. "Now that sounds like old times."

∞

They were married in the Seton family chapel at Winton Castle shortly after midday on Wednesday the twenty-sixth day of June. Less than forty-eight hours after Bruce had his great victory along the Bannock Burn, Joan was seated at the dais enjoying her own moment of happiness and triumph.

She'd done it. She'd not only done her part to help win this war by uncovering key information, she'd helped to bring Alex back into the fold right in time, and found something she'd never thought to have: a future with the man she loved.

It felt like a dream. She was happy. Truly happy for the first time in as long as she could remember.

Since arriving this morning and being swept under the very comforting and capable wing of Alex's mother, Lady Agnes, Joan had been bathed, fed, rested (forced to take a nap, for goodness' sake!), had her cuts tended and ribs wrapped, dressed in a beautiful gown of blue silk, and given a beautiful jeweled circlet to wear in her hair.

She hadn't lifted a finger for any of this—which was probably a good thing, given how exhausted and weak she was. But if she ever wondered where Alex got his solid efficiency and at times overprotectiveness, she need look no further than her new mother-in-law.

Joan did not warm to people very easily—her guard had been raised for too long—but it seemed Alex and his mother were the exceptions. She had a feeling that she and Lady Agnes were going to get along very well together, although a glance down at the end of the table made her wonder whether they would be living under the same roof for long. The two fair—slightly graying—heads were bent quite closely together, and with the way Lady Agnes was smiling, she looked more like a girl than a woman of six and forty.

Alex, seated at her side, leaned over to whisper in her ear. "I would like to take credit for that smile, but it seems to be directed at my mother."

"Who is that man she is seated with?"

Alex frowned. "Sir Alan Murray. He was one of my father's most trusted captains and has served as the keeper of the castle for years."

"Hmm."

"What does 'hmm' mean?"

She shook her head. Men could be so blind sometimes. "Your mother is an attractive woman. I didn't expect her to be so young."

"She and my father were married as children. She had Chris when she was thirteen."

Much like her own mother, Joan thought sadly. But from what Alex said, his parents had had a good marriage.

"Why?" Alex asked. "You don't think . . . ?" He glanced down at the couple with mild horror on his face.

She laughed. "It took me a while to realize my mother had her own life to live, too. But I'm glad she's happy."

He considered her words for a moment. "I suppose Murray is a hell of a lot better than MacRuairi."

"Alex!" She swatted at him and scowled. "He'll hear you, and you promised to try."

"I will. But what about him? He stood up in the wedding ceremony—right when the priest called for objections, damn it! Bloody bastard!"

Joan bit her lip, trying not to laugh. "He didn't end up saying anything."

"Only because you shot him a look of death."

She feigned affront. "I did no such thing, and I don't have a look of death."

He shivered, ignoring her protests. "I just hope you never look at me like that."

"Try to get along with Lachlan, and you won't give me a reason."

"You make it sound so easy."

She grinned. "Don't whinge, my love, it isn't knightly. And besides, my mother will help. She has always liked you."

"I would say she had impeccable taste if it wasn't for . . ." He looked down the table at MacRuairi, who was still shooting daggers at him.

"Alex!"

"All right, all right. I made a vow—albeit under duress."

She blinked up at him innocently. "I don't know what you are talking about."

"Tears and pitiful looks won't work all the time, sweetheart."

She tried not to smile. But they had *this* time. She knew she had to do something drastic or the two men might have come to blows during her wedding ceremony. Alex had backed off, but only after she'd pleaded—tearfully—with him to not let it ruin their day.

"The ceremony was beautiful," she said. Even with Lachlan's not-so-timely interruption.

He reached over to sweep a tendril of hair behind her ear, but she knew it was only an excuse to let his fingers brush her cheek. "You are beautiful. The most beautiful woman I have ever seen."

She blushed at the compliment—and the obvious sincerity with which it had been given. "Well, I suppose I look a good sight better than I did this morning. Thanks to your mother."

His face darkened. "God, Joan, I am so sorry. If I hadn't been so damned stubborn—"

"It wouldn't have changed what happened to me. You told me yourself what Margaret said."

They'd been watching Joan for a while. In a fit of pique after Alex's threat to claim her inheritance, Alice had voiced her "suspicions" (which ironically weren't real suspicions—she had no idea Joan was *really* the spy) to her husband, who had in turn confided in Despenser. But the moment Sir Adam had accidentally confirmed her identity, Joan's chance to leave was gone. Nothing Alex could have done could have changed that. Ashamed of her part in Joan's capture, Alice had told Margaret that Joan had left. Fortunately, Margaret hadn't believed it. Eventually Margaret had worn Alice down, learned that Joan was in the pit prison, and sent a note to John Ross. But Alice had redeemed herself somewhat. It was she who'd put the note in her brooch, and she who'd kept the soldiers busy under false pretenses and given the keys to Margaret to let Joan's rescuers in and out.

"My fate was sealed before you left," Joan told him. "The only thing that would have changed was that we would still be fighting this war."

He shook his head. "Christ, you sound like Raider."

She didn't miss the unconscious use of Boyd's war name. "He is obviously a very smart man." Her teasing smile softened. "But none of what happened was your fault, Alex. We both made mistakes. I was stubborn, too. I thought I was too good to get caught." She smiled. "I also thought one man couldn't make a difference and change the war. But I was wrong. Very wrong." She was so incredibly proud of him. "Please, don't let what happened cast a pall over this day."

He nodded, but she knew better than to think it was over. She almost pitied the man who'd done this to her, knowing that Alex would not let it go unanswered.

She looked down the table of her fellow Guardsmen and suspected he wouldn't be alone. "I'm glad they stayed," she said.

"They did it for you."

"I think maybe not just for me?" She'd seen him talking to the others after the ceremony, and it was clear something had changed.

He shrugged. "Maybe."

A swell of happiness rose inside her. She knew what that shrug meant. If Alex wasn't back with the Highland Guard now, he would be soon. She had faith in him.

She didn't think it was possible to be any happier.

She was wrong. An embarrassingly few hours later—Alex had utterly ignored their duties as hosts and left the feast well before it was over—she was lying in her husband's arms more content (and sated) than surely any person had a right to be.

Although maybe she'd earned it. Maybe all the difficulties, hardships, and disappointments in her life had brought her to this point. Maybe she wouldn't be experiencing this kind of joy if she hadn't experienced the alternative.

Alex caressed the naked skin of her shoulder while pressing his mouth to her hair. "What are you thinking about?"

She propped up her chin on the back of the hand she had planted on his chest to look up at him. Her golden knight. The man who'd renewed her faith in honorable men. It was a heavy mantle of expectation to wear, but she knew he was up to the task. "You. Me. The future. That I've never been so happy in all my life."

"Oh."

"Oh?" she repeated, surprised by his tone. "You sound disappointed."

He grinned rather devilishly for someone who was supposed to be a paragon of honor. "I was rather hoping you were thinking about ways to make me break more vows. That last one was rather . . . effective."

"Well, when I bent down to examine that 'scratch' you weren't going to tell me about"—Lachlan had some explaining to do for that!—"it seemed a good place to start."

"Oh, it was. And nearly a good place to end a few minutes later."

She grinned. "I guess that means I was doing it right?"

"Sweetheart, with your mouth on me like that there is nothing you could do that wasn't right."

"That's good, because I had an idea when you were behind me in the saddle."

Alex swore, and she looked up at him and frowned. "What was that for?"

"For what you are about to do to my stamina. This isn't going to last long."

But he was wrong in that. It would last forever.

Epilogue

Berwick Castle, Berwick-upon-Tweed, July 17, 1328

THE SPIDER HAD spun her web.

Robert the Bruce had lived to see the day that at times—too many times—he feared would never come. Twenty-two years ago, when things had seemed their darkest, he'd learned an important lesson in perseverance from a spider in a cave to never give up. Today that lesson had paid off.

As Bruce listened to his four-year-old son and heir, David, repeat the vows that would bind him to his seven-year-old bride, Joan of the Tower, Edward II's youngest daughter, he knew that his long struggle was over. The die that had been cast twenty-three years ago at Lochmaben Castle had finally stopped rolling.

He'd won. He'd *won*.

"We did it, my friend," he said to himself, thinking of the young churchman who'd met with him that late August day in 1305 to bring him the news of William Wallace's death. But William Lamberton, the Bishop of St. Andrews, Bruce's longtime friend and supporter, wasn't here to see it. He'd died two months ago—eighteen days before the treaty with England had been signed. The treaty that after nearly three decades of warfare had put in writing what Bruce's victory at Bannock Burn fourteen years earlier had established: Robert the Bruce was king and Scotland was a free and sovereign nation. This marriage between the Scot Prince and English Princess was only an added jewel on his crown.

But it was a crown that had come at such a cost. Too high a cost, perhaps. As the king sat in the chapel, surrounded by his friends, family, and most loyal followers, he could see the ghosts of those who had given their lives to see this day. Great patriots like William Wallace, Simon Fraser, Andrew Murray, Christopher Seton, and the Earl of Atholl; loyal supporters like Lamberton, William "Templar" Gordon, and Neil Campbell; and the most painful of all, four of his brothers—Edward had died a few years after Bannock Burn in Ireland—two sisters, a daughter released from captivity only to die a year later, and his queen, who'd survived her long imprisonment to give him three children, dying just last year.

He could even see the faces of the enemies he'd vanquished—John "The Red" Comyn, whose fatal stabbing had launched Bruce's bid for the crown, Edward I of England, the self-proclaimed Hammer of the Scots who'd nearly destroyed him, and Edward II of England, the king against whom he'd won his great victory, but whose favoritism toward Sir Hugh Despenser had eventually led to his downfall and murder last year—reportedly by a hot poker up his arse—on the order of his queen and her lover, Roger Mortimer.

So many lives lost, including—soon—his own. Aye, the veil between life and death was merely a shadow now, for the Bruce was dying. And everyone knew it.

One by one during the wedding feast, his friends, family, and loyal supporters came to pay their respects. His two lieutenants led the way—James "the Black" Douglas, who'd brokered this treaty with the English with his wife, Joanna, and Thomas Randolph, Bruce's nephew and the man he had named protector for his young son and heir, with his wife, Isabel. His kingdom was in good hands with the two men who had helped him win it.

But even before Randolph and Douglas there were the fabled warriors of the illustrious Highland Guard. Men whom he and Lamberton had handpicked to form a secret army before he made his bid for the crown. That it worked had surprised him. How well it had worked he could never have imagined.

They'd been through so much together. These men better than any others knew how much this moment meant—and how much it had cost him.

There was Tor "Chief" MacLeod, the fearsome leader of the Guard who had rarely left the king's side during his most perilous hours, and his wife, Christina, who'd once saved Bruce's life by alerting him to a plot by Comyn.

There was Erik "Hawk" MacSorley, the always-jesting seafarer whose skill at evading the English navy had enabled Bruce to flee Scotland and live to fight another day, and his wife, Ellie—Bruce's sister-in-law—who kept the half-Viking, half-Gael in line.

There was Arthur "Ranger" Campbell, the scout with an eerie ability to sense things whose information had enabled Bruce to win a great victory against the MacDougalls, and his wife, Anna—the daughter of the MacDougalls—who had been forced to break with her family to save the man she loved.

The next man in line was Lachlan "Viper" MacRuairi, the onetime ruthless mercenary turned loyal supporter, and his wife, Bella, who had spent two years in a cage for her part in putting a crown upon Bruce's head.

Behind them was Magnus "Saint" MacKay, the do-anything Highlander and the toughest man Bruce knew, and his wife, Helen "Angel" Sutherland, the healer of the Guard, who had proved her own toughness when she had led Bruce through the Highlands after being attacked by a team of assassins.

Next was Helen's brother, Kenneth "Ice" Sutherland, the onetime spy who'd brought Bruce key information about the English campaign. He's also brought the young Earl of Atholl back into the Scottish fold when he'd married his mother (and Bruce's former sister-in-law), Mary of Mar.

Mary's twin sister, Janet, followed. She was one of Bruce's best couriers, passing information while pretending to be a nun, when she crossed paths with the greatest tracker in Scotland, Ewen "Hunter" Lamont. Together they'd warned Bruce of an English plot to take him captive at an English parley.

Narrow escapes. He'd had so many of them.

Like Wallace before him, Robbie "Raider" Boyd had every reason to hate the English. He'd served as Bruce's enforcer, taming the wild Borders. But he'd met his surprising match in the "Fair Rosalin," the beautiful (and very English) sister of his worst enemy.

Bruce's own daughter came next. Cate, the natural daughter he thought he'd lost, but who had been "found" by Gregor "Arrow" MacGregor. MacGregor's near-perfect aim with a bow had come in handy more than once. Although Bruce couldn't help teasing him about being back at the scene of his biggest failure: when they'd lost the chance to take Berwick Castle because MacGregor hesitated to shoot a dog.

Bruce's kinsman Eoin "Striker" MacLean, who had planned most of Bruce's battles and attacks for over twenty years, approached with his wife, Margaret. The couple had spent most of the early years of the war apart—with Margaret thinking Eoin dead—but had reunited in time to help Bruce take Dumfries Castle and vanquish his long-time enemy, Margaret's father, Dugald MacDowell.

The newest member of the Guard, Thom "Rock" Mac-Gowan, whose ability to climb anything had helped Bruce take Edinburgh Castle by surprise just before Bannock Burn, came with his wife, Elizabeth, Douglas's sister.

Finally, the last two Guardsmen approached. He owed both of them so much. Joan "Ghost" Comyn, for all the information she'd passed over the years, and Alex "Dragon" Seton, for his part in Bannock Burn. If Alex hadn't come back when he did, this day might never have come.

Alex had proved his loyalty many times over the years and had become one of Bruce's most trusted advisors. He'd been one of the signatories on the important "Declaration of Arbroath," which had declared Scotland's freedom in a letter to the pope eight years before, and just last year Bruce had named him governor of one of his most important castles—*this* castle, as a matter of fact.

He could see the concern in both their faces as they approached. Joan bent down first to kiss his hand, and then when he indicated, to kiss him on the cheek. "Congratulations, sire. This has been a long day in coming."

He scrutinized her closely. There were remarkably few lines on her face for a woman who was in her mid-thirties. But she looked tired. "You have not been keeping yourself up too late, preparing for all this? I know it was a big undertaking that I asked of you."

It was not every day a lady was asked to host a royal wedding.

She smiled. "We were honored, my lord. And truth be

told it was not the wedding keeping me up the past few nights, it was Margaret." They'd named their daughter after her cousin who'd helped her escape this very castle all those years ago. She was here, too. Margaret Comyn had married John Ross a year after Bannock Burn—she'd made the de Beaumonts see the benefit in having her be in Scotland rather than England to claim her part of Joan's English inheritance. Joan shot Alex a look. "Her brothers were telling her ghost stories again. I wonder where they got them?"

Alex's expression was a tad too impassive. "I have no idea."

"You have to admit, it is fitting," Bruce said, fighting his own smile.

She scowled at him. "Then I'll make sure to send her your way when she wakes up screeching like a banshee."

Bruce just laughed. "How many do you have again? Between you and the rest of the Guard, I have lost count of all the progeny."

Clearly, Joan didn't believe him. "You know very well we have six. And I'll wager you can name every one of them— and every one of the others, too."

"Well, that isn't too hard. Half of them are named Robert," Alex pointed out.

"Or William," Bruce added. The loss of William Gordon all those years ago had never been forgotten.

Joan didn't say anything, still staring at him. Finally, giving up—which is something Bruce didn't do often—he said, "Thomas, William, Alexander, John, Margaret, and . . ."

"Robert," Alex finished with a grin.

"I hear from Boyd's daughter that there will be a marriage to celebrate soon?"

Joan rolled her eyes and shot Alex another look when he started coughing to hide his laughter.

"What?" Alex said, sobering. "Don't look at me, it's not my fault."

"Aye, but you take far too much pleasure in it."

Apparently, Boyd's very beautiful nine-year-old daughter had developed an infatuation with their ten-year-old son and was convinced that they were going to marry.

Alex couldn't resist taunting Boyd with jests about what would happen when they were older, and that he hoped his son had as much honor as they did.

Alex thought it was hilarious; Boyd failed to see the humor. If Alex had ever wanted retribution for the ill-treatment Boyd had given him in the early years of their pairing, he had it.

The seemingly ill-fated partnership between the hate-everything-English and the young knight from Yorkshire had ended up working out, after all. They were as close as—and sometimes fought like—brothers.

Boyd had been instrumental in helping Alex regain his place in the Guard. Although it was Joan who'd helped him repair the damage that had been done with Lachlan. It happened right about the time they put their first son in his arms—the child they'd named after him. William Lachlan.

Bruce looked down the table at Lachlan and his wife. "How is your mother? I know coming here was much to ask of her."

"She wouldn't have missed this for the world," Joan said with sincerity that they could not question. "In truth, I don't think coming back to Berwick bothered her as much as she expected. It was a long time ago." She looked as if she were remembering something, too. "The ghosts of the past have faded with so many years of much happier memories."

He only wished he could say the same. "She deserves it."

As if sensing his maudlin thoughts, Joan asked, "Sire?"

He shook off the concern. "Don't listen to me. I am an old warrior who has seen his life's great work accomplished and now doesn't know what to do with himself. Which reminds me . . ." He turned to Seton. "Tell Chief I have one more mission for you."

Alex didn't hide his surprise. "My lord?"

"Now that the pope has finally agreed to lift the interdict and my excommunication, I would like to go on a pilgrimage to Whithorn."

His words had made them both visibly distressed—or perhaps sad was the better word. For they recognized the truth: that this would be Robert the Bruce's final mission.

His work was done. It was time to join his ghosts.

"We will be ready, sire. *Airson an Leòmhann.*"

The battle cry of the Highland Guard that had rung out more times than he could remember. For the Lion.

For Scotland.

AUTHOR'S NOTE

THE BATTLE OF Bannockburn is one of the most important battles in Scottish history. With the seven-hundred-year anniversary in 2014, there has been increased interest and scholarship in what is often hailed as one of the greatest Scottish victories (or worst English defeats) in history. I was fortunate to be able to take advantage of quite a few of the new books on the subject, as well as attend the "Bannockburn Live!" anniversary celebration, which featured some wonderful reenactments of the battle. One of the highlights for me was coming face-to-face with Sir Alexander Seton—or at least the reenactor playing him. I'm sure I probably scared the poor guy with my excitement.

Sir Alexander Seton, a Scottish knight who was fighting for England, did famously switch sides at a critical juncture on the night after the first day of battle. The information he provided helped persuade Bruce to fight the next day. Seton's key part in the battle was related by Sir Thomas Gray in *The Scalacronica*, a historical chronicle written about forty years after Bannockburn. This Sir Thomas Gray is the son of the English knight Sir Thomas Gray, who was taken prisoner by the Scots on the first day of the battle—he is the prisoner who I have addressing Alex as he goes into Bruce's tent—who was presumably in a position to know.

Alexander Seton is usually said to be the brother of Bruce's closest friend, Christopher Seton, who was taken prisoner and executed after Methven in 1306. He is also probably the same Alexander Seton who entered into a band with Neil Campbell and De la Hay (Thomas or Gilbert) in 1308 to support Bruce "till the end of their lives" (*Robert Bruce and the Community of the Realm of Scotland*, Edinburgh: G.W.S. Barrow, Edinburgh University Press, 2005; p. 291).

This promise didn't last long for Seton. By November 1309 he is in England, receiving a "cask of wine" for his "sustenance," along with other notable Scots in the English service such as Sir Adam Gordon (also one cask), Sir Edmond Comyn (two casks), Sir Ingrim de Umfraville (four casks), and Malise of Strathearne (four casks) (*Calendar of Documents Relating to Scotland, Vol. III (1307–1357)*, edited by Joseph Bain, Edinburgh: H.M. General Register House, 1887; p. 23).

What caused Seton to defect to the English after signing the band isn't known, although it is certainly conceivable that the no-win, catch-22 situation of the Border lords played a factor. There were many Scots who thought their best bet was with the English, and given the circumstances you can't really blame them. No one could have predicted Bannockburn. Whatever his reasons, after Seton's timely return to the Scottish fold during Bannockburn, he serves Bruce faithfully until his death.

After the battle, Seton was rewarded by the king with more lands in East Lothian and was appointed a steward in the royal household. As I noted in the epilogue, Seton is one of the signatories on the seminal Declaration of Arbroath (". . . for, as long as but a hundred of us remain alive, never will we on any conditions be brought under English rule. It is in truth not for glory, nor riches, nor honours that we are fighting, but for freedom—for that alone, which no honest man gives up but with life itself"), a precursor to our Declaration of Independence, and is appointed governor of the Castle of Berwick in 1327. The marriage of Prince David to Princess Joan did indeed take place at Berwick Castle the following year. Bruce dies about a year later, on June 7, 1329, but he is said to have been ill for some time.

Most sources name Seton's wife as a daughter of Francis Cheyne, but a reference in a genealogical chart said that she was the daughter of Isabel, the daughter of John Comyn, Earl of Buchan, and Isabella MacDuff, which gave me the idea for the connection and my fictional Joan. Readers of *The Viper* will recall that most sources say that Isabella MacDuff and John Comyn did not have any children.

Alice and Margaret Comyn, Buchan's nieces, were his co-heiresses. The fight over the Buchan lands in Scotland would eventually lead to what is known as the Second Scottish War of Independence from 1332 to 1357. Margaret Comyn was a ward of her brother-in-law de Beaumont when she was married sometime around 1315 to John Ross—a loyal Scot. As a result, she lost her claim to the Buchan lands in England. It seemed strange to me that she would be allowed to marry a Scot. Although it gave de Beaumont the English lands of Buchan outright, it gave her an easier claim to the Scottish lands, which he also craved. But it did give me the idea for her part of the story.

I hope the members of the Seton family/clan will forgive me for adding a wyvern to their arms, but early on I needed a good war name and, well, I liked Dragon.

The attempt by Edward Bruce to take Carlisle Castle that Alex foils in chapter 2 happened the week after Easter 1314—around the sixteenth of April. Edward Bruce was sent to Cumbria by his brother to harry (possibly for nonpayment of tribute) and gather supplies for the army. While doing so, he makes something of a haphazard attempt on the castle.

Historians don't agree on the exact dates for Edward Bruce's siege of Stirling Castle, but the April raid in Cumbria could have been either after he makes his agreement with Sir Phillip Moubray (the former Scot patriot now holding Stirling Castle for Edward II) or during—possibly to relieve the boredom of the siege.

Conventional wisdom has viewed Edward Bruce's truce with Sir Phillip Moubray, whereby the Scots would lift the siege on Stirling with Moubray agreeing to hand over the castle to Bruce if he was not relieved by St. John's Day, as a major tactical blunder on the part of the king's brother. The eager-for-battle, aggressive, hotheaded, and impatient Edward Bruce (who is said to have hated sieges) essentially throws down the gauntlet to the English, forcing the very thing his brother had been trying to avoid for eight years.

But recently, some historians have suggested that perhaps it wasn't a blunder at all—that Edward Bruce's actions were actually directed by his brother. Historian and author Chris Brown posits that Bruce might have deliberately chosen Stirling as a target for Edward II, and then spread the news of his dismay with his brother as a means of propaganda to not alert the English (*Bannockburn 1314: A New History*, Chris Brown, Gloucestershire, England: The History Press, 2009; p. 216). Not only does the truce give Bruce a place to wait and prepare for the English army, which at this point Bruce already knows is marching, it also gives him the benefit of terrain of his choosing, and he doesn't have to spread his men out.

When coupled with the gauntlet Bruce himself had

thrown down the year before, threatening to forfeit the land of all the Scots fighting for Edward II if they did not submit to him within a year's time (which he knew Edward II would have to respond to), and the fact that the Scots left the English unmolested on their march to Stirling—completely forgoing their usual guerrilla tactics—I think it's a very sound theory and decided to go with it rather than the conventional wisdom of an Edward Bruce blunder.

After the execution of Edward II's favorite, Piers Gaveston, Earl of Cornwall, in 1312 by some of his barons, the king seems to have been in a period of mourning. Although he had a few favorites in between—Roger d'Amory, Hugh de Audley, and William de Montacute—I decided to bring forward the much more important (and better known) Sir Hugh Despenser the younger, whose "reign" as favorite probably didn't happen until a few years later. He did fight at Bannockburn with the king, however, having been offered the big plum of the earldom of Moray—for which he reportedly brought along furniture, as I mentioned in the story.

I also pushed back Despenser's marriage. At the time of *The Ghost*, he would have been married to Edward II's niece, Eleanor de Clare. Eleanor was the sister of Gilbert de Clare, Earl of Gloucester, whom Edward II accuses of being cowardly and who was killed on the second day of Bannockburn without his surcoat.

Like Gaveston before him, the favoritism shown to Despenser by King Edward II, and Despenser's own greed and quest for power, will earn him the enmity of the other barons. But Despenser's influence will prove even more destructive to the king than Gaveston's, eventually leading to Edward II's forced abdication early in 1327 in favor of his son Edward III at the hand of Queen Isabella and her lover, Roger Mortimer.

The pair are said to have had Edward II killed later that same year—the official proclamation went out in September—but there is some debate about whether he was actually kept alive. Similarly, although the hot poker up the bum story of his manner of death has passed into history and was circulating not long after Edward II's supposed death, recent scholarship casts doubt upon it.

Also like Gaveston before him, Despenser's reign as favorite does not end well. He, too, was executed—in some descriptions quite gruesomely—after a trial before Queen Isabella and Mortimer.

It is a fascinating period of history, of which the above is only a taste. Much has been written on the Despensers' war, but I highly recommend the very readable biography of Roger Mortimer by Ian Mortimer, *The Greatest Traitor: The Life of Sir Roger Mortimer, Ruler of England: 1327–1330* (New York: Thomas Dunne Books, 2005).

In *The Ghost*, one of the key uncertainties and information that Joan is trying to uncover is whether the powerful Earl of Lancaster will answer Edward II's call to muster and bring along with him his five hundred cavalry. To put that number in perspective, that is about the same number in total that Robert Bruce had at his disposal. But Bruce's cavalry were "light" horses and not the "heavy" armed warhorses of the English. The overall numbers for the armies at Bannockburn are disputed and vary widely, but an estimate for the English is about 12,000 to 15,000 infantry and 1,600 to 2,500 horses. The Scots were at about a third to a half of that: 5,500 to 7,500 infantry and 350 to 500 horses. In any event, I probably overstated the "mystery" of whether Lancaster would show, as he was a hardened opponent of the king. He did refuse to answer the muster himself and sent only the minimum required men for his service.

Lancaster, a direct descendant of Henry III, and cousins with Edward II, held five earldoms (Lancaster, Leicester, Derby, Lincoln, and Salisbury) and was one of the most powerful men in the kingdom. He was the leader of the baronial opposition to King Edward II and had a hand in the death of Gaveston. He opposed Despenser as well, but this time it was the king's favorite who came out on top. After being taken prisoner in battle, Lancaster was brought to trial and executed by Despenser and Edward II in 1322.

Reducing one of the great battles of Scottish history to a few pages wasn't easy, but I tried to stay as close as possible to the accepted history of Bannockburn as I could, while simplifying and trying to make it understandable. It wasn't an easy task.

There are some controversies and unknowns, however, including the location of the battle itself. But a recent archeological investigation undertaken by the BBC in anticipation of the anniversary lends support to the Carse of Balquhiderock as the battle site.

The great chivalric moment of Bruce in meeting the reckless charge of Sir Henry de Bohun and felling him with one blow of his battle-axe also isn't universally agreed upon. In one of the primary English sources, *Vita Edwardi Secundi*, written in the decade after the battle, the chronicler states that Sir Henry was trying to return to his men when Bruce struck him down, and his squire who tried to save him was also killed. Not surprisingly, I like the other version better.

As the circumstances of Clifford's death are also unclear, I gave him the chivalric death I thought he deserved by pairing him with Sir Giles d'Argentan, reputedly the second-best knight in Christendom, who did die as I described by essentially going down in a blaze of glory. After seeing King Edward II safely away from the battlefield and knowing the battle is lost, the great knight can't contemplate fleeing and returns to lead one last valiant charge.

As significant and important as the victory was at Bannockburn for Scotland and Bruce—essentially putting God's stamp on his kingship—it was the de facto rather than the de jure end to the war, which didn't come until the treaty fourteen years later.